THE COMMISSAR

THE COMMISSAR

A NOVEL OF STALINIST RUSSIA

By

GRIGORY VINOKUR

TWAYNE PUBLISHERS, NEW YORK 10003

For Information address the publisher:
TWAYNE PUBLISHERS, INC.
31 Union Square, New York 10003

Library of Congress Catalog Card Number: 65-18221

Manufactured in the United States of America

Composition set by Slugs Composition Co.

Printed by Profile Press

Author's Note

This book has been translated in collaboration with my wife Tillie Young, who was always at my side in my joys and in my sorrows. For her invaluable encouragement and guidance I wish to express my deep appreciation and gratitude.

* * *

This novel is a fictional treatment of events that actually occurred. I played an active role in the performance of duties imposed by the Soviet government and the Communist Party. As a Soviet writer, I faithfully followed Stalin's line in literature in my books, short stories and articles published in Moscow, Minsk and Birobidjan. In the thirties, I was one of the young Communists who were sent to reorganize collective farms, and in World War II, I served as an officer of the Red Army.

The hero of this novel is a Jew, the writer and commissar, Mikhail Kruger. Though this is his story, it is also the biography of the Soviet regime under which I lived.

The idea for this novel came to me while I was in the trenches at the Central Front between Voronezh and Stalingrad. Later, recuperating from a war wound, I spent many days and nights weaving the plot. In 1945 when I settled in Moscow after my release from the Red Army, I continued writing the novel, but I soon realized that this work could never be published in the Soviet Union under Stalin, because those who criticized as friends were treated as enemies.

Like so many others, I loved Russia dearly. I was a loyal citizen and a devoted Communist, but for as long as I could remember, I was torn between my loyalty and belief in communism and my loyalty and belief in Judaism. Gradually the conclusion became clear: I could no longer continue to live two lives.

I left Moscow and moved to a border town where many refugees gathered for repatriation to Poland, Rumania, Czechoslovakia, Germany, and other countries. Unshaven, with unkempt beard, and wearing a tattered, brown coat tied with a thick rope around the waist, I succeeded in passing as one of the refugees. I hid the manuscript in an old burlap sack among my other few possessions and thus managed to smuggle it out of Soviet Russia. After much wandering on the face of the globe, I was fortunate enough to arrive in the United States, where I married and became a citizen in 1953.

I did not dare bring the novel to light for fear of Stalin's reprisal against people who had helped me and who could be recognized easily despite the fictionalized treatment. After the death of Stalin and the subsequent active de-Stalinization program in the Soviet Union I decided that the time had come for publishing it.

GRIGORY VINOKUR

January 7, 1964

Contents

THE PRINCIPAL CHARACTERS OF *THE COMMISSAR*

MIKHAIL KRUGER, *a Soviet writer*
BORIS GARBER, *Mikhail's close friend and aide to Josef Stalin*
POLYA GARBER, *Boris' wife*
NATHAN WIEDER, *Chief of the Cheka, the Soviet secret police*
JOACHIM SCHULTZ, *a professional soldier*
IVAN IVANOVICH IVANOV, *Commander of the Moscow Military Academy, later Commander of the Soviet armies defending Moscow and Stalingrad*
YEKATERINA (KATYA) PETROVNA IVANOVA, *the Commander's wife and Mikhail's benefactress*
PETYA IVANOV, *the Commander's son and a Red Army officer*
ANTON SEMIONOV, *Party Secretary of the provincial village of Krasney-Bor*
SVIATISLAV POPOV, *chairman of the Village Soviet of Krasney-Bor*
KSENIA DIMOVA, *a Komsomol (Young Communist) of Krasney-Bor*
PINCHAS LEVITT, *a political commissar and Party Secretary of Birobidjan*
ANDREI KRIVOSHAPKO, *a Ukranian agronomist*

PROLOGUE

The majestic white marble palace on Morozlyevsky Street opposite Alexander Park, which extends to the very shores of the magical Black Sea, had survived the Revolution surprisingly well. Its richly appointed rooms remained as before; only the dark, unsmiling portraits of the scions of the Romanov dynasty, rulers of the Russian Empire for more than three centuries, had been removed. In their places now hung lithographed likenesses of Lenin and Trotsky.

Gone were the racks of native and imported wines and freshly stocked iceboxes which had filled the cavernous stone cellars in the days when Tsar Nicholas II, "Nicholas the Bloody," might visit Odessa. Now the palace was the prison and the seat of the Cheka, the political secret police created by Lenin to ferret out counterrevolution, espionage, and banditry.

Mikhail Kruger lay on the cold cement floor of the cellar which had previously housed the Tsar's private stores. It was the night following the third day of his imprisonment. There still had been no hearing. In the small cell lay about thirty other people, among them a few bandits, a retired Tsarist general who had refused to serve the new Soviet regime, a Greek Orthodox priest accused of counterrevolutionary propaganda, and an old rabbi who had refused to close his school. Many were there without knowing why they had been arrested or how long they would be held.

Mikhail was the youngest, though he appeared older than he was. His full mouth and upper lip were already covered with a dark blond moustache. He walked with a heavy gait and his tall sparse frame was slightly bent, as though he carried a weight on his shoulders.

The other prisoners had been astonished to find a boy of

seventeen among them. When he was thrown into the cell, they all crowded round him plying him with questions.

"What are you doing here?"

"I was arrested for robbery."

One of the bandits drew closer and slapped him on the back. "Did you rob a bank?"

"No. Not a bank. A bakery."

"A lot of money?"

"No, no money. Only bread."

"Bread?" The bandits laughed. "And you're trying to tell us that's what you're here for?"

Mikhail couldn't understand why they didn't believe him. What kind of people were they? He turned on them in anger.

"Don't you know what's going on?"

"The Reds are killing the Whites, and the Whites are killing the Reds, that's all I know," said one of the bandits.

"And the food here is nothing like it used to be," added another.

The priest, who had been sitting quietly watching the scene, suddenly admonished the men.

"Why don't you let the lad talk? Tell us, my son. Just what did happen?"

"My father is dead," Mikhail said. He hesitated a moment and sighed. "He died of hunger. My mother is sick, and I have two younger brothers and a little sister who depend on me. If it were not for my friend Boris we would all have died of hunger."

"Who is this Boris of yours?"

Mikhail straightened up and threw out his chest.

"Boris the Strong. He's a member of the Komsomol, the Young Communist Party, and he made me a member, too. When we had no bread to eat and no soap to wash with, and we were all starving and filthy, Boris organized a gang, and every morning we raided a bakery and helped ourselves to some bread. Boris said that the private bakers are only speculators who suck the blood of the poor."

Another prisoner interrupted.

"How come they got you and not the others?"

"This last job," Mikhail boasted, "I pulled myself. Boris is working in a factory now. He is head of the Special Division there."

"A commissar!" a hoodlum sneered.

"I never would have been caught, either," Mikhail added, "but the son-of-a-bitch baker informed on me."

His cellmates quickly accepted Mikhail as one of them. When he asked about getting a hearing, they told him he would no doubt get one "soon enough."

"Look at the 'Man with a Thousand Names,' " a bandit said jokingly, "he gets a hearing every day."

Mikhail had watched this man with the sensitive face and the manners of a gentleman who had openly declared himself an enemy of the Reds and whose hatred was so intense that it had driven him into a state of melancholia. At his arrest the authorities had found on him a dozen false documents each bearing another name. He had refused to reveal his true identity, so every other day the guard would open the cell door and call out one of the pseudonyms. "Nikolayev!" he would shout and the "Man with a Thousand Names" would answer: "That's me." He would smile happily and go unresistingly to the cross-examination and return crushed, beaten, and covered with blood. Two days later the guard would call: "Kotlov!" and the unfortunate one would respond: "I'm Kotlov." And so it went with other names such as Nichayev, Dimitrov, and Zindov.

He had just been returned to the cell after another interrogation and from where he lay Mikhail could hear him breathing heavily. Suddenly the guard threw open the heavy iron cell door for the second time that night.

"Kruger!" he shouted. There was a murmur and stirring from the other prisoners.

"What—what is it?" Mikhail asked drowsily.

The glare of a flashlight blinded Mikhail; a heavy boot dug into his side. The guard laughed raucously. "Poor little caged bird," he said. "Get moving. We don't play favorites here. We have dozens like you, all enemies of the state, and we have no time to waste on them." With these words he seized Mikhail by the collar, yanked him to his feet, and shoved him out of the cell.

They marched down a long, gloomy corridor. After what seemed an eternity, they stopped. The soldier opened a door and pushed Mikhail into a brilliantly lit chamber. The contrast between the dazzling light and the dark corridor made Mikhail's head swim; for a few moments he swayed on his feet. When he steadied himself, he saw a room full of white brilliance. The floor, walls, and ceiling were so bespangled with crystalline, shimmering star designs that the room seemed to be floating in a haze of frosty snow crystals. It was empty except for one corner, where a man sat behind a desk piled with documents. On one corner of the desk lay a revolver. Above the man hung a flag flanked by lithographs of Lenin and Trotsky. Mikhail could hardly keep his eyes open because from somewhere in this corner a high-powered spotlight shone directly into his face.

A voice came from the desk, but to Mikhail it seemed to come on the beams of the light.

"Prisoner, step forward!"

Mikhail stepped forward. The light seared his eyeballs mercilessly, blinding him. He turned aside.

"Trying to escape, eh?" The voice behind the light was like low thunder. "Thief! Bandit! American spy!"

American spy! Involuntarily, Mikhail's hand went to his coat pocket. The letter to his uncle! He had forgotten to mail it, and they must have taken it from him while he was asleep. They won't understand, he thought. They'll think my mother has a "rich" brother in America. They'll think—but how could I have refused to write that letter for her when she was so sick and could not see well enough to write it herself? Even so, all I asked for was some food and clothing and maybe even help to get us to America where everything seems so wonderful.

Now it was all clear to him. For stealing the bread he might have been released after a routine interrogation. But the letter was incriminating evidence. Devoted young Communists were not supposed to divulge the truth about circumstances in the new Soviet paradise.

The spotlight was suddenly turned off. The room went black for a moment. Someone took Mikhail's elbow, pushed him up to the desk, and sat him down on a chair. Before him loomed a man in full Cheka uniform. His eyes were pitiless as he seized a document from the desk and shook it under Mikhail's nose.

"Here, smell it. This is the letter you wrote. It's proof in black and white. You have betrayed our Soviet Motherland. You have betrayed us to the American capitalists."

"My mother wanted me to write this letter to her brother," Mikhail remonstrated. "My father is dead, and we were all starving. She was only asking for help from her own brother. Is that a crime?"

"Be silent when I speak!" the interrogator bellowed. "You have now been trapped by your own words. You have engaged in anti-Soviet propaganda. Confess!"

"No!" Mikhail's head was beginning to burst. He held it tightly between his clenched fists. "No! Never! Please listen to me, Tovarisch—"

"Don't you dare address me as 'Tovarisch.' To you I am 'Citizen.' "

Mikhail repeated after him: "Citizen Interrogator."

"No excuses!" the interrogator interrupted, waving the letter in the air. "You wrote there was no bread but plenty of lice. This is the poisonous humor of a provocateur. Do you expect us to pardon that? You are mistaken. This is no time for pity or sentiment."

"But it's the truth, Citizen Interrogator."

Mikhail tried to penetrate the man's brutality. "Do you have a mother? Do you have younger brothers or a little sister? Could you watch them starve, covered with filth, eaten up by lice, without a drop of fuel to boil water or a piece of soap to wash with?"

The interrogator cleared his throat and roared.

"You viper! Scum of the earth! Where the hell were you during the civil war?"

"At home," Mikhail answered timidly.

"Why weren't you at the front?"

"But that was two years ago."

"So?"

"But I was only fifteen then."

"And how old are you now?"

"Seventeen."

"Seventeen?" The interrogator looked him over suspiciously. "I don't believe it. You look a lot older. You must be at least twenty."

"My birth certificate can prove it."

"Papers. More papers. They are forgeries. Your papers are as fraudulent as your words."

"Citizen Interrogator, I protest—"

"You protest! The saboteur, the thief, the American spy protests! Ha, ha, ha!"

"That's a lie! I'm a—"

"Prisoner Kruger. I and I alone will decide what is a lie and what is not. We know exactly who you are and we know every move you make. We've had our eye on you for some time now. We know your crimes and we also know the penalty for them."

The interrogator rose, lumbered over to the door, kicked it open violently and shouted,

"Guards! Take this degenerate out of here and throw him into solitary."

The cell in solitary was damp and it reeked of foul cabbage and rotten potatoes. There was just room for Mikhail to move around. At first he was tormented by loneliness and thoughts of what might happen to him. But soon he stopped thinking. He no longer paced the floor, but lay huddled numbly in a corner. After a while, he lost all sense of time. When the guard brought him his food—a crust of black bread and a dish of muddy soup—he devoured it and relapsed into motionless torpor. He became a clod, drained of all human desire.

Days flowed into nights and weeks into months. Sometimes it seemed to Mikhail that he had been in this cell all his life and at other times that he had been brought here only yesterday.

One day, two soldiers came, dragged him to his feet and shoved him out of the cell. Mikhail looked at them without recognition, swaying on his feet while the cell door was being locked behind him. Then, as he stumbled forward into the corridor, a faint sense of the familiar stirred within him. It was that corridor stretching endlessly into the gloom and the steady thud of boots on stone that slowly rekindled in him the flame of life.

He was led into a hall that contained the furnishings of a court of justice. There were several rows of benches and in front was a dais reached by several wide marble steps. On the dais stretched a long table covered with a red cloth, behind which stood three chairs. Several pads of white paper had been carefully placed on the table. To the right of the steps stood a man and a woman and behind them several Chekas with rifles. Mikhail was brought over to join the two prisoners, and another soldier with a riflle took his stand behind him. He wondered why they had grouped him with these people whom he had never seen before.

A side door opened, and three men emerged. This was the Troika, the triumvirate of the Cheka whose ruthlessness and cruelty were already legendary throughout Odessa. Two of them were in civilian clothes and the third, a heavy, powerfully built man, was in military uniform. They marched to the long table and took their places. The military man, Tovarisch Joachim Schultz, sat in the middle. Schultz was a native Russian of German parentage. He was the principal aide of Tovarisch Nathan Wieder, Chief of the Cheka, and his name was always coupled with Wieder's, as Trotsky's name was linked with Lenin's.

At Schultz's right sat the Second Secretary of the Odessa Communist Party, Tovarisch Bronislav Kovalchuk, a man with a carefully groomed brownish-black goatee trimmed in the manner of Trotsky. The beard gave Kovalchuk, who was barely twenty-five, the dignity and security he needed to cope with his important role in the Party.

To the left of Schultz sat the Second Representative of the Odessa City Soviet, Tovarisch Dmitri Andreyev, a tiny, emaciated creature with heavy spectacles on his nose. He was a "perennial student," a man who studied without end and without result. Actually, Andreyev had dreamed of becoming a judge, but since he had spent more time attending the underground meetings of the Bolsheviks than the lectures at the University, he had never succeeded in earning his diploma. Nevertheless, when the Bolsheviks seized power, the University granted him a diploma and he became an authority on legal theory for the Party, the government, and the Secret Police.

The session of the Troika was officially declared open by a soldier who began with the words, "In the name of the Bolshevik-Communist Party and the Soviet Government. . . ." The rest of the sentence was uttered in a kind of bewildering jargon spoken so rapidly from memory that it sounded like drumbeats.

Joachim Schultz rose from his chair and cast a baleful glance over the three prisoners. Then he called out in a heavy, bass voice:

"Accused Kolosov!"

"Here!" the prisoner in the gray coat answered.

"So, now let us see. Age forty-eight. Former chief engineer of the Municipal Electric Plant." There was a slight pause, then suddenly Schultz's words boomed out with exact precision: "For engaging in sabotage you are hereby sentened to be shot! Guard, remove him to the death cell."

The soldier standing behind the condemned man took his arm. Kolosov stood pale and exhausted, without the slightest desire to resist or defend himself. Andreyev raised his hand, then lowered it. "Wait one moment," he called to the guard. Then, fixing his gaze on Kolosov, he said: "Do you want to stay alive?" The man in the old, gray coat looked at Andreyev and the other two judges with empty, glassy eyes. He seemed to grasp with the last remnant of consciousness that he was being subjected to further torment, that he would not be allowed to die so easily, not until he had "confessed" and given them the names of the other "saboteurs."

"What do you want from me?" he mumbled.

Andreyev began to speak rapidly: "On the night of April 28th on the occasion of the convention of the District Committee of the Communist Party, when Party Secretary Tovarisch Shumak made his speech about the electrification of the country, at that very moment the entire city was blacked out and the machinery of the plant where you were the chief engineer suddenly broke down. Confess! Who collaborated with you in this act of sabotage?"

"That was not an act of sabotage. It was an accident." Kolosov summoned his last ounce of strength and in an agonizing whisper pleaded, "Why do you refuse to understand?"

Andreyev was about to ask another question and perhaps even unwind a bit of judicial procedure, but Kovalchuk stroked his foppish beard and broke in sharply:

"Stop coddling this counterrevolutionary swine. Time is short."

Kolosov was quickly led out.

Schultz again consulted his notes. Then he called out:

"Accused Maria Maslinova!"

As there was no answer, he struck the table with his fist and repeated louder than before.

"Maria Maslinova!"

"Here. Here I am," answered the slender blonde standing next to Mikhail. Her voice was deep-throated and her pale face was tranquil and composed. There was a dreamy, faraway look in her deep-set eyes. The long confinement in a cell and the many interrogations had neither hardened her nor robbed her of her attractiveness. Though she was still in her early twenties, she already had behind her years of devotion to the Communist Party.

Schultz read off one of the principal charges against her. "Your father, General Maslinov, has declared that you persuaded him to decline a military post. Do you confess this to be true?"

Maria looked at Schultz with all the loathing and contempt her gentle nature could muster. "I don't believe my father would say anything that wasn't true. Why don't you show me his confession and prove to me that it is in his own handwriting?"

Kovalchuk jumped up from his chair. This time he even neglected to smooth his pampered beard. "You papier-maché intellectual," he foamed, "you are being addressed by a representative of the Communist Party and the Soviet Government. Our word is sufficient. We are not required to submit documents or signatures."

"I demand that you show me proof," Maria insisted. "Lenin teaches us to put no faith in words."

"You whore! You should have your mouth washed before uttering the name of Lenin."

Maria could feel her blood beginning to boil. "You milksop!" she retorted. "Cut off your beard so that everyone can see that you still should be feeding at your mother's breast."

"For this member of the elite," Kovalchuk said through clenched teeth, "the penalty is liquidation. This aristocratic bitch masqueraded as a Party member. Her so-called heroic deeds at the front were nothing but bribes with which she bought the trust of those whom she betrayed. That is how she was able to act as a spy for her father, the Tsarist general. She has been caught redhanded. We cannot afford the luxury of coddling traitors. The sentence of this Revolutionary Tribunal is death!"

Andreyev, the puny little man with the huge spectacles who himself was a descendant of the former Tsarist nobility, kept a discreet silence and let his two colleagues deal with this case. He dropped his bespectacled eyes to the red tablecloth and busied himself writing hurriedly with his bony little hand. Had he stopped to read what he had written, he would have seen the same word scribbled over and over again: "Shoot, shoot, shoot."

Mikhail was so stunned by what was going on that when Schultz called out his name he didn't recognize it. The soldier standing behind him nudged him and said, "Answer when spoken to."

Schultz, impatient now, looked up from the table and repeated, "The accused Mikhail Kruger!" Then his impatience turned to anger and he spelled it out. "K-r-u-g-e-r!"

Mikhail shuddered. He had a horrible feeling of awareness. The other two prisoners had been led away. He was alone before the Tribunal. A cold chill went through him. His teeth chattered. With trembling voice he said, "I—I am Mikhail Kruger," and burst into heaving sobs. His will was broken. His knees sagged under the weight of his body. He saw the face of death and he so wanted to live. He sank down to the marble steps of the dais, threw back his head, his eyes gaping at the three judges, and cried out in a heartrending voice, "I want to live. I'll do anything, but spare my life."

Andreyev grabbed his spectacles from his nose and bent over to whisper something in Schultz's ear. Schultz let out a laugh like a horse's neigh, leaned over and whispered the message into Kovalchuk's ear. Kovalchuk fondled his beard and looked into space for a moment. Then he nodded twice.

All three judges rose and began to file out. When they reached the door, Schultz suddenly pivoted around and bellowed at the soldier who stood behind Mikhail: "Throw him into the death cell!" A sadistic smile crossed Schultz's lips as the soldier led Mikhail away.

The death cell was very large and, although it was dark, Mikhail could feel its vastness. Opposite the long wall—against which the condemned were shot at close range—he could discern great windows that had been boarded up to shut out any light. Despite this, thin, silvery strands of a full summer moon had slipped through the chinks of dry wood and cast a pale luminescence over the room.

Mikhail peered about him. In a far corner lay a figure covered by an old, gray coat. He recognized the engineer Kolosov. He seemed so quiet that Mikhail wondered whether he was breathing. He turned from Kolosov and as his eyes became accustomed to the gloom, he was able to make out another figure. It was Maria. She sat in one corner of the floor, her shapely legs drawn up and her hands clasped under her knees. Her eyes, which were almost hidden by her long lashes, seemed to be fixed on the door as if she were waiting for someone. He went to her and lowered himself to the floor beside her.

"What is your name?" she asked him in her deep voice.

"Mikhail," he said. "Mikhail Grigorevich Kruger."

"Kruger? Is that German?"

"No, Jewish."

"A Jew? You don't look it—I noticed you at the trial."

He was pleased. "And I watched you too."

"Did you?"

"Yes. I admired your courage."

"I just told them what I thought of them."

"I wish I could have done that. Instead, I behaved like a child."

"How old are you?"

"Seventeen."

"You look a lot older."

"I've often been told that."

"What sort of 'counterrevolutionary' crime did you commit?" she asked, but before he could answer she covered his mouth with her soft hand. "No, don't tell me. I'd rather not hear it." Then, with an anxiety she tried to hide, she added, "You are not afraid?"

"I am not afraid now."

"I'm glad. We must be brave, Mikhail. We must not let them think we died like cowards."

In the stillness Mikhail turned to look at Kolosov. "Is he asleep?" he whispered.

"Yes," said Maria quietly, "engineer Kolosov is asleep, fast asleep."

"Is he ill?"

"He's better now. The pain is gone."

"Did they torture him much?" Mikhail shuddered.

"You said you are not afraid." She smiled a forced, wan smile. Stretching her hand out, she touched him tenderly.

"I wonder how anyone could sleep at a time like this." His courage was beginning to fail him again. "I couldn't. I must think, think."

"It is too late for thinking now," Maria answered, dolefully. She nodded toward the corner. "Kolosov has stopped thinking. His heart gave out before the end. He is dead."

"Dead!" cried Mikhail and he crept closer to Maria as though she could shield him from any harm. He seized her hands in a gesture of desperation. She freed herself, put her arms around him with motherly tenderness and pressed his head to her bosom.

"Don't be frightened—and don't frighten me, Mikhail. There is nothing left for us to fear. We have only a few hours. It won't be long."

He raised his head from her breast and looked into her face. From his lips came a soft whisper. "I'm not afraid for myself. But what will happen to my poor mother and my brothers and little sister?"

"Dear, sweet boy." She held him in her arms and rocked him back and forth as though he were the child she had never cradled. Then she stopped and looked down at him. She allowed herself to see what she had known before, that he was not a child or a boy. She bent down and touched her cheek to his. Then her lips found his.

A delicious warmth went through his body suffusing every muscle. He had never felt this kind of warmth before. It wasn't the warmth of a cloak or the sun but something deeper and inexpressible. He had never before been held in a woman's arms, nor had he ever dreamed it could be so intoxicating. He felt the world vanish as in a mist and he soared higher and higher into another sacred, exotic, and magical world in which there was no fear of death because there was no death. This was a world of impelling, irresistible, unending life. He murmured, "No, Maria. We are no longer afraid of anything. Together, there can be no fear."

Maria buried her head in his shoulder and dug her nails deep into his flesh. Tears ran down her face. She knew death awaited her. Still, she wanted to suffer the joy of love she might have had, had she lived.

It was now his turn to protect her. He held her as in a vise, locking her within his own private world. In this world there was no death. The sky was filled with hazy, blue clouds and he was a prince in raiments of gossamer gold walking on a carpet of air with the princess in his arms. Her eyes were like twin sapphires, her body fragrant with myrrh, her hair glowing and silken. Her lips were like a draft of strong, sweet wine. Around them hovered white-winged angels circling about him and his princess in a heavenly dance, and singing a paean of praise to the universe. And as Mikhail held Maria in his arms, a paean burst from his lips and he sang from the depths of his soul, the age-old song of praise to the Maker of life, of heaven and earth, the praise sung by angels and men to the God of the Universe: "Hallelujah! hallelujah! hallelujah!"

Maria had stopped weeping. She clung to Mikhail as though his body were a rock of refuge, listening in awe to his song. She kissed his hands, his eyes, his brow. Then she began to sing, first slowly, hesitatingly, then stronger and stronger.

And as their linked voices rose on the night and were carried down the dark, endless corridors of the prison, the words cast a spell over all who heard. It was the sound of peace, of universal brotherly love for all those who were in bondage, whether Christian, Moslem, or Jew. And those who lay in the dark cells heard and understood and their hearts awoke. And they who were condemned to die, sang together: "Hallelujah! Praise to God! Praised be the name of the Lord!"

And as the prison walls rang with song, Mikhail and Maria, locked in their embrace, grew silent, until at last they sensed that their moment, short as it promised to be, had come.

"Take me," Maria said softly.

Mikhail kissed her with all the unleashed passion of a man no longer a boy, with all the instinct and ardor of the lover. "You are my love, Maria," he whispered, his trembling hands groping for unfamiliar places. As he found what he sought, the lovers shuddered and as flesh met flesh, Mikhail felt as though his body were rising from the dead. Life had just started; semen imprisoned in his virgin body had found a sanctuary. He felt a happiness he had never known before.

Afterward they lay silent, their passion exhausted, their bodies filled with sweet languor. Slowly reality, like a sharp knife, began to cut into their consciousness. They felt this together, as though it were a common pain. And they knew that the time for confession was near. They separated and lay silent for a while longer. Suddenly Mikhail sat up and listened. "Do you hear something, Maria?" He jumped up and began to pace the floor of the cell. Maria sat up too and followed him with her eyes. Presently she called to him, "Come here, Mikhail. Sit down near me"

He sat down.

"Dear Mikhail," she said tenderly, "I heard something too. I'm afraid our time has come. Do you think it would make us feel better if we prayed?"

A heavy thud of boots beyond the door grew louder. The lovers looked into each other's eyes. Now they saw death. Their hearts stood still. Maria leaped to her feet and began to run back and forth in the cell like a trapped animal. Mikhail sat as though glued to the floor. Suddenly Maria stopped before him and seized his hands, just as Mikhail had done before.

"Do you know the psalm, 'The Lord Is My Shepherd'?"

"Yes, Maria."

"Say it with me, Mikhail."

Together they began: "The Lord is my shepherd. I shall not want. He maketh me to lie down in green pastures. He leadeth me beside. . . ."

The words froze on their lips as the door clanked open. Three soldiers, guns in hand, stalked in. Maria kissed Mikhail once, deeply. Then she tore herself away and flung herself into a corner of the cell, falling to her knees and crossing herself rapidly, again and again.

"Mikhail Kruger!" one of the soldiers called out.

"Here," Mikhail's voice quavered.

"Come with me," said the soldier, pulling Mikhail to his feet and leading him out of the cell.

Once again Mikhail walked down the interminable corridors of the palace cellar, through a silence broken only by the hollow sound of his footsteps and the echoing thud of the guard's boots. Then the silence was shattered by two rifle shots in quick succession and a shriek of agony. Mikhail collapsed into a heap.

"Maria," he gasped. He lay motionless, his face against the stone floor of the corridor, that final shriek searing into his brain. The soldier bent over and yanked him to his feet. "Stop acting as if you're the one who's been shot instead of that female aristocrat back there," he said sardonically. He prodded Mikhail. "Keep moving, we have an appointment. Tovarisch Nathan Wieder, Chief of the Cheka, wants a word with you." He looked scornfully at Mikhail and added: "Although I can't understand why he would waste his time on the likes of you."

They stopped before a white door embossed with a twin-headed eagle and a crown. The soldier knocked. The door was opened by Wieder himself, a dark-complexioned, middle-aged man with black, curly hair.

"Come in," he said to Mikhail. He dismissed the soldier with a gesture and motioned Mikhail to sit down on a finely upholstered, yellow leather sofa. The room had formerly been the private office of the Tsar; now it was the office of the Chief of the Cheka. Wieder walked about the room for a while. Then he stopped in front of Mikhail and stood looking down at him. Mikhail was startled by the man's eyes. They were dark, soft, almost tender and in their depths lurked the shadow of some inscrutable grief. His voice was kind.

"Kruger," he asked quietly, "do you think you might be able to forget the experience of this last year?"

"A year?" Mikhail was stunned.

"Yes. You were brought to us a year ago. We are releasing you. But for certain reasons, I am advising you to try and forget. It never happened. Unless I have your word, I cannot undertake the responsibility of releasing you."

Mikhail choked. Convulsive tremors of joy, pain, and relief racked his body. "I promise," he whispered.

"Very well, then. Be a man. Understand, speak little, keep your eyes ahead of you and look neither to the right nor the left." He paused. "About your family, I regret to have to tell you that your mother passed away. They tell us she was ailing. As for your brothers and sister, they were taken to a government home. They will be raised there and given an education. There is no need to worry about them."

Mikhail felt a sudden grief mingled with a blinding fury. But he clenched his teeth and fought it down. Everything was very clear now. Understand, speak little, and keep one's eyes ahead. The price of life.

"When did she die?" he asked in a dull voice.

"Some time ago."

Mikhail's eyes grew hazy and the veins stood out on his forehead.

"Where can I go?" he asked in bewilderment.

"That is what I want to talk to you about," said Wieder. "But first I might as well tell you that you owe a great debt to your friend Boris Garber. Not your life, because you would not have been shot. You were thrown into the death cell to teach you a lesson. But you would have gotten at least ten years if Garber hadn't convinced us to give you another opportunity to prove your devotion to our Soviet Motherland."

Wieder went to his desk and picked up a letter which was

written on white paper engraved with a red letterhead, the official stationery of the Secret Police. He folded the letter, enclosed it in an envelope, returned to the sofa and sat next to Mikhail.

"Kruger," he said earnestly, "I want to help you. You have nowhere to go. I don't want you to return to the streets of your neighborhood. It would serve no purpose. You have no one there now. Not even Garber is there any more."

At these words a dark shadow crossed Mikhail's face. "What has happened to Boris?"

Wieder smiled good-naturedly. "Don't worry. Nothing has happened to Garber On the contrary, he has a future in the Party. He has a strong character and he knows what he wants. A pity he doesn't have your education and intelligence, Mikhail." The Chief of the Cheka put his hand on Mikhail's shoulder. "We need devoted, patriotic young men. Moscow is rounding up the superior element in the Party and in Komsomol. Tovarisch Stalin is doing the same."

Mikhail looked questioningly at Wieder. "Stalin?"

"He is the General Secretary of the Central Committee of the Party." Wieder hurried on. "In Moscow there is a committee whose sole purpose is to sift through hundreds of candidates to find the best youth for positions in the capital of our great country. They are looking for young Communists with good education. Unfortunately we have very few of those. Two of my friends with whom I fought in the Civil War, Professor Maslov and Colonel Ivanov, are on the committee. I recommended your friend Garber to them. Although he lacks education, I saw that he was suitable material for Moscow. I hear that he is doing very well and has even found himself a wife."

This bit of news was so unexpected that Mikhail could not control his emotion. He stammered as he cried out, "Boris married? It seems only yesterday that we shared our secrets together."

"It's been exactly a year," Wieder reminded him, "and we have kept our eye on you. But you must forget that you have been here. If some day you meet me or anyone that you have seen here, you do not know us. Remember that! As for your future, let me explain. The Army is looking for officer material and the Cheka is seeking prospective agents, counterspies, and police officers. Our land is encircled by capitalist enemies, and we must defend our hard-gained revolution. We must prepare, train, forge from among our own ranks, young Communists who can enter the military, political, and economic branches of our government." He stopped suddenly and examined Mikhail closely. "And what is your opinion, Kruger? Would you like to study at a military academy or at a school for the Secret Police? Which will it be?"

The question was so sudden, it seemed to drop from the clouds. Mikhail sat motionless and numb. The deep dimples in his cheeks had disappeared during his imprisonment and his face was now pale and drawn. His light-brown eyes darkened. Slowly, however, he straightened himself. Yes, he had come to a decision. He was going to risk his freedom but he had to speak out.

"I would make a poor soldier or secret agent," he began timidly. "My dream has always been to be a writer. At the gymnasium I got the highest rating in composition and creative writing." He ended limply.

"So? Excellent! The Revolution can use young talented writers, too. But that comes later. Now we have to think of the Army and the secret service. I have come to the conclusion that you are not suited for our department as an agent, but for the Army you will do fine. In any case, if you don't turn out to be a good cadre officer, I'm sure you will make a good political commissar. I suggest you volunteer for the Red Army. You will study at the Moscow Military Academy. You're a bright young man, Kruger. Some day I expect to see you as a political commissar or maybe even a general."

"I don't want to be a commissar or a general," Mikhail replied flatly. "If I have to, I will serve my two years as an ordinary private."

"Your wishes be hanged!" Wieder's voice rose. "Perhaps you didn't understand me before. I have my quota to fill and only a reservoir of illiterate louts to draw from for officers' training at the military academy. You are a likely candidate. Now do you understand?"

Mikhail could see that he had no alternative. "I understand and I accept."

"That's the spirit, Tovarisch Kruger." It was the first time in more than a year that anyone had addressed him as "Tovarisch." It showed that his loyalty was no longer questioned. "Now listen to me. You are free and your prison record has been destroyed. If you should ever be questioned, you may answer that you have never been arrested. Furthermore, we will credit the two years at the military academy toward the required military service in the army. Then if you see that you are really not fit for a military career you may resign and choose something else that you have your heart set on. The most important thing is to be loyal and devoted to the Revolution and to avoid any indiscretion; to know when to speak and especially when to be silent. And if your destiny leads you to becoming a writer, then write whatever benefits our Party and country and disregard your personal sentiments." He shook Mikhail's hand.

"I promise to serve my country and the Revolution in the best way I know how," Mikhail answered earnestly.

Wieder rose and handed the letter to Mikhail. "And now," he said, "go to headquarters. You will receive the necessary papers." He shook Mikhail's hand. "Good-bye and good luck."

Mikhail put the letter in his pocket, turned and walked out of the office. He passed many guards on his way out of the palace but no one tried to stop him.

It was almost morning outside. Mikhail began to walk. Then he stopped and looked back at the white marble palace. He had gone in there one day in the early summer of 1920 a naïve boy and he had left his boyhood behind him in those dark caverns. He gazed about him. It was summer again. In Alexander Park, swaying trees and glistening, dewy green leaves greeted him as he walked. The sun rose from the sea in joyous splendor, bathing the awakening city in its heavenly glow.

PART ONE

Purging the Counterrevolutionaries

CHAPTER ONE

It was Mikhail's tenth spring in Moscow and it seemed as though he were tasting its beauty for the first time, like a lover who only grasps the depth of his passion on parting from his beloved. In a few minutes he would be on a train speeding toward the provinces by order of Josef Stalin, now the First Secretary of the Communist Party and Premier of the Union of Soviet Socialist Republics.

On his way to the railroad station, Mikhail took one last look at the city he had grown to love. The Moscow River, spanned by broad stone bridges and flanked by steep embankments, was teeming with boat life. Along the banks, under blooming white acacia trees, elderly couples sat on benches and basked in the sun. And over the entire scene loomed the silent Kremlin, its white bulwarks, its cloisters, and high, thick walls rising like a specter between the river and the vast, empty Red Square.

The Kremlin. Its presence fell like a shadow across Mikhail's morning. He was uneasy about his mission and reluctant to leave the security he had found in Moscow. But there was nothing to be done. Stalin's whims were law and they were absolute. He hurried on to the station.

The Bransky Voksal waiting room was jammed with people, packages, sacks, and valises. Most of the travelers were peasants from the villages, in Moscow on a holiday. A few of them still wore their fur coats. About a hundred young men and women were huddled in a group, chattering and singing the current lusty, unmelodic Bolshevik tunes or breaking into old Russian and Ukrainian folksongs. A few soldiers with harmonicas and balalaikas sat with their jackets unbuttoned and played, while others reeled and swayed to the rhythm of the peasant dances. Some of the peasants cracked nuts, chewing the kernels with gusto and spitting out the shells on the ground. In one corner of the station a group of girls were busy delousing each other's hair, crushing the lice they found between their fingernails with passionate satisfaction. A man who was standing nearby watching the girls said to his companion:

"Hey, 'Koom.' What do you think? Is this the bread we were promised?" He cackled, pleased at his own joke.

A man wearing a red cap and carrying a big broom pushed through the crowd, shouting, "Make room, you tramps, while the station is swept!" Two soldiers with rifles followed him and cleared the station. In a few minutes the sweepers left and the travelers swarmed back into the station. Then a bell clanged and the station gates swung open. The passengers surged onto the platform and rushed toward a waiting train. The easy camaraderie that had prevailed in the waiting room was quickly dissipated in the wild scramble for seats. The cars were choked in the space of a minute. Soon even the standing room was exhausted and the remaining passengers were forced to clamber up to the roofs of the cars.

Mikhail remained standing at the gate, hypnotized by the sight of a thousand people taking a train by a frontal assault. The "new" Russia never ceased to amaze him.

When the platform was cleared of the stifling crush, he walked past the long line of packed, rickety passenger and freight cars to a new, freshly painted coach which carried the inscription:

FIRST CLASS. RESERVED SEATS. FOR OFFICERS AND COMMISSARS OF THE RED ARMY, DULY AUTHORIZED PARTY MEMBERS, AND GOVERNMENT OFFICIALS ONLY.

What a luxurious feeling to be a commissar! Mikhail thought. He climbed aboard and located his compartment. Both berths were vacant and he saw that he would be traveling alone. He was glad, for he was in no mood for conversation. As he walked to the window, there was a shrill, piercing whistle. The locomotive heaved a deep sigh and gave off a cloud of white steam. The train began to move slowly and Mikhail was on his way to the distant village of Krasney-Bor.

The train was soon out of Moscow and its suburbs and plowing through the endless Russian plains. Mikhail stood with his face glued to the window as the flat green fields monotonously passed before him. It was as if the train were motionless and the scenery racing backward. His mind, too, began to race backward. He was glad that he had left the Moscow Military Academy and at long last had decided to study at the University. Yet, where was he now? On his way to a provincial village to straighten out the mess created by Stalin's harsh and thoughtless collectivization of the peasants.

Almost reflexively, Mikhail looked about him, as though even his thoughts might be picked up by a suddenly materialized secret police agent. He saw, with a feeling of relief that he despised even as he acknowledged it, that there was nobody in the compartment.

What was he doing on such a mission? He wanted to be a writer, not a commissar. That's why he had left the Academy. Maybe his friend Boris was right. He ought not to give up the security of a career or a profession until he was famous.

The Military Academy is a golden opportunity for you, Mikhail, Boris had argued. A *fine career and a promising future. Why do you have to throw it away?*

Even the Colonel's wife, Yekaterina Petrovna, had told him: *Mikhail, you know how much I value your talent, but why give up your military career? The Colonel thinks you will eventually make a good officer.*

The thought of the Colonel's beautiful wife warmed Mikhail. He recalled their first meeting, when the Colonel had invited him to tea.

You may not believe it, Yekaterina had said, *but I once wanted to become a writer.* Now she would sponsor him because she liked his stories. *Come and see us often,* she had told him when he left.

With the Colonel's permission, I shall be delighted, he had replied.

Don't you think the Colonel would give his permission? she had teased. *I hope you put no faith in the stories you hear about my husband. He really is not so harsh as he seems. As head of the Academy he must be strict, but to know him well is to love him. So come to see us often and do not worry about the Colonel.*

Is that an order, my Colonel's wife? he had asked, lifting her hand rather awkwardly to his lips and kissing it. She had not withdrawn it.

Not an order, Mikhail, but my profoundest wish.

The telephone poles flashed by, visible for a split second against a blue-gray sky. Mikhail noticed a shepherd tending his flock and the sight brought his mind back to his mission. The peasants were revolting against the overly strict collectivization program, in which all possessions and products became the property of the state kolkhoz. And now Stalin was sending 25,000 young Communists, students like himself, to the villages to rectify the mistakes and bring order to a chaotic situation. In an Open Letter to *Pravda* Stalin had laid the blame on the village commissars—who else could be blamed? Stalin was infallible.

Daylight faded. The sun went down and the earth turned dark. Mikhail left the window, stretched out on his seat and closed his eyes. The train chugged on; stars began to cast their far, silvery beams in the night sky. Mikhail wondered what awaited him in Krasney-Bor. How successful would he be in dealing with rebellious peasants? It was his first big challenge. Ever since leaving the Academy he had been a student at the University—*a perennial student,* Boris had called him.

Perhaps Boris was right. Even his writing had suffered, despite Yekaterina's encouragement. What he needed was experience—how else could he write about life, about the new Soviet dream? The question was, could he command respect among the bitter, hardened peasants? And what would happen if he failed? The enormity of his task overcame him; he didn't want to think about it any more. He fell asleep to the steady clickety-clack of the iron wheels.

Mikhail had been asleep for several hours when the train stopped with a sudden jolt. Amidst much shouting and cursing, the locomotive was uncoupled. Mikhail heard a voice shouting: "The god-damned locomotive went dry! Bring me some water!"

There were many such stops at small way-stations and even

in the open countryside. Sometimes the water gave out, sometimes the coal. The farther they got from Moscow, the harder it became to fire the engine; the train kept losing speed, began to crawl, and finally came to a dead stop. The whistle blew and a wild tumult broke out. Mikhail was startled out of his sleep once more and made for the window. Armed soldiers were prodding the passengers out of their cars and forcing them to push the train. No one in Mikhail's car was disturbed.

It was nearly dawn. Mikhail opened the window and let in a draft of cool, fresh air. He saw a sprawling field of scorched earth and a toppled tractor standing like a monument, a symbol of a newly crushed peasant revolt. Involuntarily, an ironic smile crossed his lips. "This is a job for Boris, not for me."

Meanwhile the train, powered by two thousand hands and legs crept onward, a thin wisp of blue smoke rising gently from its quiescent engine.

CHAPTER TWO

Krasney-Bor was really two villages. Krasney, with its old wooden houses and ancient white stone church, lay in a green valley bordered by thick woods and dung-colored hills. A sluggish stream separated Krasney from the cluster of clay and white brick houses with straw roofs and the church with bulging cupolas and gilded crosses that constituted Bor. Beyond Bor stretched miles of fertile land furrowed by the plow.

The two villages had been united for as long as the oldest inhabitants could remember. And at last the poor peasants of Krasney (who were predominantly of Great Russian stock) and the rich peasants of Bor (who were mostly Ukrainians) had found something on which they could agree: a determination to resist the attempts of the kolkhoz to take over their lands and goods.

The issue of *Pravda* featuring Stalin's letter had not yet reached the village, nor had the circulars arrived from the Central Committee announcing that 25,000 young Communists with "full powers" were being sent into villages like Krasney-Bor to "straighten out the stick" which the local commissars had bent to the breaking point. Therefore when Mikhail introduced himself to the Secretary of the Village Party Committee and to the chairman of the Village Soviet, both of these commissars regarded him with suspicion.

"Here are my credentials, Tovarisch Secretary. I am authorized by the Central Committee of the Party to inspect your activities."

They were standing in the Village Soviet, a red-brick building festooned with portraits of Lenin and Stalin. The Village Party Secretary, Anton Semionov, immediately surmised the situation. Like most party functionaries he was accustomed to trimming his sails to fit the prevailing wind. "Oh!" he sputtered obsequiously. "From the Central Committee! All the way from Moscow! From the Kremlin! Oh, Tovarisch Kruger, you are more than welcome."

Mikhail, taken aback by Semionov's fawning, smiled good-humoredly at him and started to explain the purpose of his visit. "Tovarisch Semionov, you have undoubtedly read Stalin's letter in *Pravda*," and he held up the newspaper. "It was written especially for the village commissars. And for the peasants," he added, almost as an afterthought.

Popov, the chairman of the Village Soviet, examined Mikhail's credentials and glanced at *Pravda*. "Tovarisch Kruger," he said in a trembling voice, "we have not received the newspaper yet. We are far from Moscow and it takes weeks before *Pravda* reaches us. But believe us," and his eyes welled up with tears, "we have carried out every order of the Soviet Government to the last letter. We have done it with absolute Communist piety and devotion."

An orthodox Communist is like a disciplined soldier. He does not question the orders of his superiors; he obeys them blindly. Mikhail had observed this in Odessa and Moscow and now he realized village commissars were no different. He was impressed by the extent of the diffusion of party zealousness.

Tovarisch Semionov, a man in his forties with a bushy, blond moustache that hung down and completely covered his mouth, rubbed his white, pampered hands together and boasted.

"Tovarisch Kruger, our village is in the vanguard of the country's collectivization. It is true that we still have a few outcasts who resist us and refuse to voluntarily enter the kolkhoz, but we are giving no quarter to these counterrevolutionaries. We are forcing them to make this decision and I guarantee that they will eventually submit."

"I see," said Mikhail, with pointed sarcasm. "You are forcing them to enter the kolkhoz voluntarily."

Semionov could not decide whether this young commissar from Moscow was angry because they were using force to get the peasants into the kolkhoz or because some peasants still resisted the kolkhoz.

The Village Soviet chairman, Sviatislav Popov, a thin, sallow Siberian by birth and a sailor by vocation, a Communist sent into the village some years ago, hastened to satisfy any doubts Mikhail might have.

"Tovarisch Kruger, rest assured that this village will rid itself of every single counterrevolutionary and saboteur. We are sweeping all of them out with the iron broom of the Revolution."

"And I suppose," Mikhail said, "your revolutionary broom has swept out a great many peasants who refused to enter the kolkhoz voluntarily."

"Peasants?" Popov neighed angrily. "I don't call them peasants. They are kulaks, exploiters, agents of the world bourgeoisie. They are being purged out of here."

"Are you sure they are actually kulaks and counterrevolutionaries?" Mikhail asked. "Perhaps they are poor and honest peasants who in their ignorance, cling to their own little pieces of ground, their own cows, their own horses. Perhaps the pain of voluntarily giving up the only thing they can call their own is more than they can bear. Perhaps they do not understand that without this private ownership, their lives—the life of the kolkhoz—will be better. For such peasants an educational drive is in order. What they need is enlightenment."

Semionov was not a clever man. Like so many others, he had swallowed the Communist faith and now that faith was like a ramrod which held him rigid and made his motions puppetlike and grotesque. These robots were ready to destroy without mercy, to spill the blood of young and old if only they could send to the Kremlin, to Father Stalin, a report that the tasks imposed upon them had been fulfilled with absolute precision and the utmost speed. And Semionov, as indeed so many others, could not dream that the stick which he had swallowed was no longer straight and that he was about to choke on it.

"How dare they refuse to part with their property?" he demanded. "When the Party orders that the villages are to be collectivized, the order must be obeyed without question! Anyone who resists a Party decision is a counterrevolutionary. Lenin taught us that whoever is not with us is against us. And Tovarisch Stalin teaches us that if in a group of one hundred people there is one traitor whose identity is unknown, then it behooves us to destroy the entire hundred to make certain that we have rid ourselves of the traitor. Revolutions are not fought with kid gloves, nor can Socialism be built by soft-hearted ninnies. There is no easy road to success."

Mikhail heard him out and decided to drop the discussion. It was already late in the day, and he was travel-weary. He asked Popov what accommodations had been arranged for him. There was no hotel in Krasney-Bor. It was the custom for the local commissars to offer important visitors accommodations in their homes or locate a suitable room in one of the more attractive peasant houses. Both commissars first offered their own homes, "for as long as you stay," but Mikhail thanked them both and declined their hospitality.

"You see," he explained, "my mission is so delicate that it would be healthier for all of us if in carrying out my duties I avoided exposing myself to any suspicions of opportunism."

Popov and Semionov exchanged significant looks. Popov hastened to say,

"As you prefer, Tovarisch Kruger. We have many fine houses here and we will find a suitable room for you." He gave Mikhail's hand a friendly tap. "Come with me."

"Wait," said Semionov. He went over to a small desk at which a young girl had been sitting and typing all this time. The Party Secretary wiped his blond moustache; his gray eyes blinked. "Ksenia," he said sweetly, "your house is large and clean; only you and your mother live there. Maybe you could provide lodgings for Tovarisch Kruger. He has been put in charge of our village. He has been sent here from Moscow, by the Kremlin—by order of Stalin himself. Your mother should be happy to accommodate so important a guest."

Until now, Mikhail had not looked at the girl. She was evidently the office secretary for the Village Soviet and the Village Party Committee. She was fresh and bursting with health, but she reminded Mikhail of an animal that had been trapped and domesticated. Her flaxen hair, worn loose, cascaded over her bronzed shoulders and onto her white embroidered peasant blouse. Her light blue eyes were set far apart in a round, full face. Except for a pointed chin, she would have been beautiful. Neither Mikhail's presence nor the importance of his position seemed to make any noticeable impression on her.

He walked over to her and smiled. She raised her eyes from the typewriter and forced herself to smile back at him.

"A wonderful idea!" Popov cried enthusiastically, grasping at this opportunity. "Your guests have always praised your mother's cooking very highly, Ksenia."

"If you wish," the girl replied without looking up. "My mother has never objected to the guests you have sent us."

Ksenia's mother, Prosia, was accustomed to receiving guests sent over by the Party Committee and the Soviet. She treated them all with the same cordiality. She assumed that Mikhail would be pleased with his room and her cooking and that he, like the others, would reward her with several rubles when he left. But she was startled to find that this commissar was so young—and yet, as Popov had explained, he was a very important personage.

Prosia's husband had fallen in the battles against the White Guards, and as the widow of a Red Army hero she was treated with the highest respect. She received the maximum pension, and a job was provided for Ksenia in the office of the Village Soviet and Party. Between the pension, Ksenia's job, and her own cooking and washing, she managed a respectable living.

Prosia loved great cities, having been in Moscow once in her youth, and she tried to raise her only daughter in an "urban" manner. She did not work in the fields like the other peasants, but instead cultivated the garden near her house. In general, she felt herself very close to the village authorities and in fact was the only inhabitant who approved the outrages committed against the peasants by the local commissars. She was convinced that the abolition of private property among the peasants was a just cause, that the drive to bring the peasants into the kolkhoz, even against their will, was linked to the very ideal for which her husband had made the ultimate sacrifice.

Ksenia's mother brought out Mikhail's dinner. The bowl of steaming hot potatoes and the dish of cold, refreshing sour cream were more than welcome. Prosia noticed the earnest attention Mikhail gave this simple meal. She decided she liked him. Not for herself, of course, although she thought of herself as still desirable despite her forty-odd years—some of her guests had made romantic overtures towards her. This boy was too young for her, but he might be suitable for her daughter, and it would do no harm for Ksenia to leave the village and live in Moscow where life was so much better.

Ksenia sat quietly at the table. This was her usual manner. In the village she was considered reserved, different, a snob. Actually she was frustrated. She resented spending her days at the typewriter in the red-brick building. She was a Komsomol, of course; nevertheless, she despised her two employers, Popov and Semionov, and the frenzied impersonal brutality with which they carried out the directives of the Party and government. She longed for the time when she could be free to do as she pleased, go where she wished. But she dared not speak. She had no one in whom to confide, least of all her mother. So she nurtured her smoldering resentment until it became a burning hatred of the village commissars.

Ksenia studied Mikhail as he ate. If he is a commissar, she thought, he must be as cruel as those she worked for—perhaps even more cruel since they had sent him here from Moscow on an important mission. Yet he had a kind face—and see how eagerly and childishly he attacked his food. Once or twice Ksenia caught his eye and she thought she saw loneliness there. She knew what it was to be lonely, for the village youths regarded her with fear and suspicion and never came calling on her. How she envied the village girls who had beaux to go strolling with on a lovely night like this. Wouldn't it be nice, she thought, if this young man—even if she didn't like him—should ask her to go out for a stroll and all the villagers should see her? It would then be their turn to envy her! Should she ask him when he finished eating? Perhaps if she went alone he would offer to accompany her. Or maybe she could turn the conversation to the problems of the village so she could find out how he felt and what he thought.

Mikhail sensed the girl's restlessness. As soon as he had eaten, he surveyed the white-plastered interior and vaguely patted the heavy, old-fashioned table, pausing in his gesture long enough to examine a group of three portraits on one wall—Lenin and

Stalin, framed in red velvet, and between them, framed in black, the master of the house, Ksenia's father. They hung there like holy images, ikons of the Russian Orthodox church. Then he looked at Prosia and a moment later at Ksenia.

"I feel very much like taking a walk. Would you care to come with me, Tovarisch Ksenia?"

Prosia smiled, "Do you hear, daughter? You have been invited."

Ksenia nodded unbelievingly and stood up. Mikhail took her by the hand and drew her out of the house. It was as if there had been a tacit agreement.

Overhead, white clouds sailed on an ocean of blue sky. The earth was hushed, but now and then a gentle rustle like a woman gliding by in a silk dress, broke the silence. It was the enchanted music of a green tree, trembling at the touch of a sudden breeze. The two young people walked together without a word; they realized that words would sound hollow in the stillness that surrounded them. Hand in hand, they wandered through the twisting lanes of the village. Ksenia led the way. A full moon slowly floated upward to meet them. Suddenly they stopped and looked at each other as though they had been strangers before but were strangers no longer. He sought her eyes. They were sad, sadder than he had hoped he might find them.

"Is there something wrong?" he asked.

"Let us walk a little farther," she said. "I have something to show you."

They came to the river, its current so lazy that it seemed motionless. In the distance a hound bayed. A second hound answered, then a third, and in a few moments the night was filled with the sound of howling dogs. It stopped as suddenly as it began.

"Was that the village symphony concert?" Mikhail asked, smiling.

Ksenia nodded in her earnest way. "It's from the village. We get the same chorus every night."

They held each other's hand and looked down into the water for a long while. Darkness settled and a chill breeze sprang up. Ksenia shivered. Mikhail extended his arm to protect her from the cold, but she twisted away and walked on. He did not insist but let her go. She stepped down to the bridge that linked the two villages and leaned against the railing. His eyes remained fixed on the stream below. Suddenly, a shriek from a small, lop-sided stone shack not far from the river broke the stillness. Mikhail went white and started after Ksenia. She was leaning back against the bridge railing, her eyes filled with tears.

"Ksenia!" he cried, bewildered. "Tell me! What's going on here?"

Since she did not know the exact nature of Mikhail's mission she had not dared tell him how she felt about the handling of the peasants. Now she would have to take that chance.

"You will have to forgive my weakness. It is not pity for counterrevolutionaries that makes me weep when they are put to torture. It is hard to explain. I just cannot bear the thought of human suffering."

Mikhail seized both her hands. "What are you saying? What counterrevolutionaries? Who is being tortured?"

"Those who will not join the kolkhoz of their own free will," she sobbed, "are tortured until they submit." Mikhail looked astonished. "Yes, they even torture peasants in the office of the Village Soviet. They torture them back there, and if that does not work, they bring them here to the stone shack to finish the job."

"So that's it!" Mikhail's astonishment had given way to anger. "Ksenia, you are to tell me everything you know about this. My reason for coming here is to see that justice is done and to put an end to the despotic rule by village commissars. Moscow has entrusted me with this duty."

Now Ksenia was no longer afraid of him. She told him all she knew.

"The kolkhoz is not only taking all land but also cows, horses, wagons, pigs and even hens—in short, everything. This leaves the peasants nothing for themselves. They are starving. If you went into the home of any peasant, you would see children who are swollen with hunger. The peasants have become terribly embittered; they have set fire to the kolkhoz granaries and to the kolkhoz stables, burning the cows and horses alive,

They cry that they have been robbed of their goods and livestock and if they cannot have them, no one else will."

There were more cries from the stone shack, and now they could hear a string of curses interspersed with such words as "counterrevolutionary," "saboteur," and "kulak."

"The swine!" Mikhail's grip tightened on Ksenia's hand. "They will pay for this. Illegal trials and secret torture chambers! Those bloody tactics will turn every peasant in Russia into an enemy. Semionov and Popov will both rot in jail for this."

A wave of confidence surged through Ksenia. She had been right after all. She had not been a traitor, but a good Komsomol and Communist. The proof was before her eyes—Mikhail Kruger, a genuine Party man, a Communist of stature and merit, sided with her and felt as she did. With such a man she could go to the far ends of the earth! But now his condition was dangerous. He was enraged, and he might act rashly.

"Calm yourself, Mikhail," she said. "Anger will accomplish nothing. You will have to exercise iron discipline and control. Do you wish to see for yourself what is happening? Come. I will go with you. Whatever lies in store, we will face it together."

He pressed her hand in his. "It was a lucky day when I met you, Ksenia."

They went up to the stone shack and Ksenia knocked at the door. A voice, Semionov's, shouted:

"Who is it?"

"It is I, Ksenia. Open up."

A second voice, this time Popov's, answered sharply.

"You, Ksenia? What devil gave you the itch to come here?"

"It was no devil. There is a man with me, Tovarisch Mikhail Kruger. I advise you to let us in."

The door opened at once and Mikhail and Ksenia stepped in. They found themselves in a large room, with walls of huge, rough-hewn stone blocks and a cement floor. The place was bare except for a tremendous table built of heavy red wood and a big bucket of water. On the table lay a man with a ragged, mottled beard and wildly staring eyes. He was naked to the waist and strong ropes bound him to the table. His face and chest were smeared with blood and from between the toes of his black and swollen feet jutted bits of charred paper. When his tormented eyes fell on Mikhail and Ksenia he shrieked:

"For the mercy of God, tell them to stop this torture."

Semionov and Popov grinned darkly at one another and turned to Mikhail with an air of subservience.

"This one is a kulak who has been agitating the peasants not to join the kolkhoz," Semionov explained.

"He is also the one who burned down the bread warehouse," Popov added.

Mikhail turned to the two village commissars, his face livid with fury.

"If this peasant is in fact a kulak and a saboteur, he should be tried before a revolutionary tribunal. Why was he not turned over to them? Who gave you the right to torture people? Instead of explaining the meaning and value of the kolkhoz, you would rather flog, beat, kill, and torture. You are not building a kolkhoz, you are destroying it."

He went over to the table and looked down at the peasant. "Untie him and see him home safely. This is an order. Exactly what time is it now?"

Semionov stood bewildered, cringing, his face ashen. His hand shook as he took out his watch.

"It is nine o'clock, Tovarisch Kruger."

Popov, too, was in a state of shock. Both commissars were convinced that they had only been carrying out the orders contained in the secret circular which they had received from the Kremlin. Spare no one it had said. Who had rescinded this order? There had been no warning. The earth had suddenly crumbled beneath them.

"I repeat," said Mikhail harshly, "see this peasant home. Then call all the Communists in the village to a closed, emergency session of the Party and Komsomol. I give you exactly two hours in which to call this session. I will address the meeting and issue instructions as to the correct method for gaining peasant cooperation."

He walked out, leading Ksenia by the hand.

CHAPTER THREE

The village Communists assembled in the meeting hall of the red-brick building. They were about forty strong, the so-called cream of the community—the village intelligentsia, the peasant-village vanguard, a privileged forty out of a population of about five thousand.

A sudden, emergency night session of village Communists was an extraordinary event. The suspense was great. The order to attend had gone forth by every possible means of communication and had traveled with lightning speed. No one was exempt. And every man and woman in the hall knew that beyond the four walls of this gathering, in the stirring, rebellious countryside, there was not a single Communist.

Ksenia, as usual, sat up front to record the minutes of the meeting, her notebook and pencil on the table before her. Next to her were Semionov and Popov. At the other end of the long table, alone, was Mikhail. Behind them hung a single, white-framed portrait on a red wall—the low brow, black moustache, and grim eyes of Stalin. As they waited tensely, there floated into the hall from some remote village street, the faint sound of revelry—boys and girls who never meddled in politics and spent their evenings carousing and dancing to the music of the balalaika and harmonica. This and the distant baying of a hound were the only sounds that broke the stillness in the meeting hall.

Semionov finally turned to Mikhail with a questioning and deferential air. Mikhail nodded his consent and Semionov got to his feet and rang the bell.

"*Tovarischi, Partaytsi e Komsomoltsi!*" He paused a moment, inhaled sharply and continued, "the emergency session of the Party and Komsomol of the village Krasney-Bor is hereby declared open."

Everyone rose, boomed out "The International" in a businesslike way and sat down again.

Mikhail surveyed the faces of these village Communists. They were all so stern and smug—a gallery of faces grown hard with pride and a sense of privilege. His eyes narrowed. "Comrades!" he began, "as your Party Secretary has reported, my purpose in coming here is to provide you with the correct methods for carrying out the collectivization program. What do we mean by correct? I have with me the *Pravda* which contains the letter of our leader Stalin. In this letter he states that the commissars in the rural districts have failed to understand their obligations and as a result have crippled the entire program of collectivization. I want you to note that the letter bears the caption, 'Dizzy with Success.' How was it possible to cripple so clear and simple a program and to bring chaos and disorder to the villages? It could only be done by bending the straight stick of the general Party line to the breaking point. And who did this? The ignorant, inefficient, and criminal local commissars. They, and they alone, have brought ruin and havoc to our country. The evidence is all around us. The poor peasant has been deprived of everything, including his last cup of flour and his last goat. Do you call this the correct way to establish the kolkhoz among the villages?"

Semionov could not contain himself. He rushed toward Mikhail brandishing a document.

"Here is the directive," he shouted, "the secret directive which we received, instructing us not to spare anyone who refused to join the kolkhoz. Up to this moment no new directive has been issued to us. And if someone in the Central Committee, in the Kremlin, has blundered, that is no fault of ours!"

This gave Popov the courage to shout in turn,

"The high and mighty commissars commit blunders and then throw the blame on us. It never fails. If they are wrong, they blame their subordinates!"

"Silence!" Mikhail thundered. "I don't question the fact that the old directive uses the expression 'do not spare.' But does it direct you to beat and torture? That is your personal interpretation of the decision of the Central Committee I say—"

He got no further. From the street came a roar, followed by shrill cries of "Down with the murderers!" "Down with the kolkhozes!" Then a rock came crashing through a window, striking someone's head and covering him with blood in an instant. The audience froze. Before anyone had time to recover from the first shock, more rocks came hurtling into the hall showering the occupants with splintered glass. There were blood-curdling yells:

"Turn over to us the dirty Jew from Moscow!"

"Surrender the Jew Kruger!"

"No one will get hurt if you hand over the Jew commissar!"

Mikhail grasped fully what had happened. This was an insurrection. The peasants were in revolt and his own life hung in the balance. He also understood that they would not be satisfied to kill him alone, the outsider, but when they had destroyed him they would make short work of their local Communists. A battle was inevitable and the time had come to use force. The assembled Communists were on the verge of panicking. Glaring at Semionov, at Popov, at the frightened Communists before him, Mikhail shouted:

"What are you waiting for? You brought this on yourselves—now let's see if you have the guts to smash it!" He pulled out his revolver. "In the name of the Bolshevik-Communist Party, I order you to take up arms and defend yourselves." Then he fired in the direction of the window.

Ksenia rushed toward him as someone in the mob fired back. She grabbed his hand and pulled him down with her to the floor. They crawled under the table, and from this cover Mikhail emptied his revolver into the street through the broken window.

The local Communists dropped to the floor for safety. The few with revolvers fired at the mob through the smashed windows. The rioters responded with an occasional shot and a hail of rocks, bricks, and chunks of metal. In the midst of the battle there was a tremendous explosion nearby, followed by a sheet of flame that lit up the entire village.

"They've blown up the kerosene tank!" Semionov screamed. "The kerosene for the first kolkhoz tractor!"

"Our tractor, they have destroyed our tractor," sobbed Popov.

The tumult around the building subsided as the frenzied peasants began to stream toward the raging fire. The kolkhoz warehouses were burning fiercely. Here were retribution and sport combined! It was a spectacle they could not resist.

The revolt ended as quickly as it had begun. However, had the men who ignited it been more persevering, it might have ended differently.

Just two hours earlier, Semionov and Popov had obediently dragged the battered and bleeding kulak, more dead than alive, to his home. They had been watched by a ragged, unkempt, hirsute peasant who habitually wandered through the village streets. On the breast of this man hung an iron cross. His lips were fixed in an inane smile and his eyes were full of grief. He was the picture of a soul gone mad.

He had once been a priest, known as Father Timofei; now he was known simply as the Man of God. He roamed aimlessly, a homeless derelict, sleeping in the stables, which now stood empty because all the cows and horses that were still alive had been locked up in the big, new kolkhoz stable. He usually babbled childishly, but occasionally he had spells of lucidity. At such times he could stand and recite whole passages from the New Testament or from Tolstoy.

Some villagers claimed the Man of God was not really insane. After all, the Bolsheviks had not arrested and killed him as a counterrevolutionary, despite the fact that soon after the outbreak of the Bolshevik Revolution, when the Ukraine was occupied by the armies of Kaiser Wilhelm and a hetman called Skoropadsky had been placed on the throne in Kiev, the priest Timofei, staff in hand, a pack on his shoulders and an iron cross on his chest, had journeyed from village to village, preaching for all to hear: "The Germans are the messengers sent by the Lord to save us from the Communist Anti-Christ!" When the new Bolshevik-Communist forces swept the German invaders from the land and conquered the hetman's Ukraine, the obstinate priest mysteriously dropped out of sight and was forgotten. Then, some time later he had reappeared, wearing the look of a madman, his hair and beard wild, his clothes torn and filthy and the iron cross hanging from his neck on a rusty chain.

And so Timofei, the idiot priest, while roaming through the streets that night, had seen Semionov and Popov dragging the peasant between them. He shrank into the shadows and watched. He recognized the victim at once, Stepan Bulba, a prosperous peasant whom neither words nor blows could force to join the kolkhoz. The Man of God could not overlook so strange a procession. Where were the Anti-Christs taking Bulba at so late an hour? He would follow them. He moved like a ghost from fence to fence. Neither of the commissars noticed him; they were too busy arguing and trying to hold up Bulba's sagging body.

"Tovarisch Popov, I am afraid this saboteur will not last until we get him home. Look at him. He's half gone. It's like dragging a corpse."

"Nonsense, Tovarisch Semionov. He is a healthy peasant. They all hang on to life. Don't worry, he will survive."

"I hope so, or it will go bad for us with Tovarisch Kruger."

"Do you think he is really a big wheel in Moscow?"

"He certainly acts like a big commissar."

"You are missing an important point. He is a Jew. I can tell because he speaks Russian like one of those intelligentsia, like a professor."

"I thought he was a Jew. His name doesn't sound Russian at all."

"He could be dangerous. There is no telling what plans he may have up his sleeve."

"We'll find out when he makes his speech at the meeting in a couple of hours. He will have to show his hand."

They stopped before a gate leading to a small flourishing garden and a pleasant white cottage with a green tin roof. Unlatching the gate, they dragged the peasant along the path and propped him up against the door.

"Hey! Natasha! Your stupid man is back."

"Open up, Natasha, and get your husband."

The door opened and a middle-aged peasant woman came rushing out.

"Stepan," she screamed, "you've come home! Thank God you are free!"

But Stepan did not answer. He swayed back and forth with buckling knees and then fell forward. His wife managed to pull him inside. Semionov and Popov vanished.

Natasha undressed her husband as he lay on the floor, dragged him to a bed, and ran into the kitchen to prepare something that would help revive him. When she came back with a pot of boiled milk, he was already dead. She ran outside, shrieking.

"The commissars have killed my husband, my Stepan!"

Peasants came running from all the neighboring houses. The mad priest saw that the time was ripe. He rushed down to the village, collected a handful of drifters on both sides of the river, and led them back to the cottage of the dead Stepan. The cottage, the garden, the street—all were soon alive with a great mass of humanity.

Once again the Man of God saw himself as the pastor at the head of his flock. He launched into a sermon:

"Our Gospel teaches us: 'For nation shall rise against nation and kingdom against kingdom.' This is the time of great tribulation, the time of the Anti-Christs, Bolshevik-Communists and Jews. O my brethren, a Jew has come down upon us from Moscow, a young Satan; and he will help Semionov and Popov drive every single peasant into the kolkhoz. Then will be hell on earth. All private dwellings will be destroyed and a new house will be built, a commune for all people. You will all sleep together and cover yourselves with one huge blanket. For any man to have one woman will be forbidden, since in a commune 'mine is yours and yours is mine' and everybody will be wallowing in sin. . . ."

He was answered by a deafening roar of approval. The din was so great that although he continued to harangue the mob he could no longer make himself heard. His own cohorts, who had circulated among the crowd, now went to work, inflaming even more the hatred that the peasants felt for the village commissars who oppressed, tortured, and murdered the innocent. And as if this were not enough, the Jew from Moscow was the last straw! Great cries arose from the crowd, to avenge the death of Stepan, to slaughter the Communists, to burn down the kolkhozes. Above all, kill the Jew!

The enraged peasants, armed with stones, sticks, shovels, rakes, a few rifles, and anything else they could lay their hands on, now divided into two distinct groups. One group made for the red-brick building where all the Communists were holding their emergency session and the other for the warehouse in which the tractor and the kerosene tanks were kept. In all the noise and confusion that followed, no one noticed that the idiot priest and his henchmen, who had pledged their lives for the peasants' cause, had quietly removed themselves from the scene and taken to their heels, leaving the two masses of onrushing peasants leaderless.

The kerosene tanks exploded and a conflagration swept through large areas of the village. It was a great, roaring fire. Chunks of flame soared across the night like gigantic, golden birds. The peasants reveled in the spectacle like gleeful children. They demanded little of life—a crust of bread—their own—and a measure of joy which came from a gushing stream of vodka and from lusty songs and dances—from a fire, a blazing inferno with its thousands of yellow, flickering tongues, a thing of beauty and fascination that held them in a hypnotic trance. The peasants watched and revolt died out. For once, they were grimly satisfied.

Mikhail quietly put in a call to the nearest city for a fire brigade and a Red Army Riot Detachment.

CHAPTER FOUR

The following day there were mass arrests in the village of Krasney-Bor. Every peasant identified as having taken a direct part in the violence was thrown into jail, as was the idiot priest. Still, Mikhail was worried. The riot had been suppressed, but he still had to face a showdown with the local commissars, whom all the Communists in the area were sworn to obey. In this struggle he might meet with another kind of resistance, more subtle and more deadly. He would have to charge Semionov and Popov publicly with the commission of crimes. Most of the peasants, he knew, would be afraid to testify. Ksenia, the prime witness to the operations of the Village Party and Soviet, would not hesitate for a moment, but he was afraid that the commissars, their backs to the wall, might have her assassinated.

"Ksenia," he urged her, "go to Moscow—at least for a while. I will give you a letter to friends of mine, people you can trust. Go while there is still time. When I need you I can send for you."

But Ksenia refused to leave.

Prosia, who understood the danger her daughter was in, pleaded with her. "You are my only child and so young. You don't understand politics. Why did you get mixed up in it?"

"On the contrary," Ksenia answered stubbornly. "I understand it very well and I walked into it with my eyes open. Furthermore," she added, turning to Mikhail, "I think if a mass meeting were called and I spoke to the peasants, they might believe me. I think I can put an end to this horrible confusion about the kolkhoz. The Communists among them are all peasants themselves, and if you can handle Semionov and Popov, everyone else will hear me out."

Mikhail thought the matter over carefully. A mass meeting with Semionov and Popov acting in their official capacities might be dynamite. But a mass meeting backed by a heavy show of military force with the Red Army commander as co-chairman and a carefully prepared agenda might solve the problem.

"Very well," he declared, "I will call a mass meeting, provided that I can get more militia."

The mass meeting was scheduled for the following evening at the village clubhouse. Semionov and Popov showed remarkable alacrity in accepting the idea. It was their last chance. If they could get the priest and the rioters out of jail to testify for them, they might be able to swing the meeting to their advantage. But it would have to be done quickly or not at all.

An hour or so before the scheduled meeting, Semionov came running to Prosia's house, cursing Mikhail under his breath for flatly refusing to postpone the meeting. He was exhausted from the exertions of the last twenty-four hours. Things had not gone well. The officer in charge of the Riot Detachment had refused to release the priest, despite Semionov's authority and his insistence that no tribunal would ever convict an idiot. If only he could persuade Mikhail to release the priest! He had to see Prosia and talk to her. Time was short.

Prosia was alone. She watched Semionov hurry up the path and shuddered. She had once been very intimate with the Party Secretary. Now, as she greeted him, she forced a smile to hide her fear. Semionov looked about him half expectantly, half apprehensively, and sat down at the table.

"I see that both Ksenia and Kruger are out. That's quite a love affair." He laughed coarsely. "He's clever, that Kruger. I hope he survives his cleverness. I've come to warn you, Prosia. If you know where Ksenia is, get in touch with her and tell her she has got to keep her mouth shut at the meeting. Otherwise I cannot guarantee her safety. If she speaks, there are those who feel that she is not too young to die. We have been trying to get her alone, but she sticks to Kruger like glue, and half the time we don't know where he is. Stop her from going to the meeting if you can, but if you mention my name I tell you that your own life won't be worth a kopek. I don't give a damn whether she sleeps with Kruger or not, as long as she keeps her mouth shut!"

"You have no right to accuse my daughter of indecency," Prosia cried, forgetting her fear. "She is not like other girls. And since when are you afraid of anything that Ksenia might say?"

"It's not her, it's that cunning Jew bastard. All our trouble comes from these Jews."

"Jew, Jew!" Prosia said with scorn. "That's all you can say. And you call yourself a Communist. Since when does a Communist consider the Jew inferior to a Russian or a Ukrainian? Go away, Semionov, you make me sick!"

"Kruger has converted you too!" Semionov pounded his chest with his fist. "I am a Communist, a true Communist. I have dedicated my whole life to this ideal. But it doesn't follow that Communists must say 'thou' to the Jews who have wormed their way into the Party. The counterrevolutionary Trotsky is also a lousy Jew. And our leader, Stalin, knows exactly how to take care of him. Someone will know exactly how to take care of this Jew Kruger, too."

The full impact of Semionov's words suddenly struck home. Prosia stared at him; she could think of nothing to say. At that moment the door opened and Mikhail came in followed by Ksenia. He was pointing a revolver at Semionov.

"Semionov," he said, "you have a loud and filthy tongue. You are under arrest. Put your Party card, passport, and revolver on the table. If you have anything further to say, save it for the Central Committee. Resist and I will shoot you down like a dog."

Semionov's head sank to his chest. He stood there for a long moment. Then, without a word, he laid his revolver, passport, and Party card on the table. Mikhail took them, and said contemptuously:

"You are a much worse scoundrel than I thought. I knew that you were brutal and stupid. A fanatic who murders heretics is easy to understand. Even conspiracy can be condoned under certain inhuman pressures. But you are a reactionary and an enemy of the State. You will be taken into custody as soon as the new Red Army units arrive."

Semionov raised his head. "Red Army units?" he asked dully.

"Red Army units. Within the hour. You are to stay here under house arrest." He motioned to Ksenia and Prosia. "Come with me."

Outside, Prosia asked Mikhail why he had left Semionov behind, alone and unguarded.

"There's no point in my taking him into custody myself," he explained. "He won't run away. Without his passport and Party card he is like a man in chains. In the meantime, you had better stick close to me just to play safe. We are going out to meet the Red Army."

A quiet evening was settling over the countryside. An intermittent drizzle filled the air with a faint mist, and a balmy breeze blowing across the fields carried gentle hints of the cold weather in its wake. As seen from the outskirts of the village, the twin Russian and Ukrainian communities, one of white shacks with straw roofs and the other of brown cottages with tin roofs, seemed to Mikhail to symbolize a blending of Russian winter and Ukrainian summer.

Prosia was stricken by the burnt-out fields, where charred and broken cornstalks waved mutely in the wind. She wrung her hands. "Woe is me, the saboteurs have burned the bread out of our fields."

"Hush, mother," Ksenia said kindly. "Let us not call them saboteurs, but rather lost and confused peasants whose lives have been poisoned by our commissars."

Mikhail gazed down the road which split the fields in half. The Red Army would be coming along that road to restore order to a rebellious village. Heads would roll. Mikhail hated the thought. It violated everything he stood for. But his own life, Ksenia's life, and the lives of untold hundreds were at stake. It had to be done.

They had not long to wait. A white dust cloud rose in the distance and before many minutes had passed, they heard the tread of marching soldiers.

CHAPTER FIVE

Krasney-Bor was completely encircled by Red Army troops. The men who made up these units had been carefully groomed for this kind of job. They were well fed, fully trained, and hardened. In their code of discipline there was no room for leniency; they were simply a smooth fighting machine on a special assignment for the G.P.U.

The mass meeting had been scheduled for seven o'clock. By six-thirty, the peasants slowly gathered in front of the locked doors of the village clubhouse under the watchful eyes of Red Army guards, awaiting the arrival of the commissars and "the Muscovite, Kruger." The club manager, an aged peasant who had once been a schoolteacher, waited for the signal to open the doors.

The first to arrive was Semionov. He was escorted by two soldiers with fixed bayonets. A wave of surprise went through the crowd. Semionov was under arrest! The effect was electric. The sight of Semionov coming to the meeting under guard achieved in one tactical stroke what might have cost hours of agitation and persuasion at the meeting itself.

"This is the end of tyranny!"

"Hurrah for Mikhail Kruger! He is on our side!"

"He will abolish the kolkhoz!"

"Back to private ownership! No more starvation!"

There was a sharp report as one of the soldiers fired his rifle into the air.

"Shut up!" a sergeant bawled at the crowd.

The peasants quieted down but their mood was buoyant.

Mikhail arrived, accompanied by Ksenia and the Commandant of the Red Army troops. He was greeted by tumultuous applause. His reception bolstered his confidence, and he quickly gave the signal for the doors of the clubhouse to be opened. The peasants followed Mikhail's group inside, pushing and shoving for seats. The building, which had formerly been a church, was too small to seat everyone, so the latecomers overflowed the aisles, jammed the doorway, and crowded around outside the open windows.

Popov, the official chairman, called the meeting to order and recognized Ksenia as the first speaker. He hoped that even though Semionov had been arrested, he had been able to frighten the girl and her mother enough to make them passive. But he was wrong.

"I am the child of peasants whose fathers and forefathers were peasants," she began calmly. "Here in this village, my ancestors were born and labored. Here I was born and grew up before your very eyes. My father laid down his life in your behalf when he fell in battle against the White Guards."

She paused and looked at the assembled peasants significantly. On the dais, Popov looked pleased; her speech sounded innocuous enough. "But our village," Ksenia added, changing her tone, "like many other villages, has been struck by a great catastrophe. Evil and ignorant people have found their way into the Party, and self-seekers have become the commissars of our village."

Popov straightened in his chair. He looked at Semionov, who avoided his eyes. Mikhail recognized the familiar phrases used in the Party brochures which he had noticed strewn around the desk in the office where Ksenia worked.

"The tyranny of these malicious and shameless men has driven you into crime and turned you into enemies of the Soviet Union," Ksenia continued. "But I say that you are honest and hard-working peasants and that you love the Soviet Union. Your own eyes have now seen the guilty in chains. You have seen that the Bolshevik-Communists have spared not even the Party secretary, Semionov himself. And now," she pointed at Mikhail, "an authorized agent of the Central Committee of the Party, Tovarisch Mikhail Kruger, one of twenty-five thousand handpicked men, all of whom are among the most advanced and loyal Communists in the land, will clarify for you the situation that has arisen in the kolkhozes and you will realize that freedom and justice reign in the Soviet Motherland."

Mikhail stepped up to the rostrum to a storm of applause and hurrahs. Waving a copy of *Pravda*, he cried in a ringing voice:

"Tovarischi peasants, men and women! I hold in my hand a historic document. It is an open letter which our beloved leader and friend, Josef Vasyrionovich Stalin has issued to the press. But it is not merely a letter. It is his explanation, addressed to all peasants of Soviet Russia, Soviet Ukraine, and all the other Soviet Republics. This explanation has been written in a manner so masterful, so wise and yet so simple, that everyone without exception, can understand its exact meaning. This letter which Stalin has written to you is called 'Dizzy with Success.' In it Stalin explains that those who were entrusted with leadership—the commissars, the Party secretaries and the Soviet representatives in the villages—have robbed and beaten without authority, forcing the peasants into the kolkhozes against their will. And then these opportunistic commissars have sent reports to the Kremlin announcing that their villages have achieved total collectivization. This is what our wise leader, Tovarisch Stalin, calls 'dizzy with success.' For what kind of success is it to drive peasants by force into the kolkhoz?"

He stopped suddenly as a thought flashed through his mind. Had he the right to say this? Was this not demagogy? And if he were telling lies and half-truths to these simple people, what could he tell his own conscience except that demagogy was more than words. It was a way of life. He went on:

"I assure you that neither the Soviet government nor the Communist Party nor, above all, our beloved leader Tovarisch Stalin has brought this evil upon you. It was your own vulgar and selfseeking village leaders who bent the stick out of shape. You have now seen for yourselves and will continue to see, that everyone who has bedeviled you will receive his just punishment. From this moment on you are free to direct your village life as you see fit. To those who choose to remain individual owners we will restore the land and goods taken from them by the kolkhoz. Those who choose to remain with the kolkhoz will henceforth receive a parcel of land adjacent to his house, one cow, two pigs and five hens for private use."

Mikhail went back to the table and sat down. The clubhouse shook with applause and conflicting shouts of yea and nay. Popov snatched a document from his breast pocket, hurled it on the table and transfixed it with his forefinger.

"Tovarisch Kruger," he said, trying to make himself heard over the din, "I am certain that you are fully aware of this secret directive. Semionov read it to us word for word at a closed session of the village Communists. And now you arrive with a letter by Stalin, a letter merely printed in the press and not directly addressed to our village leaders. You want us to believe that the blunder was not committed by the Central Committee or by someone in the Kremlin but that we, the village commissars, are responsible? Why make us the scapegoats? Is this our reward for honestly and loyally executing every instruction contained in the secret directive? It should be obvious to you, Tovarisch Kruger, that you have no grounds for arresting Semionov."

"You are mistaken, Popov. Apart from the commission of wrongs against individuals, which you consider debatable, the charge will also be counterrevolutionary conspiracy." He paused a moment to let his next words sink in and then added with quiet anger, "There are others, known to both of us, who have opened themselves up to that charge."

Popov went as white as a sheet. Without a word, he got up and left the meeting.

The noise in the clubhouse was now becoming unbearable. The peasants were quarreling bitterly amongst themselves, and only the presence of the troops prevented fighting and bloodshed. The military commandant, who till now had been sitting quietly at the rear of the platform, leaped forward, pounded on the bell and roared in a voice like a bassoon:

"Qu-i-e-t p-l-e-a-s-e!"

The peasants shrank back in their seats and there was a sudden silence. They saw for the first time that Popov was not in the chairman's seat. In their bickering and confusion they had failed to notice his exit.

The commandant turned to Semionov, who was still guarded by the two soldiers. "You have heard the accusations. Have you something to say?"

Semionov shook his head angrily. "*Nyet!* Not here."

The commandant again rang the bell. "The floor," he announced, "is now open to criticism and self-criticism. If anyone wishes to have the floor, he may address himself to the chair. If there are no speakers, we will declare this meeting closed and tomorrow morning at eight you will each come in person to the Soviet and declare your intention as to joining the kolkhoz. Does anyone wish to have the floor?"

In the silence that followed only one hand went up, a gnarled, work-hardened peasant hand.

"You may have the floor," boomed the commandant.

The peasant, who sat in one of the rear seats, got up slowly, shamefacedly, and looked about him. The others all twisted their necks to stare at him. There was curiosity, surprise, even suspicion on their faces. He was only one of them, a mere peasant. What suddenly made him feel so important?

"I would just like to ask a question—" the peasant stammered.

"Speak up, man," the commandant encouraged him. "You are among friends."

The peasant whacked himself on the head with his fist. It loosened his tongue.

"Is it true that we can either join the kolkhoz or stay out of it?"

"Correct," said the commandant and burst out laughing. "Come now, speak your mind. Out with it."

"And if we don't join up, do we get back everything that was taken from us?"

"Correct," the commandant repeated, but this time with an air of caution.

"But how can anything be returned to us?" asked the peasant. He paused a moment and then as if driven by the conviction that there was no answer to his question, blurted out, "How in the world can you give back to us what has been completely destroyed, burned, robbed, and scattered?"

"If there is nothing left to give back, it is your own fault," the commandant replied sternly. "You had no right to start a rebellion, to burn your own livestock and goods collected in the kolkhoz, to poison your own horses and cows and kill all your hens. You will now have to wait until the government sends aid to this region. But I guarantee that every man, whether he remains an individual owner or joins the kolkhoz, will receive what he requires."

"That is all I wanted to hear," said the peasant. "In that case I am for joining the kolkhoz."

"Bravo!" shouted the commandant in his deep voice and began to clap his hands.

The rest took up the applause. There were enthusiastic cries of "Long live our kolkhoz," "Long live the collective," and "Long live the genius Stalin." The Komsomolites and Party members had taken up strategic seats among the peasants and these slogans now came thundering from every part of the hall. The effect was contagious, whipping the downtrodden villagers into a frenzy of approval. The clubhouse shook with "Long live the kolkhoz!" It was unanimous.

Mikhail leaned over to the commandant and whispered, "The whole village will now join the kolkhoz. The peasants really do not have any alternative."

"So it would seem," replied the commandant. "But I think you ought to check on Popov. Find him. He's been gone too long. When he left he looked as if he had belly cramps. You go for Popov while I calm the peasants and close the meeting. I must make sure that they disperse quietly."

Mikhail left and the commandant turned to the peasants. "And so, Tovarischi peasants, we now close this meeting by singing 'The International,' after which you will all return peacefully to your homes."

He sang the first few bars in his vibrant bass voice: "Arise, ye prisoners of starvation . . . ." The peasants took up the song with gusto.

When Mikhail returned, the clubhouse was empty except

for the commandant. There was a look of tragedy on Mikhail's face and his lips were trembling. He could barely speak.

"What's wrong, Tovarisch Kruger?"

"Popov has hanged himself."

"He what?" The commandant's hand went automatically to his revolver holster, then dropped to his side. "You say he hanged himself?"

"Yes. In the club manager's office. He threw a rope over a beam and hanged himself."

The commandant regained his self-control. "That scoundrel!" he said. "What a mess to leave me with. He might at least have waited until they shipped him out to Siberia. Well, I guess there's no help for it now. I am going to post a guard over him. This is to be kept absolutely quiet, you understand? After dark we'll move the body out of the village. There is no sense in stirring up any more excitement among the peasants."

But by morning all Krasney-Bor had learned about Popov's suicide. There was no reaction. The peasants' hatred had burned out, leaving the ashes of resignation. They dutifully reported to the Village Soviet office, where Mikhail and the commandant warmly shook the hand of each one and directed him to Ksenia, who sat with a new kolkhoz registry book open before her. Mikhail could not help observing that the villagers showed more apathy than enthusiasm when it came to signing the registry book. They reminded him of lost sheep. He watched them put down crosses, circles, or some other mark of identity against the names which Ksenia wrote into the book. They were joining the kolkhoz, after which they would accept the praises and compliments of the new leaders, doff their caps respectfully and go home to celebrate the event by drinking vodka.

That evening, Mikhail sent a wire to Moscow, announcing that the village of Krasney-Bor, which was under his jurisdiction, had once again achieved one hundred percent collectivization through a reorganized kolkhoz and that peace and order had been established.

CHAPTER SIX

One evening Mikhail and Ksenia were lying on a haystack staring up at the blue-black sky that hung above them. The smell of fresh-cut grass mingled with the scent of apples and honey from the nearby orchards. Mikhail was counting the shimmering, flickering stars that seemed brighter in the reflection of a full moon. Ksenia was playfully winding a piece of straw around her finger.

"I guess you'll be leaving now," she said to him suddenly.

Mikhail hesitated before answering. He had been trying to think of a way to broach this subject. And now Ksenia had come right out with it. It was just like her, he thought.

"I must wait for my orders," he said finally.

"From Moscow?"

"Yes. I requested replacements for Semionov and Popov. When they arrive, I suppose I will be called back to Moscow."

"How long do you think it will be?"

"I don't know. A few days, a week—"

Ksenia tossed aside the piece of straw she had been toying with and shifted her weight slightly away from Mikhail. He sensed her disappointment and, secretly pleased, raised himself on one elbow and took her hand. He felt awkward. He didn't know exactly how to phrase what he wanted to say. He wasn't even sure he knew what he wanted to say. He had never before felt this ache in the pit of his stomach. They had known each other only a short time, and yet he wanted her; he loved her, he was sure.

"They will have to find themselves a new typist," he said. It was a line he might have written for a story, and now that he had said it, he was more uneasy than ever; he felt out of character.

"Oh?" Ksenia said with surprise. "What do you mean?" For

a fraction of a moment she thought that perhaps this young commissar had found fault with her, too. Then her instincts assured her that this was a man, not a commissar, lying next to her. "Do you mean . . . ?"

"Well, if you would like to come to Moscow with me," he hesitated.

"Moscow! Mikhail! Moscow—Och ma! Mikhail, how wonderful." She threw her arms around him and held him tightly. "Do you mean it, Mikhail? I've always dreamed about Moscow. I've read about it in our histories, and Mama was even there once."

It takes so little to make her happy, Mikhail thought. Aloud he said tenderly,

"Yes, yes, I'll take you to Moscow, my little dove. You will see Moscow with your own lovely blue eyes."

"And you, Mikhail, what will you do? Will you go back to the University? Will you continue with your writing?"

"Yes. I will continue with my studies—and my writing."

"But where will we live? Will we have to live in the students' quarters at the University?"

"No, Ksenia. We'll get a small apartment. I have friends in Moscow. My best friend is very high in the Kremlin, the right-hand man of Stalin himself."

"Who is that?"

"His name is Boris Garber. We grew up together in Odessa."

"It that where your family is, in Odessa?"

"I have no more family. My mother and father are dead and my younger brothers and sister are in a government home in Siberia. I visited them last year. They didn't even remember me," he said sadly.

"Poor Mikhail," Ksenia said in such a way that Mikhail could not remain sad. "But your friend, Boris—what about him? Is he as good looking as you?" she teased.

"Probably not," Mikhail answered in mock seriousness. "Anyway, he has a wife and child."

"What is she like?"

"A bright girl and a good Communist. She was a secretary for the Commissariat for Heavy Industry when she met Boris.

She's pretty too—although not as pretty as you," he added, pinching Ksenia's cheek.

"But isn't Boris young to have such an important position? Stalin's right-hand man!"

"It's a long story. When Lenin died, you know there was a struggle between Stalin and Trotsky. Stalin controlled the Party machinery. He gathered around him a hard core of young, dedicated Communists that he was sure would be devoted to him. Boris had the good fortune to be at the right place at the right time."

"And where were you at this time?"

"In the Moscow Military Academy."

"You, Mikhail, a warrior?"

"Yes, it is strange. You can imagine how I hated it. I have wanted to be a writer ever since I can remember; the army is not for me. But it was the only way out of—" he caught himself in time—"Odessa."

"It must have been unbearable."

"No, not unbearable, just confusing—although I didn't realize how confusing it was until years later."

"What do you mean?"

"Well, the military exercises were tough but consistent. There was an enemy; you knew who he was, you got yourself in fighting condition; and then you fought him. But the political indoctrination was not so simple. The Political Commissar at the academy was Professor Feodor Alexeivich Maslov. He is now at the University, but then he was just beginning his career. He looked like a simple, good-natured peasant, but he spoke like a true revolutionary orator. I remember a story he used to tell in his course on the history of the Red Army. This was just before Lenin died."

Mikhail looked around and lowered his voice.

"It was an account of how, when the White Tsarist Cossacks marched on Petrograd to quell the Revolution, Trotsky singlehandedly halted the attack. He rode out alone, on his white stallion to meet the Cossacks and with the voice of a lion roared: 'Brother Cossacks, you are peasants. How can you resist our Revolution that offers you land, bread and freedom? It is not Lenin who is your enemy, but they, the generals, the bourgeoisie. Fight *them*! Kill *them*! And come with me to our brother Lenin!' And they did.

"Professor Maslov told the story with such fervor that we would rise and stamp our feet and shout, 'Long live Lenin and Trotsky!' "

"It's a wonderful story," Ksenia said.

"A few years later, at the University, I took a course in Russian history with the same Professor Maslov. He told the same story—only this time Stalin was the man on the white horse, *Stalin* was the man who persuaded the Cossacks to come over to the Revolution."

Ksenia clapped her hands over her ears and whispered fearfully, "Don't, Mikhail, don't tell me any more. I don't want to hear it. It's dangerous."

"When I asked Professor Maslov why he had changed the story, he said that history changes and he had changed with it."

"Perhaps if Professor Maslov changed his mind, we should follow his example."

"It's not as simple as that, Ksenia."

"You don't like Professor Maslov, do you?"

"On the contrary, he is very likable. He is an opportunist, but in some ways, in order to survive, we are all Maslovs."

Mikhail lay back in the hay and there was silence for a while. Finally, Ksenia asked,

"How did you get into the University?"

"Boris. He has a great deal of influence. He didn't want me to leave the Academy, but he arranged it when he saw how determined I was. And Colonel Ivanov, the Commandant of the Academy, knew I wanted to be a writer, not a soldier."

"And he spoke for you?"

"Yes, he was a wonderful person—like a father to me."

"You were lucky."

"Actually it was his wife, Yekaterina Petrovna. She read some of my stories and encouraged me to write. She is a cultured woman who has studied at the University. I would have tea with her and we would discuss literature and my writing. Without Katya I don't know—"

"*Katya*? I thought she was the Colonel's wife."

"She is, but she is much younger than the Colonel, perhaps only a year or two older than I."

"And he allowed you to see her?"

"He arranged it."

"*Alone?*" Ksenia was really interested now.

"Yes, but it was not what you think. Ours was a spiritual relationship, a meeting of souls—" Mikhail realized immediately that he had used the wrong word. "Mind" would have been a better choice; Ksenia would not understand—or perhaps she would understand too well, better than he.

"You were in love," she said flatly. She was sitting up now.

"Yes and no." Mikhail propped himself on his elbows. "It was a platonic love; we enjoyed each other's company." That was the way it was, wasn't it? he asked himself. "At any rate, nothing happened," he added aloud.

"You are still in love with her," she said coldly.

"No, Ksenia. I told you how it was with us. I swear I never even touched her. I just admire her very much and when you meet her you will see why." He reached out and tried to embrace her, but Ksenia tore out of his arms, jumped off the haystack and ran toward an old oak tree at the far end of the garden. She encircled the trunk with her strong arms and resting her head against it, she sobbed as if her heart would break.

Mikhail, left alone, felt an icy void and a deep longing. He waited for a few minutes and when Ksenia did not return, he went looking for her. He saw her near the tree, pathetic, outlined in the moonlight. He offered her his hand. "Come, dearest. Come, my love. Come back." And like a groom leading his bride to the altar, he led her back to their trysting place.

In the distance the songs and dances of the young village folk reverberated in the stillness of the night.

Mikhail held Ksenia locked in his arms. Her bronzed, full face so near to his shone in the brightness of the night. He caressed her and she welcomed the touch of his hands on her body. She lay her blond head on his chest and pressed against him with her firm young breasts and in the coolness of the summer night the warmth of her body excited him. He fondled each strand of her hair and kissed her eager lips. She shuddered and clung to him as his hand probed. Ksenia was like nature itself, unfeigned and guileless; Mikhail was her first love. After every lover's ecstasy, they lay quietly in a half-dream, then made love again.

With the dawn they both fell into a deep sleep. Roosters crowed, shepherds drove their flock into the pasture, a tractor lumbered along, a truck whirred by, but still the lovers slept.

The sun was high in its zenith when Ksenia's mother approached the haystack and announced,

"Come on, you two. Get up. It's past noon."

CHAPTER SEVEN

The new secretary for the Village Party Committee and the new chairman for the Village Soviet that Mikhail had requested did not arrive immediately. Instead, two newspapermen came and spent an entire week investigating the situation in the village. Within a few days of their departure there appeared in the press a sensational account of "the rich and charming village of Krasney-Bor, where peasants have attained happiness by converting their community into a thriving kolkhoz." There were photographs of Mikhail and Ksenia, the story of their lives (which described Mikhail as a lifelong peasant), their work, their heroism in the village. Each article ended by saying that the village of Krasney-Bor had petitioned the Communist Party and the Soviet government to bestow upon Mikhail and Ksenia decorations of merit for their unstinted and devoted labors in bringing peace, order, and prosperity to the collectivized village.

But Mikhail's work in the village was not over. There were still a great many problems to be settled. Food had to be brought in to feed the starving peasants. The kolkhoz land had to be resurveyed and the work in the fields had to be organized. A new tractor was needed. The situation in the village in no way resembled the glorious account in the press, but the peasants no longer rebelled. They adapted themselves to the new life and bent their necks under the yoke of the kolkhoz. The Moscow press gave prominent coverage to Krasney-Bor, holding it up as a model kolkhoz in a model village—a shining example to all the kolkhozes and all the villages in the entire Soviet land.

Five months went by. Mikhail, absorbed in the life of the village, dressed like a peasant and grew a beard. His speech grew provincial. He even stopped caring whether some day news would arrive that he could return to the University, to Moscow. He thought seriously and earnestly of marrying his lovely Ksenia, yet somehow they never got around to it. The stress of daily life was too great. After a while they simply began to live together as man and wife. There was no ritual, no formal celebration. It was as though their kind of world did not allow it. His "marriage" was in harmony with an accepted custom in the reborn Russia which required no further ceremony beyond the nod of mutual consent by a man and woman and binding on neither.

On free evenings Mikhail and Ksenia would go for long walks. Always, as if by instinct, their steps would lead them to the bridge that spanned the river between the two villages. Arm in arm they would stand silently and watch the slow-moving stream go by.

One evening by the riverbank, Mikhail pointed to the deserted stone shack which had been used to torture recalcitrant peasants and said to Ksenia,

"You must remind me first thing in the morning to have that miserable shack taken down. We don't need that prison any more."

A smile of gratitude and deep tenderness crossed Ksenia's face. Mikhail was touched by that smile. Maria—proud and brave Maria—had smiled at him like that. He trembled as he recalled Maria, and beads of cold sweat stood out on his brow.

Ksenia, sensing something, moved into his arms. "You frighten me, Mikhail. Sometimes I don't know you." She stood up on tiptoe and kissed him. "Why are you so upset, dearest?"

"Perhaps because I hate war and brutality and I know what prisons can do to you. I was never really meant to be a commissar."

"Yes, I know. You are a writer, a scholar. You want to write and study and now you have been trapped in this village and you can't escape. I understand. But what can you do? It is what they call Party discipline. You should know that better than I."

"And yet," he answered softly, "I am grateful for my exile. I have found you here."

The heavy winter descended. Silent, biting frosts gripped the village. The trees were anchored in dazzling ice, the river frozen solid and covered by snow on which the children frolicked.

The village now had a new Soviet chairman, Party Secretary and kolkhoz director. The entire administration was in new hands and Mikhail's mission as commissar plenipotentiary was over. There was nothing left but to return to Moscow. But the Central Committee of the Party was still reluctant to release him. In the last few months the kolkhoz had made remarkable progress and the Kremlin authorities were anxious to keep Krasney-Bor in the limelight as a model village and model kolkhoz. The Kremlin grew lavish in its aid and subsidies. It provided tractors and materials for the construction of homes, a new club, a school, and a hotel. Food and clothing began to pour in. A new cooperative sprang up, with a store and even a movie theater. The peasants were inspired with new life and worked hard. They knew that elsewhere people were suffering and that dissatisfaction with the regime was increasing daily. But the inhabitants of Krasney-Bor with their bellies full could easily forget that other cities and villages were being ravaged by hunger.

Mikhail now had a great deal of time on his hands. He was impatiently awaiting orders to return to Moscow.

"Were there any calls for me?" he asked Ksenia each day.

"None, Mikhail."

"The kolkhoz, the Soviet, the Party committee?"

"Not a single call, Mikhail."

"Apparently they can get along without me. I am no longer needed."

One day, after the usual breakfast exchange, there was a knock on the door. It was the village courier. He was a one-armed Komsomol with shaggy hair protruding from under his army cap. He was very proud of his handicap and boasted of having lost his arm in the war against the White Guards. It gave the poor boy a great sense of importance and he strutted around the village like an unofficial commissar rather than what he was in fact: a messenger boy for the real commissars.

He held a telegram in his hand. His face was flushed and he was so overawed that he could barely speak.

"Tovarisch Kruger! A telegram for you! From the Kremlin! From the Kremlin itself!"

Mikhail grabbed the telegram and took it into his room. The others stood around too frightened to utter a word. The first to recover was Ksenia's mother. She got up from the table saying,

"If this is really a telegram from the Kremlin, it must be something secret. We must not ask Mikhail any questions. This means you too, Ksenia," she added. "Mikhail may be your husband, but he may have secrets even from you. If he sees fit, he will tell you about it himself." She eyed the courier sternly. "What are you standing around for? You've delivered the telegram. Your business here is finished."

The talk about secrecy was superfluous. The one-armed "commissar" had done his job only too well and by midday the whole village rocked with the news that Mikhail and Ksenia had been called to Moscow to be decorated for organizing one of the best kolkhozes in the land.

PART TWO

Stalin's Banquet

CHAPTER ONE

It was a year since Mikhail had seen Moscow and when he finally got off the train with Ksenia and looked around him, he was strangely disappointed. He had been homesick for the big city. Now the noise, the hurrying crowds, speeding automobiles, the dense rows of high, solidly massed structures, the flamboyant signs glorifying Soviet achievements and the unreal portraits of Stalin cast a pall upon him. But for Ksenia all this was new and exciting; it was for her even more beautiful than she had dreamed.

Mikhail sent the luggage containing their few belongings to the hotel room which had been reserved for them and suggested that they walk from the station to the hotel. He saw Ksenia's happiness. He would show her fabulous Moscow, Red Moscow, the metropolis of the Kremlin. Let her thrill to the wonder of it, this young companion of his who was looking forward so eagerly to the new, the better life.

The hotel was old and still retained an elegance dating back to the Tsarist days when it had served the Russian aristocracy. The Soviet regime had converted it into a guesthouse for the new "proletarian" aristocracy. It was used by government and Party commissars, both civil and military, who came to Moscow under orders. The hotel was their temporary residence for longer or shorter periods, as the case might be.

The room allocated to Mikhail and Ksenia was large and sunny. The furniture was old-fashioned, of heavy, red-lacquered wood adorned with finely carved figurines. The window looked out upon the gilded cupolas of the cloisters that rose above the Kremlin.

Ksenia could not take her eyes off the scene. Below her was the wide expanse of Red Square and directly opposite was the Lenin Mausoleum in its lugubrious black granite that blended

—despite the distance—with the gray Eastern baroque of St. Basil's Cathedral. This was her Russia, the mysterious Russia of storybook fame, exotic, heroic, inscrutable, come to life before her eyes.

Mikhail had already received word that he and Ksenia were to present themselves at two o'clock the following afternoon at President Kalinin's salon for their decorations. Mikhail was more than a little apprehensive and disturbed. Why were they being singled out for such commendation? What they had done was important, but he knew of really heroic deeds which had never even been acknowledged. All his life achievement and reward had been hazy concepts; now he was suspicious of his own elation over the proposed decoration. He decided to see Boris immediately. He was anxious for Boris to meet Ksenia anyway, and his friend, who had attended so many of these ceremonies at the President's palace, might be able to explain why this extraordinary honor was being bestowed upon himself and Ksenia.

A maid in a black silk dress and white apron answered Mikhail's knock and led him and Ksenia into a small living room. There was an air of official gravity about the apartment, typical of the residence of an exalted Party functionary, a commissar of the first rank. Boris, as usual, was sitting with his head buried in the *Pravda*. At the sight of Mikhail he rose and embraced him warmly. He was a powerful, broad-shouldered man with a large head and coarse features which added to the rugged character of his leathery face.

"Ah, Mikhail, so you are back at last! And this is the young lady you told us about." He bowed slightly in Ksenia's direction and stood back to appraise the couple, holding Mikhail's arm firmly. Mikhail could see that although Boris had not changed physically, his manner had become a little more rigid. He gave one the feeling that he knew the value of silence.

Boris' wife, Polya, who had been supervising the preparation of dinner, advanced to greet them. She hugged Mikhail, and then Ksenia. "I am so happy for you both," she said, trying hard to be convincing.

Polya had changed a great deal in her few years of marriage.

She had been gay and vivacious when she met Boris, and these traits, so foreign to his own personality, had quickly endeared her to him. Boris had found in Polya exactly what he wanted —a charming if not pretty girl, warm, aggressive and a bit talkative in a very pleasant way. She wore bright colors to set off her dark hair and eyes, and her clothes were more stylish than most. She was educated and well read, perhaps almost to a fault. She came from a wealthy Jewish family, but to Boris the fact that she was a member of the Communist Party more than made up for her former wealth. Boris was not passionately in love, but he needed someone like Polya to be with at all times. As for Polya, she quickly recognized in Boris all the traits of deep-rooted responsibility and surmised his importance in the Party. He appealed to her practical nature.

Boris and Polya had understood each other very well. He knew what she wanted and she knew what he needed. After their "marriage," which was simply a registering with ZAGS of their intention to live together, Boris and Polya had fallen into a pattern of the new Soviet way of life: constant work leavened by devotion to the Party. Then a son, Victor, had been born to them, and shortly after, Boris, the proletarian who had fought against being "exploited," had hired a maid. Polya's hands soon had become smooth and plump and useless.

Now Mikhail noticed a look of resignation in Polya's once vivacious eyes. She has too much leisure time, he thought.

After the introduction, Polya took Ksenia's hand. "Come, Ksenia," she said brightly, "let us leave the men to talk. I'll show you the rest of the apartment."

"You have found yourself a nice wife," Boris said approvingly when the two women had left the room. For a moment he was again the good old Boris, Boris the Strong who protected his friends and took them under his wing. But the moment passed and Mikhail sat face to face with Boris the Communist. He studied him closely. The trembling hands, the bitten underlip, the dark circles under his eyes, struck him as symptomatic of a deep, inner conflict. Here was a man who showed signs of sleeplessness, of mental strain, of eternal vigilance.

"You approve of her?" Mikhail asked.

"I do. I'm glad to see you married. Is this a free love marriage or are you registered?—though it doesn't matter either way. If you are smart, you will have children, a lot of children so she can keep busy, so she won't begin to—well, never mind —I think you get my point. Do you want to stay in Moscow or are you going back to the provinces?"

"I don't know, Boris. I suppose it depends on the Central Committee. They will decide my future."

"But tell me, what would you like to do if you had your say in the matter?"

"What would I like? Well, let me put it this way. I was very anxious to get back to Moscow. But now I am confused. Moscow was once a great, beautiful city, and I was a student thirsting for knowledge. I wanted to be a devoted Communist and patriot. True, I had certain doubts and disappointments, but your friendship helped me weather them. I think I could have learned to live with them and gone on being contented. But now things are different somehow. Moscow seems part of a dark and sinister world. Take tomorrow's ceremony, for instance. I cannot shake off the feeling that the honor we are about to receive may some day backfire. How do I know that the very thing for which I am being decorated today may not be called counterrevolutionary tomorrow? Popov, the Soviet chairman of Krasney-Bor, was as patriotic as you and I. He only carried out orders, and when the policy was changed, he became an enemy of the state. He hanged himself. So how do I know how or where I'd be better off?"

Boris' voice when he spoke was gruff with affection.

"Mikhail you reason well, but far too much. Remain in Moscow. You are not a man for the provinces. Besides, it will keep you near me. You're the only one in this forsaken world with whom I can speak without fear of being heard all over Moscow. That is how things are these days. All men watch each other, and Stalin watches all men. Not that I disapprove. It has become a necessary part of our life. We must be silent. We must be vigilant. In this Stalin is our teacher and we are humble pupils at his feet. For he is the master of silence, the master of the unspoken deed. He is the greatest of all men. As for you, Mikhail, get your decoration and then you will see. I suggest that you remain in Moscow."

Boris returned to his *Pravda*, signifying the end of the discussion and setting an example of the virtue of silence.

Mikhail browsed casually among Boris' bookshelves. He noted an increase in the number of encyclopedias and Russian-English and Russian-German dictionaries and the absence of many familiar editions on history, literature, and party politics. No doubt they had been banned by the "Glavlit"—the Central Censorship—as counterrevolutionary literature and Boris had burned them and restocked his library wherever possible with "corrected" editions. Mikhail deliberately ignored the missing editions, but he was curious about the dictionaries.

"Since when this sudden interest in foreign languages, Boris?"

Boris raised his eyes and looked at Mikhail over the edge of his newspaper. "Well," he answered matter-of-factly, "I am interested in German and English. They will come in handy." And he went back to his newspaper.

A telephone rang in Boris' private study. Ksenia came back as Polya picked up the receiver. They all could hear her conversation through the open door.

"Ah, Katya, my dear! We've been expecting you—what's keeping you?—Yes, they're here—His wife? She's with him. You'll love her. A wonderful girl—In half an hour, then—The Colonel? Boris? Hang on."

Polya came back and motioned to Boris. He got up, walked to his private study and shut the door behind him.

Boris' practice was to have Polya and no one else answer the telephone. He never spoke until he was satisfied that Polya had identified the person who made the call. He took no calculated risks. This was only part of the system of checks and counterchecks of which his life consisted.

Ksenia was intrigued by Boris' mode of living. He was to her a symbol of power which excited within her an ambition that Mikhail tried hard not to notice.

After a while Boris returned. He looked about him out of sheer habit, as if to see whether the same people were still in the room, took his seat again and said to Mikhail, "Ivanov is leaving for Turkey. Katya is coming alone. Go in there and pick up the phone. The Colonel wants to talk to you."

Mikhail went quickly into the study and picked up the receiver. "Colonel Ivanov!"

"Mikhail, my boy! I'm glad to hear you're back in Moscow. And I hear you've brought back a charming wife. Congratulations! Yes, and for the decoration, too. I have always felt you were cut out for honors, Mikhail. I only hope my own son—" His voice tapered off momentarily. "Well, I'll have to say good-bye now," he resumed. "I'm sorry I can't see you, but I have another foreign assignment. Turkey this time. We shall meet when I return. Meanwhile, take care of yourself, and have some teas with my wife and son. Good-bye, Mikhail." There was a click on the other end of the wire and Mikhail replaced the receiver. When he returned to the living room, Boris and Ksenia were making polite conversation.

"Moscow is a wonderful city, Tovarisch Ksenia, isn't it?" Boris was saying. "I imagine you have already discovered our fine capital."

Ksenia gave him a fetching smile. "Ah, yes, Tovarisch Garber. I find it a magnificent city. I already feel as if I couldn't breathe anywhere else."

Boris laughed hollowly. Since working in close secrecy under Stalin's personal direction he seemed unable to take any statement at face value.

"So you like Moscow, eh?" he said.

"Very much, Tovarisch Garber."

"Call me Boris. All my friends do. Remember, you are Mikhail's wife and he is, well, how shall I say it—like my brother."

"I know that," she said, and then asked point-blank, "Can you do anything to have him recalled from the village? I'd love to settle in Moscow."

"It's not a bad idea to settle in Moscow," he said, glancing at Mikhail. "Tell me, Ksenia, what sort of work would you want Mikhail to do in Moscow? Have you anything in mind?"

"Of course I have. I would like him to study at the University until he is graduated. That's what he wants to do."

"And how about your own plans?"

"One of my plans is to study medicine and become a doctor."

Boris laughed out loud. It was almost a genuine laugh; he was more relaxed than he had been in a long time.

"I've never heard anything like it," Boris said. "Everybody wants to study. It's the new fashion to live in the gymnasia and the universities. And who, may I ask, is going to do the work? Take me, for instance. I work hard in the Kremlin. Or Stalin, who works like no man I know. He is no university graduate either and yet he is far more informed than a hundred university men put together."

Polya looked at Boris strangely. "Did you have anything to drink? Something must have loosened your tongue this evening."

He became silent again. Drink? His instinct for self-preservation did not permit it. He rarely drank any more. He shunned it because there was a minute risk that a single drink, somewhere, somehow, would cause him to slip, to drop his guard for an instant. And because he loved to take a drink, especially when others drank with him, he crushed the temptation with an iron will. He had schooled himself to the point where he was invulnerable. Even in his own home where the bottle of vodka was always on the table, he had to be perfectly sober, constantly alert, ever ready to command and to obey should he receive a sudden call from the Kremlin. He could remember the few times he had permitted himself to drink alcohol —when his wife had presented him with a son, when he had received his first decoration—the Order of Lenin—from the hand of Stalin himself and occasionally when Mikhail had come to visit him and he had said more than he should have.

Tonight is another such night, he thought. He reached out and downed a full glass of vodka. His khaki jacket, which had been buttoned up to the neck, he now thrust open. He sat upright with his wide, awkward hands on his knees and in this pose his likeness to Stalin was striking. A black, drooping moustache was all that was needed to complete the resemblance.

"I suppose," he continued to Mikhail, his voice thick, "that we should produce our own intellectuals. Maybe it's not such a bad idea for Ksenia to get a higher education. A peasant girl wants to become a doctor. Excellent!" Then he abruptly changed the subject. "Tell me, Ksenia, how are things in your village? How is the collectivization program going?" He winked. "Is it true that one hundred percent of your peasants joined the kolkhoz voluntarily?"

Ksenia looked at Mikhail, who tried to signal her with a slight shake of the head, hoping that Boris would not notice. Boris did and grinned.

"Yes," she answered glibly, "the entire hundred percent did just that."

"I see. That was a piece of good work for which your names have now been added to the roster of Heroes of Socialist Construction." He leaned over, slapped Mikhail on the back and lowered his voice. "One hundred percent, eh? Down here we know exactly how you got those results. I never thought you had it in you. You did a good job, Mikhail. You're a real hero and your activities are well known to the Kremlin, including the way you handled that revolt. And all the time you had me believing that you were a softy. You're a shrewd article, Mikhail! Anyway, tomorrow at this time you will be sitting here with an Order of the Red Labor Banner on your chest and your little girl will be the proud possessor of a medal for heroic work."

The doorbell rang and the maid went to the door. She opened it a crack, which was as far as the heavy chain would permit. When she saw who it was, she quickly unfastened the chain and opened the door wide.

Yekaterina Petrovna came in, her reddish hair covered with a bright shawl. Mikhail's heart skipped a beat. Katya had never lost that mark of noble breeding which put her in a class apart. In the proletarian milieu of Communist generals, diplomats and commissars, this daughter of former Tsarist aristocracy had never become proletarianized, although she was now a member of the Communist Party and was addressed as Tovarisch Katya.

"Ivan is sorry he couldn't come," she said. She kissed Mikhail on the cheek. Upon being introduced to Ksenia, she embraced her and declared in a serious voice, "I know you love him, Ksenia. Never stop loving him. He is gentle and can be easily hurt. He is a fine writer. The love of a woman who is right for him can make a great man of him. Indifference and betrayal can destroy him."

Ksenia resented Katya's public advice, but she answered politely, "I understand him. Of course I love him."

The table was already set. Katya and Polya sat at one side, Mikhail and Ksenia on the other. Boris, as master of the house, sat at the head of the table. The supper, served by Masha the maid, was excellent. Boris ate a great deal, but by now sobered up, drank none of the superb liquors that graced the table. Mikhail ate and drank heartily. The women ate sparingly and did most of the talking.

The metropolitan Soviet woman had by now begun to lose enthusiasm for the proletarian mode of life and manners. She spoke less and less of "free love," simplicity of dress, and the vanity of cosmetics, and instead snapped up copies of outdated fashion magazines from London and Paris.

"That dress," Polya was saying enviously, "looks beautiful on you, Katya. But the low neckline—well it does strike me as just a shade too bourgeois."

"That won't hurt the revolution," Ksenia quipped.

"My dear Polya," Katya replied with a knowing smile, "you don't realize. This is the latest Parisian style. I saw it in the Paris fashion magazine I borrowed from the French consul's wife. You should have seen the dresses worn at the banquet given for the Turkish ambassador. Not only the foreign women but our own as well. Our women even wore gold bracelets and diamond-studded brooches."

"I can understand their wearing all this at a Kremlin banquet," Polya replied. "We don't want the female bourgeoisie to think that we are paupers and that we have no taste. But I don't see why we have to dress up in bourgeois finery among ourselves."

Ksenia did not agree with Polya even though she liked her better than Katya. "I think you're wrong, Polya. Why shouldn't we put on our best clothes among ourselves? We don't work in factories, so why not be well-dressed every day?"

Katya smiled approvingly at Ksenia, and turning to Polya

she said with a twinkle in her eyes, "You wouldn't want to have your hair cut short, put a cap on your head and march through the streets like a man, would you?" Polya shuddered. "I see the idea doesn't appeal to you. No woman likes to show herself with colorless lips when a bit of lipstick can add so much to them. And how about that unmistakable odor of French eau de cologne which I detect? Don't tell me Polya, that you have gone slightly French yourself."

Polya laughed. "Well, I didn't say that I was in love with the women's styles that made them all look like commissars. But to go overboard and swallow the bourgeois fashions is just as bad. We must keep a distance between them and us."

"The distance to which you refer is in our ideology, in our outlook on life, not in our clothing." Ksenia blurted out. "We are the future rulers of the world and all its wealth will be ours. We'll dress in silks and satins to our hearts' content and wear gold rings and earrings set with pearls and diamonds. We should be proud that we, former workers and peasants, will be better dressed and look better than the bourgeois women."

"Bravo, little one!" cried Katya. "Bravo! I am glad to see that the younger generation of Communists has a taste for beauty and elegance."

As if to prove that she was what Katya was referring to, Ksenia rose from the table, walked over to the mirror, eyed herself admiringly, set a few stray hairs carefully in place, then strolled back to her chair without uttering a word.

Mikhail and Boris kept out of this discussion, although they hadn't missed a word. But in the heat of argument the women had begun to drink and polite amenities were no longer being observed, so Boris tried to steer the conversation into other channels.

"Katya," he remarked casually, "I understand that congratulations will soon be in order."

"Congratulations?" Katya was taken by surprise. "I don't understand."

"It would not surprise me that after your husband's return from his mission you were to wake up and find yourself the wife of a general."

"Merciful God in heaven!" Katya almost screamed, making

her usual appeal to the deity when overcome by emotion. "You say my husband will have the rank of a general?"

"Definitely. But I tell you this in strictest confidence," he cautioned out of the deep-rooted habit of secrecy, despite the fact that this news was no longer a secret.

"I won't breathe a word, not a word." Katya's voice choked and tears welled up in her eyes. "I'll even try hard not to believe it."

Ksenia suddenly became aware of the gulf which separated her from this woman who wept for joy at the thought of becoming the wife of a general. This noblewoman who had become a "Tovarisch" was from a world that was alien to her, a village maid. Still, she had much to gain if she could win her over.

Upon leaving, Ksenia embraced Katya.

"I do hope, Yekaterina Petrovna," she said with a forced smile, "that we shall become very good friends."

"That would make me very happy. Do call me Katya. All my friends call me that."

"It would please me very much, Katya."

"And I wish you all the happiness in the world."

On the way home, Mikhail chided Ksenia. "I watched you tonight and I didn't recognize you. Where is that simple country girl I fell in love with?"

"Would you like me to feel and act inferior? Why don't you want Katya and Polya to behave like country girls?"

"I'm talking about you. I'm proud to have a beautiful and well-dressed wife, but don't play the snob. I saw signs of ambition, almost greed, in you tonight. I didn't like it. It's not becoming to an idealistic Komsomol girl."

"I forbid you to talk to me this way." She stamped her foot. "I want to get all I can out of life, and you will not stop me." She hurried ahead and Mikhail followed, calling after her,

"I don't mean to stop you. In fact I want you to get all the pleasures out of life, but be patient. I once read somewhere that all things come to them that wait."

"But please Mikhail, don't make me wait too long." She smiled, completely disarming him. At this moment he was ready to place the world at her feet.

One of the first places he took her to was the Tretikov Art Gallery. They stood at the famous painting by Repin, "Ivan the Terrible and his Slain Son." Ksenia contemplated the picture, her eyes riveted to the spot where the blood trickles from the son's head as the father, Ivan Grozni, embraces him. Had the Tsar felt any regret after having murdered his own son, Ksenia wondered?

"How horrible!" she muttered in an almost inaudible whisper.

Mikhail turned and stared into her face. It reminded him of that day in Krasney-Bor when they had heard the cry of the peasant being tortured by the village commissars. Her clear blue eyes were clouded now as they fixed themselves on the portrait. The white blouse she wore was partly unbuttoned, and he could see her shapely breasts heaving. She shuddered.

"But it's great art, you must admit," Mikhail offered.

"It's still horrible," she repeated.

"Anyway that was in our past history. That's why we had a revolution—so that we would never again have another Ivan the Terrible."

Ksenia eyed him curiously. Then she grimaced, saying, "I hope our new young Soviet painters will find more pleasant subjects to depict."

He was glad to hear her reaction. He reassured her, "Socialist Realism, as Stalin said, will afford our creative artists an opportunity to give us art that will be more pleasant."

It was twilight when they left the gallery. They came to the park around the walls of the Kremlin, not far from the Moscow River. They found an empty bench and they sat looking dreamily at the quiet flow in which a setting sun was being carried away on the ripples of the water.

CHAPTER TWO

The following day at exactly two in the afternoon, in the reception hall of the Chief of State of the All-Soviets, Tovarisch Kalinin, President of the Soviet Union, there took place the ceremony in which over fifty young Communists received their awards. They were a mixed and colorful group drawn from many nationalities in the Soviet Union. All of them were tense with exhilaration and fright. They could hardly be blamed. To be invited to a reception and ceremony in the Kremlin of Stalin, the palace of Kalinin, or even the private homes of the mighty commissars, was a supreme honor granted only to the elect. It was like being ushered into the Holy of Holies, and of all of the Communists in the land, few had ever seen that glory. As for the others, the non-Party millions of the far-flung Soviet Union, they dared not dream that any among them would ever breathe the same air as the Communist ruling class, the exalted, the omnipotent elite—the commissars.

On the dais sat Kalinin, peering at the assembled guests with his myopic eyes, his tapering, white goatee trembling with age. Next to him sat the renowned writer, Maxim Gorki, recently returned to his native land, today an honored guest. Not a man in the hall had forgotten that Gorki had fled from the Bolshevik Revolution and sought refuge abroad, that he had quarreled bitterly with his old friend Lenin, and denounced him to his face as an "evil dictator" and "traitor to the working class." Now he was back, publicly a friend and follower of Stalin. There was something mysterious and incredible about this turnabout of the world-famous Russian writer and humanitarian. Among other dignitaries on the dais were also the careworn and eternally preoccupied philosopher Bukharin and the long-faced and subtle Karl Radek.

Everyone was waiting for Stalin. But as yet neither he nor

Boris was in evidence. And now the dais was suddenly illuminated by beams from huge spotlights. The full-length portrait of Stalin, ringed by fiery red banners with emblazoned hammers and sickles, shone forth in sacred splendor. The orchestra commenced the hymn of the Communist world movement, "The International." The assembly rose in a body and added their voices to the brass, the drums, and the cymbals in an immense incantation that grew until it was a roaring volcano.

The singing ended, leaving a peculiar hush punctuated by scattered coughs. Kalinin faced the assembly from his perch on the podium, holding his trembling pince-nez to his nose with one hand and gesturing with the other. He spoke quietly, his voice reaching through the cavernous, gravelike stillness to every corner of the hall. To the fifty or more young Communists who were drawn up on one side of the dais like a stone phalanx, he uttered these words:

"Young heroes of the Soviet Motherland! Your heroism in fulfilling the commands of our Father Stalin has given the greatest impetus to the development of the kolkhoz in our beloved country. In carrying out your tasks successfully you have not only defeated the backward, who would have bogged down the program, but also the hotheads, who would have run away with it. It is to your intelligence, vigilance, and efficiency that we owe the stupendous triumph of our collectivization program. I bring you the greetings of your government and the formal acknowledgment of its gratitude."

There was a heavy surge of applause after which Kalinin proceeded to read off the names of the award recipients and the stipulations of the awards, each man or woman stepping forward in turn to be decorated.

When the decoration ceremony was over, the young heroes and heroines marched off the dais and took their seats in the reserved first row.

It was at this point that Stalin emerged, the members of the Politburo clinging to him like shadows. Behind them came several men difficult to identify, but Mikhail recognized Boris. It was a dramatic entrance, and the assembly went wild with enthusiasm.

"Long live our leader, our guide and savior!"

"Long live the Father of all peoples, Stalin the beloved!"

"Taller than the highest mountain is our Stalin!"

"Our Stalin is the sun, the life-giving sun that warms the earth!"

"Our Stalin, forever!"

Stalin stood on the dais, looking dark and grim. He gazed at the frantic, cheering crowd of his worshipers and satisfaction melted the flint of his countenance. Honor and reverence—these were the glories in which he bathed his soul. Once more he heard the cloister bells, the sacred bells which he had heard as a novice in the priestly seminary. "Praise to the Lord" they had rung. "Praise to Stalin" said the bells, "to the Lord of men." A smile pervaded his mask. He approached the podium, which Kalinin had discreetly vacated, and raised his clumsy hand. Silence wrapped the hall. His guttural Caucasian rasped like a saw as his lips began to move:

"The enemies of the people have left no stone unturned to derail us from the track of collectivized economy." He paused, put one hand behind his back and the other on his breast between the buttons of his khaki jacket. "The confiscation of the great landed estates was the first act of the October Revolution, as recorded in the decisions of the eighteenth convention of the Party. The transition to the kolkhoz was the next logical step . . . ."

He went on and on. The end of his speech was marked by an unprecedented ovation, after which the orchestra played a military march. To crown the event, famous artists of the Bolshoi Theatre for Opera and Ballet gave a performance. It was impossible to deny the impact of the entire event. Mikhail and Ksenia—indeed everyone present—left the hall more dedicated Communists than they had entered it.

The next day, Mikhail and Ksenia went to the cadre division head of the Central Committee to inquire about the possibility of their remaining in Moscow. Mikhail had decided to complete his studies at the University.

The division head was a stout man with fastidiously manicured fingernails and a florid, smiling face. He was dressed in an imported urban suit. Mikhail's request seemed to puzzle him. Almost all of the twenty-five thousand Communists that had been sent into the provinces had by now been recalled. But most of the fifty who had received decorations had been ordered to return to the villages and to consolidate their achievements. The smile quickly faded from his face. He looked Mikhail and Ksenia over from head to foot with the air of a great commissar and told them they would have to wait. He left them standing for a considerable time, but when he returned he was again genial, florid, and smiling.

"Yes, Tovarisch Kruger, you have special permission to remain here in Moscow for the purpose of completing your University studies. Report to this office in a day or two to receive your documents. The technicality which held them up should be cleared up and properly recorded by then. You may stay one more week at the hotel. Have a good time. You have earned a vacation after a hard year in the village."

"Thank you," said Mikhail, "that is exactly what I had hoped for."

The fat man pressed Mikhail's hand warmly. "Good-bye, Tovarisch Kruger, have a nice time."

Mikhail held on to the official's hand. "And what about Ksenia Dimova? What is the decision on her?"

"Oh, Dimova—now that was the most puzzling thing. Her orders were also delayed for reasons that are still not clear to me. But she is not a Party member. She is a member of the Komsomol and so I checked with them. The Komsomol Central Committee has ruled that she must go back. Her work in the village is very important."

"No!" Mikhail shouted, "I refuse to have her go back to the village. She is my wife and her place is with me."

The man broke into a short laugh which ended in a squeak. "Tovarisch Kruger, I am surprised at you. A hero, carrying an order of merit and ready to lose your temper because you will be separated from your wife!" His manner became stern. "When ordered by the Party you must be prepared to lay down your life. By comparison, giving up one's wife is a petty matter. Besides," he added, gathering up his rosy cheeks in a dimpled smile as a charming idea struck him, "there are plenty of girls in the Soviet Union."

"Yes, and why don't you tell me that there are plenty of men, too?" Ksenia interrupted hotly. "I am going straight to Stalin himself. I will make him tell me whether the statutes of the Party and Komsomol require that a man be torn from his wife. And what sort of language is that: 'there are plenty of girls in the Soviet Union?' You are treating us like dogs, not people."

"Calm yourself, Tovarisch Dimova," the official answered sharply. "You may be a heroine with a decoration, but remember that the Party can punish as well as reward. You are wasting your breath here. Go scream in the cadre division of the Komsomol."

"Very well," she replied, suddenly docile. "I will go directly to the Komsomol."

She had been struck by a thought. There was no point to this useless bickering. There must be another way, and Mikhail had the one connection which made it possible—Boris. She noticed that Mikhail had his own thoughts on the matter. In fact, he was smiling.

"Excuse me," Mikhail said calmly. "I just realized that the whole thing may be a misunderstanding. Actually it is my own fault. You see, I have never reported to the Party office that we were married."

Again the fat man went to the cabinet and pulled out Mikhail's file. He extracted a form and examined it.

"It says 'single,' not 'married.' As you say, you should have reported it. I shall have to correct the file."

He crossed out the word "single" and wrote in the word "married," grinning at Mikhail. "You won't have to report it to the Party office. I'll do it for you. You are no longer unattached. Officially, you are now married."

"I wonder whether you would do me a favor. Frankly, I wouldn't want to waste time going to the Komsomol cadre division. Perhaps you would be kind enough to take care of the matter for us. I presume this will make a difference in the ruling on my wife's case. You have the authority, since you represent the Party Central Committee, which either confirms or rejects the decisions of the Komsomol."

"Not so fast, my friend. I have just learned that you are

married and I agree that in such a case I have the authority to make the final decision. But we must go through channels. The Komsomol record at this point states that she is to return to the village. First I have to inform them about your married state and register their reaction. Wait here and don't go away."

"Thank you so much," Ksenia purred, giving him a coquettish smile.

The official looked at Ksenia, flushed a deep red and swallowed several times. "I wouldn't worry too much," he assured her. "I am convinced that everything will be all right."

He was gone for a while. When he came back, he seemed pleased with himself.

"I telephoned the Komsomol cadre division and left orders that you were not to be compelled to return to the village. As it turned out, this was unnecessary. The confirmation was already there, only they had as yet failed to enter it. They don't have our efficiency. Ksenia Dimova, you have permission to remain in Moscow for the purpose of studying medicine. I congratulate you. By the way, which one of you is related to Tovarisch Boris Garber? He seems to take quite an interest in both of you."

Mikhail looked the official steadfastly in the eye until he was sure the other cringed slightly.

"Ah, Boris Garber," he said nonchalantly. "Let us say he is just a friend of mine."

They shook hands like old friends before parting.

Mikhail and Ksenia left the cadre division office in high spirits. They were both aware that they had just made another friend, a powerful commissar, the man in charge of the cadre division for the Central Committee, who might be helpful one day. At any rate, Mikhail was amused and, for once, not too critical of what a little influence could accomplish.

Finding an apartment was a long and tedious affair in Moscow, so they were very happy when Yekaterina Petrovna offered them part of her own house. Her husband, she explained, was still in Turkey. The few nights he had stayed over in Moscow he had found it impossible to sleep at home. He already wore the uniform of a general, although for unknown reasons the promotion had not been published in the press. There must be some sort of political strategy involved, she imagined. The general had told her that he would be very glad to have Mikhail and Ksenia in his home. He expected to move his family to Turkey and from there, possibly to Germany. The international situation was such that he might have to stay abroad indefinitely. Stalin himself, Katya confided to Mikhail, had said that if the situation warranted it the whole family would have to settle abroad.

"Naturally I want someone to keep the apartment for us. I am greatly attached to it and would hate to give it up. It is good to know that whenever we return to Moscow our own home will be waiting for us. We cannot see ourselves living like transients in hotels."

Mikhail was delighted, for it relieved him of a gnawing anxiety. It would save him hours of waiting in the government's housing division in order to register his name and then months, perhaps years, of waiting for new houses to be built and his name to come up, only to find—in all probability—that he had been displaced by a more important commissar.

His only disturbing thought was, how would Ksenia and Katya get along with each other?

CHAPTER THREE

Mikhail studied hard at the University to make up for the year he had lost in Krasney-Bor. Most of the time, he yearned to be elsewhere. His dreams carried him far away from Moscow, to some distant place where he could quietly write and then come back to Moscow to publish his books. He knew in his heart that the dream was vague, that the long arm of the Kremlin reached everywhere, but it was a dream that nourished his soul and kept it alive. Once his reputation was established, he could become a newspaper correspondent and travel the length and breadth of the Soviet Union. It even occurred to him that they might send him abroad, into the great, wonderful world beyond—a thought so staggeringly remote that he quickly banished it and settled for the Soviet Union, which was vast enough for years of happy wandering. Boris—yes, Boris might some day make this possible. And he clung to his hope.

One day Mikhail had to do an assignment at the library. This day, a Friday, was destined to burn itself into his memory for the rest of his life. It was a day of disillusionments, conscious and unconscious, which split him in two. It was to be Mikhail's Black Friday.

He went to the University library and took out Stalin's recent book *Leninism,* a collection which included his commentaries on the works of a number of polemical articles. Mikhail had to prepare a paper for his class on one of the articles, "Marxism and the National Question."

There was complete silence in the library. Young men and women sat at long tables in the reading room pouring over books, newspapers, and periodicals. Large, low-hanging electric lamps cast their light around the heads of the readers. From time to time the rustle of pages being turned broke the silence and the sound was like a sandstorm in the desert.

Mikhail read and another storm gathered within him, a storm that wanted to burst from his breast.

"Marxism and the National Question" set out to prove that the Jews were neither a nation nor a people, that they must be assimilated and disappear, that they should be given no encouragement to maintain their culture and traditions. The conclusion was openly anti-Semitic. "Jews," said Stalin, "do not understand one another nor do they help one another either in peacetime or war."

Mikhail pushed aside the book, bewildered and revolted. He felt like a man who had recently discovered a treasure and now that treasure had been snatched from him. Or perhaps it was the feeling of a devoted son who had believed in his father as one believes in a god who is omnipotent and omniscient, who is benevolent and just. Suddenly the son sees him for what he really is: a crafty, ignorant, insidious liar.

Sinking his head into his hands, Mikhail sat for a long time motionless and numb, his eyes darkened. His face became pale and drawn. His back rounded over in a hump and he now looked like a stone figure in a sedentary position. For a few moments he was incapable of thought. But slowly his eyes lit up again and the color in his cheeks reappeared. He straightened up, his head high with determination. He was going to get at the truth!

Mikhail was well informed on the subjects of Jewish history and the Jewish people, and he had been reading a great deal about the new Jewish autonomous state which was being established in the Far East—the territory called Birobidjan. And what he was reading just now in Stalin's book was a contradiction and a complete denial of what actually existed.

Unbelievingly, he leafed through the pages over and over again. Now he was convinced that his identity was threatened, dishonored, defiled. His head began to throb and, as the room grew dimmer, the words zigzagged into light and dark lines. A wave of nausea rolled over him and he slammed the book shut as if a foul odor exuded from it. He leaned back for a while and through half-closed eyes fixed on the empty chair opposite him, he suddenly became aware of a pair of large, clumsy hands clutching the arms of the chair. In the semi-darkness, a familiar face was staring at him.

A hoarse, guttural voice that seemed to come from beneath the black, drooping moustache, echoed in the stillness of the room.

"Who are you?"

By now having recognized the figure sitting across the table, Mikhail answered hesitatingly, too stunned to speak.

"I'm Mikhail Kruger . . . a good Communist . . . and a good Jew."

"*Nyet!* There is no such thing as being a Communist *and* a Jew." The massive hands closed into two fists.

"But to be a Communist and a Russian, to be a Ukrainian Communist, a Georgian Communist, a Polish Communist, a French Communist, an Italian Communist—that is permissible? The exception then, is only for a Jew?"

"How dare you speak to me this way? To me, Father Stalin, god of communism, the greatest of the great, the wisest of the wise, the mightiest of the mighty! How dare you?"

Mikhail now fearlessly stared back at the angry "commune-god." "I dare because of the tradition I have inherited from my forefathers. Jeremiah dared to defy the King of Judea and his false prophets. Elijah shouted in King Ahab's face, 'You murdered.' Nathan dared to find fault with King David. And I, Mikhail Kruger, dare also to complain and demand."

Stalin squirmed in his chair as if he were sitting on hot coals. His mouth twisted in controlled fury. "Why doesn't your own friend Boris Garber complain? He is also a Jew but he agrees with all my theories and undertakings. Even on the 'Jewish question' he is with me one hundred percent."

Mikhail's laughter filled the room. "Boris Garber? You call him a Jew? Perhaps, but in name only. He's like a stone in a barren desert, neither nourished by centuries of Jewish tradition, nor blooming with centuries of Jewish wisdom and knowledge, nor stirred by Jewish exultation and despair. His impoverished, ignorant father never gave him a Jewish education and the street made him what he is. His passport carries the word *Yevray* because he was born a Jew. He's a Jew only in his papers."

Stalin walked over and put his huge hand on Mikhail's shoulder. His tone was mellow. "Then I'm right when I say that the Jews are a 'paper nation.' "

"That is not true!" Mikhail drew back in anger. "*You* say it because the leaders of the Socialist-Communist movement before you said it and those following you will probably repeat it. We have our Boris Garbers, but there are also millions of Jews who want to remain Jews. And just as a Russian who is also a Communist wants to remain a Russian, so a Jew who is also a Communist wants to remain a Jew."

Stalin sat down in his chair again and repeated mockingly, " 'To remain a Jew.' Just what does that mean?"

Ignoring Stalin's mockery, Mikhail thought a moment and then said, "It's really a way of life. Jews believe that one man must help another even if he himself is helpless or in trouble. We believe in righteousness and that the world is based on ideals of justice. A Jew believes in family love, in hope and in learning. These are part of the great heritage of our forefathers—Abraham, Isaac and Jacob. Millions of Jews here in Russia and the world over conduct themselves in this tradition. And if communism wants to destroy this way of life, then I say that it is barbaric, a new kind of anti-Semitism against which I will fight with my body and soul."

Stalin tugged at his moustache and his eyes flashed. "Mikhail Grigorevich, you are advocating an out-dated, out-moded way of life. How can you call us anti-Semites when we want to improve your lot, to give you something better. You Jews should adopt the new Russian Communist culture, the *new*, I say, because your old way of life is reactionary."

"That's not so! Jews have never been reactionaries. Nearly three thousand years ago it was the Bible that promulgated the democratic idea that power belongs not to a king, a hero nor a leader, but to the people. The Bible warned against taking up the sword and proclaimed the principle of peace. And you say that the Jewish way of life is reactionary? If that is so then I am convinced that you are a liar and an anti-Semite."

Raising his fists to strike Mikhail, Stalin rushed at him. Mikhail stretched out his hands to ward off the attack and with all his strength tried to thrust Stalin back.

"Is this the Communist 'way of life?' " Mikhail shouted. "Instead of debating with your opponent in a civilized manner, you let your fists speak for you. That is the way of murderers and highwaymen."

Stalin gave no reply. He let his fists fall on Mikhail's shoulder and pounded, pounded, pounded . . . .

Mikhail opened his eyes. Above him stood a middle-aged woman vigorously shaking his shoulder. "Hey, Tovarisch, the library is no place for sleeping. This is a reading room. Besides, it's late and we're closing."

Mikhail dashed out of the library. He walked with giant strides until he grew tired. When he came to a park, he sat down on a bench. His thoughts were filled with the "dialogue" in his dream and brought him back to the reality of the article by Stalin that he had read in the library. If Stalin says the Jews are neither a nation nor a people and should be given no help to maintain and develop their culture, why was Birobidjan created for the Jews? Had Stalin abandoned his earlier views? But his new book *Leninism,* which had appeared only this month proved that he had not changed his anti-Semitic attitude.

There was only one place Mikhail knew he could go to air his doubts. He went straight to Boris. There was no other person he could turn to.

"I want to talk to you, Boris."

"Go ahead! Which shoe pinches this time, right or left?"

"Both," said Mikhail. "I can't walk."

"Well, tell me about it."

It was at such moments that the two old friends revealed their thoughts to each other and tried to clarify to themselves the justice of the general Party line. Till now there had been no serious disagreement between them. Polya always left them alone during these discussions.

"Have you read Stalin's book, *Leninism*?"

"Of course, Mikhail!"

"And the article 'Marxism and the National Question'?"

"Yes, all the articles. What about it?"

"I think it's a lot of rubbish!"

Boris sat up wild-eyed, his fists clenched. This time Mikhail had gone too far. "Shut your mouth!" he growled. "Never say that again! Have you gone mad? Idiot!"

Without a word Mikhail jumped up and stormed out of the room, slamming the door behind him.

It was many weeks before he visited Boris again.

While Mikhail attended the University, Ksenia, who had matriculated for premedical courses at the Institute for Medicine, was enjoying herself immensely. She had picked up the expressions and mannerisms current in student circles. She mimicked everything, including the gestures. When she heard that Katya had received permission to depart for Turkey with her son and that the apartment with all its rich furnishings would be hers for two years, she was overjoyed. She stretched out her arm with the thumb stiffly erect and almost screamed,

"I swear by my thumb, it's going to be wonderful!"

Yekaterina Petrovna laughed. "Try not to use that expression, Ksenia. It's quite vulgar, you know."

"Vulgar?" Ksenia seemed astonished. "Not at all. You are just old-fashioned and still believe in affected mannerisms. You even choose your words as I would a string of pearls. At the Institute everybody uses these expressions. Why, even the professors are less careful of their language than you are."

"I still insist that both the gesture and the expression are vulgar. You can have good manners and still be a good Communist or a good student of medicine. I refer you to the articles in the *Komsomolskaya Pravda* on the role of the Soviet intellectual. There is a reference to Lenin's remark that we have a great deal to learn from the bourgeoisie. We must reject the bad and take over the good from them—their culture and good manners. A proletarian needn't ignore these."

"You don't say!" Ksenia retorted sarcastically. "In that case I shall be very careful of what I say in your presence from now on. But you understand that it will not be easy, since after all I come from lowly peasant stock and not from the Tsarist aristocracy."

Katya abruptly left the room.

Mikhail, who had overheard the entire conversation, was glumly silent. He had seen the antagonism between Ksenia and Katya grow day by day. More than anything he wanted them to be good friends, but he was unable to do anything about it. The fact was that Ksenia was no longer the same in his eyes. It was not exactly disillusionment that he felt. It was something else. More and more he found it necessary to explain Ksenia away, to find excuses for her. Her passionate drive to become an urbanite was not unusual; Russian and Ukrainian villagers were leaving the countryside in droves to settle in the cities. But her efforts to acquire a veneer of sophistication had been almost frantic. He saw in her the signs of an inordinate egotism and vanity which had lain fallow for years and had now come to the surface. He didn't want to believe it, but it was no use; he could not deny the evidence of his own eyes. Nor could he deny that Yekaterina Petrovna also saw what he saw and that her genteel spirit recoiled from this brazenness.

So he was puzzled when, a few hours later, the two women not only seemed to have patched up their differences but had become quite intimate. Watching them, one would have thought that they were lifelong friends. Mikhail threw up his hands and decided that the ways of women were unfathomable.

When Katya and her son left Moscow to join General Ivanov in Turkey, there was a tearful parting. Both women threw their arms about each other and wept bitterly. Mikhail was half-amused and a little revolted. He was sure that they would much rather have bitten than kissed each other and he avoided their eyes for fear that they would notice his reaction.

Katya embraced Mikhail and kissed him, saying, "Mikhail, no one knows what the future can bring. You may have to leave Moscow. In that case, leave the key to the apartment with Polya. She would be the only person on whom I could depend. I don't know how long we will be abroad. The general says that everything depends on the international situation, whatever that means."

Then she drew back and made a gesture that would almost have been the sign of the cross if her hand had not suddenly dropped to her side. She took one last look at the apartment, opened the door, and walked out.

A shiny, black limousine of the Commissariat for Foreign Affairs was waiting for her at the curb. A chauffeur in military uniform sat stiffly behind the wheel. Next to him, squirming and restless, sat Katya's thirteen-year-old son Petya. He was badgering the chauffeur. "Why don't you tell my mother to hurry up? I want to see my father."

The chauffeur turned his head slightly, saw Katya coming toward the car and nodded respectfully in her direction.

"Your mother is here."

A few moments later the limousine pulled away. Katya had a last look at the windows of her apartment. Mikhail was waving goodbye. She waved back and her eyes filled with tears.

The limousine disappeared, and Mikhail, who kept looking down the empty street, repressed a great desire to weep.

CHAPTER FOUR

Mikhail's dream of writing in some quiet, far-off place away from the tumult of Moscow did not materialize. He therefore set to work on a novel based on his experiences in Krasney-Bor, isolating himself each night in a separate room in the Ivanov apartment. Judiciously, he wrote only that which was safe, suppressing everything else. The villains and heroes, magnified out of all proportion, stalked about as if on stilts and into the vacuum of their souls he blew the foul air of the Kremlin. It was difficult and exacting labor, requiring the utmost vigilance and skill. His bitterness dissolved in the constant act of creation.

Ksenia became accustomed to living with a writer. She learned his habits and made no protest. Besides, she was engrossed in her own studies, having completed her premedical courses and become a full medical student at the Institute. She had inexhaustible energy. She studied hard and made excellent progress, but at the same time never missed a single concert or banquet given by the students. In addition, Polya, with whom she had become very friendly, would take her frequently to the parties and receptions given by the commissars, where the two women had privileged entry because of Boris' high position.

Thus, in time, Mikhail and Ksenia began to live parallel but separate lives. There were days when they did not see each other. And when they did come together, they made love to one another in a desperate, compulsive passion.

As Mikhail prepared for his final examinations, he noted the faces of his fellow students, pinched, sleepless and wan with the fear of failure. And deeper even was the fear of success. For to those who planned a future for themselves, success had its own terrible uncertainties. To what remote corner of this enormous country would they be ordered? A student, like a worker, a peasant, or a soldier, was subject to all the commands and decrees of the Party and government. When he received his diploma he did not explore his own future. He waited for the order that would tell him when and where to go.

Mikhail's first novel, *Village Man,* appeared as he was finishing his examinations. The press praised it. They found a few stylistic defects, but after all, they agreed, the main issue was not sentence structure but the structure of human beings in this day and age. And beyond question the characters in this novel were true Soviet villagers, the new peasant types, the kolkhozites so masterfully portrayed by the author. Here was a new man, a Communist, emotionally and spiritually different from the traditional peasant. For here was a man rooted in the soil but ready to destroy and conquer worlds in order to unfurl the flag of communism over all creation. And in praising this work the critics did not fail to mention one of Stalin's casual remarks about writers, that "writers are the engineers of the human soul." Mikhail Kruger's novel, the critics concluded, was a model social blueprint, the best current work to date on collectivization; and the author justly deserved to be designated "engineer of human souls."

The professors and students at the University flocked to congratulate Mikhail on the success of his book. He received many slaps on the back, devout looks of admiration, and his hand was squeezed innumerable times. But Mikhail was still too numb, too disturbed, and distracted by the terms "engineer of human souls" and "social blueprint" to enjoy his triumph. *You are a liar and a fraud,* he thought. *You are an engineer, not an artist. Draw yourself up proudly, salute and bark: 'Mikhail Kruger, Engineer, reporting!'*

Even though his success probably had assured his position as a Soviet writer, and might even lead to the traveling he yearned for, it gave him no rest.

Shortly after Mikhail's triumph, Boris and Polya came to visit him. Boris pulled a bottle of brandy out of his pocket and plunked it on the table.

"Mikhail, you are the man of the hour and I congratulate you. Your book has raised quite a fuss in the Central Committee of the Party. So far nothing but praise and more praise.

Let's soak up your victory in a little brandy. I am proud of you, Mikhail. Very proud. I've known all along that you had talent. I knew it from those crazy, intellectual obsessions you had even as a child. Drink up, Mikhail! And Ksenia, drink a toast to this man of yours and give him the kiss one gives a conqueror so that my eyes can feast on it. And Polya, raise your glass and kiss him too, with my blessings. Drink, all of you, and I will join you in spirit at least, for I regret I cannot drink with you now. I am due at the Kremlin tonight and have to remain sober."

Ksenia had dressed with unusual care that evening. Her thick, golden hair was pulled loosely back in a chignon and her Paris-copied, tight-fitting dress was the color of her light blue eyes. Mikhail couldn't remember ever seeing her look so exciting. He longed to hold her in his arms.

"Did you dress up just for me?" he asked bitterly.

"Yes, of course, dear. Now that you are so famous I want you to be proud of me," she teased.

"Why don't you tell him the truth, Ksenia?" Polya nudged her. Then she turned to Mikhail. "We are taking her with us to a party at the Kremlin. I hope you don't mind."

"That's right, Mikhail," said Boris. "There will be a celebration at the Kremlin today. I know how you dislike those parties, otherwise I would have mentioned it to you. I don't care particularly about them either, but I couldn't very well refuse. It's not too late, if you want to join us. I can arrange an invitation for you."

"Count me out," Mikhail answered with irritation. "I couldn't take it right now. Perhaps some other time."

"Please come with us," Polya urged. "Perhaps Stalin will be there and you can present him with a copy of your book. Boris will introduce you to him."

"Wonderful!" cried Ksenia, enchanted with the idea. "You must come with us. Please make him come, Boris."

But Boris was suddenly gone. He had disappeared into another room, dropped into an armchair, and was sitting there brooding. Polya, from long experience, understood instantly. When Boris smelled danger, he abruptly withdrew. He would now refuse to come out of an impenetrable silence. Whether he was host or guest, this habit was immutable. Polya knew her evening would be spoiled.

"Go in to him and see what's wrong," Polya begged Mikhail. "He might tell you. Perhaps I shouldn't have spoken so familiarly of Stalin. You never know. My husband is a sphinx. One never knows how much to say and how much to choke down. Everything presents some kind of danger to him. Everywhere he sees enemies of the Party and the government. He acts like the sole custodian in charge of the security of the Soviet Union. He always dictates the time of speech and the time of silence, the amount of speech and the amount of silence. What else is there left to dictate? I find living with him more difficult each day. I am so sick of it."

Mikhail refused to listen. "I will hear no complaints about my best friend," he said. Then he went into the next room, pulled up a chair and sat down beside Boris.

"Let's have it, Boris. You were in a good mood only a minute ago. What happened?"

"I hate prattling women!" Boris burst out.

"What have they done? You can tell me, can't you?"

"That wife of mine." Boris was burning with anger. "Presenting your book to Stalin! Bah! He has more important things to do than to read every book that comes out. Books are summarized and digested in reports submitted to him. As often as not he reverses literary and public opinion. He has not spoken yet. Nobody's opinion counts at the moment."

"But Polya meant no harm," Mikhail said quietly.

Boris stared at him. "When will all of you learn? One does not glibly speak of just seeing Stalin or asking to see him. If he wants you, you will be called."

"Well, he won't be able to call me because I won't be here to call," Mikhail announced curtly. "I'm leaving Moscow after all. I've decided to travel through the country, to see Siberia and stop over at Birobidjan." Mikhail had been thinking about this for some time and now the words were out.

Boris jumped up as if he had been sitting on a stick of dynamite. "You fool," he shouted. "Always going from one trap to another." There was utter contempt in his eyes. "You have finally convinced me that you have a consummate genius for finding trouble, especially when it is not looking for you. Birobidjan! Of all places!"

"What do you mean? Explain yourself! What's wrong with going to Birobidjan? Tell me, once and for all."

"Not now, Mikhail. I don't think you're worth the effort," Boris snorted, "but remind me the next time we meet and I will give you a full explanation—and basta!"

He turned and stormed back into the room where Polya and Ksenia were waiting. "Let's go," he snarled, "or we'll be late. I've left that idiot husband of yours in the next room to stew in his own genius. After he has thought it over, I will have a little talk with him." He took both their arms and roughly escorted them out of the house. They left without a backward glance.

CHAPTER FIVE

At the Kremlin the party was in full swing. It was no ordinary banquet given by a Kremlin commissar. This was a wedding. The chief of the Kremlin Guard, General Smirnov, had received the personal blessings of Stalin to celebrate the marriage of his eighteen-year-old daughter to the young and handsome Captain Makarov. Naturally, the affair was a highly restricted one and invitations had been issued only to intimate Kremlinites and—for this colorful and unusual occasion—also to their friends. Both Stalin and his spouse were expected to put in an appearance and participate briefly in the festivities.

The chief of the Kremlin Guard occupied a house that stood not far from the high Kremlin wall on the banks of the Moscow River. Pairs of armed guards, in shifts, kept a 'round-the-clock watch over it. A little distance away stood two cube-shaped buildings of more recent construction. They looked like twin prisons. One was for the exclusive use of Stalin himself. The other was for the use of his family.

Alelyuyeva was far younger than Stalin and a true Russian beauty. Stalin, however, had never been seen with her in public. By his own orders, the wives and children of commissars, generals, and important Party functionaries who worked in the Kremlin—whether they resided within or without its walls—had not been permitted entrance to Kremlin banquets. Of late he had rescinded the decree and, reversing his stand, now compelled his subordinates to come with their wives and children unless otherwise instructed. He also ordered that the most attractive ballet dancers and the finest opera singers be made available for these affairs. At the same time he also doubled the military guard and the number of secret police agents in the Kremlin.

There was peace and quiet in the land. Outside the Kremlin walls the vast populace knew nothing of Stalin's private life. No one knew exactly who his wife was and how many children he had. Everyone wondered about it, but no one spoke about it, and no one probed into it, for it was like opening the door to fear. It was wiser to think: Stalin stands for everything that is good. He is great and he is mighty. Stalin is like a god. Does one ask God whether he has kith or kin?

The actual marriage ceremony consisted of a solemn speech delivered by the secretary of the Kremlin Party unit. In it he recalled that the villages were by now totally collectivized, that industry was making giant strides in the cities, that in time the United States would be overtaken and surpassed, and that the Red Flag of Communism would be unfurled over the entire globe. Into his political tapestry he artfully wove the names of the bride and groom, praised them as loyal young Communists and ended his speech with a toast to their health, the health of the guests, and the health of the Father and leader, the paragon of virtue and intelligence, Tovarisch Stalin. Everyone shouted "Hurrah," "To your health," and "Long live Stalin" and proceeded at once to eat and drink.

Stalin sat in a seat of honor next to the newlyweds. He ate little and drank less. He was an enthusiast of dance and song. He listened carefully to the singers and followed every movement of the dancers, never failing to cast quick glances at the guests in the meantime. If his roaming eyes paused for more than a few seconds, it was to focus on the delicate bosom of some pretty woman. When this happened, he would slowly lower his lids, pick up a glass and take a short sip of wine.

Behind Stalin sat two swarthy men with longish, somewhat crooked noses and thick hair as black as pitch. Their moustaches hung down and muffled their mouths completely. Typical men of the Caucasus—either Georgians or Armenians—they bore a strong resemblance to Stalin and were his personal bodyguards. Seen from some distance by anyone who had never seen Stalin, they could easily be taken for him. Wherever he went, these two men went with him. When he left the Kremlin in his car, his doubles rode behind as decoys to mislead a possible assassin.

Stalin's wife, the buxom and beautiful Alelyuyeva, sat at another table with a high Kremlin official. She ate steadily, drank a great deal, and maintained a lively conversation. The man who faced her seemed to be enjoying her company, looking deeply into her eyes and smiling rapturously. She never once looked in Stalin's direction.

Boris, Polya, and Ksenia sat at one of the farther tables along with a number of military men and civilians, most of them with colorful decorations pinned to their chests. Polya had already met them on other occasions. Boris now introduced Ksenia to these men and the effect was instantaneous. Their eyes traveled from her glorious head and piquant smile to her half-naked bosom above which dangled a single ornament—the gold medal for heroic work suspended from a scarlet band that encircled her bronzed throat. No one could guess how her heart thumped with fright at being in the dread presence of Stalin himself!

Boris, in his black tuxedo, looked like an American playboy who had strayed into the Kremlin by accident, an illusion partly offset by the proud, fierce tilt of his big head and the Order of Lenin pinned to his lapel. He sat motionless except for an occasional twitch of his huge arm muscles and he said almost nothing. For the most part he kept his eyes fixed on Stalin.

As for Polya, who was well-groomed and wore an expensive dress, neither her charm nor her apparel drew any notice. There were too many women in the Kremlin that night who could without effort be called charming and well-dressed. It was Ksenia who attracted attention and drew all eyes irresistibly to her.

Stalin rose abruptly. Everyone else hastened to rise, some of them with barely enough time to drop their forks and spoons. But Stalin waved them back into their seats, folded his hands behind him and began to pace up and down the big room. The two bodyguards who had sat at his rear now stalked him like two shadows. Ksenia, who had taken more than a few drinks and found that the room swam a bit, watched the strolling and wheeling trio and was intrigued by the uncanny likeness these men bore to one another. As they walked back and forth she finally decided that there must be three Stalins and she took another drink to clear her head.

The trio seemed to be following a pattern. With each turn of the room they stopped at a different table, nodded slightly, smiling thin, miserly smiles that sneaked out from under their moustaches and passed on. When they came to Ksenia's table, however, they paused for a considerable time. The gold medal rose and fell on her full, daringly exposed bosom, and the trio stood rooted. Ksenia began to tremble with fear and excitement and could barely control herself. She gazed up at one of the three with eyes that were full of the sacred flamc. Hc, like the other two, wore plain khaki and had shiny, peasant boots on his feet. As she sat there the days of her childhood came back to her and once again she was kneeling beside her mother in church, gazing with adoration at the naked figure on the cross. Her mother had told her that it was God.

One of the men spoke to her.

"What is your name, my child?"

"Ksenia," she answered softly, in a voice of prayer.

"Ksenia—a beautiful name! And that medal? What is the deed for which you have received this rare award?"

"It is for helping to establish order in our village and organizing a successful kolkhoz." Her courage began to revive. "For extraordinary achievement beyond the call of duty," she finished breathlessley.

"Ah, very interesting indeed," said the man in plain khaki, his eyes fixed on her. "You must give me a first-hand report on this kolkhoz in full detail."

The trio left the table. For a short time they circulated about the room without stopping and then made for the door. They were gone.

This was a signal for the real festivities to begin. The tables and chairs were carried out or pushed against the walls. A band of musicians, dressed in evening suits and carrying their full complement of violins, drums, saxophones, and other brasses, trotted in and took their places up front near the bride and groom and began to blare out Russian dance music. The company threw themselves into one dance after another. The excitement grew high. As the music became louder and the rhythms faster and more explosive, the scene turned into one of wild hilarity and abandon; the cries, the foot-stomping, the spinning and hurtling of bodies from one partner to another mounting into an orgy of self-forgetfulness.

Boris alone stood still, his shoulders backed against the wall, his brows knitted in deep worry. He was aware by now that Ksenia was nowhere to be seen. When Polya, always conscious of him, stole a glance at his face, she tore herself away from the whirling dance.

"Ksenia is gone," Boris told her and then added quickly as he saw her go white, "I absolutely forbid you to make any inquiries."

She stood next to him, trembling. A few moments later their host, the chief of the Kremlin Guard, approached them.

"I have a report for you, Tovarisch Garber. It's about the young woman who came with your party. She is going to be delayed for a while. Nothing serious. Some official matter, I presume. She will be escorted to her home later."

The man's tone was smooth and reassuring. Boris, by clenching his teeth, managed to keep a straight face, but Polya drew in her breath sharply. They both understood.

When General Smirnov left, Boris turned a stony face on Polya. His lips barely moved as he spoke.

"Control yourself. You look so shocked!"

"Take me home, Boris, I beg you."

"You can't go now. I'll decide when it is safe to leave."

"What shall I do? I'm frightened, Boris!"

"Dance!"

It was past midnight when Mikhail got the telephone call. It was Boris.

"Did I wake you, Mikhail?"

"No, I haven't gotten to bed yet. I'm celebrating my own banquet with your brandy."

"I wanted to tell you not to worry. Ksenia will be home later."

"Why? Isn't she with you and Polya?"

"No. We're at home but Ksenia wanted to stay on. Someone will take her home."

"Someone, you say? Who is the someone?" There was a note of fear in his voice.

"Don't ask stupid questions." Boris forced a cackle. "Nobody will take her away from you."

Mikhail's fear turned to anger. "Is that all you can say? I know what 'later' means."

"It means nothing, you fool!" Boris shouted and slammed the receiver.

Mikhail remained sitting motionless for a long time. Gloom and despair enveloped him. He remembered now that Ksenia had gone off without even saying good-bye to him. What had happened to their idyllic love? And how eager she was to enjoy herself at the Kremlin, as if she were playing some game. It was all Boris' fault for inviting her.

He went to the window and flung it open. The evening, shining clear and bright, was brightened further by lamps that lit up the streets and the park opposite the house. To Mikhail, looking down from the fifth floor, the people on the streets and in the park seemed like so many smallish creatures swarming and foraging about without aim or reason. He turned from the window, sat down at the desk, propped his elbows on it and laid his chin in his hands. He stared through the open door into the next room. The bottle of brandy which Boris had brought as a gift stood on the table. Its bulging belly and long drawn-out neck, made a weird caricature. He blinked as the bottle and glasses began to bob and sway, and he shut his eyes as he thought he saw the glasses execute a sharp, mocking tattoo. He lunged from the chair, stumbled to the open window, leaned out, drew in a long breath of air and gazed down at the park. On a tree-sheltered bench a couple sat locked in an unashamed, passionate embrace. A drunk staggered along one path bellowing hoarsely what was intended to be a song, followed by a troop of youngsters who shrieked their appreciation. On another path young men and their girls strolled by, singing. Mikhail closed his eyes tightly, searching desperately for some thought. It was like staring into a vacuum. With a gasp, he ran out toward the bottle, seized it by its long neck and poured out a brimming glass of brandy. Glass in hand he ran back to the window. Again he looked out. There had been laughter and ribaldry and the throb of life. But the moment had fled. The park was still, the streets almost empty except for a few hurrying pedestrians. Ah, yes, the lovers were there, knowing only each other and wrapped in their comforting embrace under the sheltering tree. Opposite them, on another bench, lay the drunkard, his nose tilted to the sky.

Mikhail was alone. He saw that now. With a slow gesture he raised his glass. He raised it higher and higher, his eyes fixed in an empty stare.

"I drink to you, O Universe!"

He swallowed the brandy in one gulp and hurled the glass through the window. He waited, swaying, and heard it shatter on the ground below. He went into the other room, and leaned heavily on the table with both hands until his knuckles were white and bloodless. He shook his head back and forth. Gently he picked up the bottle and lifted it to his lips. He drank with slow deliberation, relishing each mouthful. As he drank, his temples began to throb unbearably. His throat burned and his limbs felt as though they were filled with boiling lead. As he drained the last drop, he sank to the floor and lay there with his head between his hands. A low, gasping sob came from his lips.

"Evil, evil, evil is the world!"

He pounded his breast with his fist.

"And what is man but a beast of burden forever, a beast under the lash!"

He lay there all night on the floor, swooning, waking, wracked by fits of weeping and laughter. Finally, at dawn, exhausted beyond endurance, he sank into a sleep beyond pain and deep as death itself.

Ksenia had been dancing with someone, a thin, young man with the sorrowful, effeminate face of a eunuch. After a while he had said softly, "Come outside. You are privileged to see the entire Kremlin, on the highest authority." Her tongue was tied, her head swimming with confusion and excitement. The grip of his fleshless hand as he led her out of the spinning, swaying crowd, was like steel. She did not recall walking down the empty alleys of the Kremlin. But she did remember coming to a house, climbing the stairs and being left suddenly alone in a dark corridor. A door opened and she heard a voice say, "Come in."

She stepped across the threshhold. The room in which she found herself was large, its gloom suffused by a strange, green light. The objects in it were blurred and indistinct, but she could see two windows covered by what seemed a heavy, red-plush curtain, a writing desk that stood between them, a bulky, leather armchair in one corner and a wall covered from floor to ceiling by bookshelves. She also saw a leather divan against another wall on which a man, dressed in a silken robe, sat facing her. She could not tell whether she had seen him before.

"Come here. I've been expecting you. I want you to tell me all about the kolkhoz." The tone was one of a command.

She recognized his voice. He was one of the three who had spoken to her at the table. Obediently she came and sat down next to him, thinking vaguely, This is very curious. To be ordered in the middle of the night to discuss a kolkhoz where I haven't been for almost two years.

She was silent for a few moments trying to collect herself. It occurred to her now that there must be some truth in the rumors that circulated among the simple folk that the leaders in the Kremlin never slept but worked day and night for the welfare of the country.

"I am waiting," he said.

"I left the village two years ago," she managed to explain. "I'm afraid my information is no longer timely."

He got up and went into the next room. As she watched him go, she suddenly realized that he wasn't interested in what she had just told him. She had a strange feeling that something was wrong. Her throat was so parched. Her head ached badly and an uneasiness began to gnaw at her. Why had she been brought here?

The man was back, bringing a tray, a bottle of liquor, and two glasses.

"Let us drink to your health."

Ksenia reached out for the glass he gave her. "To your health," she repeated as in a trance, her brain fighting to ask, "Who are you?"

They drank and he set the tray on the desk. Then he sat down again next to her and took her hand in his. That gesture helped to clear her head. Before the liquor and whatever else was in it had taken effect, she was unmistakably aware of her reason for being there. She could not deny to herself that despite the risk and the danger, she was flattered to be here. She waited expectantly and with drowsy indifference for his next move. He was speaking to her.

"What kind of work do you do?"

"I don't work. I'm a student at the Medical Institute."

"Indeed! Isn't this examination time?"

"Examinations are over." Her manner was cautious and discreet. He would learn little or nothing about herself or Mikhail. She would answer curtly, if possible with yes or no. Her mind was still clear enough to grasp that this was a game of intrigue, but a game she was beginning to enjoy.

"And have you passed all your examinations?" he asked.

"Yes."

"I see. And besides passing examinations, what else do you do?"

"Nothing."

"Nothing? You are very modest. Such modesty is unbefitting a Bolshevik and peasant maid who is clever enough to become a doctor. What you are doing is very commendable. We need a new Communist intelligentsia. We must have our own doctors."

"I know that."

"That pleases me." He squeezed her hand. "In fact, you please me." In the dimly lit room she could feel his eyes devouring her. Ksenia's veins were slowly filling with a sweet torpor.

He sat for a while softly caressing her hand and arms. When he finally drew her to him, her head sank on his breast and she did not resist. She could hear his strong heartbeats and she felt his hot hands as they passed over her bosom fondling her and she offered an answering passion as his caresses grew more urgent.

In a hypnotic state, she followed him into another room, removed her clothes and got into bed. She dozed fitfully and each time she awoke, the reality of the situation forced itself into her consciousness. The man lying next to her had none of Mikhail's tenderness; he lay on her like a clumsy animal. His behavior was beginning to disgust her. Why was she here in bed with this stranger? she thought. She began to reproach herself, but she slipped into abysmal blackness. The next time she awoke, she found herself alone.

She sprang out of bed and got into her clothes. She hurried through the next room; its high bookcase, leather divan, and large desk between the two windows made her shiver. She opened the door, passed down the corridor and came to the steps she had climbed the night before. The thin man with the effeminate face was waiting for her. She recalled vividly how he had danced with her and finally brought her here. She had only the haziest recollection of having passed through dark streets. The rest stood out with brutal clarity. She realized it was pointless to question this man.

He took hold of her arm. "I am to escort you home."

Parked outside was a closed, black limousine. Ksenia got in and huddled into one corner of the seat. The man asked for her address. She breathed a sigh of relief as the limousine left the Kremlin and started to roll through the city streets.

The car stopped in front of her building. Ksenia left the car, ran up the five flights of stairs—the elevator was not working again—and burst into the apartment. When she saw Mikhail lying on the floor in his clothes, the empty bottle of brandy at his side, she went numb. He lay face down, his head on his arm and his feet spread wide apart. She looked down at him, remorse and pity struggling within her. Then with a gasp she ran into her room, threw herself on the bed and burst into tears.

CHAPTER SIX

Some weeks later Mikhail and Ksenia went to visit Boris. Polya invited Ksenia into the kitchen for a glass of tea. In a very short time both women were deep in the gossip peculiar to the new Soviet aristocracy. There was no mention of politics; they no longer had the slightest interest in politics. Their greatest source of entertainment, with the possible exception of clothes, was small talk—both pleasant and unpleasant—about the husbands and wives of other Communists. Sometimes there was news about one or another of their friends giving birth to children without being able to positively identify the father. But Ksenia, who usually relished such tidbits, seemed too upset to enjoy them today. There were faint stirrings within her and she tried to suppress her fear of the inevitable. If she could only be sure the child was Mikhail's, she would be happy. But ever since that night in the Kremlin, certainty was out of the question.

She sensed that Polya suspected her condition. This in itself did not disturb her because she knew Polya would keep her secret. Besides, Polya herself had often hinted that if she ever met a man who interested her, she wouldn't hesitate a moment about having an affair. Only her fear of Boris, who was so righteous and moral about such matters, might restrain her. No, Polya's suspicion did not bother her. What worried her was that she could no longer hide from herself what she soon would not be able to hide from others.

As for Polya, she had overcome her shock at Ksenia's disappearance at the banquet. She was thinking about Mikhail, who might easily be duped into fathering a child he had never conceived. But above all was the fear that if something *had* happened to Ksenia that night, the consequences could be disastrous to all of them. She had to find out how matters stood.

"How I envy you, Ksenia," she began, cautiously. "There was a time when I, too, had plenty of admirers, but none of them ever spirited me away."

"What do you mean?" Ksenia asked, startled.

"I'm talking about that night at the Kremlin when you suddenly disappeared," Polya blurted out.

"So? Why should you envy me?"

"It was all so romantic!" she teased. "If you only knew how dull my life is, you would understand what I mean. Boris really doesn't need me. Women don't interest him, and I least of all. He is married to his work. He never makes love to me any more. I feel so undesired. I'm beginning to think no man could find me desirable again."

"Then why don't you find out? Boris need never know."

"Ah, Ksenia, you don't know Boris. He is like a dog in the manger who won't eat and won't let anyone else eat. I don't dare. I would never have believed a Communist could be so straitlaced."

"Well, at least he is jealous. Whatever else is wrong, his jealousy is a sign that he loves you."

"That's small consolation, you'll admit. I can't go on starving for a little affection while my husband expresses his impotent love by being jealous."

"Aren't you exaggerating a little, Polya?"

"It's the truth, Ksenia."

"If it has gone that far, I think a woman should help herself."

"And do what?"

"Anything that will save her from starvation."

"Anything? Even a love affair?"

Ksenia reddened. She felt as if this time Polya had deliberately touched her wound, but she controlled herself, tossed her head and shot back flippantly, "Yes, even a love affair."

"Then what would you say to an affair between Mikhail and me?"

Ksenia's eyes narrowed. She looked at Polya contemptuously and avoided a direct answer. "I've seen the way you look at him."

"Don't tell me you are jealous too."

"Not a bit, though you know how much I love Mikhail. At any rate, I wouldn't suffer like some women if I discovered he had a love affair now and again. Of course I wouldn't want to lose him."

"Then what really worries you is that he shouldn't leave you. Am I right?"

"Right."

"In that case, you have nothing to fear. I could never take Mikhail from you because I don't think I appeal to him. Besides, he needs you too much and I couldn't hurt him. Could you?"

Ksenia didn't answer; she just looked at Polya.

"Something is wrong, isn't it, Ksenia?" Polya continued. "You haven't been the same since you went to the Kremlin with us that night."

"I am glad that Mikhail and I will be leaving Moscow," Ksenia answered evasively.

"What are you running away from?" cried Polya impatiently. "Unless it has something to do with what happened in the Kremlin that night."

"Yes and no. You can take it any way you like. All I know is that I am sick and tired of Moscow and can't stand the sight of the Kremlin!"

"Quiet, Ksenia, lower your voice."

"At first, when Mikhail wanted to travel and write about Birobidjan I was heartbroken. But now I can hardly wait for him to straighten out his affairs here."

Polya burst into laughter. "Poor, miserable, lovable idiots!"

In the meantime another conversation was taking place in Boris' private study.

"You and Ksenia are a pair of real lunatics," Boris was saying. "Where are you running? Just when your big chance arrives you walk out on it. Moscow is suddenly too hot for you and you get an itch to see the world."

Mikhail had been waiting for Boris to bring up the subject

of Birobidjan as he had promised. Since he had not mentioned it, Mikhail reminded him:

"Boris, you owe me an explanation about Birobidjan. You remember? The night of the banquet."

Boris snorted nervously. "For the life of me I can't understand this sudden interest in Birobidjan. You are a Russian writer. Your first book made a good impression and all your stories in the journals have so far been praised. Now is your chance to amount to something. You can have a life free of care and earn a good living with your pen. You don't have to accept any jobs where police inspectors and commissars watch every move you make. You could be your own boss. Instead you begin straining at the leash. Everybody else would be dancing for joy, but not you. You prefer to go looking for trouble."

"That's just what I mean," Mikhail replied, shaking his forefinger at Boris. "It seems very odd that you should remind me of trouble the minute I ask you about Birobidjan. Now you have really aroused my curiosity to see for myself what's going on there. You and I, we are both Jews, and it is natural for a Jew to want to know what is happening in a territory established for Jews."

"Don't include me in the category of Jews," said Boris, frowning.

"As you wish," Mikhail conceded tartly. "I will accept the fact that you are not a Jew. However, let me remind you that your passport contains the word 'Nationality' and next to it the word 'Jew.' So you see that in one form or another, whether we like it or not, we are considered Jews after all. To that extent we are justified in having some interest in Jewish problems."

"You are absolutely hopeless," Boris growled and buried his nose in his newspaper, indicating that he would waste no more time on nonsense. But Mikhail was not to be discouraged. He reached out and gently took the newspaper from Boris' hands.

"Boris, I speak to you as a friend. Why do you bury your head in the sand? Is there anything in that newspaper that talks to you of our friendship? Would you, for instance, cover your face with this newspaper if I told you I were leaving and had come to say good-bye?"

"So! You are on your way already." Boris grinned. "You won't even give me the privilege of staying angry with you. Very well, what is it you want to know?"

"Why is it that the mere mention of Birobidjan makes you furious? Has Stalin given some directive about it?"

"I have no idea."

"In that case why do you object to my going there?"

"It's just that you writers are an eccentric lot and won't stay put. You are always looking for the other side of the mountain, always following the elusive. The reason I get furious is that my words are wasted on you. If you want to see the world, go ahead and see it, for all I care. But as your friend, I would rather you didn't get tangled up in this business they now call Birobidjan. Take my advice and don't accept any official assignments that have anything to do with it. Everything connected with it is nebulous and unpredictable."

"Then how do you explain the fact that hundreds of Jews are being sent there every day?"

"I can offer no explanation."

"And I think that for some reason you prefer not to explain."

"You think! You probe! Why don't you let well enough alone?"

"In the meantime there are rumors that over forty thousand Jews have settled in Birobidjan," Mikhail went on as if he had not heard Boris' last remark.

Boris laughed sarcastically. "Why is that so remarkable? Add a hundred thousand Russians, about two hundred Ukrainians, sixty thousand Koreans and several thousand Tunguses and Kamchatkans—all of whom were either born there or migrated into that country many years ago—and you will see how insignificant your figures are. Birobidjan is an outpost on the banks of the Amur. What lies beyond the River Amur? Manchuria. And who rules over Manchuria? Formerly China, today imperialistic Japan. With that kind of neighbor we cannot afford to desert our borders. They must be populated, manned, and defended, and that takes people. Birobidjan is a buffer state. I trust that you follow me without too much difficulty."

"And that's the whole story?"

"Isn't that enough?"

"Stop covering up, Boris. If that's all it is, why did they go through the trouble of proclaiming it an autonomous Jewish region with Kalinin giving speeches, explanations, and promises of all kinds while Stalin writes that we don't have to do anything for the Jews?"

"Then you have Kalinin's word for it. I can only add," Boris continued impatiently, "that the government has formed a committee of Jewish representatives, good Communists. The function of the committee is to spread the word among the Jewish masses that whoever wishes to may voluntarily settle in Birobidjan. The Party and government has no intention of forcing anyone, but whoever has the will and the desire to settle there will receive financial aid and assistance to get there."

"Boris, I want the truth. I've got to know," and Mikhail put the question again slowly and deliberately, "What is the policy on Birobidjan?"

There was real admiration in Boris' eyes. He had never known Mikhail so determined. He had always thought of him as rather weak and undisciplined. "So you insist on knowing Stalin's private policy on Birobidjan? You ask me to tell you openly what no man in Russia dares to ask himself?"

"I happen to know," Mikhail said, "that Stalin issued a call for volunteers to settle in the new city of Komsomolsk, which is situated not far from Birobidjan. But in all this time he has neither asked nor ordered anyone to settle in Birobidjan itself. There must be a reason."

"If you understand this much," Boris pointed out, dropping his voice, "then you should be able to draw your own conclusions. Why, then, do you insist on going out there? It should be enough that I have warned you to steer clear of the whole Birobidjan idea."

"But—"

"No buts, Mikhail."

"Does this mean that you can't trust me?"

"If you must know, nowadays a man can't even trust his

own mother." Boris put his arm affectionately around Mikhail. "And if the Kremlin ever decides to dismiss me and orders me shot against the wall, I might suspect, in my last conscious moment, that I owe it all to you, since you were the only person to whom I had confided certain secrets which are locked up in the deepest vaults of the Kremlin. You will do me a favor, Mikhail, if you free me of this horrible thought. I cherish you as a friend. You are an honest, straightforward man, and that makes you different. It is a difference which I prize highly and I am grateful for your friendship. What more do you want?"

Mikhail felt a tightening in his throat. "Nothing more, Boris. Nothing at all. We won't talk about it again. I'm really sorry for you."

"You pity me?"

"Well, I don't exactly envy you your job. You are a slave to the Kremlin, even though you are a great commissar."

Boris got to his feet and began pacing up and down the room. Finally he stopped in front of Mikhail.

"If it's pity you feel, I don't want it. That's the one thing I can't take, even from a friend." His face was white and his fists clenched. "From now on, if I decide that it is important for you to know something, I will inform you. And I shall do so not in order to feed your literary curiosity but to avoid having on my conscience the death of a naïve and honest comrade. So you want to know Stalin's stand on Birobidjan? Let me explain Stalin to you. I will tell you what I know or think I know. He is both mentally deranged and a master craftsman in every area of intrigue. He suffers from persecution mania. At the same time he is an unequaled political leader, the genius of our time. Try and get the picture. He is a man who inspires the greatest fear and the blindest devotion. They are inseparable if one is to stay alive. And I love him. He is my God. And this God has now moved his finger. The purge has already begun. In a short time thousands of loyal and sincere Party Communists will be denounced by the purging committees as enemies of the people. The aim of this purge is to wipe out the entire old guard of the Party, all of whom were close collaborators of Lenin and Trotsky. Stalin will spare only the young who know nothing and remember nothing. He knows that the old

Communists are laughing at him. They do not laugh openly but in secret; they keep the laugh buried in their hearts. They laugh because Stalin has declared himself a god and because they know that he is not Lenin's heir but a usurper and impostor. They will neither forget nor forgive. And so they laugh, biding their time, because they feel that Stalin will overreach himself and that he is doomed. But what they do not know is that he is doomed only if they stay alive. This is their fatal error. But we, the young ones, whether we stumble on these truths or not, will remain alive because we do not share this grudge and we take Stalin seriously. He knows that he can trust us to carry out his great plans of Socialist construction without the slightest risk of sabotage." Boris paused and poked his finger into Mikhail's chest. "These plans will be carried out without the old guard. Therefore, first and foremost, you are to avoid any association with them. I don't want to lose you."

"Yes, Boris," said Mikhail growing impatient, "but what has this to do with Birobidjan?"

"I'll get to that. I know you are familiar with Stalin's article, 'Marxism and the National Question.' "

"Yes."

"I want you to note that although Stalin has introduced changes in his other texts, this one not only remains unchanged but Stalin hasn't the slightest intention of changing it. On this issue he is adamant. No Jew, no matter how vacillating, alien, or deadened in his national feelings, will have any trouble peeling off the Marxist shell to find the anti-Semitic core. Even I, who refuse to have any traffic with Jews and Jewish problems, felt it at once. Stalin states flatly in this article that the Jews are not a nation, they do not help one another in time of war or in time of peace and that for the so-called culture of this tissue-paper nationality there is to be no sponsorship. In the face of this, what are our stupid Jewish Communists clamoring for? Apparently they do not understand simple Russian. They are told '*nyet*' and run around like rats in a trap trying to force a '*da*' out of Stalin."

"Then why," cried Mikhail, "is the government playing up Birobidjan?"

"That's one of the puzzles I myself can't figure out. And that's the truth, Mikhail."

"Then if that's the case, I have all the more reason for going."

"Yes, if you go only as an observer." Boris thought for a moment, then instructed him. "If you decide to go out there, I want you to report to me what you find. But under no circumstances accept any official assignment. Don't get tangled up in any political or opportunistic intrigues."

"There is just one thing more," Mikhail said, feeling somewhat relieved. "It has nothing to do with my desire to see Birobidjan. I have heard that General Joachim Schultz has been sent to the Far East to the Baikal-Amur zone as one of the generals of a separate Far Eastern Red Army. Is he the same Joachim Schultz who was once the Deputy Chief of the Odessa Cheka?"

"Yes, he is the same man. You also ought to know, and this may surprise you, that Nathan Wieder is now the new Communist Party Secretary there."

"Nathan Wieder? The former Chief of the Odessa Cheka? Someone is playing the devil's game."

At that moment, Polya and Ksenia rejoined the men. It was time for Mikhail and Ksenia to leave. Boris put his big, heavy hand on Mikhail's shoulder and said,

"Come and see me tomorrow. I expect to have a free evening unless—unless something special comes up. At any rate, take a chance. I see now that nothing will cure you of your wanderlust, so before you take off let's talk things over again."

"I'll stop by tomorrow night," Mikhail promised.

CHAPTER SEVEN

The next evening Mikhail went straight to Boris' house. He was not at home. Polya let him in; the maid had gone to a movie. Boris had called to say that he would not be home for supper and that some business matter would probably keep him busy till after midnight.

Although he was disappointed not to find Boris in, Mikhail accepted Polya's invitation to stay a while. He was in high spirits and he wanted to share the good news with someone. He had just been notified that some newspapers and magazines had agreed to publish his impressions of Siberia and the Far East.

Mikhail sat down on the divan and Polya came and sat next to him. She passed her hand playfully through his light-brown hair, while her eyes rested on his fair, gently molded face.

"To tell the truth, Mikhail," she said, "I'm glad you didn't find Boris in. Maybe now you will sit and talk with me like you do with him. Tell me about your trip. When will you leave? May I know or is it a secret?"

"Well, what do you think?" he teased. "Boris is not the only one entitled to secrets. I have a few of my own."

She laced her arm through his. "Mikhail, don't pull a Boris act. Remember this is me, Polya, and I'd like to have at least one friend with whom I can talk and who talks with me just for the sake of talking, without being afraid of disclosing some terrible secret."

"I was only joking, Polya. I hate secrets myself. Boris wanted to give me some advice about the trip. He knows the Kremlin's stand on the places I want to visit better than I do. And I wanted to tell him that I got some writing assignments for pieces on the eastern provinces."

"Oh, isn't that wonderful," Polya cried. She tightened her

hold on Mikhail's arm. "How I envy Ksenia going to all these adventurous places. We never go anywhere, and I am dying of boredom cooped up in this commissarial bureaucracy."

"But Polya, you have all of Moscow—the museums, the shops, the gall—"

"I'm bored because my soul is empty," she said suddenly, looking directly into Mikhail's eyes, "Maybe my salvation is to be loved."

Mikhail felt uncomfortable. Polya was behaving like a young widow hungry for a man. He wanted to see her happy but he didn't want to get involved. From their very first meeting years ago, Polya had let him know in devious ways that, stifled and frustrated, she was reaching out for love. He had resisted her enticements out of respect and consideration for Boris, and then he had met Ksenia and he thought there no longer would be any danger. But for some reason, he still felt strangely vulnerable. He smiled at Polya and gently embraced her.

"You're so nice," Polya said. "Be good to me, Mikhail." She touched his face. Her body was close to his. He could feel his maleness rise. He could not ignore her soft caress nor the desperate longing in her voice. "What is it you want?" he whispered hoarsely.

"I want to be a woman," she cried out. "Do you understand?" She looked at him with restless impatience. "I need someone to love me."

"What about Boris?" Mikhail stammered.

"It's you I need."

"Polya," Mikhail said roughly. "You know I wouldn't want anything to spoil our friendship." It was like a slap.

"Don't worry, Mikhail." Polya said, now completely in control. "I know that I can't depend on someone else for my happiness, and to share it is not always wise. I must find some other solution, but I'll try not to hurt Boris."

"I'm glad. Boris needs you."

"I know he does, but the days are dry and the nights weigh upon me."

"Why not go back to work, Polya? You will become interested again in what's going on in our country and in foreign affairs and you will have less free time on your hands."

"Oh, no! Boris would never allow that. He likes to find me at home when he comes."

"Then he loves you."

"In a way."

"In what way?"

Polya's face became pale. She avoided the question. Mikhail gently stroked her hand, and with deep feeling he asked,

"Tell me Polya, have things gotten worse between you and Boris?"

"Much worse. Haven't you noticed it yet?" There were tears in her eyes. "He has completely changed in this last year. He has become hypnotized, bewitched. All his love he gives to Stalin. There is nothing left for me. He doesn't need me at all. Look at him closely, Mikhail, and you will see a dead man. He may appear strong and manly, but behind this illusion is an ascetic with fixed, glassy eyes—a mechanical man, a robot. It's as if his soul were taken from him that horrible night," she continued sobbingly.

"What night?"

"The night the 'traitors' were shot."

"Ah—"

"I remember that night so vividly. Boris came home very late and instead of going to bed as he usually did, he went into his study. I waited and waited but he didn't come. Finally I got up and went to him. I found him pacing up and down. When he saw me he shrank back in fear. It wasn't like Boris at all. Then he broke into a loud cry and walked slowly toward me. Like a lost and tired child he laid his head on my shoulder and sobbed. This was the first and only time I ever saw him weep. I led him to our room, undressed him, and put him to bed. I held him in my arms and tried to comfort him. He clung to me, trembling and whimpering."

Polya closed her eyes, exhausted and tortured by the memory. Mikhail wanted to console her and take away her pain just as she did with Boris, but all his words died in his throat. He could only murmur,

"Don't worry, Polya. Everything will work out. You will see."

It was getting late and Mikhail made a move to get up, but Polya pleaded, "Don't leave me yet, Mikhail!"

"Polya, be reasonable. You must understand—" He was becoming uneasy. "Ksenia is waiting for me. You will tell Boris I was here."

"I understand," she said.

As Mikhail reached the hall stairs he heard a car pull up to the curb and then, after a moment of silence, pull away with a roar. He passed through the vestibule, opened the heavy, ornate door and found himself face to face with Boris. He tried to avoid his eyes, nursing within him a sense of shame and guilt. He forced himself to be casual. "So there you are, Boris! I have been waiting for you in your apartment. I thought you weren't coming home at all."

"Sorry, but it's not my fault. I was busy. In fact, I'm over my head in work." Boris shook his hand. "But I'm glad to see you, Mikhail. Suppose we walk a while. I'll take you part of the way. It will do me good to take a stroll and get some fresh air after a hard day's work."

"Boris, you work too hard. They ought to pay you double overtime."

"Overtime? I don't think of the salary. The work is important and for the most part cannot be postponed."

They left together. Boris lived on a quiet, renovated street where new houses were restricted to technical specialists and political commissars. The pavements were wide and bordered by young trees on which greenish-white buds were beginning to sprout. A bright sky full of shimmering stars hung over the city. Mikhail and Boris walked slowly through the neighboring streets toward the new botanical gardens. They were in the shape of a five-pointed star. In the center was a fountain with water cascading over a conglomeration of rocks. The two friends found an empty bench nearby and sat down.

"You know," said Boris, "often after the car brings me home, I don't go upstairs but come here and sit on a bench for a long time before going back to the house. I watch these peaceful waters flowing over the rocks and feel refreshed."

"Yes, water soothes and purifies."

"Purifies?" Boris questioned.

"And sanctifies," Mikhail added.

"Perhaps. I've never thought too much about it. I never had

the time to study religion. There's nothing in Marxism that teaches us about the holiness of water."

"Well, it doesn't matter nowadays anyhow," Mikhail smiled. "The question is not whether water does or does not sanctify, but whether we have a piece of soap to go with the water so as to keep decently clean."

"Why? Do you feel so unclean that there isn't enough soap for you?"

Mikhail was taken aback. It was as though Boris had sensed his guilt. "I wasn't talking about myself," he hastened to add. "I meant the country in general. The little things that each person needs are still scarce."

"Don't worry, my friend. What is scarce today, we'll have plenty of tomorrow. Our industry is growing day by day. Not only here, but in Siberia, where you are going. You will see for yourself."

"That's exactly what I hope to write about. I haven't told you the good news yet. I have been given assignments from the *Star*, the *Bolshevik*, and even *Izvestia* to send back articles on my impressions of the Far East and Siberia. They have practically named me their correspondent—with the approval of the Central Committee of the Party, of course."

"Of course," Boris repeated. "But remember what I told you. Only on a temporary basis and as a free-lance writer. Always leave yourself an open door for retreat."

"Naturally. I have no desire to remain there."

"In that case, Mikhail, I really envy you. It's good to be a Soviet writer, isn't it? You're free as a bird and the gates of our great country are open for you."

"Even the gates of Birobidjan?"

"I was waiting for you to bring that up," Boris said as a shadow crossed his face. "I have thought a great deal about our conversation last night and I have decided that perhaps, after all, you are right to stop over in Birobidjan for a short time. And my real reason in wanting to talk to you today is this. As a favor, I would like you to report to me personally when you come back from your trip. I don't want you to tell me something I can read in your articles. I want your own personal reaction to the problem of Birobidjan." Then Boris got up and stretched. "Well, it's pretty late and I must get back before my Polya begins to think that I am out whoring somewhere."

Mikhail rose too. "Would that be bad, seeing that it is only natural?" he asked cautiously.

"Oho!" Boris grinned. "What do you take me for—one of your writers? Not that I have anything against writers. I understand them. It's just that they are morally weak. Although, in all fairness," he added quickly, "we have plenty of playboys among our Party workers and government officials, I must admit." He shook Mikhail's hand, said good-bye, and left him standing there.

Mikhail watched him go. Boris' hand had been heavy, clammy, and lifeless. Not the hand, he thought to himself, that could caress a woman.

CHAPTER EIGHT

It was just before they were ready to start out on their journey that Ksenia suddenly confided to Mikhail that she was pregnant. He was thunderstruck.

"Why didn't you tell me before? Why did you wait until now when we're all packed?"

"Aren't you pleased?" Her voice was brittle.

"Pleased? I'm jubilant! Overjoyed! And I love you for it." He swooped her up and spun her around and around as he kissed her eyes, her nose, her mouth. "And you will make it a boy, won't you?"

"I didn't say I would make it anything," she snapped.

Mikhail set her down abruptly. "What do you mean?" Already he had seen himself in the role of a father. Ksenia would bear him a son and he would give the boy a fine upbringing. His son, he mused, would be spared the misery and deprivation of his father's childhood!

"Just what do you mean, Ksenia?"

He saw gloom and despair cross her face. Her chin trembled as she spoke. "Please don't hate me for what I'm going to say." She swallowed hard. "I don't want this child."

"In heaven's name, why?" he shouted at her. "We can afford it. We'll stay in Moscow. We'll cancel our trip. Now we can live like other people. If it will make you happier, we can even rent a house in the suburbs. A house and garden. Many writers are moving out into the Moscow suburbs. You will be among the elite—I know how much that means to you."

"I'm sorry, Mikhail, but I've made up my mind." She began to cry. "I've decided to have an abortion, before it's too late."

"You're insane! It's against the law. Besides you will be taking a terrible risk." Mikhail couldn't understand Ksenia's attitude. And she looked so helpless and frightened.

"There are doctors who will do it for money," she said.

He drew her close and looked into her sad eyes. "Tell me, Ksenia. Why don't you want a child?"

She could not bring herself to tell him. She lied. This was not the time to have a child, she explained. Later, perhaps. It would tie them down permanently and she wanted to be free for a while yet. She wanted to see the world now, while she was still young. She hoped he understood.

It struck Mikhail that Ksenia, despite herself, might be deliberately reacting to the fact that they were not really married, that it meant a life without guarantees or security. She knew that even Polya had registered her marriage in the Moscow City ZAGS and that Yekaterina Petrovna was officially married. Perhaps, he reasoned, Ksenia felt she was losing face, that this free love arrangement with him made her feel insecure and inferior.

"Ksenia," he suggested, "let's go down and register our marriage."

"Don't be foolish!" she cried. "Does the mere act of registration bring a guarantee of a stable family life? How can registration be binding when divorce can be registered just as easily? The only difference is that marriage costs three rubles and divorce fifty. No, Mikhail, that is not the answer. If love should die, registration becomes an empty gesture. I am more sure of you although we are not married, than many women are of their legal husbands. I am sure of you because I love you and know that you love me."

"Then if you love me, why do you refuse to bear my child?"

"We're not ready now, Mikhail."

"But you know how I love children."

"I beg you, Mikhail! Please! Let's not discuss it any more. I've made up my mind."

Her eyes were full of pain. She turned her back on him, went to the window and looked down into the street. He followed her and put his arms around her.

"Ksenia," he said to her after a while, his voice trembling, "you are an adult and I don't have the right to stop you. You do as you think best. I just want you to be happy."

She turned slowly. "I am terribly grateful to hear you say

that." Then she sighed, glad that it was finally settled. "It will take about two weeks. If anyone asks about me, I have gone to visit my mother."

"As you wish, Ksenia."

"Polya knows a doctor and she will make all the arrangements. I will remain until it is all over. And don't worry, Mikhail."

"So you have entrusted Polya with all the details and left me completely out!"

"You forget that she is no stranger, but a dear friend—yours and mine."

"Of course. She is our friend, as you say," Mikhail said.

CHAPTER NINE

Two days after his distressing talk with Ksenia, he came home from a visit to the Writers' Club to find her gone and a note in her handwriting.

> "Dear Mikhail:
> Phone Polya. She will explain everything. Forgive me, but I must go through with it. I love you and will always love you.
>
> Ksenia."

He stood looking at the note for a long time, his mind refusing to accept what his eyes read, even though he had expected it. Finally he went to the phone and rang up Polya.

"It's all over, Mikhail. Don't worry. Everything is fine. Would you like to come over? Or would you rather I come to you. I have the time now."

"I'd rather you came here." He tried to keep his voice steady.

"Get hold of yourself. I'll be right over."

She arrived shortly, sat down opposite Mikhail and said,

"Stop worrying. Ksenia will be home before you know it. Everything went off on schedule. It may be better this way."

"Who is the doctor?" Mikhail wanted to know.

"A friend of mine."

"Is he reliable?"

"Very. Boris knows him too. Take my word for it. Everything is just perfect."

"Does Boris know about it?"

"No, we thought it best to keep him out of it."

"I never believed she would do it." He spoke as if his heart would break. "Why did she do it, Polya?"

"I don't know."

"Women usually confide in one another. She must have told you something. Why did she do it?"

Her answer was to put her arms around him so he would not detect the lie that was in her eyes.

"It's the usual story," she said hesitatingly. "It could happen to anyone."

Mikhail was annoyed. "Stop talking in riddles," he said, disengaging her arms from around his neck. "If you have anything to say, come out with it."

Polya was frightened. She knew she had to be tactful and give Mikhail the story bit by bit. She hastened to assure him that by the "usual story" she had only meant that there was nothing unusual about a woman going into panic at the thought of giving birth.

"And in fact," she went on cautiously, "suppose there had been something unusual about it, which of course was not the case. Well, it would not be as tragic as it sounds."

"Are you keeping something from me?" he cried out. He seized Polya's wrists. "In Heaven's name, tell me what you know!"

"Don't be a fool, Mikhail. I don't know anything and there is nothing to know. What is it you want? Can't you leave well enough alone?" She pulled away from him. "You're hurting me!"

He had to get at the truth, to know why Ksenia had agreed to do such a dangerous thing. "Maybe I left her alone too much. That's the trouble."

"Now you sound exactly like Boris. He can come and go as he pleases. I can't question him, but he must always find me at home."

"Is there anything wrong in that?"

"In a way."

"In what way?"

"You men allow yourselves every liberty, but when you discover that we have done the same, then you are ready to commit murder."

"So now the truth is out!" he gritted.

"I'm glad it's out! She's no better than I am—"

He took hold of her shoulders and began to shake her

violently. "*Ti Styerva! Shlukha!* You tramp! It was all your fault!"

Polya tore out of his grip. Her face was hot with anger. Sparks of rage flamed in her eyes. "You are nothing but a savage and jealous bourgeois," she said. "I thought you were head and shoulders above the others. Now I see that you are an ill-mannered boor and I want nothing more to do with you." She stretched out her hand and struck him across the face. "*Nyegodyi!* Bastard!" and she started to run out.

Mikhail ran after her and put his arms around her. His face had turned ashen, but his voice was calm. "I'm sorry, Polya, we both lost our tempers. Forgive me." He kissed her mouth, stained with salty tears. "You're good. You're a devoted friend. I understand now— It happens sometimes—But I was not prepared for it. Now you can tell me. I promise not to be angry again."

They sat down. Now she looked at Mikhail, his head bowed in anguish, with the same compassion as a mother looking at her fragile child. "This was not the kind of affair you think, Mikhail. Maybe I was wrong but I thought it would be best to hide it from you. The Kremlin is involved in it."

He lifted his head and looked at her face in astonishment. "The Kremlin?" was all he could ask.

She told him the story.

"Believe me when I say that she does not even remember who led her away from the dance, where she was taken or with whom she spoke," she concluded. "Nor does she recall who it was that slept with her. It was a nightmare, mad and worse than witchcraft. That's her secret. That is why she did not want to have the child. She could not be sure that it was yours. Can you understand that? If you are the man I really think you are, she will never find out that you know and you will forgive her."

Mikhail suddenly felt very tired and void of any feeling. He wanted to be alone.

"Please go home now, Polya."

For the next ten days, Mikhail neither read nor wrote; he gave himself with utter abandon to the pleasures of the flesh.

He took perverse delight in abusing his body as though that were a form of revenge for Ksenia's betrayal.

Ksenia arrived in the afternoon of the eleventh day. There was not a trace of sadness or regret in her clear blue eyes. The light of day and the play of sunlight were on her face. Her body was still round and full and about her was the fragrance of blossoms. To Mikhail, who was now completely purged of all rancor, she had the allure of a woodland nymph.

She stretched out her strong, bronzed hands to him and he took them and kissed each finger tenderly in silent adoration. Life began for them once more—a quiet, happy and busy life. They prepared to leave Moscow for distant places, eastward toward the outermost edge of the earth. And like children they dreamed of strange lands and customs and men.

PART THREE

Birobidjan—
The Phantom Republic

CHAPTER ONE

A single track ran from Moscow to Vladivostok. The train ploughed through the vast black, loamy lowlands and miles of hilly pasture land dotted with cattle and climbed into the Urals, a weaving, soaring mass of blue granite and lush evergreen forest.

"There is infinite treasure in those mountains," Mikhail said to Ksenia. "Enough to turn the world into a paradise."

"What sort of treasure?"

"Metals, minerals—iron, copper, gold, platinum, granite, topaz, amethyst, malachite, bluestone, carbon—"

"What good is it if it lies buried in the mountains?"

"Wait and see, Ksenia, it will not be long before we dig it all out."

"You mean our country will become rich?"

"Rich beyond words."

"Does that mean that everybody will be rich?"

"Probably. If the country gets rich, it follows that all its citizens will get rich."

"And what about the capitalist menace? Even if we dig all these metals and minerals, how can we improve the lot of the individual if we are forced to defend ourselves against capitalist encirclement?"

Mikhail did not reply. He recognized the familiar Party line. Ksenia learned very quickly by rote and repeated slavishly what she learned. In a sense, he was glad. It was safer for her.

And so the train crossed the Urals and descended into the Siberian steppes. Day after day it jogged across the endless reaches of Siberia. It was summer, and the songs and tales about a cold Siberia covered with eternal white snow and beset by howling winds and twisting storms had not prepared him for the flaming sun and fields sweet with the fragrance of tall, green wheat standing ready for the peasant's scythe.

At last one evening the train slowed down until it barely moved. They had reached Lake Baikal. That night the passengers stood at the train windows, enraptured by the beauty of the lake. All night the train crawled along the edge of the enormous lake, its placid, luminous, crystalline waters reflecting the image of the long train and the peering faces. It was a night of clear sky full of twinkling stars. Another sky lay sunken in the depths of the lake and was washed by its waters. And when the dawn broke and turned the stars to pale gold, a fiery glow, suffused in a scarlet and blue-green mist, spread over the lake. And then the sun lifted itself boldly from the waters and shed its light over the world, bringing daylight.

Soon Lake Baikal was behind them and they were moving toward the Amur River and the Manchurian border. The region between Lake Baikal and the Amur was filled with hundreds of prison camps. The train conductors now walked through the cars accompanied by the Cheka militia, now called the G.P.U. The doors and windows were locked and the order given:

"It is forbidden to look out!"

But as soon as the conductors and guards left the cars the passengers rushed to the windows. Behind huge enclosures surrounded by barbed wire thousands of ragged men dug the earth, split rocks and, spanned onto wagons like horses, pulled and strained at incredible loads. Armed guards stood around and barked orders.

"I don't understand, Mikhail," said Ksenia, frightened. "Who are all those people?"

"I am confused myself." Mikhail replied. "Perhaps these are the counterrevolutionaries we hear so much about. I'll ask in Birobidjan."

Meanwhile the train plodded through miles of swampy forest in which pines, oaks, and maples mingled their greens, yellows, and reds in a soft, continuous web. Gnats and flies filled the air. Then suddenly the train passed a clearing dominated sharply by a tall hilltop from which a series of mounds, shaped like cupolas, swept downward and away in a gentle slope broken only by the swirling current of a river on whose banks a tiny village of wooden shacks had spread. Beyond lay a hundred miles of rolling steppe and then once more a matted tangle of hilly forest—the Siberian "Taiga," in which jungle and desert alternated.

At dawn the train pulled up before a curious oriental-looking, white railroad station set like a doll house at the edge of a bleak forest. Two large, red-lettered inscriptions in Russian and Yiddish, spelled out: BIROBIDJAN. Mikhail and Ksenia disembarked. "So this is the golden portal to the cities and towns of a future Jewish republic in the Soviet land," Mikhail said.

They walked down the wide, long avenue—the only avenue—of the new city. It was flanked by wooden, two-story houses. The avenue was unpaved and wooden planks served as sidewalks. The streets cutting the avenue at right angles were narrow and muddy. By looking to the right or the left as they passed, they could see the big, one-story wooden barracks which housed the thousands of new "voluntary" immigrants. Ragged children played in the filthy streets and women waited in long lines at the water pumps to fill their pitchers. Men stood in the open doorways, scratching themselves. The smell from the nearby outhouses permeated everything.

The only hotel, which stood at the end of the long avenue where the Biro River uncoiled itself, was also a two-story affair but differed from the other depressing structures in that it boasted a coat of greasy white paint and had a red-lettered sign: HOTEL. As Mikhail and Ksenia entered the lobby, a pleasant young Jew with a pair of old-fashioned pince-nez perched on his nose came forward to meet them. He scrutinized their passports shortsightedly and then declared,

"We have no rooms available. The hotel is filled to capacity with persons of authority—commissars from Moscow, Khabarovsk, and Vladivostok. I can do nothing for you."

Ksenia was tired and unhappy and angry because Mikhail, reluctant to secure reservations in a hotel or a private house, had not wired the Birobidjan Party Committee that he was en route. Mikhail's manner and attitude on this whole trip had irritated her deeply. At the waystations, where there were long delays, he would disappear for hours at a time seeking information. He was looking for trouble, she felt. And now why didn't he simply show his Party card? And if he had not insisted on removing their Orders, then the bespectacled young man would bow and scrape and miraculously produce a room. But no, there he was, still finding out, still testing the attitude of officials by waving a ten-ruble note before those myopic eyes.

The hotel manager pocketed the ten rubles deftly and smiled. "If you will wait here I will let you know shortly. Perhaps someone has decided to check out." He took off his pince-nez and his quick steps echoed down the corridor.

Ksenia burst out, "Why do you torture me? I'm half-dead with fatigue."

He took her hand and, despite his own general mood of disappointment, tried to reassure her. "Getting a room is our least worry. Please be patient."

"Why did you remove the Order from your jacket and force me to take my medal off? What are you up to? You are after something, and somebody is bound to misinterpret your peculiar behavior. Then you will be sorry. I won't play this game any more. It's not for me. Either stop right now or I'll pick myself up and go back home."

Mikhail put his arm around Ksenia.

"If one wants to find out the truth," he said, "anything is justified. A writer is like a sleuth. Sometimes he must even act the scoundrel, or the clown, to find out what he wants to know. The opportunity has been offered to me and I must explore it."

"Mikhail," she replied, quietly but firmly, "you must stop this nonsensical talk. You were not sent out here as a police inspector. You came here as a Soviet writer. Instead you are acting like an undercover commissar."

Mikhail laughed. "You worry too much, Ksenia. You can trust me to be careful and not get us into any trouble."

The hotel manager was back. He replaced his pince-nez, adjusted them carefully and looked at Mikhail and Ksenia with a self-satisfied air.

"You are in luck, comrades. Someone has just checked out —in fact, you have the best room at our disposal, with all conveniences."

The "best" room had a tremendous window overlooking the Biro River, a huge, iron double bed and a tattered mattress. There were also a white table, two white, freshly painted chairs, and a big, ancient, plush-upholstered armchair. The blanket smelled strongly of napthaline, but the pillowcases were clean, white, and freshly ironed. The water and water-closet facilities, although hidden somewhere down the long corridor, were considered an improvement, since until recently the hotel, like all the houses in the flourishing city of Birobidjan, could offer nothing better than a pump and an outhouse.

CHAPTER TWO

Mikhail's first visit was to the Birobidjan Party Committee. When he entered the secretary's office, Nathan Wieder got up from behind a desk and came forward with outstretched hand. "Tovarisch Kruger, I am delighted to have you with us. I have heard a great many splendid things about you. I am also quite familiar with your publications and I don't mind telling you that I enjoyed reading your novel. We could use men like you in this territory."

He detained Mikhail a long time in friendly conversation, but he never indicated that he remembered Mikhail as the destitute lad who had been arrested by the Odessa Cheka. Mikhail was relieved that Wieder either did not recognize him or preferred to give that impression. There was no point in raking up the painful past.

"And so," Wieder said thoughtfully as he looked through Mikhail's papers, "the Central Committee has given you an opportunity to come to Birobidjan without any commitments—you are a guest and nothing more." It was a statement, but there was a tone of inquiry in Wieder's voice which made Mikhail realize that the secretary could not readily believe that such a privilege was granted merely for the asking, that he was already speculating about the powerful connections Mikhail must have to secure such documents.

Mikhail was slow to reply. To tell anyone about Boris was out of the question. He studied the Party secretary—the face wrinkled and furrowed with constant thought, anxiety, and dissatisfaction, the shoulders stooped with care, the hands somewhat unsteady. Rumor had it that the job as secretary of the Birobidjan Party Committee, after so many years of experience as administrator of the Secret Police, went against Wieder's grain. But the Central Committee had arbitrarily assigned him to the post and shipped him out to replace Pinchas Levitt, who in turn had been shipped out to Vladivostok as commissar in charge of Far Eastern transport.

Wieder was not only disgruntled but deeply troubled. His former deputy chief of the Odessa Cheka, Joachim Schultz, who had been appointed commander-in-chief of the special, independent, Far Eastern Red Army, had deserted after a series of defeats along the border and had prompted a Kremlin investigation of his command. His flight had been traced to Manchuria, then to Japan, and then to Germany. Schultz had not only been Wieder's Cheka deputy but also his close friend, and his defection now cast a long shadow over Wieder's own life. From long experience, he knew what to expect. First would come suffocating, invisible pressures, then quiet, deadly persecution and finally false public accusations. When they would come was unpredictable, but he knew that they were inevitable. He was an old and devoted Communist. Like so many of the others, he would be arrested and liquidated.

As Mikhail hesitated before replying, Wieder asked: "How long do you intend to remain here and how will you spend your time?" He smiled gloomily. "The Party would like to cooperate with you in every way, even in your personal undertakings."

"I want to acquaint myself with local conditions and the mode of life," Mikhail explained. "My purpose is to write a book. But as I gather material for it I expect to forward correspondence and articles to various Moscow newspapers and periodicals."

"That is an excellent idea," Wieder agreed, "but as long as you remain here you are still obligated to subordinate your personal aims to the directives of the regional Party."

"According to the documents which I have just shown you," Mikhail answered forcefully, "you have no authority to impose a commitment upon me. I am a free-lance writer and I will accept no jobs here. Nor will my wife accept any job. She is traveling as my private secretary and she has her hands full as it is. She will report tomorrow and present her Party credentials."

Wieder got up from his seat and put his hand on Mikhail's shoulder. His face glowed and for a moment he seemed young again. This was the old Wieder, Mikhail thought, the man who had freed him from the dungeon and opened the road of life before him. He could have sworn that Wieder was secretly pleased, having done his duty and discharged an abhorrent formality demanded by his position, and that he suppressed an impulse to show his recognition and recall their first meeting. But his tone did not betray him.

"Tovarisch Kruger, I would be the last to force you to accept an assignment which interfered with your creative work. You are fully aware of the Party's concern for the welfare of Soviet writers who are, in the words of Tovarisch Stalin, 'the engineers of the human soul.' At the same time it is my duty to warn you that in accordance with the requirements of Party discipline you must register with us and comply with all general Party regulations in force, regardless of whether you are in your permanent domicile, in transit, or in a place of temporary residence."

"I fully understand and agree."

"Fine," said Wieder, taking his seat again. "Tell me, have you found an apartment? It would please you to know that we have a house under construction for our writers and that it will be finished shortly. We have quite a number of young, talented writers. We also have here the well-known novelist and playwright Sergei Kupets."

"Kupets? Here?" Mikhail asked.

"Yes," Wieder replied evenly, "he is here working on a scenario about the 'untamed' taiga."

"I see," Mikhail said and he wished he really did. Kupets was an established writer. Mikhail had met him once or twice in Moscow. He had disliked him instinctively and had avoided further contacts with him, and later Boris had told him to handle him with care because he was also a G.P.U. agent. Mikhail wondered what a G.P.U. agent was doing in Birobidjan. Surely he wasn't just writing a scenario.

"Tovarisch Kupets will be delighted to know you are here," Wieder said. "He tells me he is bored by the provincial mentality in Birobidjan. The house will be finished in a few days and you can take an apartment there as a guest writer. You know, Tovarisch Kruger, a great many people come only for a visit and decide to settle here."

"How about those who come here to settle permanently and are disappointed?" Mikhail asked.

"I would rather not discuss that aspect at the moment. You are a writer and we will let you probe into these matters independently."

"That is one of my intentions."

"Who knows?" Wieder said pointedly. "You might even come to the conclusion that if people try to leave after a while it is not the fault of the region or the administration."

"Tovarisch Wieder," replied Mikhail, looking him straight in the eye, "I have come here to see Socialist construction. That is the mutual aspiration of all good Communists. If by chance I point out some of the inevitable difficulties which arise in the realistic execution of this great work, it is for the purpose of promoting its success."

A look of admiration passed over Wieder's face. The ambiguous, half-bitter smile that just barely wrinkled his lips was more difficult to interpret.

"Tovarisch Kruger, allow me to wish you success in your undertaking. But you must excuse me now. I am extremely busy. If you need anything, don't hesitate to call on me. In the meantime, please report to Professor Gottlieb, the executive committee chairman. I am sure he will be happy to receive you."

The regional offices of the Birobidjan Soviet and the Party executive committee which carried on the administration of the future republic were in another wing of the same building. Professor Gottlieb was a tall man in his forties with a mop of black hair, fine black eyes, and a pleasant ringing voice. He greeted Mikhail warmly.

"I have been expecting you, Tovarisch. The Party secretary has just phoned me. Also, the Publication Department in Moscow has written me that you have promised to send material dealing with the situation here. Please sit down. I am anxious to hear about your first impressions of Birobidjan."

Mikhail took the seat offered him while his glance roamed

around the office. It was bare and simple, with very few papers in evidence, either a sign of great efficiency or a lack of work, he could not tell which. Or, he thought, it indicates a great deal of work being carried on in the heads of men who are afraid to write things down.

"So far," he told Gottlieb, "I have no impressions. I only arrived yesterday and have had no opportunity to see anything." He looked somberly at the man and past him through the window at the smooth hill looming up in the midst of an empty plain that bordered the taiga forest. "I hope I will be able to write many wonderful things about Birobidjan."

"Ah, Tovarisch Kruger, let us face it. We are undergoing hardships, very severe hardships. At the same time we are also making tremendous strides. You will see our schools, the theater we are building, the tailor shop, the wagon shop, and you will admire our kolkhozes, which are second to none—"

"Tovarisch Gottlieb," Mikhail interrupted, "I can well understand your enthusiasm and I hate to inject a sour note, even in my ignorance, but I am told that this very building and the new railroad station were built not by the Jews who were sent here but by the convicts from the Baikal-Amur prisons."

The professor's face grew dark. He brushed his hand over it as if to wipe off a cobweb. "Yes," he admitted, his voice vibrating with suppressed anger, "when Pinchas Levitt was Party secretary here these things did not happen. They started as soon as Nathan Wieder took his place. Everyone knows Wieder's past history. He is accustomed to dealing with convicts. He is a policeman and to him Birobidjan is simply another place which the government and Party have ordered him to police. But to me and others like me Birobidjan is part of a Jewish problem and the goal of a lifetime."

Mikhail felt a great deal of sympathy for this scholar who had given up a scientific career on behalf of a republic for Jews under the sponsorship of Soviet Russia. Mikhail understood that Wieder and Gottlieb were at loggerheads, and he saw immediately that the honest but naïve Gottlieb was no match for the Party secretary.

"The solution," Gottlieb added enthusiastically, "is to

build and to keep on building. Consider, my friend, that a bare five years ago this very spot was nothing more than a taiga infested with wolves and bears and filled with swamps and mud. All this we have transformed into a city. Only a few miles beyond the city is the taiga and the mountains. And I say that for this land, for this gift to the Jewish people, we must bow down in humble gratitude before the Party and the government. We will have a home in this land and we will become a nation like all other nations. The dream of gathering in the Jews, a Zionist dream that cannot come true in a capitalistic world, will now be fulfilled through the might and dictatorship of the proletariat! But one cannot bring the immigrant into a jungle. The climate is polar cold in winter and hot as Africa in summer. Only autumn and spring are temperate and mild. And in order to shelter the people that we brought in, somebody had to build houses and furnish them, even if they are only temporary barracks. And how about schools for children, hospitals for the sick, and factories and kolkhozes to provide work for the newcomers? Who was supposed to build all this? In the entire region we found barely twenty thousand permanent residents of the taiga who were of Russian and Ukrainian origin. The rest—Tartars, Golds, Tunguses, Chinese, Mongols, and Koreans—are scattered in small settlements over thousands of miles of taiga. But we did have at hand the Baikal-Amur prison camps and their countless thousands of convicts who ate and drank at the expense of the state and did nothing at all. The government decided to harness this labor force and make it useful."

"But Tovarisch, you yourself have just said that using convict labor was Wieder's—"

"No, no, Tovarisch—do not misunderstand me. The original idea was a good one. We assumed that the use of convicts would go on only until the Jewish immigration gathered momentum and enough Jewish labor arrived to take over the construction program. But as soon as Wieder took charge, he ordered the convicts to build estates for our new elite—theaters, a museum, a large library, and even a house for his private use. The people live like swine and naturally they desert in droves, but the building program for Party and

Soviet commissars is kept in full swing. You follow me, Tovarisch Kruger—mansions for the privileged, the higher echelons, but barracks for the people, for the thousands of newly arrived Jews. You may well ask why I allow this, since officially I am in charge here as executive committee chairman and so-called President of the territory. The answer is that I am nothing but a figurehead. Wieder is the real boss. He is the Party secretary and I can only do his bidding."

Mikhail did nothing to calm the outraged professor. He wanted this honest, harassed man to spill what was on his mind. It might provide the answers to a number of puzzling questions.

"Tovarisch Gottlieb," he said, "I have received reports that of late more Russians and Ukrainians are being sent in rather than Jews. Can you enlighten me as to the reason?"

The professor lowered his eyes for a few moments as if studying a document that lay on his desk. When he looked up again the shadow in his eyes had deepened. Then he shook his head as if to say: it was no longer a question of trusting or not trusting anyone. He already had been too outspoken. It might be only a matter of time before the Kremlin decided to discard or even liquidate him. What was there to lose? At least he would have the satisfaction of unburdening himself, of venting his bitterness.

"Tovarisch Kruger, I want you to understand that I am one of those rare Jewish Communists who has never belonged to any other Party. I say this so that you will grasp the full significance of what I am about to tell you. I repeat, I am a Communist. But at the same time I am also a Jew. I desire for the Jewish people what I desire for all other peoples—a homeland. And since the Soviet government has granted this land to us, I want to make sure that it does not remain a scrap of paper. How can a Jewish republic be formed here when for every ten Jews who receive permits to come in, permits are also issued to thousands of Russians and Ukrainians? On top of this they have recently transported to this region whole battalions of discharged and demobilized soldiers of the Red Army. These soldiers are being settled on this territory—which supposedly had been set aside for Jews. I now come to your question. You want to know the reason for all this. The reason is simply that the plan to build a Jewish republic has been cancelled. Perhaps someone in the Kremlin at first seriously meant to create a Jewish autonomous region here in the Far East. Someone else in the Kremlin, with greater power and authority, has vetoed it."

"And who might this someone else be?"

"This, Tovarisch Kruger, I should appreciate your finding out entirely by yourself."

Mikhail got up and walked to the window. He stood there breathing deeply and looking out into the early twilight before turning to the professor.

"Your information, Professor Gottlieb, was most enlightening," he said quietly. "I think I understand a great deal now. Above all, I appreciate the directness and efficiency with which, in your vast experience, you search for the truth and the scientific caution which you exercise before stating a final conclusion. I imagine that in time all the pieces will fit together."

"In time?" Gottlieb asked softly, as if speaking to himself. "Ah, yes. As you say, Tovarisch Kruger, in time—"

Mikhail turned once more to the open window. The taiga, wrapped in fierce, darkening colors, stretched away from the city in an undulating web of shaggy, densely wooded hills toward the red-rimmed horizon. And from everywhere came the pungent aroma of pine trees and wild grass.

CHAPTER THREE

As he left, Mikhail studied the imposing, five-story administration building. Its grandeur now struck him fully. In its scores of well-lit offices sat hundreds of well-dressed, well-fed functionaries—big commissars, little commissars, and their official lackeys. This massive symbol of the Soviet bureaucracy was in striking contrast to the narrow, stinking barracks where the Jewish immigrants were quartered. He had the impulse to rush back to his hotel, write all this down and send it off to the Moscow press. But discretion prevailed and instead he walked back to his hotel slowly, like a man with a heavy burden.

A strange looking woman was walking toward him. She wore a blue dress, the neck and sleeves trimmed with gold and silver lace. She led a child by the hand—a little girl with hair twisted into long, golden braids and wearing a white dress ornamented with filigree. She was young, in her thirties. Mikhail knew by her dress and her eager, sun-bronzed face, her heavy, unmanageable pale-brown hair, her proud, stalwart carriage, that like himself, she was a stranger in this region and not even a Russian; nevertheless he had the odd sensation that he somehow knew her.

"Forgive me," he said, as she drew near. He raised his hand in a gesture of friendliness. "I don't mean to intrude, but you see—well, you remind me of someone, of something—" He stopped short, feeling ridiculous, but she was looking at him with such natural frankness that he was able to go on. "Allow me to explain. Your clothes, your appearance, tell me that you are not of this region, nor could I place the region you come from. As a writer I am naturally curious about people and I could not resist the impulse to find out. My name is Mikhail Kruger. I am from Moscow."

The woman's eyes filled with a strange gladness. But she spoke barely recognizable Russian. With great difficulty Mikhail understood her to say that she was new in this country, that her Russian was very poor but that she hoped to learn and in the meantime she would be happy to find anyone who spoke Hebrew, English, or Yiddish.

"Your wish is granted," answered Mikhail in Yiddish, adding, "You will be able to manage with Yiddish in this region, at least partly, but of course Russian is indispensable if you want to remain in this country for any length of time."

"I realize that," she replied in Yiddish. "You don't know what a relief it is to be able to speak once more. I did not consider this difficulty when I started out for the proletarian Motherland."

She pronounced "proletarian Motherland" with such idealistic fervor that Mikhail suddenly grew tense. His instinct told him that there was something wrong here.

"You came from abroad?" he asked, although he had by now guessed her origin.

"Yes. I arrived two months ago from Palestine. I decided to leave that bourgeois country and its British imperialist masters and come to the land where Socialism is being built, in the new Jewish homeland being established in Birobidjan."

"Most interesting, Tovarisch—"

"My name is Esther Finli. Finli is my maiden name. I divorced my husband because he refused to leave his chauvinistic Palestine. We quarreled over it for two years. He is a fanatical Zionist but I am a member of the Palestinian Communist Party. Finally we decided to separate in a civilized way and I got a divorce. I was given custody of the child. Party comrades provided me with funds and I started on my journey. It is like being on a magic carpet."

"But tell me," Mikhail said, "where do you live? Can I look you up? I would like to hear more about you."

"I live at the hotel. Number 12 on the second floor. You are welcome to visit whenever you wish."

"Good, let us make it soon. I also live at the hotel, but we will be moving into our new apartment soon, and you will be welcome there."

"Since you know Russian I should appreciate your help in making up certain urgent requests and statements to the Party Central Committee in Moscow."

"I shall be only too glad to help you out."

"Thank you. My ignorance of Russian is a terrible handicap. I also seem to have run into some complications—temporary, I'm sure. They have refused to honor my foreign Party membership here although I carry my card with me and they could easily verify my status as a Party member by a telephone call or a single letter. They are not interested. Instead they tell me that without the authority of the Comintern or the Kremlin I had no right to leave Palestine and come to Russia, that it is the duty of every Communist to remain in his own country and fight against capitalism and imperialism."

"I am aware of this policy, although I must admit it has never been fully clarified. However, try not to worry. I will see what I can do for you."

"I am not worried at all. Why should I worry? When I arrived in France after leaving Palestine, the Soviet consul in Marseilles at once supplied me with a Russian visa which included the right to settle in Birobidjan. This means that I am here legally. I don't put much stock in the confused rumors that there is still some bureaucracy in Soviet agencies. On the contrary, I am quite optimistic that all my rights will be restored in due course, even if it does take a little time. But I am concerned about the child. Until a few days ago I had been receiving a bottle of milk every day for her. Now I am told suddenly that milk is unavailable. In fact I am on my way right now to see the executive committee chairman about it. Professor Gottlieb is the soul of kindness. He always hears me out and he has helped me before."

"Yes, I know him. He is very sympathetic."

"Do you know where I might at least get a banana for my child?"

"A banana?" Mikhail was puzzled. "What is a banana? I have never heard of it."

"You are joking!"

"No, seriously. We don't have any such thing."

"It is a kind of fruit, very tasty, with a yellow peel. It is rather long and is filled with a soft, white pulp. As food it is very substantial, like bread—often more so than bread—and it grows on low-hanging trees."

"I am sorry"—Mikhail was a bit shame-faced by now—"but I feel certain we don't grow this type of fruit here. Maybe," he added brightly, "it requires a hot climate."

"Yes, of course, I should have mentioned that banana trees need a great deal of sun and moisture. I would guess that in the Caucasus, in Crimea, or in Turkestan the climate is hot enough for such fruits as oranges, lemons, and bananas. Don't you import them here from the hot regions?"

"A small quantity of oranges and lemons, this much I do know. But even in Moscow they are hard to get. As for bananas, I have never heard that we grow them. So Tovarisch Finli, if I were you I wouldn't go around asking for things that are scarce and above all don't ask for things that our country does not have." He shook her hand and said, "I'll keep in touch with you."

The little girl, her big eyes fixed on Mikhail, had not said a word. Now she began tugging at her mother's dress.

"Tovarisch Kruger, I am happy to have met you," Esther Finli said in parting, "and I am especially grateful for your offer to help."

"Rest assured that we will do all we can. You are not alone. My wife will enjoy meeting you and although she is Russian and doesn't understand a word of Yiddish, she has a womanly heart and you will both understand one another on sight."

He watched them go, hand in hand, Esther Finli moving with the effortless stride of a desert nomad and the little girl stepping bravely beside her.

For a month Mikhail trudged through the city of Birobidjan and the surrounding region. He visited every town, village, and kolkhoz. He was torn between pride and disappointment. With one hand they built and with the other they destroyed. Under such conditions it was difficult to write objective articles for the Moscow newspapers, and when he finally managed to write, he found himself praising the construction and suppressing the destruction. It was a bitter pill to swallow. What is happening to me? he asked himself on the way back from the post office after mailing his articles. I find more hypocrisy but write less about it. He dismissed the thought from his mind.

Later, he became so wrapped up in the excitement of moving and furnishing the apartment Nathan Wieder had assigned him that he lost sight of the fact that this was only to be a temporary residence.

Before Mikhail's eyes the untamed taiga slowly retreated and bit by bit made room for each new house for each new settler. This miracle kept him chained to Birobidjan and made him forget that the time was drawing near for his return to Moscow.

CHAPTER FOUR

Mikhail had spoken to Ksenia about returning to Moscow, but suddenly he changed his tack. "I think it would be a shame to go back without seeing the whole region," he told Ksenia one day. "I would like to travel through the taiga and go hunting and fishing with the natives. It would give me a chance to get a close look at the people of this country."

Actually he was more interested in the turmoil on the Far Eastern borders. There were rumors of frequent attacks by Manchurian Chinese who were now under Japanese domination. There were also disturbing reports that Russian and Ukrainian kulaks, bourgeois remnants, and also Kirghiz and Uzbekian Moslem chauvinists were defecting across the borders at night and that Japan was smuggling in diversionists to further the purposes of Japanese imperialism. These intruders were being sheltered among the thousands of Korean, Chinese, and Mongolian families scattered throughout the villages of the taiga. They merged silently with the population and were indistinguishable from it. Mikhail knew that the Kremlin had issued an order to clear the Far Eastern borders of undesirable elements among the yellow races. How it was to be done interested him.

Ksenia was resigned. "We have plenty of time, if that is what you mean," she said. "We could even spend a few months here if you want to. Moscow won't run away, I suppose."

"You are so right. The paradise called Moscow will be there." He laughed at the stern way in which she suddenly looked at him. "I don't mean it that way. It's just that the thought of looking for an apartment, getting back into harness and re-establishing our life throws me into a cold sweat. At least here I am free."

"You are beyond me," she said irritably. "You keep telling me that the sight of things going on around here makes you sick and that you are disgusted with the intrigues and conspiracies. Yet you hang around as if you were bound in chains. Do you call that being free?"

"I can decide to sit right here or to go out into the taiga, if I choose, and visit the Korean villages. I call this being free. Besides, I have a feeling I'll find a good story there. They say that there are about one hundred thousand Koreans living in the taiga. No one seems to know exactly how they live. I think that *Pravda* would grab up that kind of material," he ended excitedly.

Ksenia was impressed by Mikhail's obvious enthusiasm. "Very well," she finally agreed. "We will stay if it means so much to you. But two months and no more."

"I'm sure that two months will be more than enough. I must find out all I can about this region. I may never get another opportunity."

"As you wish, Mikhail."

"Why don't you come with me? You will only be bored here alone."

"I'll manage not to be alone."

"What do you mean?"

"I mean that if you must go wandering about the taiga, go without me. I'll arrange to have Esther Finli move in with us while you're gone. They have put the unhappy woman out of the hotel. She is living in the barracks with her child."

"I don't believe it!" cried Mikhail. "That's outrageous!"

"Don't act so innocent. You promised to help her and then suddenly lost all interest. Now you act shocked. I have given up trying to figure you out. There are times I think you are a man of character. At other times I find you positively spineless."

Mikhail was silent. He realized Ksenia was right. He should have done something before this. He had just made promises. Now he decided to try to rescue Esther Finli and her child from the miserable barracks.

"What excuse shall we offer," he asked Ksenia, "for asking permission to take them in with us?"

"There are two of us in three rooms," she said. "It is nobody's business if we decide to let someone have a room. Tell them we are subletting it for all I care."

"It isn't as simple as that, Ksenia. This building belongs to the Party and government. We don't have the right to take in anyone else without permission."

"And I say that you do have the right. Besides, if you are looking for excuses, I can give you an excellent one." She looked uneasily at Mikhail. "Tell them I am not well and will need someone near me—a woman." She hesitated and swallowed hard. "I think I am pregnant."

"You think! Or are you sure and keeping secrets from me again? I haven't forgotten the first child. Out with it, now. Are you planning another abortion?"

"No, Mikhail, believe me, not this time. The truth is that I can't be absolutely certain but I have very little doubt about it."

"But that's wonderful news!" Mikhail almost shouted, unable to repress his joy any longer. "That changes everything. I will give up the taiga trip. Let somebody else get the story. We had better get back to Moscow right away. If we stay and there is a delay later on for some reason, you might find it hard to travel."

"Not so fast, Mikhail." Ksenia laughed. "Let us examine the whole thing calmly. I admit my first reaction was to run back to Moscow, especially when you talked about disappearing for weeks into the taiga. But the fact remains that we do have an apartment. Birobidjan is as good a place as any in which to have a child. And as you say, you are free, you have no official obligations. Your income is higher than that of most commissars. And best of all, I don't have to go to work. If the need arises for you to be in Moscow for a while on business, you can always go and return. Or if you want to go into the taiga, there is no one to stop you. You might even make an important literary contribution that will make you famous and raise your income. Besides—and you may think me foolish—I haven't the heart to run off to Moscow and leave Esther Finli in the lurch. It would be a crime. In fact, I have gone so far as to offer her the room. She nearly passed out with shock and relief."

Mikhail took Ksenia in his arms and kissed her tenderly. "Your heart speaks for both of us," he said simply. "We will stay. Go bring Esther Finli and her little girl."

CHAPTER FIVE

At dawn, with a rifle in his hand and a pack on his back, Mikhail launched out into the taiga. First a light snow filtered downward from a slate-gray sky and softly spread over the earth. Then the cold, bright sun came out and the snow vanished in the grip of a hard, dry frost. Mikhail climbed up on the stark, wooden bridge that spanned the Biro River. Beyond the bridge stretched swampy flatlands now solidly congealed by cold. About two miles away he could see the small mountain which the natives called "Bomba," shaped like a wide, truncated cone, at the foot of which nestled a tiny Korean village. His eye followed the curve of the mountain to where it merged with the taiga, the fierce, tangled expanse of untamed forest. Resolutely he walked over the bridge leaving the city of Birobidjan behind him. He trudged steadily over the frozen surface of the swamp until he came to the Bomba, which he slowly began to skirt, his feet plowing through the matted vegetation. He looked up. The mountain was higher than he had thought. Its sides were green but its flat top was covered by a broad shawl of snow. He made his way around the mountain until he saw about a dozen little houses half-imbedded in the earth and near each house a hollowed-out tree trunk belching thick, blue-black smoke. The singed, smoking trees and the buried houses were like something out of a nightmare, completely unreal. Mikhail stood fascinated and frightened. Then he heard the scrape of a door and an old man in a loose cloak emerged. His skin was yellow and his eyes slanted and sunken as if in glistening fat. His cheekbones stood out high and sharp and from them two strands of sparse, gray hair fell away to meet in a long, pointed beard. The man bowed before Mikhail and greeted him in a weird, mutilated Russian.

"Good morning, Commissar. Enter house. Drink hot tea. Drink and be warm."

The proximity of the town to Birobidjan had led Mikhail to expect something other than an exotic-loking old man and sunken houses and smoking trees; for a moment, he lost his presence of mind. Instead of thanking the man he blurted out,

"Tell me, good friend, what are you—Mongolian, Tunguz, Korean? Or perhaps a Gold?"

The old man again bowed, then raised his head proudly. "I Korean. Good Korean. Name Chan. I delegate this village Soviet. Chief commissar here. Live in house you see. Come drink tea."

Mikhail liked him at once. He in turn bowed before the old Korean, and followed him down into his house. It consisted of two rooms equal in size and was much larger than he had judged from the outside. The rooms were wide and pleasantly warm. Of furniture, as he knew it, there was none but there were several straw mats on the floor and against the walls were low sleeping bunks in which he saw pillows and blankets done in gay floral designs. The floor felt almost hot under his feet and he imagined that the oven was somewhere below. The partition between the two rooms did not run the whole width of the house but stopped short a few feet from the wall and there he was shown a large opening in the floor with stone steps leading down into a widening cavern. In this cavern lay the oven which supplied heat for the dwelling, the smoke being carried through a hollow tunnel underground to the tree which spewed the waste and soot out of its empty insides into the air. On this oven the family cooked food and brewed enormous pots of hot, bitter tea. On the wall near the steps leading downward, hung copper and iron pots and wooden plates. There was little else to meet the eye and yet the place had a unique oriental warmth and charm. It was spotlessly clean and from somewhere came a delicate, aromatic odor.

Chan's family sat in a circle on floor mats eating hot oven biscuits out of a single, huge dish and sipping hot tea. There were Chan's wife, two boys, and a girl. The woman seemed worn with years and withered before her time. The two boys looked like twins. It was the young girl who interested him. She was in her twenties, her skin a shade duskier than the others, her eyes black and soft, their slant not quite so prominent, and she had a shock of long thick, raven hair. Mikhail thought her beautiful.

They made a place for him on the mat. He was given a glass of tea and, because he was a guest, a separate plate of biscuits. The head of the household, Tovarisch Chan, made the introductions.

"This my oldest son—name Kim. Fourteen years. This my youngest son—name Wan. Twelve years. This my daughter—name Sana. Teacher in village school. Teach children Russian and Korean language. Sana speak good Russian. Finish gymnasium Vladivostok. Komsomol member. Good young Communist. No give age. Never give age of girl. Years of woman always what seem in eyes of man. So say wise men."

Mikhail glanced at the girl. She smiled and said in excellent Russian, "If you are interested in our school I will be glad to show it to you."

"Nothing would please me more. Everything about your village is of interest to me."

"Eat first," intervened the old man. "Get warm. Then go."

Mikhail chatted pleasantly with Sana during the course of the meal, with Chan adding an occasional word. The woman and the two boys said nothing but ate and smiled good naturedly. Mikhail studied them and as their faces grew familiar he realized how mistaken he had been. Neither Chan nor his wife were nearly as old as he had imagined and the boys were far from being identical.

When the meal was over, Mikhail thanked his hosts for their hospitality. They bowed their acknowledgment. The two boys went off somewhere. The old woman busied herself below at the oven and Mikhail sat and talked to Chan and Sana.

"Have you been long in these parts?" Sana asked him.

"No, only about four months."

"Somehow you don't seem like one of the new immigrants. You must be one of the Party or administrative officials."

"No," Mikhail explained, "I am neither a new immigrant nor an official, but a sort of guest, a temporary resident. Actually I am a writer. How long I remain depends on a number of factors and conditions or on my personal mood. I could stay a month or decide to stay for years."

"In that case you must be a happy person, Tovarisch—"

"Kruger—my name is Mikhail Kruger."

"Mikhail Kruger—" she repeated slowly. "Your name sounds familiar. I have read a novel and many stories published in the literary journals under that name."

"I am very happy to meet one of my readers," exclaimed Mikhail, somewhat startled, "especially out here in the taiga. But tell me, Sana, why do you say I am such a happy person?"

"Because you are a writer and have so many privileges. You are free to come and go as you please.

"Don't you have the same freedom?" asked Mikhail with disarming innocence. "The taiga is all yours. What if, for instance, I were to ask you to go hunting with me?"

She laughed and looked at Chan. He smiled and knowingly shook his head.

"You see," she said. "Everybody knows that I am not free to do any such thing. I am a teacher and have forty children in my school. Over and above that I am subject to strict Party discipline."

"We all Communists here," her father interposed at this point. "My daughter was partisan. Fought Japanese. Fought Kolchack. Civil War. My sons in Komsomol like Sana."

Chan hinted broadly that he would like to accept an invitation to go hunting with his honored guest. They bowed to one another and Chan led Mikhail out to the Village Soviet which, unlike the villagers' houses, was built entirely above the ground. He unlocked the door with great ceremony and showed Mikhail the place in which he was to spend the night.

Mikhail spent the afternoon in Sana's classroom. The next day, at dawn, he and Chan headed into the taiga. A pale, yellow moon still lingered low in the sky as both men, carrying hunting rifles and knapsacks, pushed their way through the tangled underbrush of the taiga. The were soon buried in forest gloom. The slumbering taiga awoke to the dull echoes of their footsteps and the restless replies of disturbed bears, deer, and jackals. A wave of fear began to sweep the jungle. As they went forward, the cries of beasts, now mingled with the desperate croaking of pheasants flying in panic from tree to tree, created bedlam around them. Mikhail and Chan halted and stood motionless until the forest grew still again. Early sunlight began to filter like a faint shower of golden dust through the thick foliage of trees. They took a few more steps. Then Chan suddenly stopped, fell to one knee and bent his head toward the wind. After a while Mikhail heard it too —the cautious, padded tread of some animal. Chan raised his rifle to his shoulder. A second later the flame leaped from the muzzle and a blast shattered the stillness in a peal of deafening echoes. Chan was on his feet running toward the prey and Mikhail instinctively followed him. They came upon it in a few bounds. Lying in a mass of rotten branches was a small, brownish-white bear, its head shattered. Chan stood over the dead animal, looking disappointed.

"Bad," he said, "very bad. Head broken."

The head of a bear was usually dried and hung on the wall as a trophy or sold for a high price. Chan was crestfallen at the loss of the head.

"Bad, very bad," he repeated sadly. "Head broken." Then he took out his knife, skinned the bear and gave the skin to Mikhail. "Gift," he announced, "for honored guest." After that he gathered wood, found a natural fireplace in a stony hollow, piled his wood in and kindled the fire. As the fire flared up he pointed to the remains of the bear. "Bear meat good, sweet." He explained that on this day he was not really hunting for himself, that on a real hunt for food and trophies whole groups went into the taiga, even whole families and at times whole villages. Mikhail gathered that Chan considered this trip as a sort of excursion in honor of a guest who had pleased him and not as a serious expedition to collect trophies. They bowed to one another.

They sat on a fallen tree trunk that was half-buried in wild grasses and piles of rotten branches torn from the treetops and blown in by the winds. The spot was only partly overgrown and formed a little oasis in the jungle. The fire crackled softly and their nostrils were filled with the delicious odor of roasted meat. Suddenly a wandering Gold emerged from the underbrush, came over to the fire and bowed. Chan bowed and graciously motioned to a place next to himself on the tree trunk.

"Sit with friends."

The Gold and the Korean did not understand each other's language although they and their ancestors had lived for countless generations side by side in the Far Eastern depths of the Russian empire. The Golds had their own peculiar dialect which contained no more than a few Russian words necessary for bare communication with other people when contact was unavoidable. Beyond that they maintained a stolid indifference. Mikhail had heard it said the Golds were a dying people, that no more than four hundred Gold families remained, scattered throughout the taiga. He studied this strange man. He was short and thin and dressed in fur pants and a fur jacket. On his head was a fur cap from under which two braids of black hair hung down to his shoulders. His face was reddish-yellow, the eyes small, black, and slanted. There was no trace of a beard and it would have been difficult to tell whether this was a man or a woman except perhaps for a certain ruggedness of feature. The jacket was held together by a rope from which dangled a leather sheath containing an ugly-looking knife. He carried a leather sack on his back and a double-barreled shotgun in the crook of his arm. He was the resourceful, solitary hunter.

But in his cold eyes there was not the slightest flicker of human interest. He took in the world of men, of animals, of birds with the same bland, neutral stare, as if he were incapable of feeling either joy or grief. He knew no hatred and he did not understand love. Neither life nor death would move him.

When Chan motioned him again to sit down, he uttered a single Russian word in a dead monotone as if it were quite foreign and meaningless but established by custom: "Thanks." Then he sat down, not on the tree trunk but on the cold earth beside it. Mikhail tried to draw him into conversation but the Gold kept answering indifferently in a steady monotone,

"No understand" and remained motionless, his eyes fixed on the roasting bear meat.

Chan nudged Mikhail and said, "Eat. Meat good. Roasted good."

"Fine," said Mikhail, coming to with a start, "let us eat."

The old Korean cut off three slabs of hot meat. They all ate with their bare hands, tearing at the savory meat with their teeth while the fat dripped down their chins to the ground. Chan produced a bottle from his pack and passed it on to the Gold who let the liquid gurgle down his throat until the bottle was empty, then looked at it, threw it away and stretched out full length by the fire. He was asleep instantly.

"Him Gold," Chan remarked. "I give him big slice meat. Eat only when hungry. Eat quick, drink quick, sleep quick. No talk."

Mikhail and Chan ate some more meat and chatted by the fire until the burning branches and tree roots had turned to a mass of glowing embers. The Korean took out his pipe, stuffed it with tobacco and lit up. He offered Mikhail the pipe and was surprised to hear that he did not smoke. In fact he turned a trifle suspicious because there was a belief in the taiga that a hunter lost in the forest could go for days without food or drink but not without his pipe. A man who could survive without smoking was considered by the denizens of the taiga to be a hero, a man of iron nerves and unbreakable will. No one refused a pipe when offered. To refuse would be to act the hero. Chan explained all this to Mikhail.

"I am not a hero at all nor am I trying to act like one," Mikhail told him laughingly. "I don't smoke simply because I don't enjoy smoking. I have never felt the need to draw smoke into my lungs. For the sake of being sociable I tried smoking a few times but I got nothing out of it. Do you understand?"

Chan was satisfied. They were silent for a while, Chan puffing away slowly at his pipe and Mikhail feeling within him the stir of a new theme for a novel about the taiga. At last Chan rose.

"We go home. Enough today. Very late. Sunday whole

family go hunt in taiga. Chan and two sons and daughter Sana. Woman stay home and cook. Come Sunday."

"Of course I shall come, Tovarisch Chan. I am grateful for your invitation."

They stamped out the fire. As they were about to leave, Mikhail turned to take a last look at the Gold. He was still stretched out and Mikhail thought he seemed as indifferent to the world while asleep as he had been while awake.

CHAPTER SIX

It was late at night when Mikhail and Chan returned to the Korean village. Snow had begun to fall and there was a chilling wind. Hazy, red stars were barely visible in a black sky. Mikhail was dead tired and longed for a hot glass of tea and to stretch out his limbs on some soft bedding. But he doubted that he could fall asleep. The day had been too exciting. Then, too, he felt unexpected pangs of homesickness. He had planned to cover a large portion of the taiga by going from village to village, but now, as he came back to the Korean village which lay so close to Birobidjan, he felt a sharp yearning to see Ksenia. He was worried about her. Had she succeeded in getting Esther Finli and her child out of the barracks or was she still alone in the apartment? Ksenia's pregnancy preyed on his mind. He felt guilty at having left her in order to pursue his own exotic pleasures. *My wife is with child,* he repeated to himself over and over. And how strange it was to call her his wife! They were not married; they were "comrades" living together. He recalled his own reaction whenever he heard a man and woman call each other "comrade" under such conditions.

They stopped in front of Chan's house and Mikhail explained that he would like to return to Birobidjan at once. Chan reminded him that it was late and that it would be dangerous to make the trip alone in a snowfall on a moonless night. Would Mikhail accept his hospitality? His house was warm, warmer even than the Soviet. He could leave safely at dawn. Mikhail thought it over and accepted the offer. Once inside, they sat on the floor which was almost hot since the oven had been fired in expectation of their return. They drank scalding tea and ate corn cakes which Chan's wife had prepared. Chan filled his big pipe and puffed away. He stroked his sparse beard with his long fingers and told Mikhail stories about the Civil War in the Far East.

When they finished their tea, they rose to retire. The two boys were asleep in one corner of the room. Chan and his wife slept in the same room. Sana slept in the other room and a few feet away from her bunk a pallet and blankets had been prepared for Mikhail. He groped his way into the room so as not to waken Sana, undressed quietly, slipped under the blankets and lay there staring up into the pitch blackness and listening to the heavy snores from the other room. Then he heard Sana move and his instincts told him that she was not asleep. He felt the stir of desire. Sana's proximity drove from his mind the anxiety about Esther Finli and the thoughts of Moscow and dulled the sharp ache of his longing for Ksenia. He could easily make love to Sana without breaking a taboo since his bed had been put close to hers in the same room.

"Are you asleep?" he whispered.

"No," answered Sana.

"Can we speak? I am afraid we might wake the family."

"They sleep soundly but from that distance you might."

Mikhail rose quickly and slipped into her bed. She opened her arms to him and laid her head on his shoulder, sighing softly, "We can speak now."

Her body was soft and warm, and Mikhail felt himself go hard. He stroked her smooth thighs and buttocks with his free hand. She shivered lightly. He wondered if this had been arranged for his pleasure, if it was a taiga custom, and he asked her if she had a man.

"We have no young men," she said. "Six months ago all our young men between the ages of sixteen and thirty were mobilized for important work and shipped into the deserts of Central Asia."

She snuggled closer to him, burying her hot face in the hollow of his shoulder. His arms tightened about her trembling body in response to her need but his passion was curiously mixed with anger. He lay in the arms of a beautiful and desirable woman and heard about the enslavement of young men. *This is the price of maturity in this cursed land!* he thought. *This is the final devastating truth. Our heritage is schizophrenia. It cannot be otherwise. For the act of every man and woman is an act of desperation and Russia is the seething empire of desperate lives.* He thought of Boris the Strong—silent, twisted, and impotent. It was a horrible image.

Sana suddenly drew away from him as if she had been slapped. He felt she was staring at him in the dark.

"You were saying," he reminded her almost harshly, "that all the young men were rounded up, shipped away and coerced into hard labor?"

"I didn't say they were coerced. I am a Communist and wouldn't use such language. The Party issued a call and Stalin himself asked our young men to mobilize themselves voluntarily for labor in Central Asia in order to convert the useless desert into a flourishing country."

"But here in the taiga you have vast, barren lands and a need for construction. They are sending in thousands of people from other regions to settle here and convert the taiga into a flourishing country. What is the sense of sending out useful workers and replacing them with others?"

"Don't ask me, Tovarisch Kruger. I am ignorant. All I know is that the government has a five-year plan for building Socialism. As people we are too small to pass judgment on the plan. We leave that to our betters. If everybody meddled and asked questions we would have chaos. There is such a thing as Party discipline. I and my father and all Party members and Komsomols throughout this region agitated and convinced our men, our brothers, sons, and sweethearts to respond to the call of our Father and leader, Tovarisch Stalin. It was a hundred percent voluntary mobilization."

Mikhail saw that it was no use. He felt helpless and excluded and keenly aware, in all his misery, how offensive it must be to lie there, cold and passionless, in her bed.

"You think a great deal, don't you, Tovarisch Kruger. Too much, perhaps?"

"Sometimes. It is an old habit—often a bit unfriendly, even lonely."

"I know about loneliness. I had a young man once. We were to be married. I don't know when I will see him again."

"Does he write?"

"Very little. I can't understand why. The last letter I received from him was two months ago. He wrote that the younger men were to be released from work and sent into the Red Army."

"I guess the Party and government know what they are doing."

"Absolutely. Tell me, are you married?"

"Yes and no. We live together as comrades."

She did not speak for a while and Mikhail had just about decided to get up and go back to his own bed when she spoke again.

"Do you know what we say in these parts about a man like you?"

"Tell me."

"When the body is filled with desire but the mind heavy with thoughts, the eyes alone remain hungry and will never rest until they are closed forever."

"I suppose—" Mikhail began, but he was suddenly interrupted by the sound of loud shooting and the terrified screams of women and children. Men shouted and cursed. Mikhail and Sana jumped up and began to pull on their clothes. Old Chan roused his family, lit the lamps and ordered everyone to stand ready.

"What has happened?" asked Mikhail, looking into Chan's eyes.

"Maybe raid, war with Japanese," Chan replied calmly.

"Nonsense!" cried Mikhail. "This is no enemy attack. Those curses were in Russian. Open the door."

"You not know Japanese in China. Officers speak Russian. Manchuria border very near."

"Quiet!" said Sana. "Listen!"

Someone was issuing commands in Russian: "Everybody outside! All inhabitants to report outside at once!" They could hear windowpanes being shattered and the splintering of wood as doors were smashed in. Sana's mother, petrified, stared at her husband. The two boys, dressed in their fur coats, stood erect, respectful, and ready, their eyes glued to their father's face.

Chan gathered his courage, opened the door and motioned them all into the street, where the Koreans, their women and children, their eyes still bleary with sleep, their bodies shivering in the icy cold, stood huddled together in a mass surrounded by Red Army men armed to the teeth. The whole village was lit up by torches.

"Why do you just stand there?" Mikhail shouted to Chan. "You are the Village Soviet delegate. Find out what this is all about."

"Delegate too small," Chan declared, waving at the Red Army men. "Big city commissar here now."

"My father is right," Sana broke in. "When they need anything in the village they first ask for the delegate's cooperation. The fact that they did not come to him means that the whole village is under arrest. They are probably moving us all out."

"Arrest and uproot an entire village? It sounds insane. What crime have you committed?"

"None that I know of. It simply means they don't trust us. There is no point in telling this to my father. He won't understand. They may transport us to the desert where our young men are laboring."

A civilian, flanked by two soldiers, stopped in front of Chan. It was Tovarisch Nathan Wieder, the Birobidjan Party secretary. He gave Chan his hand and said curtly,

"The operation in your village is completed. Collect all your belongings. You and your family will occupy a separate railroad car. The train leaves the station before daybreak."

Chan stared at Wieder without comprehension. Sana put her arms about her father. "Don't you think," she said, turning to Wieder with her eyes full of fire, "that this formal arrest of a whole village is highhanded and arbitrary?"

"Tovarisch Sana," Wieder barked, "you are to come to order at once! This is not officially an arrest. We are simply transporting you to another locale. New houses have been prepared for you there. That will be your new home."

"Here very good too," said Chan, awakening suddenly and tears beginning to stream down his face. "Why you drive out?"

"You are an old Communist and former partisan, Tovarisch Chan," Wieder reminded him sternly, "and you should be the first to fulfill every decision of the Central Committee."

"But nobody prepare, nobody ask, nobody warn, nobody come for advice. Build here Soviet-Korean culture. Make Korean school, Korean theater, Korean books and newspaper. Now all gone."

Wieder was not listening. "Everyone," he ordered, "is to take along whatever can be moved and made ready without delay. Wagons are on their way from the railroad station for your belongings. A separate wagon, Tovarisch Chan, will take you and your family to the station. You are to continue as Soviet delegate in the new location. As you see, we have provided for everything. We know that you are a good Communist and expect to extend every possible privilege to you when you reach your destination. We hope you will prove worthy of the name of Communist. We trust you. We also want you to understand that we are not using repressive measures but acting for the welfare of the community. It was necessary to do this secretly and without warning in the middle of the night because Japanese and Chinese sabotage and espionage are incredibly active and treacherous in this area. We have no time to examine you one by one and comb out the Chinese and Japanese. You all look alike. But have no fear, Chan. You will all be safe from them. It is too bad but as they say, 'One rotten apple can spoil the barrel.' You were unable to pick out the rotten apples, the spies, and so we've got to do it for you. It is better that way. You will be grateful in the end."

After this lengthy speech Nathan Wieder turned on his heel and was about to walk off between the two soldiers when he became aware of Mikhail, who had instinctively moved many yards away.

"Tovarisch Kruger!" He seemed pleasantly surprised.

"What brings you here? I had no idea that you were connected with this mission."

"I am in no way connected with this—undertaking," Mikhail answered, the last word sticking in his throat. "I am here by chance. I went hunting and stopped over in the village for the night."

"Fine, fine!" the secretary laughed. "Get acquainted with the region. That is very important for a writer. Stop in at the Party Committee once in a while. Keep in touch."

"I'll do that, Tovarisch Wieder."

Mikhail remained outside while Chan and his family went into the house to collect their belongings. He wanted to go after them, talk to them, express his sorrow. But he dared not return to the family of the hospitable Chan. He couldn't run the risk of being observed. If it were reported to Wieder that he had stepped into the house of the Village Soviet delegate, Wieder would sniff like a bloodhound and might decide that his presence in the village on the very night when secret orders were being carried out was a rather strange coincidence. Life was an ocean infested by ferocious sharks. And so the instinct for survival shut his mind and his heart and he began to walk away.

He went forward slowly, knowing that he could not avoid passing through the Koreans who were ringed by soldiers of the Red Army, uniformed GPU men, and plainclothes men. He turned aside quickly and stopped near a house with broken, gaping windows and a door that hung twisted and askew. The thick, hollowed tree in front of the house was still belching smoke. He hid behind this tree and waited.

The Koreans were carted off in small groups. Finally a wagon pulled by a team of two horses drove up. He watched the Chan family climb into the wagon. He closed his eyes as the "privileged," the Village Soviet delegate and his family, were driven off. The village was now empty. It was almost dawn. Mikhail wandered at random through the deserted village, glancing into the vacant dwellings, and at last turned away. He walked quickly until he reached the wooden bridge which led to Birobidjan. He crossed it at a run. He was driven by fear, by hatred, by a terrible desire to escape from the scene of outrage, to bury it in the past, to blot it out forever. And so perverse is the human mind in its desperation that Moscow now rose before his eyes as a haven of refuge.

But by the time he stopped in front of his house, breathing hard from his exertions, he saw with agonizing clarity, the hopelessness of his dilemma and the futility of running. The structure of existence was iron-bound. There was no sign of hope, of change, for there was no future. Fight against injustice? Suppose that he, an individual, rose up in his puny wrath and threw himself at the invulnerable monster. It would be a useless act of suicide. He now tasted the full gall of his bitterness. For it is not in the nature of the human mind to merely coexist with evil and resign itself to it. Instead, forced to face its helplessness, it invents some justification, some rationale, to keep from going mad.

Mikhail laughed out loud. Now that he had reduced himself to the proper size it might be easier to take further stock of his life. Well, he had written a book which had made quite a lot of noise for a little man. He had reputation. What is more, he wore an order of merit that not only gave him a sense of importance but special privileges. These were his rewards for conforming with some skill to the demands of the times. That these were also the rewards for shutting his eyes to reality, for curtailing his intelligence, was exactly the point. They were the price of one's conscience. Others who had lost sight of this fact—far greater writers than himself—languished in prisons and still others, commissars par excellence, the blazing orders on their chests riddled with bullets, slumped down before blood-spattered walls and were carted away to unknown graves.

He looked up soberly to the windows of his house, where Ksenia was waiting for him. *How naive I am and how dishonest,* he thought. *I was once told to look neither to the right nor to the left. I accepted it without question. Now that I should know better, I still accept without question. I was told, "To probe, examine, evaluate, philosophize, is fatal." It's all the same thing. Wieder warned me not to look, Boris warned me not to think. Aside from that life is wonderful.*

CHAPTER SEVEN

Ksenia was happy to see Mikhail back so soon. Esther Finli had not come to live with her after all and she was already beginning to feel very lonely in the apartment.

"I am sorry for Esther Finli," Mikhail remarked. "She should have been welcomed with open arms. Instead they put her and her child in the cold barracks. I don't understand."

"Certainly you don't!" Ksenia agreed. "I've known for a long time that you don't understand people, even if you write about them." She wished she hadn't said that. "Anyway, Esther was very grateful for our offer but actually it would not have solved her problem."

"I know that, but it would have helped."

"It would only have scratched the surface. They will not allow her to enter the Party. Her foreign Party membership is not acceptable here. However that doesn't matter any more now."

"I don't follow you."

"Well, she expects any day to marry Solomon Feier, the automobile mechanic from the Argentine. He is not only a good provider but loves her and will take care of her child adequately. I met him and was very much impressed with him."

"That is good news and I am very happy for her. He is a fine, honest man, someone her own equal."

"My God, Mikhail, how easily you create equals! You know as well as I do that she is superior to him. Am I your equal? You are a famous novelist and I am nothing but a village girl."

He laughed and put his arms around her. "Just listen to you talk! If you'd care to hear about my inadequacies I'll tell you about them some day. I discover new ones every day." He pinched her cheek. "As a matter of fact we happen to be exactly equal. We are in love."

The long, heavy Arctic winter settled down over the taiga. Mikhail and Ksenia had decided to wait until their child was born and then make their way back to Moscow and settle there permanently. This was the terrible winter of 1936-1937. Everywhere there appeared the bloody hand of the purge! People became distraught, hysterical, and suspicious of their neighbors without knowing exactly why. It was a kind of malady, a contagious disease, a mass psychosis—everyone was suspected of sabotage, Trotskyism, and espionage.

One victim of this massive purge was Nathan Wieder. The press carried a few words about an unspecified crime committed by the secretary of the Birobidjan Communist Party, adding that he was a close friend of the Fascist traitor Joachim Schultz, the former Soviet general who had escaped to Germany. Also convicted and arrested was Professor Gottlieb, executive committee chairman in Birobidjan. In this case, the charges were more specific. He was accused of a triple crime: Zionism—although in fact he had never been a Zionist—Jewish chauvinism, and of being an enemy of the state. The last was a crime of new vintage in the growing apparatus of Soviet inquisition.

Pinchas Levitt was recalled from Vladivostok to replace Nathan Wieder and a young Communist, an assimilated Jew named Berkowitz, was sent in to replace Professor Gottlieb. Berkowitz, without a moment's delay and as his first official act, decreed the immediate and total Russification of all Jewish institutions in the region.

Pinchas Levitt had been one of the leaders of the BUND —the Jewish Socialist Party. When the Bolsheviks seized power, he was among the first to leave the BUND in order to join the Communist Party. The Central Committee had sent him to Minsk, the capital of White Russia, where he became the secretary of the Party Committee at a shoe factory where the majority of workers were Jews. After Lenin's death, during the struggle for power between Stalin and Trotsky, Levitt had taken pains to see which way the wind was likely to blow. At Party meetings, the rank and file never knew where their Party secretary stood. When he spoke he was so ambiguous that one could not tell whether he sided with Stalin or with Trotsky. However, he always encouraged others to offer their opinions.

"This is a free and open discussion," he would say. "Every one of you has the right to express his opinion as to whether this country shall take the path of collectivized economy as proclaimed by Tovarisch Stalin or the path of heavy industrialization, as pronounced by Tovarisch Trotsky."

In the meantime he kept his own opinions to himself, explaining that as chairman of the meetings he did not wish to unduly influence others. And so the meetings succeeded one another in this fashion until Levitt realized that Stalin would be the victor. Only then did he express his opinion; he proclaimed himself a Stalinist.

Now he was back in Birobidjan. Mikhail went to pay a courtesy call on him. He was familiar with Levitt's record of equivocation, but he was unprepared for the Party secretary's air of cordiality and refinement. They chatted amiably for a while about routine matters and then Levitt said,

"I would be very happy, Tovarisch Kruger, if you would agree to make your home here. Birobidjan is an ideal place for a writer."

"But I'm only here for a short stay," Mikhail explained.

Levitt placed his hand on Mikhail's shoulder. "Perhaps you will change your mind when I tell you what's going on here."

"I've sensed something isn't right since I've been here, but I haven't been able to put my finger on it."

Levitt sighed. "With everything being turned upside down and tumbling around our ears, I must have someone I can trust."

Mikhail remembered Boris' warning about not letting himself become involved in any dubious political adventures. "I'm sorry, Tovarisch Levitt. I'm a free-lance writer and I want to stay that way."

Levitt dropped the subject and instead launched into a tirade against his predecessor.

"I left behind me a healthy Party organization," he said. "I left a flourishing Soviet-Jewish culture, language, and literature. As soon as I left for Vladivostok and Nathan Wieder took over, he ruined it. It was worse than a pogrom—so bad in fact that the Central Committee was forced to replace him and return me to office out of the sheer necessity for saving the organization."

It was all nonsense, of course; Mikhail knew that. But Levitt had spoken with such conviction that it sounded almost credible. This patent display of hypocrisy unnerved Mikhail. "Yes," he said pointedly, "it does seem that some leaders are not fit for their jobs. Speaking of unfit leaders, I suppose you have heard about the former Party secretary of the Ural region?"

"Yashinin? Oh, yes, I remember the case. He is the one who was recently—"

"Shot," Mikhail finished. "If you recall, Yashinin was one of the many people who hesitated seriously before deciding that Stalin was right. He came in with the tide at the eleventh hour. The Party forgave him, but never forgot him."

Levitt went white to the lips. "Why do you mention this, Tovarisch Kruger?"

"I was just agreeing with you and citing him as an example of an unfit leader." Having covered himself, in a fashion, Mikhail now allowed himself to speak uninhibitedly for the first time since he had come to Birobidjan. "There is just one more thing. I do not agree with you entirely and you may not like what I am about to say, but you know as well as I do that Nathan Wieder, despite his execution, was no less honest and loyal to the Party than you. In not one instance did he deviate from the Party line. He carried out to the letter every directive of the Kremlin."

"Go on!"

"I will do exactly that. Tell me, why was Professor Gottlieb arrested and liquidated? And why did they replace him with an ignorant, coarse, completely Russified Jew like Berkowitz? And while I'm at it, why don't you tell me why Wieder himself was liquidated?"

"I did not attend his trial. The papers only stated that he

was closely connected with Joachim Schultz who is now one of Hitler's specialists on Russia. True, they published no evidence of a specific crime. But I do not question the Kremlin. Would you have advised the Kremlin to take the risk of not liquidating him?"

"I will tell you how I feel about it. No one can be guilty of a crime committed by another. A father is not guilty of the crime of his son, nor any man for the crime committed by his friend without either his aid or his knowledge."

Levitt got to his feet and pointed his finger at Mikhail. "Look at you," he said, "all hot under the collar and glaring at me with the eyes of a martyr! What are you—a Jesus? Did you come here to preach about justice and injustice? We are engaged in a permanent revolution. The Red Flag has still not been raised over the whole globe. We are surrounded by capitalists and must remain vigilant. Everyone is suspect. No man is sure of tomorrow—not I, not you, no one! It is of no importance that the innocent die with the guilty, for someday we shall create an eternal paradise for all people. I have no pity for Nathan Wieder. He believed this as I do and he killed thousands without pity. If I have any pity at all it is for the naïve and pathetic Gottlieb. But even this is sheer waste of feelings in the face of universal turmoil. We are rebuilding the world. Just as a brick can fall from a building and kill an innocent worker, we too must have casualties. Does that mean we have to stop building?"

Mikhail went to the door, the blood still pounding in his ears. So Levitt the rabbit, had become a lion. This was self-hypnosis with a vengeance! He turned before leaving and said quietly to Levitt,

"Tovarisch, you have told me your new philosophy. It is one in which the individual mind and the individual soul are devoid of any value. But this philosophy is not as new as you believe. It is as ancient as evil itself. I will tell you my philosophy, which is just as ancient. There can be no social justice without justice to an individual. Without justice to one man there is no justice at all. Pinchas Levitt, we are both Jews and as Jews we have inherited a culture which abhors your philosophy. You are therefore living an abysmal lie and will need the infernal powers of the devil himself to go on living it. Out there in the wide world are peoples of many faiths striving for justice—not justice for the mythical masses which you have invented to cloak your acts of murder, but justice for every man because he is any man."

He slammed the door behind him. He had said it at last. It did not matter that he had had to plant fear in Levitt's heart in order to say it. He felt relieved; he had his reprieve until life once more dragged him down into the quagmire of doubt and fear.

And Levitt, his face still drained of color, wondered what to do with this indiscreet young commissar with the powerful connections.

CHAPTER EIGHT

In the first month of 1937, Ksenia gave birth to a boy. They named him Alexander in honor of the great Russian poet Alexander Pushkin. They fondly called him "Alenka." Mikhail sent an elated telegram to Boris and Polya announcing the birth, but the reply, curiously, read: "Congratulations on your newborn. Please come home at once. Am very lonely. Polya." Mikhail studied it and decided it must be a code. It was absurd that Polya should ask them to come. It could only mean that Boris wanted to see Mikhail urgently.

Between the birth of his son and the suspense over what news Boris might have in Moscow, Mikhail found little time to write. What free time he had was monopolized by Sergei Kupets, who had made a concerted effort to cultivate Mikhail's friendship. Mikhail had deemed it politic to respond, however mildly, to his overtures.

Kupets dropped in as often as possible, usually with a friend, Leon Kolker, the chairman of the Birobidjan Radio Committee. Kolker was a wiry, ugly little man with an air of watchfulness that reminded Mikhail of a vulture waiting for his prey to weaken enough to allow him to come in for the kill. Mikhail assumed that, like Kupets, Kolker was a G.P.U. agent.

Kupets always brought a bottle of vodka, most of which he drank himself while he expounded on world politics and literature. Lately he had begun to stay until far into the night, talking, drinking too much, and making mock proposals to Ksenia which were just short of being improper.

Once, Kupets and Kolker had been drinking since nine o'clock of the previous evening. It was now two o'clock in the morning. They were belligerently proclaiming the glories of Soviet literature; there was a thin note of tension in the atmosphere.

"Sergei," Mikhail said impatiently, "you sleep all day and drink and talk all night. When do you find time to write?"

There was a sudden silence. Kupets, who carried his liquor well, looked slyly at Kolker, then intently at his host. With his blond, rakishly trimmed beard and upturned nose, he looked the perfect cynic.

"Mikhail," he replied, "better look to your own laurels. I happen to be a finished writer. I have already launched my masterpieces on the world—three plays, two scenarios, and five novels, all of which have sold and made me notorious, if not famous. Let's face it. Writers write for money although they never admit it and always hoodwink the public into believing that they are martyred idealists. This is not to mention the lies they write into their books. My money is rolling in and I no longer have to lie to my readers—that is, until my income dries up or"—here he smiled broadly—"I decide to accept poverty and join the classic writers; something which you have not the talent to attain. You consider me a degenerate drunkard. Allow me, then, to point out a distinction which in your naïve arrogance you have failed to notice. To drink an ocean of vodka is degenerate. To drown in it might almost be noble."

Before Mikhail could pursue the matter further there was a knock on the door. "Who could that be?" he said uncertainly. He knew that he was living in times when a knock on the door at 2 A.M. was more likely to mean a firing squad than a friendly visit. *Perhaps I have been set up for the kill,* he thought. Aloud he said, "I'll answer it."

He opened the door expecting the worst, and found Esther Finli weeping bitterly and uttering incoherent sounds. "Esther, what is it?" he asked her. "What is the matter?"

"They—have—arrested my husband," she sobbed.

"What?—When?"

"Just a few minutes ago—They came and took him away—They wouldn't tell us where they were taking him—" She was on the verge of hysteria and Mikhail led her into the living room, where Ksenia poured her a cup of hot tea. Ksenia drew Mikhail into the kitchen.

"For Heaven's sake, Mikhail," she said, "get rid of those two pests. Esther is in a bad way."

"I'll do that," Mikhail agreed. He returned to the living room. "Don't worry, Esther," he assured her, "everything is going to be all right. Just tell me what happened." He turned to the two men. "I'm sure you won't mind coming back tomorrow. You understand that this woman is a good friend and if I can do nothing else I would at least like to console her. So if you will pardon me—"

"Yes, of course," Kupets yawned, pulling at Kolker's sleeve. "Come to my place. I have a bottle of vodka stowed away. Real, good stuff. Ninety-six." He shuffled toward the door, followed by Kolker. "Ksenia, my dear," he called into the kitchen, "how about a little kiss before I leave your gracious home?"

Kolker guffawed. "You are right, Kupets. This is indeed a gracious home. They don't throw you out. They just politely show you the door."

When they were gone, Mikhail turned to Esther Finli. "Tell me what happened."

Esther gave them the details. Her husband, she explained, had never been a Party member. In fact, he had never belonged to any Party. But he was a hard worker. He could fix any machine. He had built a small cottage for them and they were happy. Then suddenly the secret police had dragged him out of bed and taken him to prison. There had been no specific charges, no explanations.

This was the story. "It will be my turn next," Esther added. "Not that I care much about myself. I see that my doom is sealed. These murderers will shoot me without the slightest sympathy for my daughter—or for the child alive within me. I am resigned, for it's all I deserve for distorting the truth, for lying to myself and to others, all because I thought it would promote the victory of Communism. But what about my husband? He was always an honest, nonpolitical person. He took no sides and was never involved in any political quarrel. He lived for his work: his ideology lay in his magical hands—to build and repair. What could they hold against him? This is what destroys me."

Neither Mikhail nor Ksenia could find words with which to console the unhappy woman. Words were pointless. Action was needed. There was only one possibility—that something could be done quickly before the G.P.U. passed sentence. Mikhail could hardly wait for morning to come.

"Wait here till I come back," Mikhail said and walked out of the house.

This time he did not stop to think of his own personal risk or even of the privileges he might lose by interfering in the affairs of the secret police. With an automatic gesture he snared his sleeve in his hand, polished the decoration on his lapel and set out along the river bank in the direction of the G.P.U.

The desk sergeant looked Mikhail over, resting his eyes a moment on the shiny Order of the Red Labor Banner and asked politely, "Can I be of service, Tovarisch?"

"My name is Mikhail Kruger. I am a newspaperman from Moscow on a temporary stay by authority of the Central Committee. I must speak with the chief of the G.P.U."

The sergeant took this down verbatim in his notebook, picked up the telephone and repeated each word into the mouthpiece. Then he listened for a moment and hung up the phone.

"Go right in, Tovarisch Kruger. The chief will see you. Second floor, room 9."

The G.P.U. chief, Tovarisch Ilyushin, was a fairly young man with soft, intelligent eyes and a pinkish, smoothshaven face. He looked more like a rural schoolteacher than the local chief of the dreaded secret police. He was of the new generation of Communists, the Stalinist guard which had displaced the defunct and liquidated Leninist faithfuls. Smiling pleasantly, he waved Mikhail to a chair.

"Tovarisch Kruger, I've had the pleasure of reading your novel and I have followed your other publications with a great deal of interest."

"Thank you, Captain," Mikhail answered in an equally friendly tone.

Captain Ilyushin smiled again, nodded once and said quietly, "Please state the matter which brings you to see me."

"The matter is a rather delicate one. I must first tell you that as a conscientious Soviet citizen I know how to value the work of the G.P.U. However, since we are all human, there are times when some small but unavoidable misunderstanding might arise. I mean—"

"Yes, yes, of course. Things do happen. Please don't hesitate to be frank. We are not the devils most people imagine us to be. We are all human and can make mistakes. But our overall task is to safeguard the integrity and security of our country and Party."

Mikhail found himself liking this soft-spoken man and he felt safe. "Early this morning," he began, "the mechanic of the Kalinin factory was arrested—a man by the name of Solomon Feier. He is a friend of mine, or to be more exact, a man whom I first met in Birobidjan and who seems to me beyond the shadow of a doubt to be an utterly honest and upright person. He has received more than one Stakhanovite quota award. He is the quietest and least partisan of men. Recently he married a woman and made a home for her and her child by a former marriage. They had a dream of happiness. Yet at this moment she is at my house bowed down with grief. I feel that the whole thing is an obvious error—" He stopped because of the look on Ilyushin's face. The softness was gone. It had been discarded like a mask and Mikhail found himself staring at a stranger.

"You have come to plead for this outcast and saboteur whom the American imperialists have sent in to spy on us? Are you aware of what you are doing, Tovarisch Kruger? Or would you prefer being called Citizen Kruger? Go home and I will forget that you were here. The matter is closed."

"Tovarisch Ilyushin, I know that I have incurred your wrath. But please don't misunderstand me. I am not so abysmally ignorant as to even dream that I could come here to influence you in your official capacity. No, indeed. This is a deeply human situation and I have come here to plead to you in your capacity as a human being which the very magnitude of your position demands. After all it is I who must go back and face this woman. I was hoping that you would advise me what I could tell her."

Ilyushin gave Mikhail a cold, almost admiring appraisal, but his voice was icy.

"Tell her anything you damn please. I give you exactly ten seconds to decide whether you are out of this thing or in it."

"I was never in it at all," said Mikhail smoothly, wondering if that was his voice and his words, "at least not in the sense you mean. You know the famous writers' disease called curiosity. It seems that a writer simply cannot resist anything strange. Well, the little lady from Palestine was strange—exotic if I may say so—and I played around with the notion of including her in my next novel as a type. Besides," he added, making a gesture of futility as if the truth were at last being forced out of him, "you have been so frank with me that in all fairness it is my duty to be equally frank. Well, one thing leading to another, I gave her my promise that I would try. I kept my end of the bargain. One is willing to run quite a risk for—shall I say—so pretty a woman." How he despised himself for what he was saying!

Ilyushin gave him a genuine smile this time. "It was a good try, almost too good. If it will help your worthy cause with the little lady, tell her from me that you nearly became a hero for her sake and missed joining her husband by the skin of your teeth." He looked at Mikhail blandly. "There's nothing as effective as the truth, you know. As for your unspoken question, I can tell you that Solomon Feier will be sentenced to hard labor in a Sakhalin prison camp and"—he nodded slowly, his face still bland—"that ought to give you a good head start."

Mikhail shrugged his shoulders and got up. He controlled himself with every ounce of strength he could muster. "It never fails," he pronounced calmly. "They always get caught in the end. But that is neither here nor there. Law enforcement is not my business, although I am curious about it. We writers are amateurs in everything."

"I wouldn't go that far," the captain laughed, showing his white teeth. "I rather like writers. I ought to. I once aspired to being a poet and wrote reams of verse. As it turned out, however, the Party ordered me into criminology, trained me and, well, here I am." He shook Mikhail's hand. "Discipline comes first. Good luck to you, Tovarisch Kruger."

"Thank you for your cooperation, Captain Ilyushin," said Mikhail respectfully, thinking at the same time that the tour de force he had just executed would keep his sense of shame alive for years.

Mikhail walked home, his face burning with helpless rage. He said nothing when he came in and Esther understood at once that everything was lost. The child was with her now. Esther stared at Mikhail for a moment, then took her child by the hand and went to the door. Mikhail went after her. "A hard labor sentence may not be forever—" he began. She must have heard but did not turn around.

Esther Finli, leading the little girl by the hand, went slowly down the long street with its two-story houses, passed the splendid new railroad station, stepped between the rails and walked toward the city line. The rails stretched ahead of her for thousands of miles back to nowhere. She gazed down them with glassy eyes, picked up her child and tightly clasped her to her bosom and waited. A train appeared. It was like a small bug at first, barely crawling and emitting tiny puffs of smoke. Then it grew larger and blacker and as it moved relentlessly toward them its sharp whistle echoed in the taiga.

"Quickly my child—look up at the sky. See how pretty!"

She herself had time to throw her head back and gaze for an endless second at the fair heavens.

By nightfall the whole city knew that a mother and her child had been killed by a train which, because of this terrible accident, had left Birobidjan far behind schedule.

CHAPTER NINE

After Esther Finli's suicide, Mikhail found himself depressed and lethargic. He wanted to flee, to hide in some dark corner, to shut his eyes to the chaotic injustice he saw about him. His mind surveyed the whole of the limitless Russian continent and came to the same inexorable conclusion: everywhere was the iron Soviet rule and everywhere the deadly Party line.

"Look here," Ksenia remarked dryly after noticing Mikhail's black mood. "I don't know what you are fussing about. It's over and done with. They have left *us* alone. So what is bothering you now?"

"Do you really want to know? It's these mass arrests. Why are they doing it? They have arrested and shot high-ranking people and even workers and peasants. That's what is giving me sleepless nights. They liquidated Professor Gottlieb, the executive committee chairman, because he was a 'Jewish Nationalist.' But on the other hand they liquidated Nathan Wieder, the Party secretary, who was a Russified, assimilated Jew without even the slightest interest in Jewish problems."

"But I know all that," Ksenia broke in impatiently. "Then why don't you come to your senses and get us out of here? Polya's telegram indicated that we would be much safer in Moscow but every time I mention it, you shut me up. Why don't we do what she says? We'll feel much better back in Moscow with our old friends." She thought for a moment. "By the way, speaking of old friends, you didn't tell me what the Ivanovs wrote in the letter you just received."

"Katya writes that General Ivanov is back for good."

"How come?"

"They've returned him to army duty. He's in command of a garrison on the outskirts of Moscow. But Katya says that he is terribly preoccupied with something. He probably has his own troubles."

"Did they mention their son?"

"Yes. Petya is quite a big lad. He speaks German and English and has a strong flair for military science. He now goes to the same school with Boris' Victor."

Ksenia, returning to their original conversation, asked, "Well Mikhail, let's settle this question once and for all. Are we going to leave this end of the world or not?"

Mikhail was silent for a few moments. "I think I have a plan. Let's wait a few weeks. Then you and Alenka can start out for Krasney-Bor on the pretext of visiting your mother. I'll remain here a while longer before I leave for Moscow. It will all look very natural. Later, after I have located an apartment, I will come for you."

"Brilliant, Mikhail!" Ksenia clapped her hands excitedly. She was delighted at the prospect of returning to Krasney-Bor, even for a short time, and of leaving behind her the chaos and uncertainty of Birobidjan.

Mikhail was left alone.

Shortly after Ksenia's departure, the Birobidjan newspapers published an appraisal by the local literary critic, Solomon Balter, of Mikhail's novel and his other work. Mikhail was astounded to read that his work contained insidious anti-Soviet propaganda! As if that were not enough, on the following day a similar review appeared in the Yiddish newspaper, this time signed by two writers—Mendel Ritz and Feivel Dolin.

Mikhail recognized at once that he was the intended victim of a collective public charge. Stunned by the suddenness of the blow, his first impulse was to escape, to run for cover. But he knew this would be suicidal.

He waited for the knock on the door. Two armed G.P.U. men would come in and drag him off. This was inevitable, for such charges could result only in immediate arrest. He paced up and down like a caged animal. Once he seized the telephone, asked to be connected with the Party secretary and hung up before anyone could answer. What could Pinchas Levitt do? He could think of only one way out—to face the charge, expose it as a fraud and thereby prove his innocence.

He thought of going to the G.P.U. with his novel, his stories, and his articles to demand that Captain Ilyushin point out a single passage or word that could even remotely be interpreted as anti-Soviet propaganda. The libelous charges would be exposed and his accusers arrested for diversionism and sabotage. But perhaps this was exactly the move he was expected to make. If they were being blackmailed into writing these deadly articles against him in the press, he would only be playing the blackmailer's game.

The knock on the door was loud and sudden. He recalled the dark and filthy cell of his youthful imprisonment and he shuddered. Why had he not taken the risk and left with Ksenia and the baby? Why had he not run for Moscow long ago when it was safe? With a supreme effort he summoned enough strength to fling open the door. Framed in the doorway were Sergei Kupets and Leon Kolker. Mikhail's cry of joy died in his throat as he recalled that they, too, were police agents.

They came in. Kupets, as usual, was slightly drunk. He carried a Yiddish newspaper in one hand and a Russian one in the other. Waving both newspapers in Mikhail's face, he belched foully and yelled, "Outcasts! Poison pens! What do they have against you?"

"I haven't the slightest notion," Mikhail replied bitterly.

"You don't?" Kupets burst into sardonic laughter. "Then let me tell you. They are throwing you to the dogs to save their own skins. You weren't born yesterday. These thieves are running through the streets shouting 'stop thief!' " He turned to Kolker. "Tell him who these characters really are."

Leon Kolker pulled over a chair, straddled it, and came right to the point. "Mendel Ritz and Solomon Balter both crossed the border back in the twenties and never reported themselves to the Soviet authorities. They didn't want to be sent back to Poland or to be arrested on suspicion of espionage. But since they never informed the authorities, evaded the law all these years and, what is more, fraudulently entered the Party pretending they were Soviet citizens, concealing their true identity,"—he prodded Mikhail's chest with his forefinger and winked wisely—"who knows who they really are, eh? Now take for instance their attack on you. A public accusation! A strange move, isn't it? How would you explain it?"

"Go on," said Mikhail. "Tell me the rest."

"Certainly, I'll tell you the rest. This Feivel Dolin was once officially a Zionist. He cannot deny it. Also he knows that the ax is about to fall and he thinks that he can bribe someone into sparing his life by exposing the so-called anti-Soviet message hidden in your writings. The same holds true for the other two conspirators. But they are only fooling themselves. Everyone knows that you are an honest man, a worthy Communist, the possessor of the Order of the Red Labor Banner and an important writer."

"Thank you for the compliments, Tovarisch Kolker."

"Don't thank me, Tovarisch Kruger. I am only doing my duty as I see it. I cannot tolerate these callous and unfounded accusations against you, this vicious attempt to besmirch your character in the eyes of the Party."

Here Sergei Kupets extracted a few sheets from his breast pocket and proclaimed dramatically: "He who digs a grave for another will lie in it himself." Then he spoke in cold, clipped accents. "Now Mikhail, Kolker and I have jointly written an article which will appear in tomorrow's press. In this article we show that your novel and all your other writings have been praised by the foremost Soviet critics, that you are a great Soviet patriot, a hero with an order of merit which you received for outstanding contributions to Socialist construction both in villages and cities. We also declare that precisely such counterrevolutionaries as Solomon Balter, Mendel Ritz, and Feivel Dolin, who wear the masks of honest Communists, would invent these false charges. Finally, we expose their origin and identity."

Mikhail went white. He now fully grasped that this was a double conspiracy and that he was in the middle of it. In this deadly crossfire of accusations, someone had to fall victim. Perhaps he and his accusers had all been marked for death.

He saw with dreadful clarity what was about to happen. It was his turn to be blackmailed in a game of double blackmail. A lethal weapon had been put into his hand. Which God gave him the right to destroy others? He was numb with helplessness.

"Which among us," he said quietly, as if commenting aloud to himself, "has the right to judge, the right to cast a stone?"

Kupets exploded. "You idiot! We are trying to save you. You are nothing but a soft-brained, book-fed Jewish intellectual. These saboteurs are cutting your throat and you want us to be merciful. Kolker, show him the deposition."

Kolker pulled out a document, unfolded it and handed it to Mikhail. It was a typewritten statement, and read:

> To the G.P.U. of the Autonomous Jewish Region, City of Birobidjan:
>
> I, Mikhail Grigorevich Kruger, member of the Communist Party and member of the Union of Soviet Writers, presently in Birobidjan on an authorized temporary stay, herewith declare that the following persons, namely Solomon Balter, Mendel Ritz, and Feivel Dolin, entered the Communist Party with the intention of committing sabotage and promoting counterrevolution. I further declare that the aforementioned Solomon Balter and Mendel Ritz, both citizens of Poland, entered the Soviet Union secretly in the nineteen-twenties with the object of committing treason against the Soviet Union and that the aforementioned Feivel Dolin, former member of a Zionist party, is currently carrying on his Zionist, counterrevolutionary activities both within and without the Communist Party.
>
> I also declare that this statement is being submitted by me of my own free will as a patriotic Soviet citizen and that my purpose in doing so is to aid the Party and government in purging our country of all internal enemies. I testify that the above is a true and just statement of fact, in witness whereof I subscribe my name.

His name was typed in.

Mikhail handed the statement back to Kolker. "I won't sign."

"Why not?" asked Kolker in amazement.

"Yes," Kupets gritted, "why not?"

"Because I have no knowledge of the so-called facts set forth in this paper. Isn't that reason enough?"

"You don't need personal knowledge," said Kupets coldly. "We know the facts. You are taking our word for it, that's all. We have written an article in your defense—with our signatures, you will note. Sign this paper and our article appears in the morning press."

"The reason you were able to sign the article is that you have sufficient personal knowledge of my character and activities. You also claim personal knowledge that these men are saboteurs. Then sign your names likewise to the deposition. Why ask me to sign? Or are you forcing me to file this complaint?"

"No one is forcing you," Kupets replied smoothly. "You will do this of your own free will. The deposition sets this forth specifically—paragraph two."

"You won't convince me."

Kupets took the deposition from Kolker, thrust it into Mikhail's hand and said, "We've had enough of this nonsense. Sign it or else."

Mikhail looked about him. His throat was parched and his tongue felt like lead. Kupets and Kolker were staring at him.

"You look strange," said Kupets. "What's your answer?"

"Answer?" He swallowed hard. "I know that you are secret agents."

"So," laughed Kupets. "What of it?"

"Why don't you listen to reason?" Kolker now broke in soothingly. "We don't wish you any harm. On the contrary, we have your interest at heart. Sign and you will be free as a bird. You could even leave here today, for all we care. And if you decide to stay, no one will molest you. Not another soul will know what you have written."

"What I have written!" Mikhail laughed bitterly.

"Very well, if you must, what Kupets and I have written,"

Kolker conceded, waving his hand magnanimously, "but which you have signed."

"Why do you need my signature?"

Kupets slapped Mikhail on the back. "You are either a prize fool or a first-rate actor," he snorted. "Obviously, as agents we prefer wherever possible to have the complaint lodged by a citizen. This is routine."

"Why did you force these men to write articles attacking me?"

"Where did you get that story? They've hated you from the first day you arrived."

"You had better sign," Kolker said acidly.

"What if I refuse?"

"We will shoot you and throw suspicion on Dolin, Balter, and Ritz. They have the motive. We could easily plant the deposition around here where the G.P.U. will find it—an unsigned copy which the murderers overlooked when they stole and destroyed the signed original. This is as easy as child's play for us."

"I see you just feel like killing somebody today," Mikhail responded bitterly. Then without a word, he took out his pen, signed the deposition and threw it at Kupets. "Leave me alone now," he said tonelessly. "If you stay here another minute, you will have to kill me."

The two agents got up, exchanged smiles and shrugged their shoulders. Kupets walked out without a word. Kolker leaned over and with his forefinger spelled out on Mikhail's forehead—"moron." Then he, too, walked out, closing the door softly behind him.

CHAPTER TEN

The following day, with trembling hands, Mikhail opened the morning mail which contained the local newspaper, in Russian and Yiddish editions—*The Birobidjan Star*. The article was there, under a rather dismal photograph of him; it was signed by Kupets and Kolker, two "citizens." It praised Mikhail and condemned the libel committed against him by the "counterrevolutionaries," Solomon Balter, Mendel Ritz, and Feivel Dolin. Mikhail read slowly, almost without emotion, the identical article in both newspapers. When he had finished, he let the newspapers drop to the floor and for a while he stood looking down at them. Then casually, with the toe of his boot, he scraped them back and forth until they were a mass of torn and filthy rags.

There was nothing else for Mikhail to do in Birobidjan. He had freed himself of all his assignments in connection with this region. Now he could leave. It would only take him a few days to make the final arrangements. He was just beginning to pack late in the afternoon, when Pinchas Levitt called on him. He looked tired and drawn, as he dropped heavily into a chair.

"You had a close call, Tovarisch Kruger," Levitt said.

"I see you read the papers, Tovarisch Levitt," Mikhail replied.

"I not only read them, I edit them these days. The G.P.U. has left me with a few vacancies on my staff."

"Yes, the G.P.U. has a way of creating employment opportunities."

"I see you are leaving us, Mikhail." Levitt pointed to the packed valises on the floor.

"Yes, Tovarisch Levitt, I am on my way."

"You are leaving the furniture behind. Does that mean you intend to return?"

"No, I am leaving for good. What could I do about the furniture, anyway? I can only take what my valises hold."

"There is such a shortage of furniture and yours is expensive. It's a pity. By the way, you might like to know that I have just received a telegram from Moscow. They are sending me a number of executives and aides and an editor. It will be a relief to get the newspapers off my hands. I will be able to breathe again."

"Good, Tovarisch Levitt. You deserve a rest after all this upheaval. You really ought to consider going to a rest home for a few months."

"A rest home! I won't have that much free time. Even after this new crew arrives I will have my hands full just keeping up with my job as Party secretary." Then he suddenly asked, "What would you say if I put one of my new men in your apartment and asked him to buy the furniture? I could forward the money to you."

"Thank you. It wouldn't be bad to realize something on this furniture. I happen to be short of money. I'll have to get an apartment in Moscow and buy new furniture all over again."

"What do you plan to do in Moscow—take a job or go on working as a free-lance writer?"

"What sort of job am I good for? The only thing I am equipped to do is to write. Besides, I have a family to support. Tovarisch Stalin says, 'A writer is an engineer of human souls.' The government pays our engineers well, so I'll have to make a living where it pays best."

"As far as that goes, I am not really worried about you, Mikhail. You will manage. I am only sorry that you are leaving. I had hoped—but it's no use. I realize that Birobidjan is not for you."

"For that matter, Tovarisch Levitt, I am not sure that Birobidjan is for you either."

"You are talking nonsense, Mikhail. Even Moscow wasn't built in a day. There are difficulties, but we will overcome them."

"I sincerely hope so. I wish you the best of luck."

"You are anxious to leave, of course. But I have come to ask a favor of you."

"I am listening."

"First let me say that if you did not have temporary status I would have forced you, under the rule of Party discipline, to take the job as editor of the local newspaper. In your case I don't have the power to enforce the rule. I am therefore asking a favor of you. Edit the newspapers until the new personnel arrives. It will only be for a few weeks. My greatest responsibility is to make sure that the one Russian newspaper comes out every day. The fact is that unless I can hand over this job to someone for a while I will simply have to suspend publication, and you know what Moscow will say."

"But what about Kupets? Surely he could—"

"Kupets might have filled the bill but he has suddenly disappeared. I am told he developed an irrepressible urge to go on a long fishing trip. I don't really trust him anyway—let us say because he drinks too much."

"Yes, let us say that," Mikhail added.

"Besides all my other problems, we have to set the type by hand because no one knows how to use the linotype machine that was sent to us by American donors. And who are the typesetters? Youngsters right out of printing school. They have no experience and make hundreds of mistakes. Their spelling and grammar are hopeless, so everything goes, with the result that our paper is full of linguistic monstrosities. As you know, a grammatical error can become a political one."

"That seems a little farfetched."

"It isn't. It has happened. I know of a case where Stalin's name, because of a simple typographical error, was printed as Sralyin.* You know how things are," he explained. "I don't have to put a finger in your mouth. Somebody accused those responsible with sabotage. The typesetter, the chief proofreader, and the editor were all arrested and the newspaper was shut down. They were never seen again."

* A reference popularly associated with the Russian words relating to excrement.

Mikhail looked hard at the Party secretary. Levitt was unkempt and unshaven. He looked old. His eyes were bleary for lack of sleep. Mikhail felt a certain amount of sympathy and even admiration for this man who had been able to tack successfully with the prevailing political winds for so long. But he himself had had enough of Birobidjan.

"I am sorry, Tovarisch Levitt, but I cannot do what you ask. Editing a newspaper is a grave responsibility. I am a writer, not an editor."

Levitt sensed the futility of pleading further and he left without another word.

The cadre of eighteen men arrived—all responsible Party members—and took up their posts in the administration. The new commissars were young Communist intellectuals freshly graduated from the Party schools. They had studied and mastered every trick of dictatorship. They knew when to criticize and when to flatter, when to bully and when to connive. Under the influence of this junta of "leaders" the region began to show increasing signs of Russification despite everything Pinchas Levitt, the Party secretary, could do. Day by day, as he struggled to stem this remorseless trend, he watched the dream of a Jewish cultural revival on Soviet soil fade away.

Mikhail was ready to leave Birobidjan. His apartment was already occupied by one of the new commissars, who had brought his wife and two children. He even bought Mikhail's furniture. They allowed him to use a small room for the time being.

Mikhail found this man a pleasant fellow, at least in private life. He was on the regional executive committee and in charge of all the cultural and educational institutes. A tow-haired Russian with gray, thoughtful eyes, he seemed always buried under a pile of books, newspapers, and manuscripts, engaged in a never-ending search. The reason was obvious. Culture and propaganda being inseparable, he was up to his ears in propaganda. Mikhail discussed literature with him several times in a cautious way and a mild friendship grew up between them. He once confessed his envy that Mikhail was returning to Moscow. He and his family were homesick for Moscow, he had hinted,

One evening before Mikhail's departure he noticed that the commissar was disturbed. "Tovarisch Rockov," he remarked, "you don't seem yourself today. Is anything wrong?"

"I was instructed today to take over the job of Party secretary, and I have no stomach for it. I am an educator and my interests are cultural. The new job will harness me to things like construction, factories, kolkhozes, and Party cadres. They are not in my line."

"I don't understand," Mikhail responded, going pale. "This afternoon I stopped at the Party committee to say good-bye to Levitt, and he said nothing about being transferred to another job."

"He did not tell you," answered Rockov, dropping his eyes, "because he did not know then what was coming."

"What are you driving at?"

"He has been arrested by the G.P.U."

"Arrested? What for?"

"I have no idea. I only know that I was told to take over his job."

Mikhail felt a sudden stab of anguish.

"Levitt is a devoted Communist," he cried. "I have known of him for years. He is utterly sinless. This is madness. Today he, tomorrow I, the next day you, Tovarisch Rockov. Something must be done. We can't keep silent!"

Mikhail's fist came crashing down on the table. Rockov, frightened, tried to calm him. Rockov's wife put her arms round him, tears of pity in her eyes. "Mikhail," she said brokenly, "Mikhail Grigorevich, you mustn't say such things! You must never speak like that again. We have heard nothing, you understand, nothing! No man can vouch for another. To you Levitt was a good man and a devoted Communist, but can you swear it was not a mask? Every country has its secret police who know things hidden from the public. They must have found out that Levitt was not what he seemed. If it is a mistake they will free him. You must believe it, or it will break your heart."

"No!" He pushed her away, "No! You are kind. But we are not children to put to sleep with bedtime stories."

Rockov looked at Mikhail sternly. "Kruger," he said, "you are too highstrung. You spend too much time writing. You need a holiday. When a man is lonely the whole world seems dark. You have had a shock. I understand. But I know you are a good Communist. Our government doesn't go around squandering its orders of merit. When they gave you one it was deserved. You are still a hero in our eyes. But even heroes can get an attack of nerves. We'll forget it! We heard nothing."

"Yes," Rockov's wife added, "go lie down. You will feel better. You are among friends here. You have nothing to fear. But please lower your voice or our neighbors may hear you." She sighed. "Who knows from a man's face what is in his heart?"

Mikhail realized that his outburst was a dangerous mistake. Luckily, these people had been understanding. Others might not be so generous another time. It was not enough to say little and to look neither to the right nor to the left, as Nathan Wieder had once said in the Cheka prison. It was not enough to stop thinking, as Boris had urged. One had to do more. Somehow, one had to control the unthinkable so that it never burst from the depths to catch a man unaware.

"I am very grateful," he said, "to you both. I couldn't reconcile myself to the idea that he is an enemy of the people, of the government and the Party. It was a terrible shock. But I must have implicit faith in the G.P.U. Please forgive my conduct."

"Forget it!" Rockov smiled at him. "There's nothing to forgive."

Mikhail drank hot tea with rum, and went to his room. He lay down on the bed without undressing and fell asleep. When he awoke, the house was dark and still. Through the window he could see the smooth-flowing Biro River and the bridge that led to the taiga and the former Korean village. The night was so utterly calm and so clear that the spherical mountain which rose in massive beauty miles away, seemed to fill the frame of his window. He got up and stood for a while looking down at his valises. He was leaving this place forever; the first train at dawn would carry him away. It would be a long journey and he would have time to think. How does one control the unthinkable? How does one prevent the unthinkable from finding tongue and erupting? There must be a way. His last thought, when he went back to bed was that if he ever found the solution to this problem, his education would be complete.

He slept fitfully, glancing every few hours at the clock. It was still too early to leave for the station. But he swung his feet off the bed; as he did so he heard two distant shots. The hunters are out on the taiga, he told himself. But he couldn't stay in his room any longer. He dressed, took his portfolio under his arm and tiptoed out. Everyone was asleep. He waved his hand in the general direction of the bedrooms, though he had said his formal good-byes the evening before. He unlatched the front door, opened it and without a look back closed it behind him. As he walked down the street the thought came to him that the Rockovs would soon move to better quarters. They would inherit Pinchas Levitt's magnificent dwelling.

Day was breaking. Mikhail walked rapidly. The air had a biting edge and the surface of the Biro River was ruffled by a sharp wind. Now that his body was in motion he could not contain his impatience. He was anxious to get his valises out on the platform, and wait for the express to come in. He spurred himself to greater speed, turned off the main thoroughfare known as Soviet Avenue and took the shortcut through the alleys. He came to a large new brick building with tiny windows protected by thick iron bars and he paused to catch his breath. This must be the new G.P.U. prison, he thought, and it struck him that the shots could easily have come from here. He passed the prison, broke into a trot and went down a few more sidestreets. He saw the luminously white, oriental-looking station ahead of him and by the time he got his valises out of the baggage room and onto the platform he was out of breath. There were several passengers waiting already, though the train was not due for another half hour. Mikhail stood between his two valises, waiting.

A porter came out with a red flag to warn passengers that

the train was due in. Mikhail realized that he didn't have a newspaper. He ran into the station and bought one that had just been delivered. The print was still wet, and it smudged under his hand. He stuffed the paper into his pocket when he heard the train pull into the station. He ran for the platform, grabbed his valises, climbed on board, and found his seat. Five minutes later they pulled out of the station and Mikhail stood at the window and kept the river, the bridge, and the city in sight as long as he could.

He had the upper berth. When they were well out in the open countryside and moving steadily away, he climbed up and lay down. Through the window he looked out on the endless expanse of the black taiga. Time passed. Then suddenly the sun stood caught in the window-frame and kept pace with the train. His eyes began to smart and he had to shift his position. He turned his attention to the other three passengers who shared his compartment. They were all, he found, from Vladivostok and on their way to Moscow. They sat in deep conversation, their heads close together talking about Socialist construction, five-year plans, incredible mechanical inventions, and vast production schedules. They were so preoccupied that they had not even noticed him when he came in.

Mikhail took the newspaper from his pocket and, flat on his back, tried to read. There was the usual headlined report to Stalin on the progress of Socialist construction in city and village. Directly underneath was a brief notice from G.P.U. sources informing the public that at 4:00 o'clock in the morning Pinchas Levitt, former Birobidjan Party secretary, had been shot for treason. The Far Eastern section of the G.P.U. had established that he had for years been not only a spy in the pay of the Japanese but also a Jewish nationalist who planned to betray the Far East to the American bourgeoisie.

Mikhail hurled the newspaper through the open window. He lay back, buried his face in the pillow, and wept silently. The train hurtled on mile after mile, the huge wheels muttering, talking, repeating over and over again: "Moscow-Kremlin, Moscow-Kremlin, Moscow-Kremlin." Gradually the sounds merged and Mikhail drifted into sleep. He saw himself as a child standing in the synagogue with his father. A prayer shawl covered his father's head and he could hear him sob as he prayed: "And on this Day of Atonement it is sealed, how many shall pass away and how many shall be born; who shall live and who shall die. . . ."

PART FOUR

The Desecration of a Synagogue

CHAPTER ONE

When Mikhail arrived in Moscow he was decidedly ill. He was not only physically depleted but his nerves were at the breaking point. He found even shaving too much of an effort and he grew a beard. But after spending a few weeks with the Garbers, Mikhail felt strong enough to move to General Ivanov's spacious home, where a room was always waiting for him.

The general was as erect and stern as ever. From the top of his smoothly shaven head, the blue scar of an old wound ran down his forehead. This is the way Mikhail always remembered him. Yekaterina Petrovna seemed unusually striking; her clothes, which came from Istanbul and Berlin, were unmatched for taste and elegance. Mikhail felt a stirring that he thought he had left in the past. It disturbed him, but at the same time he did not wish to renounce it, only to repress it and savor its sweetness in secret.

Some of the diplomatic niceties in Turkey and Germany had rubbed off on the general. His speech and manners were polished. There were other changes, too, subtle changes which made Mikhail suspect there were tensions beneath the polished surface of this dignified household. There was an occasional look of pain, almost grief, in Katya's face when she felt she was not being observed; the general's affability sometimes seemed a bit forced, and he had short periods of distraction. The house was quieter than Mikhail remembered it, perhaps too quiet. There was less entertainment than one would expect for a man in the general's position. Also missing was their son Petya, who had once livened the house with his pranks. He was now a cadet at the Moscow Military Academy.

General Ivanov had developed a flair for clothes. He wore his heavy military uniform only when required by regulation. One day he surveyed Mikhail from head to toe, frowned, and turned to his wife. "Katya, please bring in the gray suit, the one I bought in Berlin."

"Why? It no longer fits you."

"Exactly the point, my dear." He made a gesture of indignation. "Take a look at the suits our Soviet writers wear. They are a blot on the national honor. The time has come to dress our writers in decent, civilized clothes. Give Mikhail the suit and let him try it on. It should fit him."

"Please don't trouble," Mikhail protested. "Thank you very much but I have enough money to buy a suit. Besides, General Ivanov, you are taller and heavier than I am. It won't fit me."

"It will fit you because I say so!" the general barked. "This is an order. You are not to countermand me. My eye is keener than yours. We happen to be exactly the same height and in Berlin I was as thin as you are—the result of too much hard work and no sleep. And stop ranting about how rich you are. Nobody here earns the kind of money which can buy anything as good as these foreign suits. We make tanks, planes, and tractors but no suits. We don't even produce enough tanks and planes, and when we do, they don't compare to those which Germany puts out. But that is beside the point, eh?"

Katya came in with a gray suit of wonderfully soft texture. "Here it is, Mikhail. Try it on."

Mikhail went into his room, put on the suit, and was amazed to find that it fitted him. He came out and Katya smiled approval. The general, a big smile on his face, waved his hand in triumph.

"Now you see before you a writer dressed in a style worthy of his profession."

Mikhail, despite his embarrassment, was truly grateful. But the general was still riding high. He went to a closet, opened it, and came back with a gray fedora. "Put it on. Don't look so sheepish."

"A hat!" Mikhail was stunned. In the Soviet Union a fedora was considered a sign of bourgeois decadence.

"I understand your qualms," said the general, "but you miss the point. It is ordinary common sense and entirely in keeping with the Party line. Just as it is acceptable at present for a Communist to be an intellectual, so it is acceptable for an intellectual—a writer, no less—to wear a decent suit and hat without feeling like a bourgeois. This is cultural progress. Enough of this beggary! We are now a world power, someone to be reckoned with. We cannot appear before the world in rags. If the whole nation cannot as yet put on decent clothes, there is no need for us, its representatives and the vanguard of the people, to wallow in mud."

So Mikhail accepted the suit and the hat. That evening they all drove in the general's chauffeured car to Boris' house. During Mikhail's absence from Moscow a friendship had developed between the Ivanovs and the Garbers. The women were fond of each other, and the general genuinely liked Boris—and there was the undeniable fact that Boris had Stalin's ear. Whenever Boris spoke, Ivanov listened closely, seeking to detect even the slightest vibration of hidden meaning in his words. Boris, as usual, was passive and reticent.

When Boris saw Mikhail in the gray suit he looked him over from head to foot and shrugged his shoulders.

"Don't you like it?" Mikhail asked.

"You look like a playboy," Boris said, "and your decoration is out of place on this kind of suit. At least remove it when you put this suit on."

"I disagree, Tovarisch Garber," the general intervened. "When the Party or government bestows a decoration, it should be worn proudly and never removed."

"In that case, general, why did you leave your decorations at home? I don't see you wearing them."

The general's hand quickly went to his breast and he laughed shamefacedly. "This is very curious. You know, I've noticed that when I put on a civilian suit I sometimes forget to wear my service medals. But then I have so many of them. Mikhail is not a soldier. He is always in civilian clothes and should therefore wear his order on all occasions to denote his position in society."

"So now it's a question of prestige. But never mind, the whole thing is petty." Boris forced a smile. "The Revolution will not suffer because of it." He motioned to the table, which was already set for dinner. "Join me, if you please," he said, then added with mock severity, "You were ten minutes late,

Tovarisch Ivanov; we were compelled to wait. It is a conspiracy to starve us."

Mikhail was pleased to see that Boris was still capable of humor. He seemed more relaxed and his words had less of that bitter edge. But Mikhail knew him so well that it was easy to detect what the others missed—a sudden tenseness in the eyes accompanied by slight neck tremors; an occasional gesture that was too wide for Boris, as if he were making an effort to throw off a finger spasm; a subtle, masklike change in facial expression which died in an instant. Mikhail sensed that Boris was under great stress despite his attempt at playing the genial host. The disease was deep. There is no way out for Boris, Mikhail thought, as long as he remains Stalin's shadow.

Dinner was served and Mikhail tried not to think about Boris. Instead he ate more than he should have, told one funny story after another and drank himself into a state of elation. Life, he convinced himself, was wonderful. His troubles were over. He had accomplished much since his arrival in Moscow several weeks ago. He had started on a book and signed a contract with the state publishing house. It was nothing more than a social blueprint done to specification. But they had paid him fifty percent cash down and he had deposited the money in the Moscow bank. He worried little about Ksenia. He had been even too lazy to write more than a letter or two, and he had sent no money because in the village her mother provided for everything. Nor did he feel that there was any need to rush about looking for an apartment. Why bother? Boris would help him. He lifted his glass and thickly proposed a toast.

"I drink to our Soviet way of life, to the Soviet family and to the fine apartments which are indispensable to both. But since it is hard even for a Russian writer, a loyal Communist, and bearer of an order to find an apartment, I also drink to patronage. I drink to it because in this society *blaht* is everything. And if I have anything I have connections." He got up, swaying, and winked at Boris. "Finally, I drink to Boris, who I hope will help me get an apartment, a beautiful apartment in one of the new buildings opposite the Kremlin." He waved his glass unsteadily at the room and his eyes suddenly filled with tears. "Do you know what will happen if I don't get such an apartment? My Ksenia will not come back to me. She will fall in love with some village Stakhanovite and will marry into the kolkhoz. I will be a lost soul. Do you want me to be a lost soul too, Boris?"

There was a terrible clatter as Boris brought his fist down on the table. "Sit down and shut up!" he bellowed. Mikhail tottered for a moment, his lips still moving soundlessly, then slowly sank into his chair. He tried to set the wineglass on the table but his hand shook and the glass turned over, leaving a red stain on the white tablecloth. Polya, smiling reassuringly at everyone, jumped up and dried the tablecloth with a napkin.

Boris, after breathing heavily for a minute, seemed calm again. He reached over and filled Mikhail's glass from the bottle. "Drink your head off, for all I care. You are my guest and it is your privilege. Make a hundred toasts. But never use the word *blaht* in my presence again. I hate it. How can a writer like you allow himself to use such a vulgar expression? So you want an apartment? You may be my friend, but I have no influence nor would I use it if I had it. No hard feelings."

Mikhail raised his glass. "I apologize for my behavior. I will change my toast." He looked into Boris' eyes. "To your health."

Katya gave Mikhail a quick glance of approval and raised her own glass. "To all our healths." They all drank, even Boris, who poured a few drops of wine into his dry, empty glass and wet his lips.

Later as they were all going into the sitting room, Polya tugged at Mikhail's sleeve and managed to whisper in his ear, "Boris loves you. He won't sleep tonight because he feels he offended you. But yesterday he asked me to tell you privately that if you went down to the Housing Office you would receive a signed order for an apartment in the new building. Simply give your name."

Mikhail felt ashamed. "He will sleep tonight," he whispered back. "This is the first time I have ever apologized to him. It is a historic event and will shock him into sleep."

"A new school of psychology! By the way, you know you

hardly mentioned Ksenia and Alenka all evening. You should be—"

General Ivanov overheard the last few words. "Why all this whispering?" he interrupted. "First Boris lets him have it and now you. What do you want of him?"

"I want to make sure," she answered, moving forward gracefully and taking the general's arm, "that he doesn't forget about his wife and son."

"Why should he remember them?" Boris snorted. "He has you and he has Katya. He's the playboy of Moscow. That is why I would like to see him settle down. When he brings Ksenia and the boy home he will stop chasing after our wives. Look at that beard he is sporting. It must drive the women crazy. He had better shave it off before he breaks too many hearts."

This tone of levity coming from Boris was so unusual that they began to laugh. One word led to another and the hilarity became explosive. They made a great deal of noise.

"We had better lower our voices," Ivanov cautioned. "They can hear us outside."

But Boris was trying to make amends for his loss of temper. "Listen, everybody!" he shouted. "You are my guests. I want no restrictions. You can shout from the rooftops. I am afraid of nobody. Enjoy yourselves to the limit. How about a song, Mikhail? You have a fair voice. Remember the one we used to sing?"

Mikhail nodded and he and Boris began, the others joining in:

> "*Zhivi, poka zhiviotsa,*
> *Poy, poy, poka poyotsa* . . ."*

In parting, everyone agreed that the evening had been a huge success.

* "O let us live, while we may,
And let us sing, while we may. . . ."

CHAPTER TWO

The next morning Mikhail was up early. All night he had had visions of his new apartment in the center of the city, within view of the Kremlin, the Red Square, and the Moscow River. In the sober morning light he found it incredible. Yet it had to be true. He washed in a hurry, thought of shaving off his beard but did not have the heart. He had to admit it really did something for his face, added some dignity and made him look more distinguished, rather foreign. He then decided to put on the gray suit which General Ivanov had given him, and removed from the lapel the glittering, gold-rimmed order with its red labor banner thinking, maybe Boris is right after all. It is out of place on a foreign, bourgeois suit. He put the decoration safely away in a drawer. He started to write Ksenia a letter, but after a few lines threw down his pen. It would be better to wait until he could include the news that he had actually gotten the apartment. Then he could send the address, describe the house and elaborate on the wonders and comforts of their new home. He glanced at his wristwatch. He was very hungry and the Ivanovs might sleep far into the morning. He would run out for a while, have some breakfast in a restaurant, and telephone his apologies if he stayed out too long. This reminded him that he would need some money, so he went to the drawer and took three rubles.

Moscow was radiant in the early morning light. Mikhail walked down the main avenue which stretched the whole length of Moscow from the Briansky to the Kursky railroad stations. He passed the gigantic tower surrounded by fine buildings set in the heart of a sprawling garden—the first Moscow University dedicated to Lenin. Beyond were the rows of workers' homes, smaller and far less comfortable than those for commissars but quite an improvement on the ancient, filthy, narrow shacks in which the vast majority of the proletariat still lived. Farther down he saw a new department store with wide show windows, a new bakery, a modern beauty parlor, a shoe store, and a dress shop. The prices in these stores were far beyond the reach of the worker, and the customers were all drawn from the elite—army officers, Party functionaries, important professionals, and high-ranking commissars.

Gradually he drew near the Kremlin. The golden crosses on the steeples of the old Slavic cloisters had been replaced with ruby-red, five-pointed stars. Within these stars were electric bulbs and at night this Kremlin sky cast a gloomy splendor over Red Square and all of Moscow. By day, too, the Kremlin made its own sky as the red stars reflected the sunlight in emblazoned red. No matter how often Mikhail watched those red stars on the steeple tops riding the Kremlin sky, he always felt their formidable fascination. When he reached the Kremlin gates, he threw back his head to take a last look at them.

The gates swung open and a car rolled out. Mikhail peered through the open gates; he could make out a clock somewhere inside. He wound his wristwatch and set it by the clock. Then he thought that as long as he was at the Kremlin he might as well walk over to the Housing Office and inquire about the apartment. But it was too early. He moved away and followed the Kremlin wall to the Moscow River, where a new bridge was under construction. There he whiled away a half hour before going back to the entrance. Just as he got there the gates swung open again, letting a car through. He checked the time. More cars came through, leaving the Kremlin. In one, he noticed Stalin sitting stiffly. Another car followed closely behind. There sat Stalin again. In complete bewilderment, Mikhail saw Stalin in a third car. Were his eyes deceiving him? Then he remembered the rumors that Stalin had doubles—decoys that were used as a precautionary measure—to confuse a possible assassin.

Mikhail really had no idea when the Housing Office was officially open to the public, so he decided to try the national library in the hope that it would open early. He could spend an hour or so reading, even stop off for a bite, and then come back. Perhaps they would give him the order for the apartment immediately and as long as he had wandered off this far, it would save him a trip later in the day. As he turned to leave, he noticed that another man who had been loitering about also apparently gave up, for he looked at his wristwatch and sauntered off.

The library was not far away. As he started to climb the steps he was suddenly pivoted around and he found himself looking into the eyes of a policeman.

"Your papers!"

"What for?" asked Mikhail, taken by surprise.

"I insist. Your papers!"

Mikhail reached into his pocket only to discover that he had no papers on him. Chagrined, he tried to explain that he had changed suits and had neglected to transfer his documents.

"A likely story. You can tell it to the G.P.U."

"You have no right to arrest me and pull me off the street," Mikhail protested vehemently. "I happen to be a Soviet writer, a Communist—and I carry an order of merit."

"You don't say!" sneered the officer. "Even an order of merit." He scrutinized him mockingly, "I must be blind. I don't see it anywhere."

"I left it home."

"A mystery, I'm sure. We'll let the G.P.U. figure it out."

He proceeded to search Mikhail, impounded the three rubles, and made a careful notation in his notebook. Then he took out a pocketknife, cut off all the buttons on Mikhail's trousers, removed his belt, and made another careful entry in his notebook. Mikhail stood there holding his trousers up while a crowd gathered and watched. When the officer was ready, he put away his notebook and yelled, "Beat it!" The crowd melted instantly. Then the policeman took out his revolver and told Mikhail,

"Start marching toward Lubyanka Street. Don't try to escape because your pants will fall and I'll riddle your behind."

"Lubyanka Street!" Mikhail cried out in fright. "But that's the Cheka—I mean the G.P.U. headquarters."

"Aha! I see you've been there before. Start moving."

As they reached Lubyanka Street and walked through the iron gates of the white G.P.U. building, Mikhail suddenly noticed the civilian whom he had seen loitering about the Kremlin. The man came forward and ordered the policeman,

"Take him to Room 7."

They passed down a long, wide, brightly lit corridor lined by steel and wooden doors. The steel doors had numbers and the wooden doors silver and gilt inscriptions. Mikhail managed to read one of these inscriptions: "Investigations Second Division—Tovarisch Petrushkin." They stopped before a black, steel door bearing the number 7. The policeman opened the door and pushed Mikhail into a small, narrow, windowless cubicle and locked him in. This tiny room was painted pure white, literally shone with whiteness. There was not a scrap of furniture and it was this emptiness which made the whiteness so maddeningly intense. Mikhail stood in the center of this whiteness, trying desperately to understand why they had suddenly arrested him. He knew one thing clearly. This was no jail but G.P.U. headquarters. He was in the building which had jurisdiction over all of the Soviet Union. They never detained people here for long. Everyone was shipped out with great dispatch.

He heard the sound of a key. The door was flung open and the civilian who had loitered about the Kremlin came in.

"Identify yourself."

"I am Mikhail Kruger, a Soviet writer."

"Don't tell me what you want me to believe. Answer the question. Who are you? I want the truth. We know you and everything about you."

"If you know everything about me," Mikhail answered, trying to smile, "then you know that I am telling the truth. Why did you arrest me?"

"What are you doing in Moscow?"

"I told you. I am a Russian writer. I write and publish here. Hundreds of people can vouch for that. I don't know what you are after. What have I done? What are you charging me with?"

"Why are you so interested in Moscow?"

"Interested?" Mikhail was confused. "Why, everything in Moscow interests me. I am a Soviet citizen, a Communist, a writer by profession and a bearer of the Red Banner. I received the decoration for helping to establish one of the largest kolkhozes in the Soviet Union."

The man barely smiled. "Do you expect me to believe that?"

"I do. That's the whole story. I swear it. What do you want with me?"

"Who sent you to Moscow?"

"What do you mean—sent me? Who do you take me for?" Suddenly his courage fled. Perhaps it was another frameup. He had to save himself, clear everything up before it was too late. Let them call General Ivanov to verify that he was staying there until he was able to get an apartment. He would not mention Boris unless there was no other way out. And how about the Writers' Union and the government publishing house? "Look," he said. "Obviously you have mistaken me for someone else. Just hear me out. Call General Ivanov. He will verify that I am staying with him as his guest until I can locate an apartment. If you are not satisfied with that, call the Union of Soviet Writers and the state publishing house here in Moscow. They know me well and they will supply all the facts about me. And if that is not enough, you can call the Central Committee of the Party itself. Why don't you write all this down? Don't I have any rights?"

The man gave him an ugly look, shrugged his shoulders and pointed to the ceiling. "There is a little box there with a machine in it. You can be heard in every office. Every word you just said has been written down. You speak good Russian—no trace of a foreign accent. You are sure you don't come from abroad?"

"I have never been abroad."

"Have you ever been in an insane asylum?"

"Do I look it?"

They both laughed and the man went out, locking the door. Mikhail inspected the ceiling and the little box. It looked more like a camera. The latest technique, he thought, a device to reproduce every detail of an interrogation. He had heard rumors of this technique but had been reluctant to believe it. Now he was convinced. The next step would be thought control. So far the Communists had shown themselves capable of everything else.

Again the door opened, this time admitting a uniformed G.P.U. guard who marched him out of the room and down the long corridor to a door with a gilt inscription. The guard knocked and the door was opened by a uniformed attendant. Mikhail found himself in a large, airy, well-furnished office. Busily writing at a desk was an official who wore a military jacket almost entirely covered by medals, decorations, and ribbons of all kinds.

"Sit down," said the official, raising his head.

Mikhail, holding up his trousers in one hand, shuffled over to the chair next to the desk and sat down. On the desk were his belt, his buttons, and three rubles.

"We have been advised through several sources," said the official, eyeing Mikhail severely, "that the man who calls himself Mikhail Kruger did not wear a beard."

"I raised this beard in the last few months."

"What were you doing around the Kremlin?"

"I was admiring the red stars on the cloister steeples. There used to be crosses there. I often go for an early stroll and happened to be passing by. It was sheer curiosity for me, as a writer."

"Do you take me for an idiot? You are talking to the chief investigator of the Central G.P.U. I want the facts. I repeat. What were you doing around the Kremlin? Talk fast!"

"This is the whole truth, nothing else," Mikhail smiled. "Obviously you think I committed or was trying to commit some punishable act. You may have your reasons, but in this case the truth is so apparent that to invent a plausible explanation would be useless. With the resources at your command you would explode it in no time and I would have to invent another, and another. I have told you the truth."

Mikhail could well imagine the machinery that had been activated the moment he made his statements in the white room. His words had been carried into every department of investigation and written down verbatim. Each commissar had acted on that portion of the interrogation which fell under his jurisdiction. Telephone calls had been made all over Moscow and even beyond—the Central Committee of the Party, the Ministry of the Interior, the Foreign Ministry, the Kremlin's Special Division, the state publishing house, the Union of Soviet Writers, General Ivanov, and even the Central Bureau for Insane Asylums. All replies had been in his favor and this information had been collated and submitted to the Chief Investigator before Mikhail had been brought to see him. Mikhail could well afford to smile as he had. The trouser buttons, the belt, and the three rubles on the desk were the symbols of his freedom—unless they were being used as bait.

The investigator was looking at him with furrowed brows and eyes of gray steel. "You are too clever," he decided. For a few moments he sat tapping his cheek with his forefinger. Then he leaned forward.

"You know of course that you have done nothing to erase our suspicions. Your answers are absurd, for you can be all the things you claim you are and still be a conspirator. Your last answer as to why you were loitering about the Kremlin would not convince a four-year-old child. On top of it, you have the gall to try to teach us our business. I have the power, for security reasons, to ship you out among the polar bears. I may decide to do so. On the other hand, I may not. It depends on how you will answer three questions." He laid both hands, palms down, on the desk. "First—why were you found without a scrap of identification? I know what you said when you were arrested. That won't do. Second—explain the meaning of that foreign suit you are wearing. Third—why did you raise a beard?"

"The answer to all three is very simple," Mikhail declared, "but I will answer them in reverse order because that is the order in which they happened. I raised the beard because I was too lazy to shave. Besides, I thought my wife might like the change. The suit is a gift from my friend General Ivanov, who brought it home from abroad. He thought I looked seedy in my old suit. Luckily this one fits. As for my identification papers, I feel rather silly about this. I have never had an elegant suit and this one was to be worn only on special occasions. But it was like a new toy. This morning I got up very early and tried it on just to convince myself that it was mine. All I wanted to do was go out, catch a bite to eat, and go right back. I took only a few rubles with me. However when I got outside, the air was so good that I simply kept on walking. Then for a while I became engrossed in the scenery around the Kremlin, especially the red stars, and was strolling back by way of the library when the policeman stopped me. Incidentally, I am still hungry."

The chief investigator passed his hand over his furrowed face and regarded Mikhail thoughtfully. It was a full minute before he declared, "I am going to release you. From now on don't twist your neck to look behind the Kremlin gates if you have no business there, even if your wristwatch is slow, because according to our clock your time could easily run out. If you should ever have business at the Kremlin, come at the proper time, expedite it and leave. We can also do without your artistic admiration of our cloister stars. We have enough cranks to deal with. Carry your papers with you at all times. Lastly"—he got up and gave Mikhail his bony, heavy hand—"if you must come around here creating suspicion, don't do it in a foreign suit. All in all, you have given us and yourself a bad headache." With a sour look he leaned over and pressed one of the black buzzers at the side of his desk. A soldier came in. The chief investigator motioned toward Mikhail. "Sew his buttons on and make sure they are all in place. I hope you haven't forgotten your old trade." Then he wrote out a receipt for the buttons, the belt, and three rubles.

CHAPTER THREE

The new apartment was on Sadova Street in a white building covered by ornamental carvings, paintings, and bas-reliefs—hammer and sickle; gun and sword; book and torch; and the like. Tier upon tier of broad balconies overlooked the neighboring streets.

Mikhail handed his permit to the building manager, who gave him the key to his apartment. The building was occupied solely by leading commissars. Mikhail's apartment had five rooms and was on the top floor. He went up in the elevator, stepped out into the corridor and found number 77 among the rows of bright, freshly painted door numbers, wondering for a moment whether the double seven was a good or a bad omen. Inside, he was startled by the cool blueness of the walls and the great windows through which the daylight still poured although it was almost dusk. Mikhail, confronted with this splendor, told himself the incident at the Kremlin had been only the deceptive dark before dawn.

He took the elevator down to the main floor and walked to the nearest barber shop to have his beard shaved off. Then he hurried back to the Ivanovs.

Katya met him at the door. "Mikhail, we were so worried. What did they want with you there? They called us!"

"It was all a mistake." He smiled. "They didn't like my beard."

"I see you shaved it off," she observed as she led him to the study. "And I liked it so much." Then she asked, "Did you finally get your apartment?"

"Yes—five rooms in the heart of town, opposite the Kremlin. It's a dream come true."

Katya looked at him with her soft hazel eyes. "I am deeply happy for you, Mikhail."

"Is the general at home?"

"He is not here. He will not be home tonight. He was suddenly called out on an urgent matter."

"This sort of thing has been been going on for some time, hasn't it?"

"Yes, something is brewing. I wish I knew what it was."

"Hasn't the general told you there is talk of war?"

"Yes, he mentioned it." She shuddered and closed her eyes. "Frankly I'd rather not think about it."

Proud Katya, always confident and self-controlled, looked so distressed at that moment that Mikhail had an instinctive urge to calm her, reassure her. He put his arms around her protectively and brushed his lips against hers.

A look of astonishment fleetingly crossed Katya's face, but she offered her mouth and her lips seemed heavy with passion. Suddenly she pushed him away and, trying to keep her composure, said, "Have you had your dinner, Mikhail?"

"No, I—"

"Then I shall have to banish you at once, unless you come in and have something to eat."

She brought him some cold meat and wine, all the time avoiding his eyes. Mikhail caught her hand.

"Won't you join me?" he said.

"No, Mikhail, I think it best not to. I am going to my room. I feel—rather tired." She disengaged herself from Mikhail's grasp and left the room.

Mikhail didn't touch the food in front of him. His eyes were fixed on the door through which Katya had disappeared. It took him quite a while to calm himself before he started to eat.

The next morning Katya went with Mikhail to buy furniture. They started with the sofa. He found it was more difficult than he had supposed. They went from store to store, but the sofas were flimsy things patched together with thin boards and covered with upholstery of the most depressing colors. Mikhail became discouraged, tired, impatient, and ready to buy anything. But Katya persisted.

"I won't let you throw your money away," she declared. "We will go on looking till we find something suitable."

So it went on, day after day. It was not until the cold snap set in and the first snows fell in the streets of Moscow that Mikhail finally completed furnishing his apartment.

The pieces which Katya had chosen were old-fashioned and of heavy, carved wood. She spent a long time matching the shapes and colors. Then, after the furniture was bought and delivered she tried many arrangements before she was satisfied.

When it was all done, Mikhail invited all his friends. Polya and Katya cooked and baked in his new kitchen while he, Boris and the general made themselves comfortable in the ornate chairs and discussed Stalin's latest speech. Stalin had said that the country had entered on the first phase of Socialism, that there were no longer any classes in the Soviet Union. It was now a classless society which ruled itself. Boris, spreading out the newspaper on his lap, dug his finger into the vital sentence: "Life, comrades"—he read aloud—"has improved, life is happier."

"Agreed," said the general. "We can't complain any more."

I wonder, thought Mikhail, whether Stalin ever walked into a worker's home and saw a large family crammed into a tiny, airless space, trying to live from hand to mouth on starvation wages.

General Ivanov turned to Mikhail. "What is your opinion? You are a writer, and you know more about the people than Boris or I. Do people feel that life is better and happier now?"

Mikhail said quietly, "Stalin is always right."

The sarcasm was not lost on Boris. Mikhail saw tiny insane fires flicker in Boris' eyes.

"What's holding up those women?" Mikhail cried suddenly. "We will starve to death." He dashed into the kitchen and came back with three glasses and a bottle of vodka. "Let's have a drink while we're waiting."

Mikhail and the general drank a toast and then another while Boris raised his empty glass twice. Polya and Katya came in with a roast and insisted on joining them in a drink.

"To your health, Mikhail!"

"To your wife and child! Wherever they may be!"

After the fifth drink Mikhail laughed raucously. "I swear on my honor that first thing tomorrow morning I'll leave for Krasney-Bor and bring home my wife and son. On my honor!"

The general's face lit up with a smile. "Your swearing on

your honor, Mikhail, reminds me of Professor Maslov's favorite joke."

"Oh please, general, do tell us the joke," Polya urged.

"You don't have to coax me, Polya," Ivanov grinned broadly. "I'll tell it." He coughed, cleared his throat and began,

"Once upon a time there was a peasant. He had a very lean cow that gave no milk. One day his wife told him, 'Mikita, why do we need a cow that gives no milk? Sell her!' So Mikita took the cow to market.

"A farmer came up to him and asked,

" 'Are you selling the cow?'

" 'I'm selling,' was the answer.

" 'Is she a good cow?'

" 'A terrible cow!'

" 'Does she give milk?'

" 'No milk.'

"The farmer turned on his heels and left. A city man standing by witnessed all this. He walked up to Mikita and said,

" 'That's no way to sell a cow.'

" 'How else?' Mikita asked.

" 'I'll show you.' And the man took up his position near the cow. Another farmer stopped by.

" 'Are you selling the cow?'

" 'I'm selling.'

" 'Is she a good cow?'

" 'I swear on my honor, she's not a cow but a piece of gold.'

" 'Does she give milk?'

" 'Milk, he asks. Not only milk, but even cream!'

" 'How much do you want for her?'

"This was more than Mikita could bear. He rushed up to the man, pushed him away from the cow, and shouted,

" 'Beat it! Scram! I'm no fool! Such a wonderful cow I don't sell!' "

Polya rocked with laughter while Boris dropped his head on his chest and cackled, "That's some city man. I can do with a man like that. He can sell a cat in a sack."

Mikhail guffawed and shook his finger at the general. "I think you tell that joke even better than Professor Maslov."

Fixing her eyes on her husband, Yekaterina Petrovna smiled benignly. "Oh, Vanya, you told that so well!"

They ate and drank and sang far into the night. When everyone had gone, Mikhail went into the bedroom. The bed was wide, of red mahogany with nude figures of men and women carved on its posts. A prince or princess must have slept in it, he thought. Then came the Revolution—The prince or princess was dead, but the bed had found its way into a government store and waited there until he, Mikhail, had bought it for a princely sum. Was he not therefore a prince? He shook his head drowsily, undressed slowly, and crept between the sheets. He was tired but found it hard to fall asleep. He was haunted by a mysterious relationship in life between form and content. It was all so paradoxical. Thus, he lay in a princely bed and felt like a prince but he was no prince. He was going for his wife and felt like a husband, but was no husband. His mind grew fuzzy. Can the form of marriage endure, he speculated, with a content of free love? But if as Ksenia had said, marriage was love, it would take any form that love took. Then any lover would become her husband.

It was all very confusing. Opening his eyes, he looked toward the window. A light snow had begun to fall. It must be falling on the village of Krasney-Bor, too. It would gather on its low rooftops and wrap itself like a white cloak round every house and every stone. The fields would lie in soft white repose, and on their bosom thin shadows of smoke would curl blue from the chimneys. He closed his eyes and listened as the snow beat rapidly on the window pane. Still sleep did not come. Ideas of form and content began to swarm again in his brain. At one point it dawned on him that in England a king reigned over a democracy and in Russia a kingless people lay prostrate in the grip of autocracy. He smiled at the contradiction, turned over on his side and fell fast asleep.

He woke late the next morning, washed, shaved, and left the apartment carrying his valise. Outside, he boarded a trolley that took him to the railway station.

CHAPTER FOUR

The village of Krasney-Bor was wrapped in icy whiteness. The river cut through its center now like a broad band of frozen snow and formed a road for the only traffic he could see—one or two cars with wheel chains and a number of sleighs drawn by scraggly horses. Few adults were about. Mikhail knew what winter did to the village. All day the peasants lay snoring on their warm ovens and no one moved even to shovel away the snow which lay roof-high. In thc evening they trudged with their wives and children to a neighbor's house to have a jolly time. The young people were out in full force, skating and sliding on ice ponds, and there were even a few couples walking arm in arm through the snowbound streets. The hoarse strains of an accordion and the strumming of a guitar told him that courting was still popular, even in a hard winter.

The news of Mikhail's arrival spread swiftly. Everybody knew of course that he had come to take Ksenia and Alenka to Moscow. It meant a big send-off party, where vodka would flow, and there would also be news from the outside world, from the great metropolis of Moscow.

Ksenia's face lit up when she saw Mikhail. At that moment he was again the leader of men with whom she had fallen in love. He must have found an elegant apartment and now he would take her back to Moscow. She threw her arms around his neck and kissed him till she was breathless.

The peasants began to arrive with their wives and children. They came and stood around shamefacedly and timidly at first, but as their numbers increased they felt more at home and occupied every available seat—the long benches by the walls, the chairs 'round the tables in the big dining room. They even sat on the floor. They were served vodka, sour pickles, sauerkraut, and steaming hot potatoes boiled in their jackets. The vodka flowed, tongues loosened, and the boasting began:

"Our kolkhoz is the richest in the entire Soviet Union."

"Our men and women Stakhanovites fulfill their quotas not merely one hundred percent but one hundred and fifty and one hundred and eighty percent."

"Three of our kolkhozites—two men and a woman—have been decorated for outstanding production."

"Success and the good life is ours—bread by the ton, vodka by the barrel, and mountains of potatoes."

Mikhail found it hard to believe his ears. He found himself suddenly alert to what they were saying. No one had any complaint or grievance. Everything was perfect. They sat there in their festive rags, the men in patched breeches and torn boots and the women in tattered, crumpled dresses and faded handkerchiefs, all poor as church mice and boasted that they were rich and living on the fat of the land. There had been a colossal change in their attitude. Someone or something had convinced these poor, half-starved villagers that they were living in a paradise. They had no sanitation and no hygiene. No street was paved. The peasant was still a slave of the seasons and the weather. When it rained he walked knee-deep in mud. The houses were smelling pigsties. Yet to these peasant-kolkhozites it had become the best of all possible worlds. Socialism had, for them, arrived. If these older peasants boasted of their new glorious life, how much more would their children who knew no other!

Yet as a symbol that the regime had not swept everything before it, there sat the old lutist, surrounded by the children. The stories he chanted were indeed strange and they believed, at least while they listened with round eyes and eager hearts. All those things had happened in the dim long ago, and if a child grew skeptical and suspected that the old bard was making things up out of his own head, he had but to look at his parents and uncles and aunts to see that they too were listening and nodding their heads, as if to say, "Yes, that is how things were in those days."

They heard him sing: "A vision, my brethren, not of today alas, but of the good old days, the good old days of long ago. It is winter, cold and white, on Christmas Eve. The angels come down and sing that God was born and in each house stands a Christmas tree with gold and silver trinkets and presents for every child, trees lit with a hundred tiny candles—white and red, blue and yellow, and all the colors of the rainbow. All dance in a circle 'round the tree. The children wear new shoes with lovely suits and hats to match. Father wears his velvet vest and across his chest lies the huge silver chain and in his pocket bulges his great silver watch. Mother wears her red silk skirt and high-button shoes. So they sang and danced, in the days of long ago. . . ."

The children looked at each other and at their parents, who nodded and wiped tears of memory from their eyes, and some said, "Yes, it is all true. That is how it was once upon a time."

"So," the lutist sang, "they danced 'round the Christmas tree and then they ate till they burst. Later, wrapped in furs, with broad sashes of bright red girded about their waists, they went out into the night. A great sleigh was drawn from the barn and three prancing horses harnessed to it, not skinny nags but horses fair and proud, for each peasant had his horse and sometimes more, and he could go sleighing when his heart desired. . . ."

"It's a lie!" cried a fifteen-year-old with a Komsomol button on his chest. "Nobody owns any horses. Ownership is a capitalist invention. It's sabotage and counterrevolutionary. Horses in this village were always in the kolkhoz stables."

The old man dropped his lute to his side. "A lie, you say! You don't believe me! Ask your father! Ivan, tell your clever son whether you once owned five horses, twelve cows, three oxen, sheep and goats and hens. Tell him Ivan, how many things you once owned."

Ivan dropped his eyes. "It is true as you say. But why neighbor, remind me of it? I live well today also."

"True, very true," the old bard chanted, raising his lute again. "Our life, they say, is good. We must not sin against the bounty of God. We are humble." He continued:

"So the peasant sat in his own sleigh behind his three prancing horses. He held the reins in his left hand and the whip in his right. With him sat his wife and children. The peasant cracked his whip and the steeds ran like the wind over the feathery snow. The harness bells tinkled, the frost bit deep, and snow-swirls blew up before them and settled slowly behind them as they flew on. They rode and they sang a song of joy:

" 'Aida, troika, snyeg pushistey. . . .' "*

The old bard struck the back of his lute with one bony hand and with the other he strummed loud and furiously, his long, agile fingers flying over the strings. Then he intoned a song of praise to God for the white peace of winter, the gift of heaven to all peasants who toiled in the fields in summer by the sweat of their brow.

The peasants and their wives, under the spell of remembering, began to sing with him and the house shook with a wild chorus of praise to something that was no longer true but for which they would always yearn.

*" 'Three horses that gallop on feathery snow. . . .' "

CHAPTER FIVE

Mikhail and Ksenia wintered in their magnificent new apartment. It was a golden season for them. Mikhail's second novel was completed and published early in 1939. It was an even more resounding success than the first. For weeks his name appeared in the columns of the daily press. The critics praised him for his ability to probe into the minds of human beings and for his artistic portrayal of true Soviet workers and peasants. He had arrived. The Union of Soviet Writers gave an official reception in his honor, which was followed by a private reception at the home of General Ivanov. Through all this Ksenia was more like a creature of air than flesh and blood. She floated. Her ecstasy lasted until the excitement died down, then she reverted to the indolence she had shown since her return to Moscow. She slept far into the day. She had no household cares, having brought back with her from the village a middle-aged peasant woman whom she trained to be a maid-of-all-work. When she was bored, which was often, she read old novels—either Russian or translations from the French—about dukes, duchesses, courtiers, royal intrigue, and the lives of famous courtesans. It was the sort of literature sold in the bookstalls on the street behind the temple of Ivan the Terrible.

Mikhail himself was not immune to the praise and flattery being lavished upon him. He began to believe that perhaps he had really created the new prototype of Soviet art. What saved him from going completely overboard was the realization that the very precision of his art, the careful detailing, the smooth polish—were nothing but a facade to hide his own aversion to what he was dispensing. The whole thing was a masterpiece of artificiality.

One morning, Mikhail received a telephone call from the Central Committee ordering him to report at once to the

Propaganda Division of the Central Committee. He dressed hurriedly and, without waiting for breakfast, dashed out of the apartment. When he arrived at the Central Committee office he was referred to the Propaganda Division chief, a tall, emaciated individual with an ascetic face.

"Tovarisch Kruger, I am transmitting Party orders to you. You are to write a novel at once," he said. "The subject is the life of a Stakhanovite in the first Soviet automobile plant named after Stalin."

Mikhail knew better than to protest that he had not the slightest familiarity with the subject. Orders were orders; this was Party discipline and he had no choice.

He went to the automobile plant and formed a friendship with one of the Stakhanovites. He spent a few nights at the latter's home, studied his idiosyncrasies and blueprinted for himself the man's mode of living. This research completed, he was ready to produce a novel ordered by the Party.

The writing went quickly and smoothly; by May the novel was finished and in July it was published. The press labeled it one of the great books in the new Soviet literature. The reviews were hysterical with praise. The book sold phenomenally well, and so much money began to pour in that Mikhail might easily have lived in leisure for a few years. But it was not to be.

On August 24, the Stalin-Hitler non-aggression pact was announced in the Soviet press. Everyone was astounded. Mikhail, Katya, Polya, Ksenia—all the Russians—had been led to believe that the Nazis were a menace to Communism. There had appeared constant denunciation of Hitler in the official press. General Ivanov and Boris knew better, of course, but the general was unavailable and Boris was evasive.

"What does it mean?" Mikhail asked Boris.

"It means that Stalin has done the best thing for our country," he replied.

"But I thought we might sign a treaty with the Western powers."

"You thought! You thought! What does the West care for us? Do you think they would bleed for Communists? Do you? They didn't even support the Czechs. Stalin is no fool! The

English may think so. They sent a junior official to negotiate an agreement. Do you think they wanted a treaty? They wanted to *talk* about a treaty and then accuse us of an unyielding attitude, and thus make easier for themselves the road to a deal with the aggressors. But I have said more than I meant to, and this is for your ears only, Mikhail. I don't know why I tell you so much. I am getting more careless in my old age."

"What will happen, Boris?"

"To me? If I am not more careful with my tongue, you know what will happen."

"No—I mean what will happen to us? What will happen on the Manchurian border now? There was a great deal of agitation there even when I was in Birobidjan."

"I will tell you what Stalin says on that subject in his exact words. He says: 'If the Japanese desire war, they can have war; if they desire an understanding, they can have that too.' "

"Which will it be, Boris? What is the next move?"

"I can't say anything more. I have said too much already. Wait and see. Everything comes to him who waits. You are a writer; you should know that."

Mikhail did not have to wait long. On September 1, Nazi Panzer divisions rolled into Poland. Sixteen days later, Red Army units crossed the Polish frontier "to deliver the Polish people from the disastrous war into which they have been plunged by their unwise leaders" and to give their "blood brothers," the Byelo-Russian population of Poland, "an opportunity to live a peaceful life."

The Party machinery ground into action. "Spontaneous meetings" were held throughout Moscow and the rest of the nation to orient the masses on the oppressive policies of the Poles in dealing with Ukrainian and Byelo-Russian minorities. The official press published accounts of "atrocities," stressing that the intervention of Germany and Russia was aimed at restoring "peace and order" and to help "the Polish population to reconstruct the conditions of its political existence."

Polish resistance to the Soviet troops was feeble. When it was all over, it was disclosed that the non-aggression pact had contained a secret protocol partitioning Eastern Europe into "spheres of influence." Eastern Poland was the Soviet Union's first spoil of battle.

Shortly after the Polish surrender, the Central Committee called in Mikhail and "offered" him what it termed a temporary position as Commissar of Culture and Propaganda in one of the key Polish cities, Bialystok. His status was to be that of a civilian attached to the army. There was no refusing it. Mikhail was now a political commissar under army jurisdiction. Without a word he accepted his orders and the next day was on the train to his destination.

CHAPTER SIX

Bialystok was not at all what Mikhail had expected. He had been prepared to meet a desperate, exploited class, a mass of ragged, starving, destitute workers and peasants who for ages had been ground into the dust by princes and capitalists. He found no such class. Everywhere he saw well-fed, well-dressed people, not only among the wealthy and educated but also among those who were undeniably workers and peasants. They lived in comfortable, decently furnished homes. The stores were amply stocked with food and clothing. Perfumes and jewelry sold in great quantities. The Russian "conquerors," both military and civilian, swarmed into the stores like a horde of hungry locusts buying up everything they could lay their hands on—shoes, butter, suits, sugar, soap, and honey. They bought watches by the score, and negligees, slips, and nightgowns, and sent them to their wives, daughters, and sweethearts. Russian women thought the negligees were evening gowns, and paraded through the streets to display their new possessions.

Mikhail bought a number of things for Ksenia and Alenka. Out of a sense of guilt and shame—the Poles' faces told him what they felt: Russia, the vaunted land of Socialism, was revealing itself a half-naked, half-starved nation going mad at the sight of plenty—he resisted the urge to buy more.

But this state of affairs was short-lived. All private stores, enterprises, apartments, and factories were confiscated and nationalized. The owners were arrested, dispatched to Siberia, or simply shot. They were replaced by Soviet commissars—managers, engineers, doctors, teachers, propagandists, and Party secretaries.

One of Mikhail's tasks was to transform all theaters, schools, and clubs into effective agencies of propaganda. This entailed selecting Soviet Communists and assigning them to key positions and recruiting and training Polish Communists and sympathizers to help implement the program among the people. He also had to plan and launch new Soviet newspapers, periodicals, journals, and books. His judgment in selecting a man for any job had to be flawless.

Mikhail worked ceaselessly—planning, editing, organizing, directing. It left him no time for his own creative work. If he had any time to observe and speculate, it was during the short visits to various cities and villages in the course of his work. One fact became evident to him as time wore on. Poland was beginning to look like Soviet Russia. The new government stores and co-operatives had the same beautifully decorated windowfronts and the same empty shelves. The well-dressed crowds were beginning to look threadbare, with pinched, careworn faces; they seemed to walk with their heads down and cast furtive glances over their shoulders.

Mikhail lived at the Hotel Ritz and since he could not predict the length of his stay in Bialystok, there could be no question of bringing Ksenia and the child. Anyway, in her letters to him, Ksenia showed no desire to leave their luxurious Moscow apartment. She raved about the expensive gifts he managed to send her from time to time, but there was no love in her words. The old feeling, which had been fading for some time, was now gone. One day he picked up all her letters and read them through, searching his own soul as he read. When he put them away, he realized that they were strangers. They had nothing in common but the child.

CHAPTER SEVEN

On the rare evenings when he was free Mikhail was usually too tired to do more than stay alone in his hotel room and think. He was by nature a pacifist with a real hatred of militarism since his days at the military academy. He abhorred the word "war," and like many Soviet citizens he was almost glad that Stalin had made a non-aggression pact with Hitler. But he also had doubts and fears. What was the price of peace? How could one be neutral about a regime that had openly declared its aim of exterminating whole peoples? How can one make peace with a tyrant and murderer?

The atrocities committed by the Nazis which he learned of from the refugees, depressed him. Sleep became a nightmare. He saw Ksenia in flight from the Nazis with the child in her arms.

One night the telephone woke him out of his sleep. There was nothing unusual about a sudden call in the night. It was the secretary of the Party committee. But the message was unusual. All Communists were to report at once, without fail, in the courtyard of the G.P.U. building. Orders from the Kremlin. Communists were to help the G.P.U. carry out city-wide raids to purge the area of suspicious and undesirable elements.

Mikhail dressed quickly. He understood what a raid of this kind meant. He remembered the night raid on the Korean villages in Birobidjan when the whole population was arrested and transported. Who would tonight's victims be?

In the courtyard of the G.P.U. building the police, the Red Army troops, and the armed civilians awaited their orders. Mikhail knew many of the civilians. They were not G.P.U. agents but top-rank Communists—factory executives, engineers, store managers, journalists, music directors, and lots of others, all hated by the people of Bialystok who made distinction between them and the regular government commissars. Tomorrow the public would hate them even more as auxiliaries of the G.P.U.

Orders were barked. The raiding party was divided into units of ten, each unit made up of soldiers, G.P.U. agents, and civilians. They were briefed on raiding tactics and were given instructions to memorize. Then the Party secretary delivered a rapid, fiery, patriotic speech. Mikhail now discovered that the city was full of wealthy bourgeoisie and capitalists hostile to the Soviet occupation. The city and its environs also harbored fugitive generals and other officers of the defeated Polish army. Further, there were suspicious characters among the refugees who had fled from the Germans, many of them criminals and counterrevolutionaries. The presence of these enemies so close to the border was a threat to the Soviet Union. They were therefore to be transported to a remote region like Siberia, where they would be rendered harmless.

Arms had been distributed to all the civilians and Mikhail, too, listened to this speech with a revolver in his hand. When the G.P.U. chief issued his final instructions, Mikhail looked down to find his hand trembling. His first thought was, I must keep out of this manhunt. His second was to recognize the inevitable. I dare not keep out if I value my life. For a moment too he was tempted to use the revolver to blow his brains out. But this was no time to die, but to fight. If he couldn't fight against this terror openly, he must fight it with cunning and guile.

The G.P.U. contingents spread quickly and quietly through the city and suburbs. It was midnight. Suddenly it was as if an earthquake had struck. Terrified shrieks filled the air. Men and women were dragged from their beds and driven half-naked into the streets. All who resisted were executed on the spot. The rest were herded to the railway station and packed into filthy cars. Doors and windows were locked and the trains moved eastward.

The raiders searched for hidden gold, American dollars, banned literature.

In one house that Mikhail's unit raided there was a young mother with her infant, both ill with fever. She did not scream when the G.P.U. agent shot off the lock and burst in, followed by Mikhail, but she lay there, her eyes glowing like coals in her flushed and feverish face. The agent ordered her to climb out of bed, take the child, and join the other prisoners outside. She did not stir. With a curse the agent grabbed her by the hand and pulled her half way out of bed.

"Your husband is a Polish army officer," he shouted. "He fought against us. Where are you hiding him?"

She got out of bed and began to dress, swaying unsteadily on her feet.

"My husband did not want to fight. He was drafted. He had to obey orders. What else could he do?"

"Where is he?" the agent demanded.

"I don't know. He has been gone a month. I haven't seen or heard of him. The child and I have typhus."

The G.P.U. agent shrank away. "Let's get out of here. She can't get away. We'll come back later. We mustn't take chances with typhus."

They left the house and joined the rest of the raiding party, standing guard over a truck crammed full of men, women, and children. The leader shouted an order and the truck moved towards the railway station.

The raid ended by dawn. The G.P.U. sat back and rubbed its hands. "The city and its suburbs," it was able to report, "have now been purged of all dangerous and undesirable elements."

Mikhail said nothing to anyone. In the morning he was in his office, engaged in "culture and propaganda," helping the Communist Party to establish the Soviet order in this Polish land.

In the midst of all this, Boris and General Ivanov appeared in Bialystok. The general was on a three-day inspection tour. Boris spent one day in secret conferences. Both managed to pay Mikhail a short visit.

"You seem to be doing a magnificent job, Mikhail," General Ivanov said.

"I do my best," Mikhail replied. "It is not easy. The people were glad to see us at first. They thought we were 'liberating' them and saving them from German oppression. They couldn't believe that we had signed a treaty with the Germans. Neither could I at first."

"Do you know the saying, 'If you cannot cut your enemy's throat, clasp him to your bosom?' It is an old Georgian proverb, and one of Stalin's favorites."

"What do you make of all this, General?" Mikhail asked.

Ivanov frowned, grimaced, and rubbed the scar on his forehead. "I am a military man. All I know is that the Red Army has had no important battle experience since the Civil War. We are depending on our superb equipment, our iron discipline and the political enlightenment in all our ranks. Theoretically we should be able to carry out Stalin's basic dictum on military strategy: In the event of war we shall strike the enemy in his own territory. But the fact remains that we have little experience and this disturbs me. That is why we are in favor of pushing our borders as far out as possible and fortifying them impregnably."

"Just what does that mean?"

"Well, Poland was one example. Now take Leningrad. It is close to the Finnish border and it is dangerously exposed. Finland will be asked to move over a bit."

"You mean a war against Finland?"

"Inevitably. It could happen any day."

Boris had sat through the discussion silently, with his brows knitted in thought and an occasional enigmatic smile crossing his lips. His face had changed. It was wrinkled, jowled, and his eyes had a dead lustre. He finally made one comment. "Stalin knows best and his genius will carry us through." It was a categorical statement requiring no answer. The discussion died instantly and in a few minutes both men took their leave.

Several days later there was another message asking Mikhail to report to the Party secretary, a fat, unctuous type who outlined the latest cultural problem:

"Tovarisch Kruger, on Kilinskego Street, opposite the new Soviet school, stands a synagogue. Through the classroom windows, the students can see the Jews bowing and scraping in prayer, with their prayer shawls held over their heads. It is intolerable!"

Mikhail said nothing. He had not yet been asked for an opinion.

"The poison of religion is seeping into the classroom," the secretary continued. "We cannot allow this. I would like to have your opinion, Tovarisch Kruger. You are a—man of sensibility, a writer—Do you think it best to close down the synagogue and prohibit prayer altogether or perhaps relocate the Jews to another place of worship?"

Mikhail tried to evade the question. "I believe it calls for an exercise of caution, Tovarisch," he said.

"Of course, of course. But we must do something."

Mikhail saw that he would have to commit himself. "The country is being taken over by slow stages," he said. "Of course, there is no fundamental need for churches or synagogues. In time they will all be abolished." The secretary smiled. "But at this point a gradual approach is indicated."

He glanced at the secretary and then proceeded cautiously.

"The religious elements here are essentially harmless. They buzz around like bees, but it is easy to draw them off with a little honey—another place of worship. The present synagogue, with a few alterations, can then be converted into a Communist youth center."

"Very interesting."

"The whole thing can be done quietly. There must be an old building somewhere in a side street where the Jews can congregate. As a matter of fact," he added, thinking that he might be able to soften the blow, "I would be willing to expedite the entire matter personally. It is a delicate job, but I think I can do it swiftly and silently."

"An excellent suggestion, Tovarisch Kruger, and I agree with you wholeheartedly. I will leave the matter in your hands and trust to your—discretion."

CHAPTER EIGHT

Mikhail went to the synagogue before sundown. It was an old-style building which differed outwardly from all the others on the block only in one respect. Over the entrance hung two white marble tablets into which the Ten Commandments had been carved in golden letters. Inside, the Jews had already begun the afternoon prayer. Old men sat on long benches with their heads bowed over prayer books. They rocked gently back and forth and mumbled and chanted individual prayers. On the dais, before a Holy Ark of carved wood which rose against a background showing in bas-relief the city of Jerusalem and the Wailing Wall of the destroyed temple, stood an old man with a long white beard and an ancient prayer shawl wrapped about his bent shoulders. In a thin, dulcet voice, he recited the Eighteen Benedictions: "Blessed art Thou, O Lord our God and God of our fathers, God of Abraham, God of Isaac, and God of Jacob . . . ." The congregation had now risen. Mikhail, standing at the rear of the synagogue, waited for the Benedictions to end and then walked down the aisle. Men looked at him curiously. He was a stranger to this congregation, their glances said, but welcome to join in the prayer.

A red-beared man in a black skull cap came up to him and introduced himself. "I am the sexton. You are here for the first time, I see. Evening prayer will be in an hour. If you have a request to make of the congregation, please don't hesitate. We welcome you."

"I must see the trustee at once on a matter of great urgency," Mikhail said.

"The trustee?" asked the sexton. He pointed proudly with a long, thin finger. "There he is. Up front. His name is Alexandrovich. He is a Russian Jew from St. Petersburg. Over thirty years ago he came down and built this synagogue. He has been our trustee ever since. It is the will of our entire congregation. Wait, I will tell him you wish to see him."

The sexton left and returned with the trustee, a tall, impressive man with a stern face and small gray beard. His voice was surprisingly mild.

"The sexton tells me that you wish to see me on an urgent matter."

"Yes. I would like to see you in private. I should prefer the congregation not to hear what I have to say."

"A secret?" The trustee smiled. "If it concerns the synagogue, we have no secrets here. Besides, what secrets would a young stranger have for an old man like me? But if you insist—"

They went to a corner and Mikhail said, "My name is Mikhail Kruger. I am here on official business for the Party and the Soviet government and I want you to listen very carefully to what I have to say."

"I understand," said the trustee, growing very pale.

"Very well. Opposite the synagogue is a Soviet school. The pupils are being educated as free citizens unencumbered by superstition or any kind of religious influence. It has now been ruled that your synagogue interferes with the development of the children. They can see you at your prayers and sometimes they can hear you. This distracts them. Apart from this, you are considered a bourgeois influence. My orders are therefore to advise you that you must move out. This building will be converted into a club for young Communists. We have also made provisions for your congregation and are offering you a location in Grodney Alley. Try to understand that there is nothing personal in this. I am only carrying out orders."

Alexandrovich listened, his figure erect and his face waxen. When Mikhail had finished, he replied bitterly,

"You are, in other words, a commissar." His voice grew strident. "For thirty years I have been trustee of this synagogue. I built it with my own hands. Now you come here and ask me to destroy it in one second. Why? We were here long before the Soviet school. If the authorities find our presence an inconvenience, why don't they open the school elsewhere? We won't move, do you hear?" He was shouting now. "We will not get out!"

The old trustee turned his tear-stained face to the congregation. "My brethren," he said, his voice full of grief, "we are being evicted. You see this man? He is a Jew, but a commissar. He has orders to evict us. They have given us another location, in Grodney Alley, in a slum, where houses are like stables. You ask why? Because our worship here interferes with the education of the pupils in the Soviet school. Another decree against Jews and another outrage, this time at the hands of a Jew. When a commissar commands, we must obey."

The Jews surrounded Mikhail, waving their hands and shouting.

"A Jew! He is a defamer of Israel!"

"A traitor to his nation!"

"He is evil. Cast him out!"

Mikhail's anguish was obvious.

"Do you think this is easy for me?" he asked. "Am I not a Jew myself?"

"You are not a Jew—you are a commissar!" one of the men shouted.

"Yes, I am a commissar. And do you know what a commissar is? A blind instrument. I obey the orders of my superiors. And you will have to obey them too. Otherwise blood will be spilled. You should praise the Almighty that it is I and not someone else who came here. I at least understand your pain and sorrow. Another commissar would not have bothered with explanations, and at the slightest sign of resistance, he would have torn down the Holy Law of the Ark, trampled it with muddy boots, and thrown it into the gutter."

The Jews shuffled their feet and looked from one to another.

"There would have been arrests," Mikhail added. "In the confusion there might well have been bloodshed." Mikhail hesitated; this was such an onerous task for him. "Don't you think I am familiar with the tragedy of Jewish life?" he asked. "If I stand before you like a prophet predicting evil days, pour your hatred and wrath upon my head and then as so often before, wrap about yourselves the cloak of exile so that Judaism may survive."

Not another word was spoken. One by one the Jews went back to their seats and Mikhail again stood alone. No face was turned to him. The dusk of evening spread over the windowpanes. Then a very old man, his shoulders bent and his beard heavy with age, rose and went to the dais. He was the rabbi of the congregation. He stood before the Holy Ark and with a sigh intoned those words of faith and consolation that have come down through the ages: "And He, being merciful, forgiveth iniquity and destroyeth not. . . ."

It was the evening prayer. Mikhail, his back to the wall in the corner of the synagogue where the worshipers had left him, listened to the hum of devotion that filled the night and felt a pain he had not known before, the pain of exile. He closed his eyes and his lips moved voicelessly, repeating words he thought he had long ago forgotten, words he had once said as a child, standing next to his father in the synagogue with a prayer shawl over his shoulders.

The hum died down. Mikhail opened his eyes and saw the trustee standing before him.

"Prayers are over. We wish permission to hold a meeting," the man said quietly. "You understand that I alone cannot decide to abandon the synagogue. I must have the consent of the congregation."

"Certainly, Citizen Alexandrovich," Mikhail sighed. "You may hold your meeting and report the results tomorrow morning. In fact, I will be here with a truck to help you move."

"So soon?"

"It is better that way. I don't advise you to delay it. It is safer."

The trustee moved toward the dais. Mikhail left the synagogue, feeling the burden of yet another betrayal on his conscience.

The following morning he went by truck to the synagogue. He climbed out and walked into the building. It was packed. The Jews, wrapped in their white prayer shawls, sat waiting in devout silence. It was a clear, sunny morning, but all the lamps burned brightly and everywhere flickered wax and suet candles. Here and there a mournful stillness was broken by a muffled sob as a Jew covered his head with a prayer shawl.

Mikhail looked for the trustee but could not find him. He went from bench to bench, searching the faces that peered from under the prayer shawls, but none turned to him. The wave of revulsion that came from each phalanx of white shawls was like an icy wind. A Jew! A defamer of Israel! They had shouted it at him and it echoed again in his ears. Mikhail hurried toward the dais. He found the trustee, a tall figure drawn up corpselike beside the Ark and dressed in white from head to toe.

"I have brought the truck," said Mikhail. "I am waiting."

The trustee raised his shawl and covered his head. "We shall do as we are commanded," he said in a muffled voice. "We are here today to pay our last devotions to this spot which has been hallowed by the prayers of thirty years. This is the moment of separation."

The white figure bowed low before the Holy Ark, and the congregation as one man, bowed low in despair beneath the prayer shawls that stretched over them like a white mantle of mourning. A swell of anguish rose and filled the temple and then subsided.

The trustee and rabbi together approached the Holy Ark. The trustee swung open the doors and waited until the rabbi first took out one great scroll of the Law before he himself took out the second. Both men turned to face the congregation, the scrolls, surmounted by silver crowns, pressed to their bosoms. There was a sudden commotion. Men rose from their seats and converged on the Ark. Each took hold of what he could—a book of the Law, a volume of Talmud, a prayerbook, a silver candlestick, a silver candelabrum, or a golden wine cup. Silently bearing their precious burdens, they went out and loaded them upon the truck. When it was over, the trustee and rabbi, each carrying a sacred scroll, climbed into the rear of the truck and sat with the scrolls in their arms. Several other Jews joined them and sat guard over the mountain of holy articles. Mikhail leaped in beside the driver, waved his hand, and the truck pulled away with a clatter. Outside the vacant synagogue stood the mass of Jews, their heads shaking with sorrow and their eyes moist as the truck drew out of sight. Mikhail did not turn his head.

The next day he filed with the Party secretary a request for a two-week leave of absence, giving as his reasons poor health and a desire to visit his family. His request was granted.

CHAPTER NINE

Mikhail arrived in Moscow on the eve of the May First celebration. He dropped in on Boris for a short visit and later went on to visit General Ivanov. Then he made his way home by the most circuitous route possible in order to mull over what he had heard. With lagging pace he wandered through the streets of Moscow, strolled along the paths of the Park for Culture and Rest, and spent some time sitting on the boulevard benches. His hunch in not going directly to his own house had been right. During his absence from Moscow, Ksenia had not only stopped paying visits to the Garbers and the Ivanovs but had offered every possible excuse for declining their invitations. She had estranged herself completely from Polya and Katya and avoided meeting them altogether. She had formed new friendships with smug overbearing minor officials and their wives. He knew more or less what to expect. He was far too prepared for the changes in her to delude himself.

When he got home, he was congenial but quietly aloof and when Ksenia told him with unabashed frankness a few hours after his arrival that she could not break a previous engagement, he was almost relieved. He played with Alenka, watched the maid put him to bed, and then read far into the night before going to sleep. He did not hear Ksenia come in.

The two weeks went by quickly. Despite the unspoken estrangement between himself and Ksenia, it was a good rest for Mikhail and he felt a twinge of loneliness at the prospect of going back alone. He proposed half-heartedly to Ksenia that she return with him to Bialystok. She gave him a number of reasons for declining.

"Yes, you have convinced me," Mikhail answered and a wave of relief went through him at the way such things worked themselves out.

Before leaving for Bialystok, Mikhail invited a few of his friends over. It was an intimate gathering—a few writers, a literary critic, General Ivanov and Katya, Boris and Polya.

The conversation turned to Petya, the general's son.

"You should be proud of your son," one of the writers said to Katya. "He will be graduated from the Academy with the rank of captain instead of first lieutenant. A rare honor."

"Yes, he seems to be born for the military life," Katya replied with a note of sadness in her voice. "He takes after his father in that."

"I envy him his prowess," Mikhail said. "As you may recall, Katya, and you especially, general, I was not much of a cadet."

The general made no comment. He did not seem impressed with his son's excellence. He was, in fact, unimpressed with the whole Russian military staff. The bitter struggle with Finland had confirmed his fears and lowered the prestige of the Russian army in the eyes of the world.

Boris, who had now grown a sparse, drooping mustache, sat puffing at his pipe. He was almost a replica of Stalin in his dress, in the inflection of his speech, in his very silence. For the most part, he sat aloof with his brows furrowed. When Mikhail saw Boris get up and go into another room, he understood. Boris wanted to see him privately. He waited a few minutes and then joined him. Boris was sitting in an armchair, staring into space, the dead pipe in his hand. His face lit up somewhat when he saw Mikhail and he forced a smile.

"You are leaving for Bialystok?"

"Yes, my leave is up."

"Are you writing?"

"No. I haven't the time."

"Too bad. Do you want to be released from the assignment?"

"Yes. Can you do something?"

"You know that I am always ready to help. It's a pity they had to turn you into a Party bureaucrat. Your job is writing and we consider you one of our best. What you are doing is ridiculous."

"Don't blame it on me, Boris. I was mobilized for this work. Party discipline, you know."

"I know. The Party will simply have to demobilize you and you will obey the order." He sucked at the dead pipe. "Likewise Party discipline."

"I'd like nothing better."

"Tell me, Mikhail," Boris asked suddenly, "is Ksenia's mother a reliable person?"

"Why do you ask?"

"I think that Polya, Katya, and your Ksenia ought to spend the summer out there. I understand that Krasney-Bor is a beautiful village with parks, a picturesque river, and an excellent climate. Why should they sweat all summer in the Moscow heat?"

"It doesn't sound like a bad idea but Ksenia expects to spend the summer in Moscow. I offered to take her to Bialystok and she argued that if we kept the apartment locked up too long, we might lose it. You know it happens now and then."

"Don't be a fool, Mikhail. Your apartment is perfectly safe. Besides, I will have you released from your assignment and you will be back in short order. I would like you to consider this as final. The women go to Krasney-Bor this summer and we will live it up in Moscow like a couple of bachelors."

Mikhail felt that something important was in the wind and he wanted to know what it was.

"I am curious," he said quietly, "about this sudden idea to have Ksenia and Polya leave Moscow. And why do you include Katya? I cannot answer for her. Why not speak to Ivan yourself? Is anything wrong? Are the women in any difficulty?"

"They are, but not in the way you think." Boris slowly lit his pipe and puffed away for a few seconds while Mikhail stared at him. "You see," he went on, lowering his voice, "we may be going to war. That is why I want the women out."

"But why send our wives to Krasney-Bor?"

"Krasney-Bor would never be bombed. It has no military value."

"I suppose you are right, Boris, and I will suggest it to Ksenia, although you know she is not on very close terms with Polya and Katya these days."

"Leave the persuasion to me," Boris said, rising, "I just wanted to be sure Ksenia's mother was reliable."

Mikhail left Moscow in a bleak mood. It was a day's journey to Bialystok and he spent most of it looking out the window. The roads were jammed with military vehicles carrying troops, supplies, and equipment—all moving west. There were also long lines of freight cars loaded with sugar, wheat, oil, and butter—all destined for Germany, under the terms of the non-aggression pact. One way or another, it was madness and Mikhail gave up trying to figure it out.

In Bialystok all was quiet. Mikhail returned to his work in the Culture and Propaganda office without enthusiasm. He waited each day for the orders of his release to arrive, but weeks went by and there was still no word from the Central Committee in Moscow. He grew impatient about Boris' ability to get him out. Perhaps Boris had in inflated notion of his own powers. He even began to wonder whether he ought to put any stock in Boris' tale of possible war. Boris, he decided, was unnerved by overwork and prostrated by the fear of committing the slightest sin against Stalin.

Early in June he received a letter from Ksenia. It came as a surprise. She wrote that she and Alenka, and Polya and Katya would be in Krasney-Bor until the end of summer. Apparently a new wing had been added to her mother's cottage.

Mikhail understood the significance of this news in a flash. He rushed out and a few minutes later confronted the Party secretary.

"You have my discharge certificate, Tovarisch?"

The Party secretary smiled and slapped him on the back. "What's your hurry? Don't you like it here, Tovarisch Kruger? We need you for a while yet."

"You haven't answered my question. Do you have my discharge?"

"Of course I have it, Tovarisch," the secretary answered suavely. "It arrived some time ago, but you know how things are. The work of the Party comes first. I interpreted the certificate not as an order but merely as a confirmation of your privilege to leave us. I thought it necessary, for Party reasons, to keep you here another few weeks. We have a number of highly important jobs coming up."

"The devil take your important jobs!" Mikhail shouted,

white with rage. "If you think the Kremlin doesn't know its business, why don't you call up and say so? If it saw fit to recall me, you had no right to keep me here. I ought to bring you up on charges!"

The secretary's fat, greasy face went green. It had been a mistake. Only a man with pull in the Kremlin would have opened up like that and made such a threat. He cringed and began to plead,

"Mikhail Grigorevich, do not misjudge me. Can you blame me if I love you like a brother and wanted to hold on to you? I will be happy to consider anyone you recommend, but you know there isn't anyone else around here who can manage the Culture and Propaganda section. They are all blockheads and each more illiterate than the next. You are a scholar. I am terribly sorry to see you go."

Mikhail's anger subsided and he realized that they ought to part on friendly terms. There would be reports by the secretary, summations and evaluations, and these would go into the record. He extended his hand.

"Tovarisch, it is my turn to apologize. We are all human. I was hasty and lost sight of our prime objective—the success of our Party work. What you did was entirely justified and I would have done the same. However, rest assured that my release is based on important considerations or the Kremlin would not have seen fit to authorize it. I am not at liberty to say more. It has been a privilege and a great personal pleasure to have been able to assist you in your work."

The secretary smiled broadly and squeezed Mikhail's hand. "Tovarisch Kruger," he said, "if I was sorry to lose you before, I am doubly sorry now. But we must face realities."

He went with Mikhail to the door and shook his hand several times in parting.

PART FIVE

The Eleventh Plague

CHAPTER ONE

Having missed the through train to Moscow and preferring not to wait for the next one, Mikhail decided to return via Minsk, where he could make connections with the Moscow Express. On June 21 he boarded the Minsk train and sat back with a sense of relief to be leaving Bialystok. He watched the rolling landscape slide by. It seemed peaceful enough. He peered into the sky; it was blue and utterly innocent, yet something in the air gave him a sense of foreboding. When night fell, he rolled into his berth fully dressed and tried to sleep. He was alone in his compartment and it made him feel peculiarly deserted and fearful, although he knew that a few steps away were many passengers—army officers, Party officials, commissars, and others. He tossed for several hours. When he finally slept, he reeled into a nightmare. Huge trumpets blared and blazing boulders fell from the sky. He sat up, drenched in a cold sweat.

But it was no dream. The train was speeding into the milk-white dawn and above brown steel birds flew, their rigid, outstretched wings bearing the sign of the swastika. The air was filled with a crescendo of long, piercing wails. The fields on both sides of the train were erupting in puffs of smoke, flying earth, and rocks. In the train, pandemonium had broken loose. There were roars, screams, and desperate cries of "War!"

The soldiers and the G.P.U. train wardens ran from car to car shouting: "Keep calm! No provocations! Anyone spreading false rumors will be shot! Keep away from the windows."

Mikhail lurched out of his berth and sprang into the aisle. Unaware that he was polishing the order of merit on his lapel with the palm of his hand, he approached a G.P.U. officer, a lieutenant who fixed his eyes on Mikhail's order and came to attention.

"I was fast asleep," said Mikhail, with a great pretense at calm. "Can you tell me what happened?"

"We don't know yet," the officer replied. "We will find out when we get to Minsk."

"How soon will that be?"

"In an hour or so, if all goes well." He bent forward, peered out of the window and scanned the sky. "They are gone for now. As I said, we might know in an hour."

Quiet was restored. The train moved ahead at top speed. The sun rose and passengers began to pull their packs and valises from the racks. A half hour from Minsk they passed through lovely suburban villages set amidst fragrant wheat-fields and seas of swaying corn.

But the skies above Minsk were filled with smoke and flames. Craning their necks out of the open windows, the passengers watched the flames and billowing smoke mount skyward. The train slowed down and finally came to a halt a few miles from the city limits. The passengers, groaning or babbling incoherently, waited for orders. These were not long in coming. The G.P.U. commander made his decision and the word was passed from car to car: "All out!"

The mass of men, women, and children began to alight, dragging out their packs and valises and dumping them beside the track. When all were out, the G.P.U. commander swung himself up on the locomotive steps and made himself heard.

"The train stays here," he shouted. "We don't know what's going on and therefore we cannot tell you, but we can no longer guarantee your safety on this train. You are on your own from this moment. Proceed as you can. I want no panic. Spread no false rumors!"

There was not a road in sight—nothing but empty fields and the parallel rails that led to a burning city. The passengers, loaded down with their earthly goods like beasts of burden, took the path of least resistance—the narrow, silvery tracks.

Mikhail had little to carry beyond a light overnight bag containing a change of clothing and a leather portfolio with personal documents. He could cover ground easily. What lay ahead of him he already guessed. The large crowd of passengers descending on the city might be rounded up and detained both for their own safety or for security reasons. He therefore forged ahead and in a little while found himself striding alone down the rails. He walked rapidly and steadily until the sweat poured down his face and back and his hands grew hot and clammy. After three miles or so, he left the rails for a road, and a half hour later was in Minsk. He stopped to look around him. There had been no destruction where he was, but the restaurants and stores were all closed or boarded up. People were hurrying in all directions. Suddenly the sky was full of Messerschmitts and Fokkers and he heard the wail of falling bombs.

The earth shook with great tremors. Mikhail began to run. Huge craters were torn up out of the streets, houses blew up and filled the air with bricks, mortar, and flaming splinters. As he ran, Mikhail heard the cries of terror and the shrieks of the wounded. He leaped over still, crumpled bodies; he fell, got up, and ran some more. Desperately his eyes sought for a hiding place, a cellar, even a hole in the ground. All around him were men, women, and children running for their lives. At last he found a cellar, crashed his way into a dense mass of humans, and was followed by a surge of bodies that squeezed him almost into unconsciousness.

Suddenly he realized that there was no real safety here. A near miss would entomb them under tons of brick and steel. He shoved his way out and emerged into the open street. The sky was still full of German planes. A mass of Russian soldiers were streaming through the city, frantic with fear, ripping off insignias, stars, braids, and every sign of rank or military identification. From every direction came confused cries:

"The German tanks are in the city!"

"The Germans are on our heels. Run for your lives!"

"It's a blitz. Every man for himself!"

Mikhail saw soldiers stop civilians in the street, tear the clothes off their backs and take to their heels as disguised civilians. A blast nearby shook him out of his trance and he began to run. Where he ran did not matter, as long as it was in the general direction of Moscow. He ran until he gasped and the pain in his side became unbearable. Suddenly he came to a halt and looked at his empty hands. The valise and the portfolio were both gone. He imagined he had dropped them as he hurtled into the cellar. They might as well have been at the bottom of hell. He started running again.

Somehow he found the railroad station. It was a blazing inferno. He turned and headed in another direction, trying to seize some idea, some hope. There were freight cars somewhere—yes, he remembered now; they were ten miles outside Minsk in the direction of Moscow. But they would be used for the evacuation of women and children. He himself would only be ordered to the military commissariat to report for duty, regardless of his city of residence. The thought sobered him and he stopped, wiped his brow, and tried to imagine where the military commissariat might lie.

There was a sudden intensification of air action. Then the German formations turned and headed west, leaving the city in flames and rubble. Mikhail stumbled through the gutted street. Government stores gaped with enormous holes, their walls caved in and the window fronts shattered. Clothes, bread, sewing machines, butter, sugar, and iron beds were half-buried under the piles of glass splinters, bricks, dirt, and burning beams. People were prowling feverishly among the ruins, foraging for food. As he watched this open looting of government stores, Mikhail recalled vividly what he and Boris and the old gang had done for a crust of bread in the days of hunger on the Moldevanka.

He was terribly hungry. Stepping in among the ruins, he rummaged for food, coming up with a loaf of white bread and a piece of liverwurst, both sticky with ash and grime. He did not try to clean them—it would have been useless—but stood there in the gutter munching them. No one stopped to notice him.

After resting a while, he stuffed what was left of the food into his pockets and renewed his search for the military commissariat. What he found was a large, three-story building which had suffered a direct hit. The building sagged as if about to collapse. The windows had been blown out and the doors ripped off. Through the holes in the walls he could see the gutted rooms, splintered furniture, and countless documents scattered about. Over the entrance hung a large dirty placard hurriedly lettered:

THE MILITARY COMMISSARIAT HAS EVACUATED TO NEW QUARTERS IN THE VILLAGE OF LIPO, NEAR SMOLIVICHI. EVERY MALE BETWEEN THE AGES OF 17 AND 47 IS TO PROCEED WITHOUT DELAY AND REPORT TO MILITARY HEADQUARTERS IN LIPO FOR SERVICE IN THE RED ARMY IN DEFENSE OF THE MOTHERLAND. ALL THOSE WHO FAIL TO OBEY THIS ORDER WILL BE SHOT AS TRAITORS AND DESERTERS AND ENEMIES IN COLLABORATION WITH THE FASCISTS

A large group of men, the majority of military age, stood around the placard. They read it over and over but no one made a move. There was a good deal of shoulder shrugging.

"It's a wild goose chase," one said.

"Who knows if they are still in Lipo?" said another.

"That's only twenty miles away. I don't believe it. Those cowards must have run at least sixty."

"Right. Take a look at those threats. They are brave enough when it comes to shooting Russians."

"Fascists! My my, what bad words they use. Why, only yesterday they ripped out our tongues for using them because Hitler and Stalin had signed a pact of friendship."

"Brothers," said one, "let us be practical. It will be dark soon and we might as well sleep here. We can't go looking for headquarters in the dark. We can decide by morning. As the saying goes: 'Morning is wiser than the night before.' "

It was some kind of solution and in short order the men had distributed themselves around the building, most of them in the courtyard and garden. Mikhail sat down under a tree on the curb and was joined by a youngish man whose face had a strong Caucasian cast. He introduced himself as a Ukrainian, an agronomist by profession. His name was Andrei Krivoshapko. He seemed not at all depressed.

"Tovarisch, stop worrying, everything will turn out fine in the end," he assured Mikhail. "The devil is not as bad as he is painted. I am not even sure that this is a real war. It is some kind of misunderstanding, or a blunder. They will kiss and make up in a few days, don't you think?"

Mikhail smiled. He liked this man who spoke words of encouragement but he was dead tired and had no desire to answer. He fell asleep with his back against the tree trunk and Krivoshapko, after gazing a while at Mikhail, stretched out on the ground nearby.

CHAPTER TWO

Mikhail woke at dawn to the sound of terrific explosions. The German dive bombers were over the city again. He stared up at Krivoshapko, who stood over him with a tranquil smile on his lips.

"War!" Krivoshapko said softly. There was a sort of pious contentment or a poetic wisdom in his tone—Mikhail could not tell which.

"You seem almost happy about it," Mikhail said.

Krivoshapko lowered his eyes and a gentle shyness spread over his handsome face. Yet in his proud, slender body endowed with a peculiar feline grace, there was an undercurrent of strength.

"Happy? No. But do you think our tears will wash it away? If it is our destiny, this war will become the eleventh plague."

"The eleventh plague?" Mikhail repeated in astonishment. "What do you mean?"

"You said you are a Jew. Don't you remember the ten plagues God brought down upon Pharaoh's Egypt?" Krivoshapko sighed. "We might add this war as the eleventh plague on Stalin's Russia."

Mikhail got to his feet. Men, women, and children were dashing about wildly with unwieldy loads on their backs, crying:

"The Germans are everywhere!"

"Bialystok and Lvov are gone!"

"German tanks are in Minsk!"

"They are arresting and killing everyone, especially Jews!"

"Run for your lives!"

Mikhail watched the mass of streaming fugitives. "We had better move on to Lipo," he said. He scanned the courtyard of the building. It was empty.

"Where are all the friends we had last night?" he asked Krivoshapko. "It's time we got started."

Krivoshapko gave him a childlike smile. "You are naïve," he said. "They all ran out hours ago. Some of them simply disappeared. Others marched out after contingents of the Red Army that came through during the night."

"Retreating Red Army units?" Mikhail queried. "Did they have full equipment?"

"Yes."

"Why, then, didn't they turn and fight?"

"It's a good question. I guess no one wants to fight, at least not yet. There is nothing to fight for."

"You can't mean that!"

"But I do. You may be older in years, my friend, but you sound young, too young, and must have lived a sheltered life. Don't misunderstand me. I am not saying that your life was a bed of roses, but compared to life as we know it, yours must have been sheltered. That is why you don't understand that they have nothing to fight for. Look at the facts. This is not the orderly retreat of a vanquished army. It is not even a rout. It is a vast mob of uniformed men trying desperately to remain alive. Many of them would kill to get their hands on a suit of civilian clothes and probably have. Thousands have deserted and thrown away their arms and identifications. This reminds me that you ought to unpin that bauble, the glorious insignia on your jacket, and be prepared to destroy your papers at a moment's notice. Come. We must get out of here."

"Where can we go?"

"Anywhere. All I know is that too many people are coming through. The Germans can't be very far away. Or do you prefer to stay?"

"It would be suicide. I am a Jew and a Communist. They will hang me from the tallest tree."

"You? A Jew?" Krivoshapko was surprised. "You certainly don't look it. Anyway—as I was about to say—your little red banner would be your death warrant. On the other hand, it might be a good idea to carry it in your pocket. You can always throw it away if you smell danger, but if we meet with a semblance of Soviet authority along the road, you can pin it on again. It might command enough respect to get us a ride on a truck or train. If we run into Germans, you will have no papers or identification, and we will both swear that you are neither a Jew nor a Communist. In fact, you are a Russian of Russians. Look at me. I look Caucasian but I am Ukrainian. It was an idiot who invented races. People intermingled thousands of years ago during the great migrations. No area on the globe has a distinct race. Jews are Egyptian, Babylonian, Greek, Roman and everything else in the world although they still call themselves Jews. The Russians and Ukrainians are Mongol, Tartar, Swedish, German, and French. The Germans themselves are no exception and—"

"Krivoshapko, I beg of you, this is no time to philosophize. You are not being practical. You have papers and can always prove who you are. I don't dare produce my papers."

"You worry too much. Thousands of people will lose their papers in this panic. It is expected and natural. Our accents are native and we look native. If we fall into German hands it might be better to have no papers."

They joined the stream of fleeing inhabitants. Wave after wave of planes flew overhead, strafing and bombing the city to soften it up for the invasion of tanks and infantry. Mikhail and Krivoshapko tried to keep a steady pace, marshaling their strength for the long journey ahead.

"Tell me something, Krivoshapko. Why didn't you leave with the others last night when the Red Army came through?"

"I didn't want to leave you alone."

"You could have awakened me."

"I didn't have the heart. You were enjoying your sleep too much."

Mikhail laughed. "Why are you so interested in me? You don't know me."

"Do you have to know someone in order to help him?"

"Who are you?"

"My name, profession, and nationality you know. You have by now guessed that I am not in the Party. My faith you would perhaps not understand. I am a Christian who also believes in the Jewish and Moslem religions. All religions are alike to me if they uphold one God and only one God. I am of the faithful. I know that God is One. But I also believe in man and in the son of man whom God has created. Man was made in the image of God but who has seen God's image? It is a secret and its color is a secret. Is it white, black, brown, red, yellow, or all colors combined? In the face of this secret, all men are equal and it is this equality which commands men to love and help one another. You are a commissar. Yesterday you could have jailed or even shot me for preaching religion. Today, in the face of death, we are equals. We need each other. It is the finger of God already restoring the balance in things both great and small and it brings me joy. This is my faith."

The earth quaked under their feet. A house seemed to rise in the air and spring apart with a horrendous blast of flame and smoke. It was close. They were both hurled to the ground and lay stunned for a while. When it was over they got up and plodded ahead.

"You know, Krivoshapko," Mikhail said, resuming the conversation as though nothing had happened, "I have met many people in my time but you are the first to express such strange ideas to me."

'I have other ideas, too. About languages, for example. I studied Latin, Greek, English, French, Hebrew, and German. I wanted to feel the taste of each language. What I found was that they used different sounds for the same human ends and I came to the conclusion that what the world needs is a universal language that would help erase the illusion of separation."

"This is an impressive philosophy," Mikhail laughed. The planes still droned overhead, but the explosions were less frequent now. Perhaps they are out of bombs, Mikhail thought.

"It is the philosophy of the world citizen," Krivoshapko declared, "and it is based on the concept of world government. It is the only way to abolish wars."

"It sounds utopian."

"Of course it is utopian! What is Socialism if not some kind of Utopia? And what about the belief in a life beyond death or in resurrection? You seem amazed that millions of intelligent and educated people put their faith in Utopias. But you are shortsighted. Take these aircraft which fly in the heavens and hurl death and destruction upon cities and upon the innocent. A mere fifty or sixty years ago they were a vision of the future."

Mikhail did not answer. He was tiring. It had been two terrible days. He still had no idea where the Germans were. He listened as he trudged ahead. He heard that new word "Blitzkrieg" repeatedly, that the Germans were invincible and were taking city after city, that the Red Army was flying like chaff before the wind and that in a week Hitler would march triumphantly into Moscow.

They passed the outskirts of the city and a few miles farther came to the prison, one wing of which was in flames. The iron cell locks had been ripped off and the prisoners herded into the prison yard. There must have been about a thousand of them. By the time Mikhail and Krivoshapko reached the spot, they had to push their way through a vast crowd which buzzed with rumors that the prisoners were being transported to a safe place.

The prisoners were being sorted into three groups—criminals, political offenders, and the sick and wounded. The prison officials, their aides, the guards, and the G.P.U. agents marched up and down shouting orders in tense, sharp voices, trying to organize and start the evacuation before the Germans staged another bombing raid. Finally columns of prisoners emerged from the yard surrounded by guards and moved away in the direction of the asphalt highway that led from Minsk toward Moscow. The refugees fell in behind them.

A few moments later, from the rear of the long column of refugees, came the sound of volleys of shots. Mikhail knew that the political prisoners were being executed in mass for fear they might revolt or help the Germans against the Soviet regime. But there was little time even for murder. More planes were coming toward them from the west.

"Hit the ground!" Krivoshapko yelled.

There was a desperate and futile scramble for the roadside and the fields bordering the road. Everything served as protection—a tree, a rock, or a hole in the ground. Most of the column did not make it in time. The planes swooped down and, in a single strafing pass, sprayed death over a long path with a sort of horrible objectivity. Then they continued on their way.

When the road filled up again there was no longer any distinction between prisoners and non-prisoners. The prison column had been dissolved among the people in the panic. The chief warden now performed his last official act. Climbing on top of an overturned wagon, he bellowed that in view of the emergency he could not guarantee safe transfer to a location immune to German air raids and therefore exercised his right under these conditions to declare an amnesty to all prisoners. Every man was to save his life as he thought best. They were free.

It was an empty gesture. None of the prisoners had tried to escape anyway. Where would they go? Now, as before, they clung to the armed guards, who now became the pathetic shepherds of a terrified flock.

Fear had glued the column together, but fatigue soon thinned it out. In two hours of steady marching under a hot sun, a small legion of the strong forged ahead and the rest of the column fell behind, strung out along the road. Mikhail was able to count in the hardcore group a few dozen prisoners, the warden, a few guards, and about a score of others, including a few women, some of them with children strapped to their backs. He turned pantingly to Krivoshapko.

"We are less than a hundred. You said war was an equalizer. Do you still think so?"

"I didn't say it equalized everything. If it did, there would be peace, not war."

Some hours later, with dusk approaching, they were more than twenty miles out of Minsk. The warden, who still felt himself to be in authority, called a halt and announced that they would spend the night in the forest a few hundred yards from the side of the road.

They settled down under trees, crept behind bushes and rocks and slid into gullies. A few even dug foxholes for themselves. Darkness fell and the hours passed. From time to time a dull, distant explosion came to their ears. Far away, over the city of Minsk, hung a dense, red glow.

Mikhail and Krivoshapko lay under a tree. Nearby was a

whimpering child. Someone groaned in pain. A snore went up from behind a clump of bushes.

Krivoshapko sighed. "Ah, Russia, Russia! Our poor, miserable Russia!"

"And yet," answered Mikhail, "Russia will survive. Do you remember Napoleon?"

"Yes, I know. Infinite Russia is invincible. But this is not only its greatest strength—it is also its greatest weakness."

"I don't understand."

"People are accustomed to think of Russia as the largest country in the world because it takes in a sixth of the earth's surface. But there is more illusion than reality in this. Those who glibly use the word "Russia" fail to see that it is an enormous empire composed of many peoples, large and small, each of whom has a natural yearning for autonomy and independence. The Ukraine is not Russia, the Caucasus is not Russia, nor is Turkestan, nor Siberia with its conglomeration of oriental peoples. Now that the Kremlin has sunk up to its neck in a great war, would it be wrong for these peoples to recover the territories which the Tsars conquered and engulfed?"

Mikhail nodded sleepily.

"Let the Kalmyks, Chuvashes, Kamchadales, and Golds take back the Urals and Siberia," Krivoshapko continued. "Let the Uzbeks, Kirghizes, Turkomans, and Tadjiks repossess Turkestan. Let the Tartars recover the Crimea and Kazan area. Let the peoples of the Caucasus—the Georgians, Armenians, Glizgins, Ossets, and Abkhazes—declare their national and political independence. White Russia and the Ukraine are ready to tear away from Russia now. And if the Chinese would demand what once belonged to them—the Khabarovsk and Vladivostok areas, then Russia itself would be no larger than Italy or France and would no longer be a world power."

"How true!" Mikhail said and then, hungry, cold, and utterly exhausted, he fell asleep.

When he awoke, the sun was shining brightly through the lattice of branches and leaves and people were milling about them beating the bushes, peering behind rocks and trees, looking for something.

"What's up?" asked Mikhail, getting to his feet.

"It's obvious," answered Krivoshapko, stretching and gazing up at the shimmering foliage. "The shepherds have abandoned the flock. The warden and guards sneaked off during the night. You might say they have left us as bait for the Germans."

They could hear the sounds of havoc far down the open road as mechanized forces—they could not tell whose, but they moved too slowly to be retreating—advanced toward them. Krivoshapko lay with his ear to the ground. Mikhail crawled over to him. "What are you doing?" he asked.

Krivoshapko got to his feet. "Listen, everybody!" he shouted to the small group which had clustered around them. "If you value your lives, listen carefully. The Germans are coming and they will be here in a few minutes. They know the woods are full of people all along the line and they might decide to reconnoiter this area because the woods are especially thick here. If they find us we will have to surrender, naturally. Understand that there are no Jews or Communists among us. We will tell them that we are all convicts who were taken out of Minsk prison, dumped into this forest and abandoned by our wardens. All women, children, and those who look like Jews will have to hide. We must stick to this story. We are all in the same boat. One false move and we are all dead. If we help each other, God will help us all. I will now explain my plan." He turned to Mikhail and whispered, "You have no time to lose. Dump your papers."

Mikhail stepped deeper into the woods, emptied his pockets except for a penknife, and ripped his decoration from his coat. He dug a hole with a sharp stone behind a tree, threw everything in, refilled it with earth and stamped it smooth with his feet. Then he found a large rock and heaved it on top of the spot. With the knife he carved two tiny initials into the tree-trunk—M.K. As he worked he heard the clank and clatter of advancing tanks and by the time he got back they were already in sight and he could make out the brown helmets of the German troops walking behind them. In a few minutes the whole formation was abreast of them. Then suddenly one tank detached itself from the rest and made for the forest, its guns belching fire. Shells crashed into the trees somewhere behind them. Everyone threw himself to the ground. Krivoshapko and two convicts crawled out into the clearing and waved white handkerchiefs at the tank. It edged forward cautiously, coming nearer and nearer until it was almost on top of them. The three men did not budge. Finally it came to a halt. A German officer lifted himself out and barked in bad Russian:

"Who are you? Speak fast!"

"Mein Herr," said Krivoshapko in German, "we are convicts who slaved in the Minsk prison for those cursed Communists. Last night they dumped us out here and took off before daybreak like a bunch of scared rabbits. We welcome you as liberators and ask for your protection."

"Jawohl!" The German brought his hand to his steel helmet in a sharp salute. Then he sprang to the ground, drew out his revolver, took a few steps into the forest and peered about him. The convicts—about thirty of them—tattered and dirty, stood together like a human shield against what might lie behind them in the forest. It was a tense moment. His revolver half-raised, the German glared at the convicts. But the stratagem had worked. His eyes were no longer roving. After a few moments he straightened up, laughed and put away the revolver, at the same time waving his left hand in a gesture of assurance at the man inside the tank.

"I see," he said. "Very well. In the name of the Führer, Adolf Hitler, I hereby declare all convicts of the Minsk prison to be free men, subject to the dictates of the German Reich. You may go as you will. Heil Hitler!"

"Heil Hitler!" they all shouted together.

The German crawled into the tank. It rumbled back to the road, turned in the direction of Moscow and moved ahead at a surprising speed past long lines of marching infantry.

Some of the group now took the highway toward Moscow, reasoning that there were more German troops behind them than in front of them. Others started back toward Minsk, thinking that since it was already conquered territory there would be no fighting. A few decided to risk starvation in the forest in the hope that somehow the situation would clear up.

Krivoshapko looked quizzically at Mikhail. "We have three alternatives. Each is a dead man's choice. Which, my good friend, strikes your fancy most?"

Mikhail shrugged his shoulders. "Let us go back to Minsk."

"It suits me," said Krivoshapko, also shrugging his shoulders.

CHAPTER THREE

They walked back together. When they arrived in Minsk, they found whole sections of the city devastated. The wooden cottages of the poorer sections were heaps of smoldering cinders, only their red-brick chimneys stood, like monuments in a graveyard. Corpses lay everywhere, strewn at random. However Soviet Street, Minsk's main thoroughfare, had come through the holocaust relatively intact. One wing of the imposing administration building had been completely gutted and Lenin's statue was now just two feet on a pedestal, but most of the building still stood. Truckloads of German soldiers armed with automatic rifles patrolled the area.

Surrender was the order of the day. Russian girls strolled arm-in-arm with German officers. The people who had refused to leave the city—Great Russians, White Russians, Ukrainians, and Poles alike—and the peasants of surrounding villages and kolkhozes bowed low to their conquerors and crossed themselves. "Thank God," they seemed to say, "we are free at last from Stalin's yoke, his kolkhozes, his G.P.U." Little did they know what lay ahead.

Mikhail and Andrei found a habitable room in a half-ruined house and settled down. The two men lived frugally on the little money they had left and waited for developments. As the weeks passed, their clothes became seedier. Their shoes wore out. Their faces became covered with stubble, then with full beards.

For the most part they stayed in their room, bored, depressed, and waiting for a miracle to happen. Inaction was sapping their patience. They listened eagerly to whispered rumors that the Red Army was about to stage a counterattack, but the German radio commentators and the collaborationist Russian press kept boasting and confirming one another by saying that the German armies were at the gates of Moscow and Leningrad, and that one-half of the Soviet Union had been conquered. It was easy to believe that the war was lost. The two men began to feel hopeless.

"We must find some way to escape," Mikhail finally said after a day of brooding.

"We can't use the roads. They are filthy with German patrols and it would be suicide. If we are caught trying to sneak through, we will be shot as spies."

"But I've got to get through. I've got to find my wife and son. I sent them to Krasney-Bor. Are they still there or did they escape to Moscow? And is Moscow still in Russian hands? Only God knows!"

"You said that your wife is Ukrainian. As yet the Germans are not molesting Ukrainians and Russians unless they put up resistance or are partisans."

"My wife is a Communist. My son has a Jewish father."

"I know how desperate you must feel, Mikhail, but try to get hold of yourself. There may be another way out. It strikes me that there are others like us and if we started looking, we would find them. I am thinking of an underground escape route, perhaps through the Polesia Forest."

"But they say the forests are full of partisans who are fighting the Germans. We risk getting involved, maybe even getting shot by the partisans for refusing to join. I would gladly join them but all I want right now is to get through to my family. I want to know that they are safe. I pray that they are still alive."

"Then let us wait until we can find out a few things."

They began to wander daily through the streets. They learned nothing, but they agreed it was better than wasting away in a room. Then one day they found an announcement which the Germans had posted on telephone poles and buildings. It was printed in three languages—Russian, Yiddish, and German:

ALL JEWS MUST ABANDON THEIR HOMES AND ALL PERSONAL BELONGINGS BY JULY 20, 1941, AND REPORT TO THE GHETTO ON THE OUTSKIRTS OF MINSK. THE NAME OF EACH PERSON OF JEWISH ORIGIN WILL BE REGISTERED AND HE WILL RECEIVE A YELLOW STAR OF DAVID. AFTER SEPTEMBER 3 ANY

JEW FOUND OUTSIDE THE GHETTO OR WITHOUT THE STAR OF DAVID WILL BE SHOT AT ONCE.

ALL RESIDENTS OF MINSK ARE HEREBY ORDERED TO CO-OPERATE IN THIS MATTER. ANY PERSON OF CHRISTIAN OR ARYAN ORIGIN CONCEALING OR HELPING TO CONCEAL A JEW WILL BE SHOT AS AN ENEMY OF THE THIRD REICH.

Mikhail looked at Krivoshapko. "This is it," he said bitterly.

"Do not lose faith, Mikhail. God will help us."

"Us? You are not a Jew. There is no reason for you to suffer."

"We are all human beings."

"No, a Jew is not a human being. Hitler has ordered our extermination."

"Snap out of it, Mikhail! No one need know who you are. I guarantee you we will escape. I feel it in my bones."

For three days Mikhail and Andrei mingled with the crowds on the pavement and numbly watched the Jews moving toward the ghetto, the old, the sick, the pregnant, the sad-eyed children. It was like a national holiday; the turnout was greater than at a public funeral. And the public made itself heard.

"Down with the dirty Jews!"

"Hurrah for the Jews wearing the Order of the Yellow Rag!"

"Kill the Jews and save Russia!"

A few ran into the gutter and struck the refugees with their fists. Krivoshapko seized Mikhail's arm and pulled him out of the crowd. They began to walk slowly away. Suddenly Mikhail left Krivoshapko's side and turned back.

"Hold on," cried Krivoshapko. "Where are you going?"

"To the ghetto," Mikhail called over his shoulder. "These are my people."

Krivoshapko stared after him. "Stop, Mikhail!" he shouted. "Wait for me!"

He caught up and grasped Mikhail's hand. "I am going with you."

Mikhail stopped, turned his head and looked gratefully at Krivoshapko. "No," he said. "I am going alone. I must. Goodbye. You are a good man and I will never forget you."

"I am still going with you."

"What for? You are not a Jew. You don't have to suffer,"

"Very well, then. I am going with you as a protest to a world that has permitted Hitler to do with people as he does."

"Another Utopian idea?"

"Apart from which," Krivoshapko went on sadly, "I am alone. I have no one. All I could do is wander again. My mind is made up."

Mikhail studied him, then nodded his head. "All right. We go in together."

It was evening when they arrived. The ghetto was nothing but a few streets marked off on the city's outskirts bordering the marshy Polesia Forest. The miserable, ramshackle houses were crammed with Jews—old and middle-aged men, women of all ages, and children. For them the order of life had ceased; soon, life itself would end.

Mikhail and Krivoshapko squeezed their way into one of the houses. The stench was unbearable and there was no floor space. They got out and wandered about for an hour before deciding to stretch out on the stony earth near the house. The two friends found a bit of ground free of stones and overgrown with low weeds. The weeds made it close and hot, but it was possible to breathe. Overhead was a blue, cold, transparent sky. The barbed-wire fences around the ghetto gave off lurid gleams as the Germans played spotlights on them. When the Germans were satisfied that all was in order, they turned off the lights. The ghetto was still. Terror is the enemy of sleep, but even terror succumbs to torpor and the people of the ghetto were steeped in torpor. There was no other way to survive.

The next morning they were marshaled for labor on the railroad to repair rails. After a few days working on the tracks, they were sent to the forest to saw down trees to be used as fuel for troop trains. The labor was inhuman. Each day was a miracle of survival. The Germans shot and hanged men at the slightest provocation. There were no trials—just a flat statement by the officer: "Disobedience to orders!"

One evening a German officer took from one of the ghetto children in Mikhail's house a stuffed toy which he apparently had been admiring for several days. The child, her eyes furious, ran after the officer shrieking, "Thief, thief, give me back my bear," and pounded his rigid thighs with her puny little fists.

Without emotion, the officer drew his revolver and shot her through the chest. "Jewish scum!" he muttered, looking down at the child who lay in a pool of blood, her mouth open and her innocent eyes staring in wonderment before they closed forever. He spat, turned on his heel and went off with the toy in his hand.

The incident affected Mikhail deeply. It gave him a purpose for surviving; he had to do something to help stop this inhuman brutality, something more than share the fate of his people. Dying, even in honor, was not the answer.

The German officer was found dead the next day. The Gestapo never discovered who killed him but twenty Jews were chosen at random and hanged in retaliation and their bodies left dangling from the telephone poles.

Lying in the weeds one early dawn, Mikhail told Krivoshapko, "Maxim Gorki once said that the word 'man' rings with dignity. How can I agree with him? It doesn't account for the men who destroy other men and their dignity. So far neither civilization nor religion has made man any better. He seems to get worse as time goes by."

"The world," Andrei argued, "has not yet come to an end, despite Hitler's proclamation that the Third Reich will last a thousand years. Believe me, Hitler cannot last. He is too evil. The earth will not tolerate him much longer."

They were interrupted by the roundup for the usual labor detail, the forest again. When they reached their destination a sudden, deadly fusilade came from the heart of the forest. It took the guards entirely by surprise. They fell to the ground and in that moment Mikhail and Krivoshapko, as if by common impulse, scrambled over a pile of lumber and crawled into the underbrush. The bullets whizzed over their heads and ricocheted among the trees as the guards recovered and tried to cut them down. But they were moving left and the partisans were firing more to the right. The guards had to shift their fire. In a minute the two were running like hares down a winding forest path and away from the sound of battle. No one followed them. They ran until they could run no more. Then they broke trail, ploughed their way through heavily wooded ravines, and, finally, threw themselves into a tangle of high grass, dense bushes, and low firs. They did not stir all day. The German forest patrols would hesitate to leave the trail, but the Germans might send aircraft to bombard the area or bring out the bloodhounds. Nothing happened. When night fell, they turned eastward in a big circle, feeling their way slowly. They crossed the trail miles beyond in the dim moonlight and headed straight into the Polesia Forest marshes. Their hope was that freedom lay in that direction, even the freedom of the Soviet regime which was, by comparison to the Third Reich, a paragon of virtue.

Suddenly Mikhail stopped. Andrei looked at him in alarm.

"What's wrong, Mikhail?"

"I just remembered that for every Jew who escapes, the Germans will shoot two others."

"That is true," answered Krivoshapko sadly, nodding his head. "I didn't think of it myself. Perhaps we had no moral right to do this. It makes us accomplices to murder."

Their eyes met for a long moment. The decision, clearly, was up to Mikhail. He took Krivoshapko's arm. "Come on, Andrei," he said, "we cannot help them in the ghetto but perhaps we can help rid the world of Fascism by living to fight another day."

Together they moved deeper into the forest.

CHAPTER FOUR

Like locusts, the Wehrmacht had devoured White Russia, Latvia, Estonia, and Lithuania in its sweep toward Moscow and Leningrad. Then Hitler, saying, "My generals know nothing about the economic aspects of war," diverted the main thrust of his forces toward the Ukraine, to tap its abundant reservoirs of wheat and coal.

At Kiev, the Germans took 600,000 prisoners in a month-long battle, then resumed their march toward Moscow. The Red Army lost another 600,000 men as the Wehrmacht continued to roll eastward. By late October the personnel of the embassies and the more important government offices had been evacuated from Moscow. Looting was widespread in the capital.

Then resistance stiffened. Fresh reserves from Siberia were flung into battle and the autumn rains left both armies bogged down in mud. The attempted encirclements of Leningrad and Moscow failed. General Ivanov, who was in charge of one of Moscow's vital defense sectors, mounted a series of counter-offensives which forced the Germans to pull back.

Stalin emerged from his fortress under the Kremlin—a secret network of escape tunnels—and showed himself in the streets of Moscow. The people filled the streets of the capital shouting enthusiastically: "Father! Leader! Hero! Savior!"

At an elaborate ceremony, Stalin awarded General Ivanov, who had just been called in from the Voronezh front, a Gold Star of Heroism, pinning it on Ivanov's breast himself. There was great applause and then the guests moved on to the banquet. Ivanov mingled with the guests in the vestibule, accepting congratulations. Almost everyone was in uniform. Boris was there but he was difficult to recognize. He had grown very thin and the top of his head was bald. His eyes were deep in their sockets and his body shook from time to time with marked tremors. The three glittering orders on his chest—the Order of Lenin, the Order of the Red Labor Banner, and the Order of the Red Star—clashed sharply with his pale, drawn face and played up his obvious anguish. He walked over to Ivanov, who embraced him and spoke to him with stiff kindliness,

"You must hang on, Boris."

Boris had lost his son at Moscow and had not yet recovered from the shock. He peered into Ivanov's eyes.

"Hang on? I suppose you are right. But I can't forget. I neglected my son. He had no father in me. And when he died I could not even go to the burial because I could not leave Stalin's side. See General, here is the decoration which Stalin gave me when I told him that my son died in battle. This red star is my dead son."

"I know, Boris, I know. It is little consolation. Stalin gives them out freely these days. What else can you give? This is war. With death in every home, how will you replace life and how console the living? My own son has just been recalled to the front. He is so young to be an officer in the front lines! If this thought can console a bereaved father, let it console you, Boris. You are not alone. In this common tragedy we are all together."

"At least if Polya were here," Boris complained bitterly. "She does not know yet, but she must find out sooner or later. At least we could weep together. Not even a postcard from the village. All communications are disrupted. I don't even know whether the village is in German hands or not. And even when I pray for Polya to be near me, I'm glad she isn't. When she finds out that her son is dead, she may not survive. I have given her nothing. I mean nothing to her. Her son was her whole life."

"Enough, Boris! Enough! Stop punishing yourself."

"And what about Mikhail? Have you heard anything?"

"Not a word, Boris. He has completely disappeared. I think he must be a prisoner somewhere."

"I hope not," Boris said. "You know the Nazis have no fondness for Jews."

The bell rang and they took their separate places at the banquet table.

The next day General Ivanov left Moscow to return to the front.

The situation was critical. The Germans concentrated heavy tanks, artillery, and planes against Voronezh, attempting to cross the Don. Ivanov blew up all the bridges. The Germans tried to cross on barges but were mowed down by artillery. Yet they kept coming, using all available watercraft, including steamboats and sailboats. They were blown to bits.

A remarkable change had come over the Russians. The same soldiers who had thrown away their arms at Minsk, now hurled themselves into battle with unprecedented fury. The same peasants who had greeted the Germans as liberators now rejoiced in their annihilation. The answer was simple—they had found the Nazis more brutal, more inhuman even than the Communist dictatorship.

But the Germans refused to quit. Again and again they threw pontoon bridges across the river, only to have them obliterated by the relentless fire from shore. The waters of the Don were red with German blood and thousands of German corpses floated on the current before the Wehrmacht finally crossed the river.

Once across the Don, the Germans pressed close to Voronezh and partially outflanked it, so that a number of divisions were able to move toward Stalingrad.

General Ivanov saw the situation as critical. He seized the telephone, was put through to the Kremlin, and asked for Stalin personally. "Stalin is busy." said a voice. "He cannot come to the telephone."

"The hell you say!" shouted the general. "You go back and tell him I must speak to him. Tell him we are faced with a catastrophe!"

In his Kremlin hideaway, Stalin sat deep in a red-velvet armchair studying a colossal globe. When he was told that Ivanov still was on the telephone, he leaned forward, located the city of Voronezh and inserted a red marker. Then his finger traced the twisting blue line which was the River Don, slid toward the former city of Tsaritsin—renamed Stalingrad by his orders—and came to a stop. He spanned the distance between Voronezh and

Stalingrad with his hand, got to his feet, and turned to Boris.

"Stalingrad must be defended at all costs. Its name means everything to the Russian people. Lose Stalingrad and we lose Russia."

Boris, a mark of grief carved into his face, turned his eyes to Stalin but said nothing.

"Speak up!" Stalin snapped.

A devoted dog will never snap at its master but will gratefully lick the cruel hand that strikes it. It was this doglike devotion which made Boris so valuable to Stalin—the same devotion he himself had once lavished on Lenin, Stalin recalled only too well. He saw his own image in Boris and he hated what he saw. Boris was still silent.

"Have you got lockjaw?" Stalin asked pointedly.

Boris smiled guiltily. "There can be no question at all. It doesn't require an answer. Stalingrad, the city that bears your name, must never fall or Russia is lost."

Stalin turned from him, muttering, "Idiot. I asked for your opinion. All you can do is repeat my own words. You are useless."

Boris was in no way disturbed. He knew that for anyone to dare to disagree with Stalin was far more than useless, it was dangerous. He was well aware that no dictator tolerates opposition and that every dictator, no matter how great—and Stalin was the greatest—craves confirmation even if his own words are aped by his followers.

"Tovarisch Stalin," Boris said, "I must remind you of the message. General Ivanov is still on the telephone. He asked for you personally."

"I have no time. Go tell him that I am busy."

"He has been told that once, but he insists. His message is alarming. He is asking for reinforcements—planes, tanks, artillery. And judging by the reports of casualties, he may need several fresh divisions to hold the line."

"He is at Voronezh and he is to stay there. Tell him to hold fast at all costs. There is to be no retreat and there will be no reinforcements. I am ordering out all available forces for the defense of Stalingrad. Tell him to mobilize the entire rural population if necessary and to fight to the last soldier and civilian. Tell him that if he disobeys my orders it will cost him his head!"

Boris went out into the anteroom. The aide handed him the receiver, saluted and left.

"General Ivanov, this is Boris speaking. Boris Garber."

"Boris? Glad to hear your voice, but I asked for Stalin."

"How is it going?"

"Bad. Very bad. I must speak to Stalin."

"I understand. Colonel Matveyev gave me your message. However, Stalin cannot come to the telephone. He is too busy, but he has authorized me to transmit his orders to you. They are as follows: you are to hold Voronezh without further reinforcements. Mobilize the rural population if necessary. All reinforcements are being routed to Stalingrad."

At Voronezh military headquarters, the general staff waited impatiently for General Ivanov to report the Kremlin's reply. When he came rushing into the dugout looking like an enraged animal, they knew that it was hopeless. Ivanov stopped before the round table, looked from one man to the next, and announced his decision:

"Unless you can give me favorable reports, I am ordering a retreat. We all know what your reports have been so far. Have you anything to add?"

They spread out the military map. Seated were the other generals and division commanders. Around them stood colonels, majors, and various other officers and aides, among them General Ivanov's son, Petya, a captain in Army Intelligence.

A tank division commander, sleek, well-groomed, and clean-shaven except for a tiny moustache under his long nose, gave his report:

"Here is the latest before I return to the front. We have five tanks left. But they are equipped with small-caliber cannon and all we have left are large-caliber shells. What are we supposed to fire with?"

One of the generals spoke next. His face under the heavy steel helmet was set in grim lines and was covered by a thick, gray stubble. His uniform was filthy and drenched with sweat.

He had just come from the front where the fighting was thickest. There was mud even on his eyelids.

"I can report on my division," he said. "It no longer exists. Major Chekov died in action. He was a good commander—irreplaceable. The political commissar is a prisoner of war. I am lucky to be here." He downed a tumbler of vodka. "I am curious to know what Stalin said," he added.

"He refused to come to the phone but transmitted his orders through a confidential aide. His orders are to hold Voronezh. Stalin is my commander-in-chief and I am only responsible to him directly. I therefore consider this order unofficial and undocumented and I am making the decision. Since we cannot defend Voronezh, we will retreat."

A general with a rounded beard and spectacles took off his helmet, wiped the sweat from his gray head and declared firmly:

"With your permission, General Ivanov, orders are orders. Are you not being technical? If the decision were mine I would perhaps order a retreat. But the order is to hold the line. I can see no alternative."

Young Captain Ivanov now asked for the floor. General Ivanov nodded. For a bare moment a look of filial love shone in the young man's eyes, then vanished as he addressed himself to the business at hand.

"General Ivanov," he said respectfully, "I am convinced we can hold out."

"Fine, Captain," replied the general with dignity. "Tell me, in that case, how long we can hold out."

"General, you are far more aware of our staying powers than I am. You know we are still strong, that we have manpower and firepower. Some divisions are operating efficiently. By redistribution we can bring our divisions to three-quarter strength. And the population is on our side. I don't have to go into detail."

"Yes, Captain, I know all that"—he waved his hand—"and so do the others. But in war, dying is not an art—living is." He looked keenly at his staff. "We could hold out for a limited time. We could inflict great damage, but we would also surely lose. Now to lose Voronezh permanently is one thing. To lose it with the aim of retaking it is quite another. I appeal to your sense of military strategy. The Germans will take Voronezh, which they will use as a support point for Stalingrad, where they are in trouble. They will release badly needed divisions to reinforce the Stalingrad offensive. But if we, still intact, mount a counteroffensive in sufficient force against Voronezh, they will be compelled to bring back divisions or surrender the city. It is highly doubtful that they can spare divisions from elsewhere since the front is too active and too extensive, and their greatest fear is a flanking movement that would entrap whole armies within enemy territory. Plainly, I am convinced that the Germans cannot maintain the attack on Stalingrad and hold Voronezh at the same time—as long as we are a fighting force. I am willing to surrender Voronezh more than once. If they persist, they will be caught in a shuttling movement with constant losses of men and equipment. Remember, their manpower is smaller than ours and time is in our favor. And when we retake and finally hold Voronezh, with Stalingrad holding out, I believe we can, at the right time, outflank them. I am therefore ordering a full retreat. I also want it to seem apparent that we are on the run." He paused. "Is there anyone here who wishes to express an opinion?" There was no answer. "Very well. In that case, the meeting is closed."

The Germans entered Voronezh without resistance. They had hardly begun to consolidate their position, when the Führer ordered several divisions to Stalingrad to reinforce the offensive there.

Stalin, after first venting his spleen against everyone around him, tried to reach General Ivanov by telephone. He found that all connections with that front had been severed and he swore that he would shoot Ivanov with his own hands for surrendering Voronezh to the enemy against orders. He checked and rechecked the movement of the freshest troops and the best equipment toward Stalingrad and issued a command that not one foot of ground was to be given to the enemy, regardless of cost.

Then, after days of tense silence, a report arrived that General Ivanov's armies had encircled Voronezh, destroyed the German supply lines, closed the trap and retaken the city in a murderous counteroffensive. It had been a brilliant stratagem and a smashing victory. Voronezh was back in Soviet hands and the Germans had suffered fantastic losses in men and equipment.

Stalin breathed a sigh of relief. He forgave Ivanov for disobeying orders and even raised him to the rank of Marshal of the Soviet Union. Nevertheless, he placed the Voronezh sector under the command of another general and transferred Ivanov —not to Stalingrad but to an entirely different front.

CHAPTER FIVE

Marshal Ivanov's new command consisted of relatively fresh and well-equipped troops. His sector stretched in a wide arc which included the village of Krasney-Bor, and as Ivanov fought toward it he kept thinking of his wife and her companions. He prayed for their survival. He also thought of Mikhail, a perplexed and troubled man caught up in the horror of war, and wondered about his fate.

The heavy autumn rains made twisting, narrow, deep-rutted roads impassable for both sides and forced a temporary stalemate. Ivanov fretted with impatience. Accompanied by his son, he had to establish his headquarters about two hundred miles from the front in the only suitable house of an obscure little village which lay along the banks of a small but turbulent river. The house had once belonged to a Russian count called Akimov, who had enjoyed a reputation as an agronomist and had conducted a number of agricultural experiments. He had died in the early years of Bolshevik rule, leaving two daughters, now in their thirties, both of whom derived from their father a deep-rooted love of the village, its soil, and its flowers. The Soviet government had allowed the two women to keep the house and site. They were now true peasants, kolkhozites, but they still occupied their "ducal estate" and were still identified by the villagers as the daughters of the famous agronomist, Count Akimov. The tradition of deference to nobility was still strong in the rural areas and this served to isolate the two women. They remained spinsters. Natasha, at thirty-seven, was like a faded lily. Sonya, thirty-three, had kept some of her youthful freshness. When Ivanov took over the house he moved the women to the upper floor, gave strict orders that they were not to mingle with the officers, moved his staff in and went to work.

It rained endlessly. Young Captain Ivanov looked out the window at the guards standing stiffly at attention, drenched from head to toe. He turned to his father, who sat pouring over military maps.

"The guards are soaked to the skin. It's almost as bad as being in a foxhole."

Marshal Ivanov raised his head impatiently. "I suppose you want me to invent a strategy against nature. We are fighting Germans, remember? God makes the rain. Against this my power is limited."

Petya Ivanov raised his eyebrows. He had never heard his father mention God before. It was very odd, but he decided not to probe.

"I mentioned the guards because of our sick list. We have more sick than wounded."

The marshal left his maps and joined him at the window. He looked at the Red Army men shivering with cold in the driving rain.

"Curse those Germans!" he said. "They came in fast enough. In three months they occupied half the country. But now they are crawling out like tortoises. They are too fond of Russian bread, Russian vodka, and Russian women. It looks as if they plan to spend a winter 'vacation' in Russia."

"It does seem that way." Petya smiled. "Do you suppose they might freeze to death while enjoying these pleasures? Napoleon did. Those winter battles were his ruination."

"Winter battles! Is this some more of your book theory? You forget that this is mechanized war in a modern age. Sure, Suvorov climbed the Alps and wintered in them while the whole world slept. Then suddenly he descended and took the French in the rear. It was great strategy. But try it today. Telephones and radios will broadcast your secret to the far corners of the earth. No, times have changed," he added almost wistfully. "We are fighting a war of tanks, planes, and submarines. The old strategy is a game for children."

"But father—"

"I've told you not to call me 'father.' At the front I am your superior officer. I should never have attached you to my staff."

"In that case transfer me to another outfit."

"I will transfer you when I see fit to do so. You are here because I can use you. Your knowledge of German is an asset and your work in Army Intelligence has been satisfactory."

Captain Ivanov came to attention. "Marshal Ivanov, there is something else on my mind. I now speak not as your son, but as an officer under your command. I call to your attention the latest issue of the *Red Army Star* which I note is still on your desk unopened. It contains an article by Tovarisch Stalin on the defense of Stalingrad. He says expressly that Stalingrad is the central strategic point of the war, for if the Germans succeed in taking the city they will have captured the key to the entire Soviet Union."

The Marshal strode to the desk, unfolded the newspaper and read the article cursorily, then hurled the newspaper to the floor. He paced up and down for a minute, then bent over, picked up the newspaper, smoothed it and fussed with it a while before laying it on his desk. He kept his eyes averted from his son. Finally, after pacing back and forth some more, he sat down at his desk, fixing his eyes on the military map.

The captain watched his father with deep concern. The marshal's actions had expressed, far better than words, what was uppermost in both their minds—the sudden transfer of an undefeated military commander to a less active theater of war.

After a while Marshal Ivanov raised his head. "Why," he asked bitterly, "is Stalingrad more strategic than Moscow, Voronezh, Kiev, Minsk, Kharkov, or Odessa? It is the process of war which creates strategic cities, not their historical fame. I can name a dozen cities, Moscow included, from which the Germans can fan out all over Russia. In war there are no cities, only military positions and theaters of action. In a war of mobility—a modern war—there are no permanent strategic points. What is strategic today is not strategic tomorrow. I say that if Stalingrad falls we can still win a war of movement, provided that the Russian soldier's will to fight is stronger than that of the enemy. But here is the strange thing. Both Hitler and Stalin are fighting a war of personal prestige and are locked in a death struggle over Stalingrad. They are both deliberately committing the same blunder and they balance each other's insanity. For Hitler it may be the final blunder. My only regret is for those hundreds of thousands of Russians who will be sacrificed."

"Then you are convinced we will win."

Marshal Ivanov smiled grimly. "No doubt. Besides, knowing the Germans, we have no alternative."

CHAPTER SIX

The Germans had decided to try to hold Krasney-Bor. They had surrounded the village with a system of deep trenches and dug-outs connected by concrete redoubts and had stationed several divisions of troops in the vicinity. General Joachim Schultz was the ranking German officer. He had established his staff head-quarters in the red-brick building which once had housed the Village Soviet, the Communist Party, and the kolkhoz administration.

Among the villagers his name quickly had become anathema. His first official act had been to arrest all leading Communists who had not managed to escape or hide and he hanged them singly on the willow trees which lined both sides of the river. Then he herded all the villagers to the river banks to view the dangling corpses.

He stood up on a tank and shouted his orders to the people:

"You are to speed up your work in the kolkhoz and provide food for the Führer's troops. All saboteurs and all those who fail to cooperate or neglect to redouble their efforts will hang on willow trees"—he pointed at the swaying corpses—"like these Communist swine."

He spoke in German, and his aide, a Russian who had been raised in Germany, translated.

"That is all. Dismissed!" shouted the general, echoed by the interpreter.

Ksenia, her mother, Polya, and Katya were there. When they got home Polya could hold out no longer and sank to the floor in a dead faint. They tried to revive her and Ksenia's mother offered to run for a doctor but Ksenia stopped her.

"The news will leak out that one of our guests has been taken sick. The Germans will get wind of it and start asking questions."

They finally revived Polya and put her to bed. She kept pleading hysterically,

"Katya, Ksenia, let us escape. We must run away somewhere. The Germans will find out who we are and will hang us."

"Where shall we run, foolish girl?" Katya kept repeating soothingly again and again. "Try not to worry. The Germans will never find out."

Ksenia's mother never dreamed that Polya was anything but Christian and ascribed her terror to sheer hysteria. She had no knowledge about Boris' activity, for with his usual foresight, he had forbidden that his name and status be mentioned. Katya, too, had kept her own secret well, merely stating that her husband was in the army. It was Ksenia Prosia was worried about. The whole village knew that her husband was a Russian writer, a Communist, and a Jew. Any disgruntled peasant could inform the Germans that Ksenia's child was half-Jewish, that his father was a Jew-Communist who had forced them into the kolkhoz and for this exploit had been awarded an order of merit by the Kremlin itself.

No one came forward with such information. The peasants' dream that the Germans would free them from the yoke of the kolkhoz had been shattered by Schultz's brutality. In fact, a few days later, the villagers devised a plan to help Katya and Polya. From the beginning their instincts had told them that Katya was somebody very important. Her distinguished bearing, her poise—her whole manner—bore the stamp of a person of great status. They asked no questions. They simply knew. About Polya they knew nothing except that she was Ksenia's friend. The plan was based on the fact that the young and middle-aged men were all in the Red Army and had left their wives and children with grandparents. Polya and Katya would separate and live in peasant homes as wives of peasants torn from the plow and drafted in the army. The Germans, chiefly on the track of partisans and patriots, would have little reason for questioning them. They would simply go unnoticed. The two women eagerly agreed.

Those were hard days for Polya and Katya. Disguised in peasant dress, they did the the housework and farm chores for their adopted households. They played their roles so perfectly that no one could have dreamed that one of them was the wife of Marshal Ivanov, a hero of the Soviet Union, and the other the wife of the Jew, Boris Garber, a top-rung Kremlin commissar and close aide and intimate of Stalin himself.

Ksenia, however, made no effort to remain inconspicuous. She did no work around the house; instead she insisted on wearing her most attractive city clothes. The Germans quickly became aware of her. The ordinary soldiers ogled and the officers schemed. When Ksenia visited Polya and Katya she reassured her friends that the Germans were only men and if the two women would only realize this, they would not hide behind peasant skirts.

One day, as the old village bard, surrounded by a crowd of peasants and their wives, sat under a tree singing old Russian songs and strumming on his lute, General Schultz passed by with his retinue of aides, bodyguards, and interpreters. The peasants all bowed low before the Germans, while the old singer brought his palm down on the strings and choked off the chord he was about to play. General Schultz stopped in front of him, and in perfect Russian ordered:

"Keep playing and don't hold back!"

The peasants shrank back in terror as if they had seen a ghost. This Nazi murderer spoke their native tongue like any Russian! Knowing nothing of his life, that he had been raised in Russia, that he had been a rabid Communist, a chief of the old Odessa Cheka and a Soviet general in the Far East, they were paralyzed by what they thought was German black magic. There was no escaping the Germans. They were masters of witchcraft!

"Go on playing, I say," repeated Schultz, looking around with malicious satisfaction at the gaping peasants.

The old man began to play the Russian "Dolya"—Fate. After a short prelude of plaintive chords, which he brought gently from the lute with his long, thin fingers, he raised his vibrant, silver-toned voice.

"*Ech tui dolya, maya dolya* . . . ."*

* "Alas my fate, my fate alas. . . ."

The general stood gazing at the lutist, then suddenly opened his mouth and began to join him in the song. After a few bars he stopped, glared at the crowd and bellowed,

"Sing, you Russian swine! Everybody sing!"

In a wild, explosive chorus the peasants thundered,

"*Ech tui dolya, maya dolya* . . . ."

The general stopped his ears with his palms. "Silence!" he roared. In the deathly stillness he peered from one face to the next. When his eyes found Ksenia, he stopped. "Incredible," he breathed. "A jewel in a dunghill." Adjusting his monocle, he bowed stiffly from the waist.

"Fräulein!"

Ksenia seperated herself from the others and stepped forward. Quietly and fearlessly, she declared,

"I am Ksenia Alexandrovna, at your service."

"Ksenia Alexandrovna! I am charmed," he answered in Russian. "As I see, you are not a villager. You are from the city, I presume."

Her sensuous lips opened in an ambiguous smile. "Yes and no, Excellency. My son and I came down from Moscow to visit my mother for the summer."

"So!" Schultz eyed her thoughtfully. A woman less vain and less naïve than Ksenia would instantly have seen through the feigned sadness which the general, after a minute of silence, now assumed.

"Frau Ksenia Alexandrovna, I regret deeply to inform you that Moscow has fallen to our troops and has been nearly razed to the ground. It will take some time before complete order is established there."

Ksenia believed him. Her blue eyes filled with tears and she bowed her head. "Merciful God," she whispered. "What am I to do?"

General Schultz pulled out his handkerchief gallantly and offered it to her. She dried her eyes. Then he took her arm and led her away.

"Have no fear, Frau Ksenia Alexandrovna. You are under my personal protection here."

Ksenia turned to him, her eyes full of desperation. "Help me!"

she pleaded earnestly. "My apartment, my clothes, all my possessions are in Moscow. Please give me a permit to return there."

"That is out of the question."

"But you said that the Germans were in Moscow?"

"That is so. But no permits are being issued." He asked her meaningfully, "Did you also leave your husband in Moscow?"

Ksenia could barely control the sudden shock she felt at his question. Her eyes fixed on the ground, she answered in a flat, even voice,

"I have no husband."

The look of sympathy he gave her masked his satisfaction. "Ah, then you are a widow."

"No, I am neither a widow nor divorced. It is just that I have no husband. He was a friend. You probably won't understand this because you come from another culture. You see, we had a custom here known as free love. Marriage was unnecessary, and we lived together as close friends. There was no mutual responsibility and either one could declare himself free at any time. One day he went away on a trip and never came back. I am free now and to tell the truth I am glad because I never really loved him. I was too young when I met him. I guess you could call it a girlish infatuation."

"So!" said the general, smiling. "At any rate, I understand this situation quite well. Of course you have no way of knowing that although I am a German, I was born and bred in Russia. I am familiar with the Soviet customs. We have free love in Germany, too." He bent over, and she could feel his breath on her cheek.

Ksenia shrank away from him as the full meaning of his words and his insinuation registered.

"No!" she cried. "I don't want this to happen to me again."

Schultz, taken by surprise, squirmed out of the situation in masterful fashion. He adjusted his monocle and bowed from the waist with extreme courtesy. His voice was a mixture of suavity and deep concern.

"A thousand pardons, my dear, if I have created the slightest misunderstanding. Trust me and calm your fears. I am only interested in helping you. If you will come to my quarters tomorrow, perhaps by that time I can arrange some way of getting you to Moscow. Understand that I am making no promises, but I will do my very best. However," he added with an air of gallantry, "your charm is such that if I do succeed in getting you to Moscow, the loss will be mine."

Ksenia, unaccustomed to such an approach, wasn't quite sure how to react, whether or not to accept his invitation. "Perhaps you are frightened of me," Schultz continued. "Believe me, I am not as bad as I am painted. I have spent most of my life in Russia and in a way I am more Russian than German. Yes, I am even a victim of the Russian fate which the old bard bemoaned. Here I am, a man almost fifty, still alone and lonely with neither wife nor child to gladden my days. I have never had the time to think of myself because I have always been dedicated to an ideal. That is how I lived my youth and manhood in Russia and this has also been my life in Germany. Would you believe me then if I told you that a general can also suffer deeply? So don't think I am not sympathetic. I understand you and I am willing and anxious to help you."

Ksenia agreed to come to Schultz's quarters the next day. By the time she reached home, she had completely convinced herself of the general's sincerity. She was surprised at his age; he looked much younger than a man who was close to fifty. And he was certainly not as bad as she had imagined. He was only carrying out orders. He was no worse than the Communists, except for Mikhail perhaps. No, Mikhail was not like the rest. But where was he? Was he living or dead? She was fond of him, but in her heart there was no longing, no pain.

That night Polya and Katya, after hearing the rumors about Ksenia's conversation with the general, stole out to visit her. Ksenia's mother, worried and frightened for their safety, was overjoyed to see them. She put the samovar on the table.

"Moscow has fallen," Ksenia told them excitedly. "Do you hear? The Germans are in Moscow."

Polya and Katya looked at Ksenia with eyes full of distrust. There was no doubt that something had happened to Ksenia. Now they believed the rumors.

Katya lost her dignity and said:

"It's a damnable lie about Moscow! They could never take Moscow. Don't believe that German liar, Ksenia!"

Ksenia was obdurate. "I tell you it is true, Katya. He has no reason for lying about a military matter. I will prove it to you. He has offered to get me a permit to leave for Moscow. Maybe I can even help both of you to get one."

"Don't, Ksenia!" Polya pleaded. "The Germans will find out who we are."

"Then I'll get one for myself," answered Ksenia shrugging her shoulders. "You may be right after all, Polya. Even if you don't look very Jewish, you ought to stay out of sight. There is a certain something by which you can recognize a Jew anywhere. There's no use denying it."

"Ksenia!" Katya said in disgust. Polya sat silent and frozen.

When Katya spoke again her voice was pleading: "I beg you not to go to the general, Ksenia. He will issue no permit to you. I know these Germans better than you do. He is a liar. He will only use you."

"Don't give me that holier-than-thou act!" Ksenia said. "Everybody lies. Why not? More power to them if they can get away with it. Your husband, Katya, and yours, Polya and Mikhail. They are all liars. Do you think Polya, that I have for one moment forgotten that wedding at the Kremlin? Can I ever forget it? I found out something that night. The greater the man, the greater the lie." Her voice was now shrill and ugly. "And you, Polya? With how many men have you slept?"

Polya, her ashen face now tinged with color, said nothing.

"And you dear Katya, Yekaterina Petrovna," Ksenia continued bitterly, "the daughter of a count who sold herself to a Russian boor just because he was a big *shishka*, a career Communist! An aristocrat sleeping with a common lout! And why are you so sweet to Mikhail? You like him, don't you? He is young and handsome. Quite a change from your elderly husband. So!—Now do either of you feel like preaching to me? Anyway, who cares?" She shrugged her shoulders again. "Soon the Germans will take over the whole Soviet Union."

Polya got up and began to pace the room, clasping and unclasping her hands. "I'm lost," she said as if to herself, her voice dull and lifeless, "but I won't show them I'm afraid. I'll know how to die."

"Don't worry, Polya," Ksenia said. "My hands are clean of blood. I can't stand the sight of it. I won't give you away. You are still my friend."

When Polya and Katya left, Ksenia's mother asked sadly,

"Tell me, Ksenia. Is it really all over with the Soviet Union? I want the truth."

"Yes, mother," she answered. "It is all over or will be very soon. The general may be lying about Moscow but he is not lying about this war. The Germans are going to win."

Her mother said nothing. Weeping silently she went into the next room and closed the door behind her.

Ksenia, after staring at the table for a while, yawned and stretched her arms. Then she went to bed and slept like a child.

The following morning she went directly to General Schultz. She learned that he had been ordered to a new post in the German capital as Director of Russian Archives and Treasures for the Gestapo. It was ostensibly an innocuous but dignified office of a scientific nature. Actually, however, the Germans had seized countless confidential Party and government documents in the occupied cities and to analyze and coordinate this information required a specialist in Communist terminology and Soviet diplomatic jargon. Schultz was the most logical candidate for that position.

The general looked forward to the job in Berlin. He longed for a social outlet and he wished to spend his declining years in a permanent place. It was now almost within his reach. He pictured himself in a warm, comfortable home graced by the presence of a congenial woman and perhaps even a child. Strangely enough he had never learned to care for German women, and he had known many. But this Russian girl, this Ksenia, who had a child but no husband, had gone straight to his heart.

When Ksenia came to him, he greeted her this time with gentility and straightforwardness. His instincts told him that only the truth would win this woman's trust.

"My dear, I have a confession to make. I know you will forgive me when I tell you that I lied about Moscow having fallen. The truth is that we caused great damage in Moscow but were forced to retreat. I do believe, however, that soon not only Moscow but all of Russia will belong to Germany. Therefore, as yet I cannot offer you any permit to enter Moscow. At this moment I can do nothing for you."

Ksenia could hardly still the beating of her heart. He had recanted his lie! There was virtue in this man after all.

"I feel deeply grateful, General, for your frankness and sincerity," she said.

"Then we are friends? And I should like it very much if you would call me Schultz, or even Joachim, if you wish."

Ksenia blushed very prettily. "I would feel awkward."

"Why, Ksenia? You see, there is so little time. I have something to tell you and I must say it before it is too late." He took her hand. "I will speak from my heart and if you do not believe me or if you say no, I will not resent it no matter how great my disappointment. I have a secret dream, perhaps the only thing in this world I could ever hope to achieve without force. As a woman you will understand such a dream. I am being recalled to Berlin to serve my country in another capacity. Wars have ended for me. For the first time in my life I can be at peace in peaceful surroundings. Come with me to Berlin, Ksenia. I am asking you to marry me. I speak to you now not as a general but as a man, and the choice is yours. Come with me to Berlin and help me realize my dream. In time we may grow to love each other."

Ksenia gazed at him as in a trance. There was nothing like this in the psychology books she had superficially read while taking her premedical course, but it was the very stuff of the countless romantic novels on which her fantasy had fed for years. Princes always fell in love with demure village maids. And now a general, a man of the world, was pleading for the hand of a lowly peasant girl. She was powerless to resist.

"I have a child," she protested weakly. "I cannot abandon him."

Schultz suppressed the elation he felt. He raised her hand and kissed it.

"Your child? How little you know me, my dear. When we marry, your child will also be mine. Now say you will come. Time is so short. I leave at dawn tomorrow."

She felt so secure and protected as he pressed her small hand between his strong ones.

"It is very sudden," she whispered.

"That is our destiny, my dear."

"Do you believe in destiny, general?"

"Absolutely. Destiny rules the world."

At dawn the next day, Schultz's car with two cavalrymen riding alongside, slowly drove up to Ksenia's house. Ksenia came out with Alenka in her arms. As soon as the general saw her, he sprang out of the car, came forward and took the child from her. A minute later the car was on its way out of the town toward the railroad station where an armored train stood waiting for them. They drove slowly, the cavalrymen on either side watching every foot of the road.

It was a dismal morning. Krasney-Bor, rigid in the vise of war, was still asleep. No one was out except the usual patrols. The sky was overcast and the trees shook their crowns heavily in the humid breeze.

There was always the danger of road mines, so the car traveled slowly. Schultz estimated that it would take about two hours to reach the armored train. Suddenly they heard the wail of falling bombs and the booming of antiaircraft batteries and they knew that the area was under attack by Soviet planes. Schultz waved to the cavalrymen and ordered the chauffeur to accelerate.

The car leaped forward and raced for perhaps a hundred yards, then suddenly exploded in a burst of flames.

The cavalrymen later reported to Colonel Von Reindorf exactly what had happened.

"We saw it with our own eyes, mein Colonel," one of them explained.

"Yes," the other added, "they were traveling at great speed down the road to avoid the bombs and suddenly—poof!"

"Was it a direct hit?"

"We believe it was a land mine. The road is known to have been mined."

"Ach, so. And the bodies?"

The first cavalryman clicked his spurs. "They are there, sir. Though, if you will permit me to say so, they now may be difficult to identify."

Under the cover of night, what was left of the four bodies was brought back to Krasney-Bor. The German command tried to keep the incident a secret, but by morning all the inhabitants of the village had heard of the tragic episode.

CHAPTER SEVEN

Mikhail and Andrei had been traveling east through the Polesia Forest, looking for the Russian lines. They came to a large clearing which had been hacked out of the side of a gentle slope. Cautiously, they crept into the clearing and began to climb the hill. Halfway up, they could distinguish peasants' huts that capped the top of the slope like a colony of mushrooms. There was nothing to arouse suspicion. They kept climbing until they stood in the village. Mikhail knocked at the first house and an old bearded peasant opened the door. Mikhail and Andrei with a wide flourish, crossed themselves. Then they whined,

"Give something in Jesus' name."

The peasant eyed them shrewdly, looked at their torn clothes, waved them quickly into the house and shut the door. "Partisans!" he said, giving them a broad smile.

They nodded. The peasant, still smiling, rubbed his hands together. "Wait here and don't worry. I'll be back in a minute."

He brought back with him a crowd of men and women. They fed the two "partisans" with bread, milk, and cheese. Mikhail asked the old man, who seemed to be the village elder, where the German lines were.

"They are well over a hundred miles east of here by now," the man said. "Maybe even beyond Moscow, if the Germans are still moving as fast as they were when they came through here. If you are figuring on crossing the German lines, you had better give up the idea. You would perish in the forest before you reached your destination."

"What are we to do?" Krivoshapko asked Mikhail.

"You may stay with us if you want," the village elder said. "I have lost two sons to the Germans. You can take their places. This is a quiet village and the Germans will not bother us—especially in the winter." He smiled. "I think it will be too cold for them."

"But by the winter it may be too late—"

"It may already be too late. But why die needlessly in the forest? Stay here. If it is not too late, you will live to fight; if it is too late—well—"

"I think he is right, Mikhail," Krivoshapko said. "Let us winter here and begin our journey east when the snows begin to melt."

"No, Krivoshapko. I think it would be wiser to move on. Winter is still a long way off." Mikhail turned to the old man. "We thank you for your kind offer. We can only stay a day or two."

They spent only a few days in the peasant's hut. There was not much for them to do, but the old man had a lively mind and they spent hours discussing literature and agronomy. Krivoshapko outlined a complete program whereby the village might increase severalfold its harvest of wheat. The old man was especially appreciative of this. The Germans never came around; the front was too far advanced and the village was too small to make it worth their attention.

Feeling rested, Mikhail and Andrei took their leave of the villagers. They were given two sacks full of bread, potatoes, bottles of milk, and cheese. They were already wearing some of the peasants' clothes.

"God bless you," Krivoshapko said as they left. "We shall never forget your kindness." Everyone hugged them and then they headed eastward into the forest as dusk fell.

They traveled all night and slept the following day in the bushes and swampweeds. Even though the front was perhaps two hundred miles away by then, they could not chance a meeting with German patrols. They would most certainly be shot as partisans if they were caught now. They kept to this pattern as the nights and days rolled by. They moved very slowly, especially in the early weeks. Food was their greatest problem and here Krivoshapko's agricultural knowledge and woodcraft enabled them to survive. He located edible roots, mushrooms, nuts, and berries which grew in abundance in the forest for those who knew where to find them. Once in a while they were lucky enough to kill a bird or a hare with a stone and they had a bit of roast game.

Then one day they began to hear the occasional distant rumble of heavy guns and the roar of planes, which told them that the front was not far off. Soon they could hear the thin rattle of machine-gun fire and the sharp exchanges of rifle fire. At first the sound of the firing confused them, for the echoes beckoned them deceptively toward every point on the compass. Slowly and painfully they learned how to distinguish among the echoes and to move toward the original source of sound. With every step and turn they felt that they were nearing freedom. The cold rains began. They no longer stopped to worry whether they would reach the German positions first. They could not guess and they were being driven by the instinct of survival. Nothing mattered but escape from the present.

At last the forest thinned perceptibly and they could catch glimpses of open country. They quickened their pace. The gunfire was closer now, much closer, but they were deaf to its menace. They climbed a hill which was still covered sparsely with bushes and they stood panting at the top. Above them was the brilliant blue sky and stretched out before them were miles of rolling fields enveloped in a haze of sunlight. For a minute, breathing their freedom, they could see nothing else. Then as they examined the landscape, they saw something that made them drop like stones to the ground. A row of heavy gun emplacements faced them only a few hundred yards away, the long cannon projecting out of the camouflage at a sharp angle.

"German or Russian?" Andrei asked, peering intently.

"I can't tell yet," Mikhail whispered back, "but I do know there is no battle going on despite that machine-gun fire. Everybody is still dug in, waiting for orders. The trenches can't be too far off."

Krivoshapko's face was wan and sad. "I don't like it," he muttered. "After all this, to come up behind the German lines would be too ironical. In either case, we could never crawl past those guns without being observed. We'd be shot before we were challenged."

"But what else can we do?" Mikhail asked.

Andrei was silent for a moment. "Nothing, I guess," he agreed reluctantly. "But we certainly can't risk it before dark. Look hard between those first two cannons, past the clover fields, toward those hills. Do you see what I see?"

"I can't be sure, but it looks as if it might be a village. It is a village. I estimate it to be about five miles away."

"After it gets dark we will crawl past those emplacements and head for the village, come what may. Do you agree?"

"Agreed."

"Then we had better memorize the terrain."

"Exactly."

They lay there all day and waited for dark, listening to the sporadic bursts from machine guns. Once in a while they put their ears to the ground in the hope that if the artillery units were dug in nearby, they would catch the sound of voices. There was no sound of human life. It was eerie and suspicious. Finally Krivoshapko remarked,

"We stupidly forgot that these guns might have been put out of action and that this may be an abandoned position. It would explain everything."

"Impossible," Mikhail answered. "That battery is in good shape and this is a solidly reinforced gun position. Besides, I think they are Russian guns."

"How can you be so sure?"

"To begin with, notice the direction in which they are pointing—away from the village, back over our heads. We have been moving through German-held territory for days over a distance greater than the range of those guns, hence it would be absurd for the Germans to point the guns in this direction. No, these are Russian guns and we are well out of the German sector. The firing that we've been listening to is between patrols. It is sporadic and keeps shifting. You will notice that much of it has died down and that it seems to be moving away from the area. Probably some German patrols have probed their way into this sector and are retreating under cover of machine guns. It's the usual routine."

Krivoshapko was impressed. "You seem to have learned a great deal at the military academy."

"I wouldn't say that," laughed Mikhail. "As a soldier I was a complete dud. It's a miracle that I remember anything at all, although I am a reserve officer with the rank of captain. How about yourself?"

"I had to take military courses along with my regular classes in seeding, planting, and soils, but I just couldn't take it seriously enough. I only got through by the skin of my teeth. I am a reserve lieutenant, but I do happen to be a good agronomist."

"I don't doubt it for a moment. And my stomach confirms it."

They waited until it was pitch black. Then they shook hands, took deep breaths, and began to crawl forward slowly on their stomachs. At intervals of a few yards they stopped, listened intently and moved again. They crept past the forest rim into the open field. After an incredibly long time, they reached and passed the first gun. It was at that moment that an arrow of light pierced the darkness and swept past them. The light disappeared as suddenly as it had appeared. Massive silence and blackness closed in. Mikhail lay panting next to Krivoshapko. Finally he crawled forward again. It was like staring into an abyss. He turned his head and waited for his friend. "Krivoshapko," he whispered. There was no answer. Then suddenly he heard voices, distant and pitched low, yet so distinct that tiny words—Russian words—seemed to etch themselves on the darkness. He buried his face in the grass, clutched the earth with both hands, and listened.

"You had better turn in, sergeant, and stop wasting your ammunition. You are beginning to see things. There's no one out there. They would have to be out of their minds—"

"Still, I wanted to make sure. I could have sworn I saw something move—"

Mikhail could not hold out. He raised his head and shouted: "Tovarischi! Don't shoot, we are Russians!"

The machine gun opened up with a deadly spatter that raked up chunks of earth and rock all around him. Then it choked off and there was a throbbing silence. Mikhail lay frozen as in the jaws of death. He knew what was coming and he prayed. It was a hand grenade and it fell short, for in the emptiness of the night his voice had distorted his location. The blast singed his forehead and the tops of his hands. He felt no pain. The silence that now enveloped him was deeper than anything he had ever known. He was wide awake at the center of nothing. He knew what death was like. It was being encased, agape and painless, in a block of wood. As he lay there, the sergeant's tiny voice again floated through the night:

"Play the light over there and stand by—They aren't firing. They are either dead or they are Russian."

"Or both," said another voice.

The searchlight was turned on and Mikhail rose to his knees. After a moment of searching, the beam picked him up. He raised his hands above his head.

"We are Russian," he croaked.

"Who are 'we?' " came the sergeant's voice.

"There are two of us." Mikhail turned around. He could not see Krivoshapko. "My friend must be wounded back there."

"Walk forward with your hands high," ordered the sergeant.

Mikhail staggered to his feet and obeyed, walking ahead toward the source of light. As he neared the trench, the searchlight was turned off and a small flashlight was shone in his face. A moment later he was seized roughly and pulled over the parapet. He was searched.

"These papers say you are Mikhail Kruger, a Russian writer and a Communist," said the sergeant. "I also see that you have the Red Labor Banner. Where did you get them?"

"I am Mikhail Kruger and these are mine. I had buried them and later I dug them up when I escaped from the Germans."

"You look as if you have been running a long time," the sergeant said. "I've seen these cases before. They look perfect. Too perfect. I'm sure you can explain everything to the lieutenant."

"Not now," Mikhail almost yelled. "I have a wounded friend back there. Get somebody to bring him in before he bleeds to death."

The sergeant hesitated. At that moment the lieutenant emerged from the dugout and stared at Mikhail. "Let him go." he ordered. "I recognize this man. I've seen his photographs in the newspapers. He is Mikhail Kruger, one of our writers. Follow me, Tovarisch Kruger."

"Thank you, lieutenant," Mikhail answered, his voice shaking, "but there are two of us. My friend is wounded out there near the gun battery."

"Call him," said the lieutenant cautiously.

Mikhail cupped his hands to his mouth and shouted several times: "Andrei!" There was no answer.

"I want a volunteer to go out there and bring in a wounded man," said the lieutenant. "It may be dangerous. We can't play a light on you."

The sergeant stepped forward and saluted. "Let mc go, Tovarisch Lieutenant. I remember the direction in which I fired."

The lieutenant nodded and a moment later the sergeant crawled over the parapet and disappeared into the night. They heard him crawling along the ground. Then there was a long dead silence. Finally they heard a heavy, dragging sound. Then Krivoshapko's body came tumbling over the parapet and rolled into the trench and sprawled face down in the dirt. The blood on his jacket was already dried and caked.

CHAPTER EIGHT

It was a long, hard pull to staff headquarters. The meadowlands rising gently toward the small village in which the Army general staff was quartered had soaked up an enormous rainfall and in places the road was a quagmire. Two straining horses dragged a wagon through the slimy ruts a yard at a time. Mikhail sat facing the lieutenant and a soldier who kept his hand on the rifle trigger. The driver sat with his rifle beside him and glanced back at them from time to time. Despite the lieutenant's recognition of Mikhail, the latter was still officially a prisoner and his freedom had as yet not been granted him. But at this moment it mattered little to him. Krivoshapko was dead and he mourned him bitterly, slowly smoldering over the irony of his death. He said nothing and sat immersed in his sorrow. He did not see the dawn break, nor did he look up when the wagon finally entered the picturesque little village of one-story, wooden houses and pulled to a halt before staff headquarters.

The lieutenant gave a sharp order and sprang out. The soldier opposite Mikhail saluted but otherwise did not budge. The driver wheeled in his seat, laid the rifle across his knees, and stared pointedly past Mikhail's head. Mikhail turned to watch the lieutenant, who was being saluted by two soldiers at the entrance of the building. He saw the lieutenant disappear inside. At that moment he looked up. There, framed in the upper window, was a woman's face. It was like a soft caress. He threw his head back and their eyes met. The exchange of glances did something for him. It had the insistence of life behind it and the awareness of his present situation as he waited grew more and more painful.

The lieutenant was back. "This way," he said, "Orders of the marshal's aide. Your papers have been turned over to him."

Mikhail went toward the house, followed by the lieutenant. The guards opened the door. An officer came forward to meet him. Mikhail did not look into his face but saw from his insignia that he was a captain.

"Tovarisch Kruger," said the captain, "at ease." The voice had a familiar ring—"Go through there," the captain said, pointing to a door at Mikhail's left. "Someone is waiting for you."

Mikhail with a sudden flash of understanding, wheeled halfway and there, framed in the doorway, stood Marshall Ivanov. The marshal and the prisoner locked in a close embrace.

A few moments later Mikhail collapsed. His body, racked and bruised by the flinty earth and flogged beyond endurance by wind and rain, simply surrendered.

He slept for two solid days and when he awoke he was desperately hungry. He opened his eyes and stared about him. A woman sat at his bedside, looking into his face.

"I am Sonya," she said, smiling.

He remembered now. She was the woman in the window.

"You were in a daze that night," she went on, "and probably you don't know where you are. The marshal asked me to give you my room—"

"Marshal? It is *Marshal* Ivanov now? That is good news. I *have* been away."

"You have been sleeping for two days. We were getting worried." Her voice, deep and throaty, reminded him of a voice he knew so long ago, but had somehow forgotten.

"We?" he asked.

She blushed slightly. "Well, we were all worried about you, so I thought I would make sure you are all right. I hope you don't mind."

"Mind? Not at all." He studied her face. She was not too young, but still attractive. It was so long since he had seen a woman. Then he shuddered slightly as he suddenly remembered. She reminded him of Maria, the girl in the Cheka prison in Odessa. He rubbed his brow and blinked as if trying to dispel an illusion.

"Are you sure you are all right?" she asked, watching him.

He reached out and patted her hand. "Of course I am all right," he assured her. "What makes you think that I am not? I've slept a long time, that's all."

"Tovarisch Kruger," she blurted out, "the truth is that the marshal had the doctor examine you. He found that you were suffering a bad case of exhaustion. He left orders for someone to look in on you from time to time and report anything unusual. We were to call him at the first sign of fever."

Mikhail was astonished. "And I slept through all this?"

"Yes. Also, Marshal Ivanov ordered me to keep watch and notify him the moment you opened your eyes." She withdrew her hand. "I must report to him now."

"Suppose you tell me first where I can get something to eat. I'm starved."

She smiled happily. "That's good. My sister Natasha, who is an excellent cook, is preparing breakfast for the staff right now. In the meantime I had better run down and report. You will also need new clothes. Your old clothes were burned."

He gazed at her and felt a familiar stirring. He admiringly noted her eyes with dark glints in them and her blonde hair that was twisted into two heavy braids. In her face he saw tenderness and compassion. The calico dress she wore added to her unaffected charm.

"Whatever you wish," he said dreamily. He closed his eyes when she left and he must have dozed a few seconds, for when he opened them again Petya Ivanov stood over him. The marshal must have looked like that a good thirty years ago, thought Mikhail as he took in the strong, determined lines of the captain's face. But the obsolete uniform which the captain wore made him blink. Epaulets, too! They were supposed to have gone out with the Revolution.

Petya Ivanov shook his hand. "Tovarisch Kruger, I am very glad to see you looking so well. My father extends his good wishes. We spoke about you often, very often. This is a happy coincidence. Now that you are back, father wishes you to remain. Frankly, I don't think he intends to release you. I have brought your uniform. Put it on and come down for breakfast. After that you will receive your orders."

Mikhail looked at the new shiny boots by his bedside and at

the uniform neatly folded on a chair. He stared at the style and insignia.

"I don't understand," he said uncomfortably, "are we dressing up for some military masquerade?"

The captain laughed. "I don't blame you. I should have explained. We just received our new uniforms. You have been out of circulation too long so you couldn't have heard that the Red Army is in the process of changing its uniform—Generalissimo Stalin's orders. We are going back to the Tsarist uniform in an effort to restore the prestige of the higher officer. In addition, the Red Army manual and the military code have been revised. It is all to the good. We had to learn through the bitter lessons of actual combat how to tighten our discipline and raise the battle efficiency of the Red Army. We had to learn that obedience to orders was paramount, that it had to be automatic and absolute, that a soldier was not someone who thought but who fought under orders. I am now inclined to go even further. The less a soldier thinks, the better."

His fanatical enthusiasm was hard for Mikhail to accept. "This is incredible," he said brusquely. "I can't see it at all. First we rip the epaulets off the Tsarist officers and now we wear them ourselves."

"Hold on, Mikhail. Not so fast. You have been out of it for a long time and haven't been in touch with our latest directives. Besides, you don't have the right perspective. There is this difference. Previously only high-ranking Tsarist officers wore these epaulets. Who were these men? They were counts, landowners, capitalists, and a few middle-class intellectuals. Today these epaulets are being worn by workers and peasants, Soviet intellectuals, Communists, builders of Socialism. On our caps we wear not the Tsarist cockade but the Red Star, the symbol of world Revolution and world Communism."

"Stalin is now generalissimo?"

Petya drew himself up. "The Supreme Soviet conferred this rank upon him."

"I see," said Mikhail. He got up and pulled on the blue, red-striped trousers. Then he picked up the jacket. "Suppose you explain these epaulets to me. I am rusty, you know."

"Well, it's all very simple. Notice my epaulets. They are

gold, with a red bar and four stars, signifying that I am a captain. Yours are identical. A first lieutenant has three stars, a second lieutenant two stars. As for the higher ranks like major, colonel, general, their epaulets are more striking but quite easy to distinguish. I know this is all new to you but you will get used to it," he added giving Mikhail an almost sheepish smile. "My father really looks splendid in his new marshal's uniform that he put on today for the first time. He is terribly imposing, which is what a marshal should be. He now commands discipline. When he passes me I can't help coming to attention, as specified in the manual, even though he is my father."

When Mikhail stood before the mirror in his new uniform, he barely recognized his own reflection. He was a dashing cavalier, an officer in a highly disciplined army ruled by ancient and immutable distinctions of rank. "Let us see what this means," he speculated. "The uniform makes the army. It signifies rank, and rank prevents men from thinking beyond certain limits. It sharply defines each man's responsibility and ensures the precise amount of dignity to match." He shook his head and smiled at his reflection. "The idea," he added, turning to Petya, "is obvious. No one may think beyond his epaulets. Little epaulets will bow to big epaulets and so on up the line. Finally Stalin, of the supreme epaulets, will bow to no one and think for everyone."

Petya looked at him strangely, and they left the room together. On the stairs they met Sonya, who was coming up, and she stared at Mikhail.

"It can't be you, Tovarisch Kruger!"

"But it is." He couln't help smiling.

"My God, what a difference clothes can make!"

"I assure you I am the same man."

She was embarrassed. "I didn't mean anything by it." She bent her head and swept past them.

After breakfast Marshal Ivanov called Mikhail into his office. It was a quiet morning except for the dull, distant rumble of artillery. Someone was playing melancholy piano music on the second floor. Probably Sonya, guessed Mikhail, his throat tightening a little. Ivanov sat facing him in full uniform, his chest completely covered with medals, decorations, and orders—a solid array of enameled red, yellow, gold, and silver. The gold epaulets on his broad shoulders bore purple zigzags and the stars which shone out of each, were real diamonds. He looked a great deal older and far sterner than Mikhail remembered him, and the high brow with its fierce scar deepened the grimness of his face. He was a formidable figure as he sat there, the model of a famous, battlewise general who held the destiny of the country in his hands.

As Mikhail waited for the marshal to speak, he experienced a sense of unreality. He saw his old life as through a mist. There was Ksenia and his son, Alenka. He tried to bring their faces, their movements, their forms into focus, but he was unable to. He thought of Boris and Polya and Katya, but they took the shape of elusive dark pantomimes; only Krivoshapko, the unforgettable, was real—agonizingly clear, always to remain.

"I want to hear your story," the marshal said kindly. "All of it."

Mikhail told him everything that had happened since he boarded the Minsk train.

"This is war," Marshal Ivanov said, when Mikhail had finished. "People are its victims. It is the tragedy of mankind. Since the world began, there has been war. Today, for man to survive, we must put an end to war." In his mind as always were thoughts of his beloved wife, Katya, and those with her—Ksenia and Polya—in Krasney-Bor, now in the hands of the Germans, but he avoided bringing up the subject.

"How will you put an end to the war?" Mikhail asked skeptically.

The marshal bit his lip. "Through the right kind of war."

"You will put an end to war through war?"

The marshal looked at Mikhail through bloodshot eyes. "The world is doomed if we lose this one. War is our only salvation before we can have a lasting peace. Hitler has challenged the world. And we, if we want to survive, must defend ourselves. There is talk of a second front. Churchill and Roosevelt have promised us this second front; they recognize that the survival of their own nations is at stake."

"I am far behind the news. Remember, I haven't seen a newspaper in months."

"We can bring you up to date in short order. I will have the newspapers of the last few months sent up to your room and also certain books, brochures, circulars, and the laws and decrees currently in force. For a while you are to do nothing but read. Familiarize yourself with facts and events and get back into the swing of things."

He leaned forward and his voice was decisive. "I have had you assigned to my staff and I am now giving you your orders. You are to serve as chief political commissar of my army. I want my men to be taught who Hitler is, how he came to power and what he stands for and I want these facts explained in terms of social and political realism. I want them to know who the enemy is and what this war is about. Your job will be to reach the minds of my men so effectively that they will be willing to go through hell on the battlefield."

Mikhail looked perplexed, and Ivanov hastened to explain:

"Don't misunderstand me. I am not talking about stupid heroics and senseless sacrifice. You can fight to the last drop of blood and still be beaten. I am talking about effective warfare and I cherish the life of every man under my command. A hero is not one who walks into certain death with a smile but one who knows the art of survival in battle. There is only a fine line between running stupidly toward death and running stupidly away from it. In the first case you have useless sacrifice, in the second a rout. The net loss is usually the same. This is one of the many things you will have to teach. You will be in regular contact with me, and we will map out the entire educational program in full detail because I consider it basic equipment in this war. As it happens, my present political commissar is inefficient. I am putting him back on reserve status—let them ship him wherever they please. You are to take over as of now."

Ivanov reached out, took a heavy envelope from his desk and handed it to Mikhail. "These are your official orders and instructions." Then he leaned back in his seat, folded his hands, and stared at Mikhail.

The marshal could not be serious! Mikhail thought. War

emergency was one thing—all men fought and he was ready to do his bit to destroy the enemy. But to be chief political commissar of an army was far beyond his ability. It was too fantastic.

"I know exactly what you are going to say," the marshal said. "You are about to plead incompetence. Don't bother. I know your capabilities and your limitations and my decision is final. With some experience, Tovarisch Kruger, you will become a model political commissar."

"There is just one thing," said Mikhail with sudden inspiration. "My rank is that of captain. It is my impression that the chief political commissar of an army must have the rank of general or colonel, at least. I don't qualify."

"Stop teaching me my business!" the marshal exploded. "Those were peacetime regulations. We are at war now."

"I insist on protesting, Marshal Ivanov. Although I have always lived with a pen in my hand, I would rather join the ranks and fight. Give me a gun and send me to the front."

The marshal shook his head. "You have your orders. This war has no front. The front is any place that can be reached by a German bomber and this includes our farms, our cities—in short, our whole civilian population. This war is being fought by everyone—the kolkhozite, the factory worker, and the soldier. In protesting this assignment, you are not thinking of this war and that each man must fight where he is most effective. You are thinking of yourself alone. It is exactly as if I, as marshal, should refuse to throw a hand grenade or use a bayonet in a battle emergency." He smiled and sighed. "After all, this is a war, not a child's game. You might be forced to fire a few rounds yourself before it is over. In the meantime, you are to take up your duties as political commissar, Major Kruger."

"Major Kruger?"

"Yes, Major. Why don't you read those documents? You will find that everything is quite in order."

Mikhail opened the envelope, glanced through the contents, got up and saluted the marshal.

"Do you understand now?"

"Yes, Tovarisch Marshal."

"Dismissed!"

Mikhail turned and went to the door. The marshal's cough stopped him and he wheeled around. Ivanov came forward with outstretched hand.

"Good luck, Mikhail. I have always known you would make a good soldier."

"Thank you, Tovarisch Marshal."

"No, not this time, Mikhail—"

"Thank you, Ivan Ivanovich."

"That's better. Go rest up a while. You still need it. Read all the material I send you. You will receive your new insignia in due course."

Mikhail grasped the marshal's hand, saluted, and left.

CHAPTER NINE

Mikhail pored over documents, maps, military texts, and campaign statistics for several days. He examined confidential reports on army morale and studies of troop behavior under stress and read through an enormous pile of newspapers. When he went to dinner, which he ate at the marshal's table, little was said. Ivanov did not probe; he merely asked an occasional question. Otherwise Mikhail was left alone, for which he was grateful. He saw Sonya a few times as she passed his open door and gave him a friendly smile. He smiled back and promptly forgot all about her.

A week later he was driven to the front, where he visited the troops in the dugouts and trenches. They gathered around him and listened attentively. He was like one of them, they decided; he spoke with an easy informality and what he said made sense. Mikhail, watching their faces, felt that his first visit to the front had come off well.

There were many visits and before long the news spread among the ranks that Major Kruger, the new political commissar was all right, that he talked sense and was willing to listen to complaints, that he liked to spend time with the rank and file and that he would fulfill requests provided they were reasonable. He had one peculiarity—he did not smoke but gave away his cigarettes. On the other hand, he could swap yarns with the best of them.

Marshal Ivanov was pleased and he said so. "You are doing something important for my men. Perhaps you can't notice any differences, but the effect is there all the same. There are a hundred little signs that only I can detect." He smiled and pointed to the pile of reports on his desk. "For instance, these are all routine matters and I get them every day, but if there were the slightest undertone of stress in any single one of these I could track down the cause unfailingly. I have my finger on the pulse of this army and I can tell you that there is already a slight improvement in morale. Keep up the good work."

One evening Mikhail came back from one of these visits to the front and found Sonya leaning against the staircase. She was crying.

"What's the matter?" he asked her.

"Nothing," she answered. "The marshal wants us all to join him at supper tonight. Hurry or you'll be late."

Mikhail left to get washed and dressed.

The table that night was decked as for a gala occasion. The tablecloth was pure white. A yellow, glistening, huge-bellied samovar stood in the center, puffing vapor like a locomotive. At each place was a crystal dish of cherry preserves, a plate laden with great slices of lemon and a tall, fragile, delicately etched tea glass. Trays were piled high with different assortments of meats. The breads were fresh and gave off a delicious aroma.

Mikhail was the last to arrive. The marshal, his son Petya, and the two sisters, both of them dressed as for a holiday, were already seated around the table. Mikhail took his place next to Sonya and noted that her face was white and her lips pressed tightly together. Her sister Natasha, who had put on her spectacles for the occasion, passed the plates around, remarking, "Eat while you can. Eat and enjoy it. There will be no food like this at the front."

Mikhail looked questioningly at the marshal, who nodded his head and explained,

"Yes, we are moving out. By dawn the whole front will be in motion."

Sonya got up suddenly, stifled a sob, and ran out of the room. Natasha took off her spectacles and wiped her eyes. "They always come," she said quietly, "and always there are others. As soon as we get to know them, they leave. It all seems so senseless."

They ate in painful silence for a while. A bit later Sonya rejoined them looking composed, almost resigned, and the mood lightened somewhat. Ivanov made a few attempts at joviality and Mikhail told some bizarre stories which sent Petya into peals of raucous laughter and made Natasha snatch off her spectacles with a gasp. The marshal looked squarely at Mikhail but he was not listening and Mikhail knew it. Unrolling before the marshal's eyes was the plan of the coming campaign.

"Would you mind playing the piano for us a little?" Ivanov asked Sonya.

"I am a poor player," she answered, half-ashamed. "However, if you wish, I will try."

"I do wish it very much," the marshal said softly.

She looked at him. He resembled her father, whom she had loved so much. Then she glanced at Mikhail, quickly lowered her eyes, and went to the piano. The marshal caught her glance. She could love deeply, he thought, and time was passing her by.

Mikhail listened to the plaintive, melancholy music and found himself wanting to be near Sonya, to touch her. At the same time, the image of Maria kept swimming up before him —passionate, open-hearted, ill-fated Maria.

When Sonya finished playing, she got up to say goodnight and their eyes met for a long moment. No words were necessary.

Later that night, alone in his room, Mikhail sat brooding in his armchair. Beside him stood his packed valises. He switched off the light and shut his eyes. The house lay wrapped in the velvet cocoon of night. He seemed to sink into the depths of stillness. *How many griefs,* he thought, *is the life of a single man? Whom have I lost and whom forgotten and whom must I forget once more? I walk among the dead as among the living, yet the faces of the living I cannot see.*

He bowed his head in thought and dug his fingers into his hair. For a long time he sat, his eyes closed, moving with infinite slowness toward the threshold of some dark cognition. Then he opened his eyes and a quiver went through his body. "I have seen the back of the truth," he said aloud, "for the face is too horrible to bear."

He got up and moved to the door, opened it, and stepped silently into the pitch-black corridor. He felt his way along the wall until he reached Sonya's room. When he touched the door he found it half open. Softly he closed it behind him and moved toward the bed. Sonya was sitting upright, a blanket wrapped around her shoulders. He kneeled on the bed, took her in his arms and glued his lips to hers. She stiffened in his embrace.

"Mikhail," she pleaded. "Tell me you love me."

He did not answer but seized her face roughly between his hands and kissed her again. Instinctively she understood that it was this way or not at all. Quickly she laced her arms around his neck and returned his kiss. He took her like an animal, recklessly, ferociously, and she gasped in pain. Later, his head on her breast, he slept, while she wept her disappointment.

Toward morning he woke and smiled at her. Gently he spoke into her ear. He did not ask forgiveness, but roused her with gentle caresses. As her passion deepened unbearably, each touch brought little moans from her throat. At the climax she cried out in ecstacy so that he had to put his hand over her mouth.

They lay quietly for a long while. Then he left her.

The call for breakfast came an hour earlier than usual that morning. It was a silent meal. The men were preoccupied with the details of departure and the women busy with serving the meal. Goodbyes were said right after breakfast. Everyone shook hands. Mikhail tried to hold Sonya's hand for a lingering moment but she withdrew it sharply. Natasha shook his hand quickly, curtly. The marshal thanked the women for their patience and cooperation, then announced that as of that moment they were officially on the march.

It was cold. The harsh wind blew across the fields with random violence. Over the earth, the ridges of frozen mud stood out like huge, hardened veins. It was battle weather.

Slowly but surely the front went into motion. There were sharp skirmishes with elusive German patrols and short, bitter engagements with German contingents which pulled back under steady pressure. The Red Army was grinding forward grimly across the dismal steppe and the general staff cars rolled behind at a snail's pace.

Day after day, the front inched ahead over endless expanses of stark, naked fields. The signs of war were scarce—shellholes in the earth, an occasional tank discarded by the roadside, and miles of severed telegraph wires. The Germans were retreating in good order, leaving nothing, and taking everything.

Mikhail knew by now that unless the front swerved unexpectedly, the line of march would take them through Krasney-Bor. He sought information about the village from Captain Ivanov.

"I cannot tell you anything about Krasney-Bor," Petya said. "I have had no intelligence reports from there."

"Is it still in German hands?" Mikhail asked anxiously.

"In the absence of authentic information it must be presumed that the village is still held by the enemy."

"And what will happen?"

"I assume that plans for its capture will be incorporated in the present offensive. Perhaps they already have been."

"How about the civilian population?"

"I know what you are thinking," Petya answered unblinkingly. "My mother is there, too. The marshal has said nothing to me, but I know that it preys on his mind night and day. Krasney-Bor, as things stand now, may be very important. If we have to take it, let us hope it will be done with a minimum loss of life to noncombatants."

"Yes—yes—" Mikhail said automatically.

"Confidentially, I don't dare think about my mother. All I have to do is watch the marshal ordering the men and equipment from position to position—all in the direction of Krasney-Bor. It is killing him, but he is doing it. I must not think about my mother, and to keep myself from doing it, I concentrate on what my father stands for. He is our marshal, winning this war. He is above sentiment. When I look at him, I know where my duty lies."

How true this was, thought Mikhail. The man loved and worshiped his mother and had to live in the shadow of a great father whom he never really knew or understood. Katya's gentleness, her sensitiveness, her abhorrence of war and violence, her poetic tenderness—all of which she had tried to instill in her son—were precisely the things he had to stifle in himself as a young Communist and patriot.

As the days passed, the signs of battle increased. They rolled over terrain on which there had been bloody engagements. The fields were still strewn with unburied corpses, shattered tanks, and overturned trucks. They went through villages that had been burned to the ground.

When they finally reached the environs of Krasney-Bor, Mikhail felt a tightening in his chest. He knew these fields. Far off where the horizon met the sky he thought he could see the contours of the twin village and the faint glint of its river. He was not sure, for the air was filled with a diaphanous, snowy drift.

Darkness fell. In the shadow of night the army of Marshal Ivanov moved on the village from three directions. It was a moonless night. The approaches to Krasney-Bor were blocked by mines, barbed wire, and staggered rows of burned-out tanks and trucks—each one of which could be a booby trap. But Ivanov was prepared. He had been able to commandeer a tiny squadron of outmoded aircraft. These he sent up first to throw down flares and strafe the fields in long furrows. Hundreds of mines were detonated and booby traps blown up. German guns began booming. But before they could find the effective range, the wires were cut and a silent, dark, immense tidal wave of men and steel surged toward the German fortifications.

The battle raged for a short time, and then the fortifications were breached. Those Germans who were not dead, surrendered. Inside Krasney-Bor the shock troops began mopping up with ferocious efficiency. A thin line of fleeing Germans were decimated by the advance troops beyond the town. The red flag was hoisted to the top of the brick government building.

There were few civilian casualties. A river of humanity streamed toward the headquarters of Marshal Ivanov, bearing gifts. The old village bard was there, chanting ballads of Russian triumph. The elders were in the vanguard, carrying pitchers of water and loaves of bread and salt to their saviors.

CHAPTER TEN

Polya and Katya came out of hiding and joined the huge crowd which had gathered before the heavily guarded Soviet headquarters waiting for Marshal Ivanov to appear. It had become Ivanov's practice to appear before the assembled inhabitants of liberated towns and for the chief political commissar to deliver an address marking the significance of the victory. When the marshal, several top officers, Petya and Mikhail emerged from the building and climbed onto the rough speaker's platform which the engineers had thrown together, the crowd greeted them with wild cheers. Katya gasped and Polya nearly collapsed.

Ivanov, looking straight at Katya, spoke less than a minute. He announced the victory briefly, stating that it was made possible by the efficiency, loyalty and courage of the Red Army, mourned those who died in the cause of freedom, congratulated the village, and gave Mikhail the floor.

Mikhail stepped forward. He had seen Katya and Polya, but was still searching the crowd for Ksenia and Alenka. The terrible fact that they were not there was beginning to seep into his consciousness. He began slowly and sorrowfully:

"My brothers and sisters, I am back where I have spent many happy days. I feel that this village is a part of me and now it has been liberated by the superb and invincible Red Army under the leadership of that heroic son of the Soviet Union, Marshal Ivanov, and the tutelage of Generalissimo Stalin. We may all rejoice—"

The villagers, who had recognized Mikhail immediately, listened to his speech intently. He spoke of the sadness of war.

"—and let us remember," Mikhail concluded, "those valiant soldiers who today gave their lives for the motherland. And let us not forget, either, those of our loved ones who died under the German yoke—" here Mikhail paused and there was a shuffling of feet, for the villagers knew, better than he, what he had come back to "—and whose memory might—"

Somewhere in the crowd a woman fainted and had to be carried away. It was Prosia, Ksenia's mother. Mikhail, standing on the platform, saw what happened, and as soon as he recognized the victim, his hands dropped limply to his sides. The marshal and Petya stepped off the platform; Katya struggled through the crowd and threw herself desperately into her husband's arms. Polya came toward Mikhail slowly, her eyes brimming with tears. He came down to meet her and she put her head on his breast and broke into loud sobs.

Later, dry-eyed and stony, he listened as Katya related the story of Ksenia and Alenka.

"They perished in one of the first air raids," she lied. "They were caught in the center of town."

"And where are they buried?" Mikhail asked.

"It was a direct hit, Mikhail; burial was not possible."

Marshal Ivanov came in and after a quick, whispered conference with Katya, took Polya into another room. Mikhail and Katya heard her sobs, "Oh my son! My Victor!"

"I must go in to her," Katya said. "Mikhail, you are a man; you are strong. But Polya is weak; she has had a very hard time here. She needs me now."

"Yes, yes," Mikhail murmured, "of course." He was staring into space, his fists clenched, his face ashen, when Katya left him.

Mikhail accepted what Katya told him as fact. He had no reason to question her story. He saw little of Polya, who was steeped in her own grief, and there was as yet little opportunity to circulate among the people, for the marshal kept him unusually busy. Mikhail was too dazed to notice that his assignments were often rather afield and only remotely connected with propaganda and army morale.

The marshal knew that if Mikhail stayed in Krasney-Bor he would eventually learn the truth and he could think of only one way to save him from that agony—a transfer. Finally he made his decision and called Mikhail to his office.

"I have a vital assignment for you," he told him. "I am sending you to Moscow with a sealed, confidential campaign report. You will leave here in twenty-four hours. In the meantime, I am sending Katya and Polya back to Moscow for their safety. However, you are to travel alone and are not to contact them in Moscow for two weeks after you have delivered your report. I have my reasons. I will recall you when I need you. I imagine that by then the front will have moved beyond Krasney-Bor and you will rejoin us at the new headquarters."

Katya and Polya left for Moscow and Mikhail prepared to follow his orders. He decided that before he left he would for the last time visit the cottage in which he and Ksenia had once spent so many happy hours. As he walked toward Prosia's house, he recalled vividly his first trip to Krasney-Bor. Then he had been young, untested, still idealistic. Now—what was he now? Certainly his youth was gone forever and his ideals were battered—He didn't want to think about it and hurried on to the cottage.

Prosia had hardly been seen in public since the coming of the Red Army. She avoided people and kept mostly to her room. When Mikhail knocked, she let him in and invited him to sit down. Her hair was white and she looked shrunken and old. Mikhail took her hands in his. She looked pleadingly into his eyes.

"Mikhail, I know you have come to say good-bye. I beg you, never think ill of us. I know that Ksenia should not have done this to you. Forgive her, Mikhail."

He dropped her hands and stared at her. Something was very wrong! In a flash he remembered silences, furtive glances, and gestures that, taken singly, had seemed slightly odd but meaningless. Now their meaning fell into place, as did the assignment to Moscow. His immediate reaction was anger; only compassion prevented him from seizing Prosia and shaking the truth out of her.

"I will never speak evil of the dead," he said, holding himself in check.

"You are a good man," she sobbed. "Your generous heart has forgiven her. Now I can mourn my daughter and my grandson in peace. She loved you, Mikhail. But she thought you would never come back. It was all the fault of General Schultz. He pursued her; he lied to her. He told her that Moscow was taken and that Russia was lost. She believed him, foolish girl. She was so terrified that she believed him. She went away with the German but she would not part with the child, whom she adored. Their car was destroyed in an air raid. Merciful God, even their bodies could not be pieced together for a decent burial. For this, dear God, the living are punished more than the dead."

She sank into a corner, her face to the wall and moaned softly. Mikhail turned and left the house.

He went straight to Marshal Ivanov, who took one look at Mikhail's face and knew that the truth was out. He nodded curtly as Mikhail saluted.

"Yes, Tovarisch Major."

"Tovarisch Marshal, I am here to request that you consider the cancellation of my Moscow assignment. I also wish to be relieved of my commissarial duties. I should prefer to be sent to the fighting front at once."

He was trembling. Without waiting for the marshal's permission, he sat down on a chair. The marshal got up and put his arms around Mikhail's shoulders.

"No, Mikhail," he said earnestly, "that is not the way. Suicide is not the solution to your problems. It is not the solution to any problem. You will be at the front some day and you will fight. I do not question your courage or your patriotism. But at this moment you are speaking neither out of courage nor out of patriotism. I want you to carry out the orders I gave you."

Mikhail was silent. Ivanov squeezed his shoulder affectionately. "The moment you have delivered your report you will start on furlough, which I have countersigned. You will rest and you will recover. We still need you. Above all, try to remember that a man's destiny is not in his own hands. His life and his death are not for him to decide. Some day you will think back on these words, which sound so empty to you now. You have suffered, but this is our common lot. I guarantee as your friend that eventually you will decide that life, all of life, is worth living."

CHAPTER ELEVEN

In Moscow, fingers of frost traced glittering cameos on countless windowpanes and bejeweled the austere walls of the Kremlin. The first snow had covered the city with a blanket of white—and German bombs had left gaping holes in the blanket. When Mikhail returned, he found his apartment building in ruins. He stood at the site for a long time, gazing at the white mountain of rubble under which lay his furniture, his books, his manuscripts and everything else that he had possessed.

He had a month's furlough, no desire to go anywhere or to see anyone and no roof over his head. What he wanted was some place where he could just lean back and collect his thoughts. He made his way to the Red Army Officers' Club, got a tiny room on the top floor, unpacked in a hurry and fell into bed.

Polya and Katya were also back in Moscow. They had arrived two days before Mikhail. Polya was already beginning to feel the weight of her loneliness. Her son was dead and her husband, more and more immersed in his secret work, rarely came home from the Kremlin. When he did, he sat in silence. Boris' face was now a yellowish-green and what hair he had left was gray. Periodically he suffered from stabbing head pains and he leaned on a heavy cane. Polya felt closer to him than ever before and each night she sat up and waited for the sound of his cane and his dragging steps.

Katya, too, had come back to a different life. With nobody left to entertain or to visit, she spent the days reading poetry or sitting in her living room rereading a small pile of letters from Ivan and Petya. Her reddish hair was now delicately streaked with gray and her eyes had a strange haunted look about them. In her reveries she wondered whether she could ever again find God in all the emptiness that surrounded her. She remembered herself as a girl kneeling in a church and again she breathed in the solace, the fulfillment and the peace of those moments. Then she took from an old trunk her ikon in its frame of hammered gold and silver, and an image of the Blessed Virgin, hung them in her room, kneeled before them and folded her hands in supplication.

"In the name of Jesus and the Holy Virgin Mary, I pray that my husband and son be returned to me. Their faith is not my faith, yet their life is my life. Forgive, merciful God, and bring them back into my arms."

Nightly thereafter she recited this prayer.

Mikhail kept to his room for two weeks, reading, meditating, trying to unwind his jittery nerves. He came out only for meals. At the end of the second week, he saw a notice posted on the bulletin board of the club:

PROFESSOR FEODOR ALEXEIVICH MASLOV OF MOSCOW UNIVERSITY AND HOLDER OF THE ORDER OF LENIN WILL LECTURE TONIGHT AT 8:15 IN THE CENTRAL AUDITORIUM ON THE SUBJECT:

"RUSSIA'S INVINCIBILITY"

ALL OFFICERS ARE INVITED TO ATTEND

Mikhail saw that he could just make the lecture if he hurried. He ran up the stairs, went into a packed assembly hall and found a seat near the door. Professor Maslov was just making his way to the speaker's stand on the stage. He looked much older and grayer, and his worn military jacket, on which the Order of Lenin hung conspicuously, couldn't hide an enormous paunch. Mikhail hardly recognized him. A wave of applause greeted the professor and he waved his hand with an air of modesty until the hall grew quiet. He began in a soft voice. Mikhail smiled as he recalled the familiar oratorical style—gentle and unassuming at first, then slowly gathering force in a rising crescendo punctuated by sharp, dramatic outbursts and leading up to a whirlwind climax, and finally a significant pause followed by a majestic coda. He listened with his eyes closed, spellbound by an hour of masterful rhetoric. Maslov came to his pause and a few moments of suspense ticked by. Then he leveled his summation at the audience.

> "Praise, everlasting praise, to those who have given their lives for our Soviet land. Our Father Stalin, our Generalissimo, genius of strategy without peer both in war and peace, will lead us onward from victory to victory. Russia is invincible because in him is the light, and the power and the glory. History has spoken through him. We cannot equal him; we can only emulate. He, and only he, holds the destiny of mankind in the palm of his hand. Long live our Savior Stalin!"

The audience broke into spontaneous applause and shouts. Mikhail found himself carried away and shouting with the rest before he remembered that the last time he had heard Maslov speak it had been to describe how Stalin and not Trotsky had ridden out on a white horse to meet the ferocious Cossacks before the gates of St. Petersburg. A pack of lies, thought Mikhail. How easily Maslov's words can charm the masses. I was almost his victim again. He got up, slipped out of the hall, which was still shaking with the thunder of applause, and went up to his room. He took down a book and tried to read. It was no use. He lay down on the bed and stared up at the ceiling. A few minutes later someone knocked at the door and he got up, resentfully, to open it.

"Tovarisch Major," said the uniformed attendant, "you are wanted urgently on the telephone. Please go to the office at once. It seems very important."

"I'll be right down."

The man saluted and left. Mikhail wondered who it might be and what made it so urgent. He went down quickly.

When Mikhail didn't come to see them, Katya and Polya began to wonder what had happened to him. Where was he? Had his train been bombed? Had he been hurt in one of the recent air raids?

"Don't worry!" Boris told them. "He is safe and holed up

at the Officers' Club. I know because it is my business to know. Now I want you to leave him alone. After what he has gone through, he is better off by himself for a while."

Katya, not wishing to irritate Boris, said nothing, but Polya came and took his hand. "Boris," she said firmly, "we have all suffered more than our share. We must not nurse our pain alone. We can share a bit of happiness. Mikhail has gone off by himself out of desperation and I know that he needs us. If you are afraid that we will tell him anything he shouldn't know, you needn't worry. I promise you we will never tell him about Ksenia."

"But he knows, Polya. He knows."

"What? How can he? It is impossible. I don't believe it."

"He knows," shouted Boris, getting angry. "I have been in touch with the marshal."

"Then he needs us more than ever. Boris, you must bring him here."

There was no answer from Boris. Instead he suddenly twisted his head in an agonizing cry and grasped the sides of his chair. His face went blue. "Get a doctor!" he whispered. "Quickly!"

A doctor was dispatched from the Kremlin. He saw immediately that Boris had suffered a stroke and ordered him taken to a hospital. Fortunately, it was a small seizure, not very serious and ten days later he was brought home in a wheelchair. His face was calm and he smiled occasionally like a man relieved of a great burden. He seemed more human, more genial, and when he looked at Polya, who ministered to his needs, there was an unaccustomed tenderness in his eyes. The doctor took Polya aside.

"He is paralyzed from the waist down," he explained. "The prognosis is not hopeful and he will probably remain this way unless a miracle occurs. However, he has an iron constitution and if he takes reasonable care of himself and avoids undue excitement, he can live to be a hundred. We will check on him from time to time. Report anything unusual."

The doctor, the nurse, and the hospital aide left. Polya went in to Boris, bent over and kissed his brow.

"I will never leave you," she said.

He nodded, pulled her head down, and kissed her affectionately on the lips. It was the first time in many years that he had kissed her like that.

"Polya, I am a realist," he said. "Once I had to live one way and I held back nothing. Now I will have to live another way." He put his hand on her mouth as she tried to protest. "No, please don't give me false hope. I saw the face of the doctor and I know that the chances of recovery are slight. I must face it. Let me tell you what lies ahead of me and you will see that it is bearable, even quite pleasant. First, I will be pensioned off for life and therefore we'll have no economic worries. Second, I have become a free man. I am free, do you understand? I can sleep at night and I can breathe by day without straining my ears for that fatal telephone call which would have summoned me to final judgment. You are horrified, Polya. Do not fear. It is all over now. I have done my work well. A grateful government has awarded me a pension for life and a roof over my head. And"—he stroked her hair—"I have a wife, still young, still beautiful. I consider myself a lucky man."

Polya shrank back, afraid that he had lost his mind. But Boris was quite sane. He smiled and took a paper out of his jacket.

"This is my passport to life. Stalin has put it in writing. Read it."

It was a letter, signed by Stalin. Stalin himself had given it to him personally in the hospital. It praised Boris for his work, expressed regret that Boris was forced to retire on a pension when the country and he, Stalin, still needed his services so badly. But as a token of reward for loyal and devoted services of many years in the struggle against all enemies of the Communist Party and the Soviet Union, he was granted the lifetime use of a house and garden in the suburbs of Moscow.

"Oh, Boris, this is wonderful," Polya said, hugging him. "You must call Mikhail and tell him. He must come and spend some time with us in the country."

"Yes, Polya, I—"

The telephone rang. In the past it would have been the signal for Boris to stiffen and send Polya to answer it. But now, with a smile on his face, he wheeled himself over to the telephone. It was a high-ranking government official who wished to express his regrets at Boris' retirement and his hopes for his speedy recovery. Boris thanked him and rang off with a humorous remark.

"This will go on for a little while," he explained to Polya. "The minister was really congratulating himself that this mysterious shadow who could walk freely in and out of the Kremlin will no longer darken his footsteps." He laughed and added: "They will all be extremely polite and friendly. They will feel relieved—until Stalin acquires another shadow."

Polya reminded Boris about Mikhail.

"Yes, of course," said Boris. "I will call the Officers' Club right now. I hope he is still there."

This was the call which Mikhail received at the club. When Boris asked him to come right away, he hung up and was there within an hour.

Mikhail was surprised to find Boris in a wheelchair. Boris told him what had happened and showed him Stalin's letter.

"At last, Boris, you will be yourself again. I am very happy for you—and for you, Polya. It is the best thing Father Stalin has ever done."

"Enough, Mikhail, enough. The past is over. I bury it. I look forward to the life of a country gentleman."

"You deserve it, Boris. And I might add that despite your illness, you look better than you have in years."

"I feel fine. Now you listen to me. I want you to pack your things and spend the rest of your furlough with us. It's about time we got together. I have plenty of time on my hands. Besides, you can help us move into our new house in the suburbs. As you can see, I am slightly handicapped."

He attempted to be the old Boris—Boris the Strong, planning, ordering and in complete command. Mikhail willingly agreed to come.

Stalin had been generous. The new house which had been allotted to the Garbers was large, airy and equipped with every modern convenience. The garden which surrounded it and the countryside beyond was white, still, and wrapped in a pristine beauty which made the war seem remote.

Boris eagerly assumed the role of lord of the manor. He seized the wheels of his chair in his powerful hands and propelled himself from one room to another and back again like a man possessed. He consulted with Polya on such things as the arrangement of the furniture, the kitchen facilities, plans for the garden, stocking the pantry, and provisions for the entertainment of guests. He was so insistent about things that she often threw up her hands in submission. He usually had his way. Mikhail, impressed by the way Boris had accepted his handicap and was even exploiting it to reconstruct his life, was shocked out of his own self-pity. He even made an attempt to write. At night he sat at his desk by the window gazing out into the hazy moonlight or letting his eyes rest on the stretches of silvery snow, then writing slowly, reflectively, until he became drowsy with fatigue.

By day, when the sun hung from a frosty sky, Polya wheeled Boris outdoors, helped him into a sled, and pulled him up and down the glistening garden paths. The days and nights went by in this manner until Mikhail's furlough was almost over.

Then, one morning, as soon as the sun had risen, Mikhail left the house and strolled through the countryside. Soon he would be leaving this peaceful haven for the deadly realities of the front and he was filled with regret. He was writing now and had found something which could only grow through the slowness of time in a climate of quiet thought. The war was an interruption. He stopped at the garden gate on his way back. Polya was there, pulling Boris on the sled. Boris sat upright, in a heavy fur coat and fur cap, looking like a huge bear. A tiny, insistent breeze shivered through the brittle, ice-locked branches. Mikhail smiled. The sled was coming toward him. "Good morning, Boris, Polya," he greeted them.

"It's better than that," Boris said. "Why only good morning? I think people ought to greet one another by saying 'good month' or 'good year.' Why is everybody so miserly about time?"

"It's beautiful here," Polya commented, breathing deeply and looking about her.

Mikhail nodded. "It will be even more beautiful in the spring."

"You are playing leapfrog with time," Boris complained. "Time is long. Why rush it? Let winter be winter."

"That's just it, Boris. Winter is paradise here and I wish I could prolong it. But at the front, winter will be hell. We thought the Germans would collapse last winter, but they didn't. And now they are threatening the Caucasus. Even now, rumor has it that they occupy half of Stalingrad."

"I'd rather you changed the subject," Boris said, squirming in the sled.

"Yes, you are right, Boris. It is not a subject dear to my heart, anyway." Mikhail took hold of the rope and helped Polya pull the sled.

"What will you do after the war, Mikhail?"

" I don't know. If I survive—"

"You will survive!" Boris said. "Do not talk foolishly."

"I hope so. There is a book I want to finish."

"You have no one now. You are welcome to live here with us. Anything you wish."

"Thank you, Boris. I don't know—"

"I would like you to come, Mikhail. It would please me—and Polya, too, I am sure." Boris stared at the snow-covered ground. "You may think me a fool, but I would not object if you two—That is, you are both young and still full of—" He could not go on. "Forgive me," he mumbled. Then he raised his head and his eyes were full of anguish. "You must understand, both of you. To accept what has become of me, I must accept all of it or nothing."

Mikhail could think of nothing to say. Polya ran to Boris and threw her arms about him. "Don't!" she cried. "Don't talk like that!"

He patted her cheek. "There, there," he soothed her. "No hysterics. Just take me inside. It's getting cold and I am very tired."

As he watched this touching scene, Mikhail suddenly became aware of the drastic change in both of them.

Mikhail remained outside, thinking. Boris the Strong. How ironic! Now he was a shell of a man. Mikhail shuddered. And what about me? What awaits me tomorrow?—He thought about Katya. Poor Katya. She's all alone now. I must see her before I go back to the front.

When Katya saw him, she received him with arms outstretched and her eyes filled with tears. "Let us hope the war will end soon and may all three of you come back safely to me. Embrace Vanya and Petya for me and tell them that I'm waiting."

He left with a gnawing at the pit of his stomach. He knew now that Katya was the one woman he had always loved, dreamed about, desired. This was the woman he might have been happy with.

How he envied Marshal Ivanov!

The following day Mikhail said goodbye to Boris and Polya and returned to the front.

CHAPTER TWELVE

Marshal Ivanov had been instructed by Stalin to move on to Stalingrad with the bulk of his forces, and that is where Mikhail headed. The train carrying him to the front was delayed en route and finally ordered to a halt amidst the rolling fields. The passengers flocked to the windows to see what was causing the delay. Most of them were army personnel whose furloughs had expired or who had been discharged from convalescent status. They had all seen action before and were by and large a serious and silent lot. There was one group, however, which made a great deal of noise and treated everyone with obvious contempt. One of the most boisterous, who had obviously been drinking, was a lieutenant Yefim Kalugin, a muscular youth with a flat face and stiff, wiry blond hair. He had spotted Mikhail's reserve and when they took their seats again, he squeezed in next to Mikhail.

"I see you are headed for the front, Major," he said. "Are you aware that there will be shooting there?"

Mikhail looked blankly at him. "I am aware of it."

"You run the risk of getting killed, you know."

"Don't we all?"

"Anyone can talk big, Major. It's easy to be a hero behind the lines. Wait till we get to the front. You may not be such a hero."

"You, no doubt, are a hero."

"At least I was wounded, once at Kursk and once at Kharkov. I wanted to be returned to my outfit but the chief medical officer at the hospital turned me down and had me routed instead into the Moscow reserves. And do you know, Major," he said, thrusting his face close to Mikhail's, "in Moscow I saw many Jews, but on the front, not one." His breath smelled strongly of brandy.

"You are drunk and a liar, Lieutenant," Mikhail said, turning away.

Kalugin flushed. "You Jew-loving bastard! That major's uniform doesn't scare me. What makes you speak up for the Jews, anyway? You know as well as I do that all the Jews are back home having the time of their lives, while we do the fighting."

Mikhail turned quickly and slapped the lieutenant's face hard with the back of his hand. The shock knocked Kalugin halfway off his seat. He got up slowly, rubbing his cheek and glaring at Mikhail. He knew better than to strike a superior officer.

"When you have sobered up, Tovarisch Lieutenant," Mikhail said, "I'll talk to you or beat the daylights out of you. I don't care which."

Kalugin drew back a few paces. "I see," he said contemptuously, "that you are not even a front-line officer, just a staff officer—an armchair major of some kind."

"I am the chief political commissar of Marshal Ivanov's army. If you should happen to be assigned to his army, I will yet make a man out of you."

This seemed to sober up Kalugin instantaneously. He suddenly changed his tone. "Tovarisch Major, I've been assigned to Ivanov's army too. We should perhaps go in together."

"Thanks." Mikhail couldn't help smiling. "But there must be others coming in with us. Maybe we'll run into each other later."

"Wait," Kalugin insisted, seating himself again, "I happen to know that you and I are the only ones going in. The other officers tell me that they have no final instructions and that they are to take their men to some allocation center near Stalingrad. That's all they know right now. But my assignment is specific. I must report to Marshal Ivanov's headquarters. I don't mind telling you," he added in a confidential voice, "what my assignment is. I am slated to be Ivanov's chief reconnaissance officer. Quite a promotion, don't you think? Not that I don't deserve it, but the fact is that my rank didn't call for it. They told me that there was no officer of higher rank available and that it was an emergency. Now they will have to upgrade me to major to save face. I'll wager on it."

Mikhail did not hear the last words. Petya Ivanov, the marshal's son, had been in charge of reconnaissance. He wondered if anything had happened to him and he felt a gnawing anxiety.

The train moved forward cautiously a few miles, then stopped again. The men were now ordered out. Ahead the horizon was dimmed by a thin veil of smoke.

"What happens now?" Kalugin asked Mikhail.

"Unless, I'm mistaken, we will have to proceed on our own from here in the direction of Stalingrad and try to make contact with our patrols."

"But where is the front?"

"Somewhere ahead, no doubt. In the direction of the smoke."

"Ah, it is an ugly business."

"You're not afraid, are you?"

"Me afraid? Anywhere you go, Tovarisch Major, I can go!"

"Well, let's stop talking and move on, then," Mikhail said. "I guess we are stuck with each other. The fortunes of war, Tovarisch Lieutenant," he added. "The fortunes of war."

The way to Stalingrad lay across a dried-up steppe with traces of early snow. There was a crude road which went in the general direction of the front. The soldiers, led by officers, tramped ahead. Shortly after, they were joined by other troop columns, cars, trucks, horse-drawn supply wagons, and tractored artillery.

Kalugin kept running back and forth along the line of march, sniffing like a bloodhound.

"Are you practicing reconnaissance?" Mikhail asked sarcastically.

"Somebody has got to find out where we are going. I asked those eagles where they were heading and they said to hell and invited me to go there myself. None of them know which army they are supposed to join. It's bedlam."

They came to a fork in the road and Mikhail took the left turn.

"What's the idea?" demanded Kalugin.

"I am simply following the artillery," Mikhail explained.

"That's a sure way of getting killed. They are always the first to be spotted."

"Well, if we are spotted, it will mean we are reaching the front." Mikhail strode ahead rapidly. "If you are worried," he called over his shoulder, "why don't you turn right?"

"Hah!" shouted Kalugin, trotting after Mikhail. "Just keep going and we'll see who ducks first." He caught up with Mikhail and the two men settled down to a steady pace. After walking in silence for a mile or so, Kalugin suddenly slapped his thigh. "I have it!" he said. "You've got something up your sleeve. You can't fool me. You must have a secret hideout somewhere. You know exactly where you are going. I say, Tovarisch Major, I have a proposition to make. How about going to the front by way of Tashkent, or Samarkand, or even Bukhara? They are safe enough, I guarantee you. I know because I was born and raised out there. It's a nice, quiet place, no front, no shooting. We can spend our days eating pilaf and shashlik."

"You are beginning to get on my nerves, Lieutenant."

"Lieutenant Yefim Kalugin, to you. You still haven't told me your name."

"If you must know, Lieutenant Yefim Kalugin, it is Mikhail Kruger. Major Kruger to you. Please don't forget that."

Kalugin stopped in his tracks. "Kruger! Did you say Kruger? That name rings a bell. But," he added as he resumed walking, "that was too long ago. Give me time and I will remember it."

"Perhaps you have read my books," Mikhail said. "I am a writer."

"Books! You must be crazy. I never read."

"It doesn't surprise me," Mikhail replied, turning his attention to the road ahead.

They walked steadily for the better part of the afternoon, passing burnt-out wagons, abandoned guns, and disabled tanks along the way. The smoke was heavier now; it hung over the entire countryside and one could almost taste it in the air.

"We will have to proceed cautiously," Mikhail said at last. "We must be very close to the front lines."

The road led sharply upward. They climbed to the top of the rise and stopped.

"You are right," Kalugin said, pointing. "We have found the front. Look down there."

Below them lay the blackened shell of Stalingrad. From where they stood, the city looked like an enormous, smoldering volcano. And beyond this abyss of destruction lay the broad, sparkling ribbon of the Volga.

As Mikhail and Kalugin were taking in this awesome sight, a soldier wearing a Red Army uniform and carrying an automatic rifle emerged from behind a rock and motioned to them to come over. His rifle was held at the ready position, and while it was not trained on them, Mikhail could see the soldier's finger was on the trigger.

"Tovarisch Major, Tovarisch Lieutenant," he whispered and saluted, when they approached him .

Mikhail breathed a sigh of relief. "Can you take us to Marshal Ivanov's headquarters?" he asked.

"No. I am not liaison. But let's go before we are spotted. They have been raising hell again. It comes and goes. They are hard to figure. On the double, please."

"I suppose they also find us hard to figure."

"Naturally. On the double, please."

They trotted downhill, the soldier pointing the way but bringing up the rear. He is taking no chances, Mikhail thought. Then along a twisting bypass which had been cut out of the hill itself, the soldier stopped before a cleft through which was visible a house, its roof covered with heavy tree branches, and its sides reinforced by piles of rock. He herded them through the cleft and they went into the house.

A captain, round-shouldered, wrinkle-faced, with eyes that shifted like two little masses of quicksilver, stood before them.

"Your papers!"

They brought them out and the captain scratched his head. "I am Captain Panyzhin, Liaison. You will have to stay at least overnight. Ivanov's men were here twice today. I can't direct you to his headquarters. I don't have the information. The fact is that nobody has any information. They have stirred up such a soup around here that what is true today is not true tomorrow. Take my binoculars and see for yourself."

Mikhail went to the window and peered through the binoculars at the battle zone. He could see spurts of flame coming out of the rubble of Stalingrad and shadows weaving in and out among the ruins. A man scurried out of a house and hurled something in front of a tank. It heaved. Then a bomb or a shell, coming from somewhere, fell into the street and the scene was blotted out in a pall of fire and smoke.

"God!" said Mikhail. He handed the binoculars to Kalugin.

The lieutenant stood for a full minute at the window. "It's no use," he announced. "I can't figure it out."

"Exactly," said the captain. "It's street by street and house by house. It's sewer and gutter and cellar. Sometimes both sides are holed up in one house, lobbing grenades down the corridors and firing from one room to another."

"And you do not know where the marshal is?" Mikhail asked him.

"All I know about Ivanov's staff is that it is somewhere in the middle of that hell, in some cellar. Nobody here knows how to reach it."

"But your job is liaison, Tovarisch Captain. Surely you must—"

"Look at the spot I'm in. I am supposed to act as liaison and to hold this hill if the Germans spot us. I have a big army here—ten men to be exact—and when we are blown up, they will cite us for heroism. Meanwhile, my orders are to quarter the replacements and stragglers until the different commands decide to pick them up. I don't know where headquarters is—any headquarters. So you will have to wait here, at least until morning. Perhaps by tomorrow the situation will change. No—I promise you by tomorrow the situation will change, but for the better or the worse, I cannot predict. Nor could the marshal, I don't think."

Mikhail and Kalugin had something to eat and tried to get some sleep. At dawn the different staff patrols came through. Once past the guards, they barged in, drank down huge quantities of tea and raw vodka and left. As each man came in, Captain Panyzhin buttonholed him and went through his routine.

"I've got two eagles looking for Marshal Ivanov's headquarters—a major and a lieutenant. Can you tell me where Ivanov is located?"

The answer was always the same. Nobody seemed to know. One man remarked, "Even if I knew, what's your hurry? They'd probably die before they got there. Let them live a few hours longer."

Mikhail, who stood by listening quietly, looked at this soldier who could banter in the face of death and thought to himself that Stalingrad would never be taken as long as there were men like these.

"Have a cigarette on me," he said, taking out his pack.

"Thanks, Tovarisch Major." He smiled and lit up. Then, as he saw Mikhail put the pack in his pocket, he gave him a sharp look, got up and saluted.

"You must be the political commissar."

"Yes, but how did you know?"

"I am in Marshal Ivanov's army. You must be Major Kruger. You don't know me but everybody knows about those cigarettes."

"Yes, I am Major Kruger."

"Allow me to call my lieutenant." He ran outside.

The lieutenant came back and introduced himself: Lieutenant Slonimov, Third Reconnaissance Aide, N-R Army."

"N-R Army?" Mikhail was puzzled.

"Yes, Marshal Ivanov's army."

"How is the marshal?"

"In excellent health, Tovarisch Major. Will you kindly step aside with me so that we can talk privately?"

He took Mikhail aside and explained. "We are permitted to identify ourselves to authorized personnel, but we are not permitted to say anything that might give a clue to the location of the marshal's headquarters. Even Captain Panyzhin is not to know where it is—no reflection on the captain, just security reasons. The outpost here is too vulnerable and the Germans torture their prisoners for information."

"I understand. How is Captain Petya Ivanov?"

"You mean Colonel Ivanov, Tovarisch. He also bears the title, 'Hero of the Soviet Union.' "

"He must have performed miracles to have been given so high a rank in so short a time."

"I am a soldier, Tovarisch, but we have rarely witnessed such heroism against overwhelming odds. If we had more Petya Ivanovs, the war would soon be over." He bent forward, lowered his voice and added with a smile, "You must know the colonel intimately but I doubt that you would recognize him now in his long moustache and his goatee. Very distinguished. Anyway, he is a hero and can look as he pleases. Someday he will go further even than his father."

Mikhail could not help laughing. "The father still shaves to look younger and the son grows a beard to look older. That's life for you. Nobody is satisfied."

"Right you are," answered the lieutenant, feeling very much at ease.

Yefim Kalugin, who had slept late, now came in clean-shaven and wearing his usual smirk. "Good morning, fellow angels," he snickered. "I see you are ready to guide us to the Stalingrad paradise. But not before I've had my morning snifter and shaken the cobwebs out of my brain. Hey, Cook!" he shouted at one of the men, "bring out a bottle and make it snappy! No faking, either. I want vodka, the genuine Russian brand and bring out a dozen glasses with it. I want to toast my fellow angels before we go up to heaven."

The lieutenant frowned and looked questioningly at Mikhail.

"He's all right," Mikhail assured him. "A very reliable officer. Wounded twice. Plenty of battle experience. It's just his manner. He's been through a lot. Allow me to introduce Lieutenant Yefim Kalugin."

Lieutenant Slonimov and his men sized Kalugin up carefully. Their lives depended on it and they knew it. If he failed to pass muster they would simply leave him behind. There was some banter back and forth as the vodka was served.

"How do you like our Stalingrad front?"

"Why, do you know where it is? Here's to Mother Russia!" Kalugin emptied his glass.

"Around here, they say."

"I might be standing on it."

"You may fall on it."

"Not without taking some Germans with me."

"Don't worry, we'll give you a chance to bury a few Germans."

"It will be difficult."

"Why?"

"I didn't bring a shovel."

It did not take them long—about three vodkas—to decide in his favor. He was a good fighting man. In this, their instinct was unerring.

While everybody was toasting Stalin and the marshal and Mother Russia, the door opened and some wounded men were brought in. Their bandages were bloody and their faces were ashen gray.

"I have to be a doctor, too," grumbled Captain Panyzhin as he began to redress their wounds. "I am everything. Now I will nurse them until the hospital detail decides to look in. If you ask me where the hospitals are, I couldn't tell you. Like the front, they are nowhere." He helped lift one man onto a cot, then stood looking down at the bloodless face and closed eyes. "This one" he added, "will lose his leg unless he gets real medical attention." He began to cross himself but stopped quickly. "He is so young," he sighed. "God help him—and us."

Mikhail and Kalugin were given rifles, rounds of ammunition and left with the patrol. As soon as they had emerged from the hill cleft into the open, they began to follow secret bypaths around twisting curves that spiralled steadily downward in the general direction of the Volga. The going was rough and in some spots they had to crawl on their hands and knees. They spanned small chasms like a herd of mountain goats and clung to tree branches as they swung themselves over deep gullies. Finally they came to a halt in a sandy nook from which they could see the Volga. About a dozen small boats were moored behind a huge rock that jutted out from the shore. The boats were effectively hidden from the opposite shore and were painted a dull, watery gray. Rocking back and forth on the current with a steady motion, at this distance they created the mirage of a small caravan of camels moving across a gleaming desert.

It took some time to reach the shore. The ground had to be

reconnoitered carefully. When the signal was given that all was clear, Lieutenant Slonimov motioned them on and ordered them to crawl slowly toward the boats. On reaching the mooring rock, they lay flat and waited while Slonimov kept his ear to the ground. Finally he pointed to one boat and whispered, "When you get in, lie down. Only one man will row. Keep your voices low. Sound travels far over water."

They lay in the boat while one soldier quickly untied the rope. In a few moments they were floating downstream. Then one man dipped the oars softly and began to row.

"What about the other boats?" Mikhail asked quietly.

Slonimov looked at him sadly. "There are other patrols in the area. Mine came over in two of the boats. Some of my men did not report back. As you see, the rest of us all fit into one boat." He raised his head over the boat's edge and examined the opposite shore through his binoculars. "If the Germans don't spot us," he remarked, his eyes glued to a fringe of trees that grew close to the bank, "we ought to reach headquarters by tonight."

There was no comment. The fringe of trees drew closer, and after a long scrutiny of the bank they beached the boat quickly and plunged into heavy vegetation that closed behind them.

It took another two hours to reach the only suburb of Stalingrad which was not occupied by the Germans. The gardens and apple orchards, vineyards and little white cottages here were still comparatively intact, still unravaged by war.

"How did the Germans miss this?" Mikhail asked.

"Don't get too confident," Lieutenant Slonimov warned him. "Soon you will see the real Stalingrad."

A half hour later they were crawling from house to house with snipers' bullets whining over their heads. The earth shook from the explosions of shells. At one point Mikhail, lying next to Slonimov behind a block of charred timber, saw a train moving across a trestle. Red flags with black swastikas inscribed in white circles hung from the windows.

"My God," said Mikhail, "that's a German troop train. Why don't they bomb it? Where is our artillery and where is our infantry? Who holds this sector?"

Slonimov shook his head. "This is the worst tangle you have

ever seen. Everybody is everywhere and nowhere. The Germans are asking themselves the same questions. Stop trying to figure it out. Save your energy. You will need it."

They ducked into the shell of a house. The walls sagged dangerously. They pushed broken furniture against the windows and reinforced the buckling struts with rubble. Slonimov placed men at strategic openings with orders to fire at anything that moved and looked German. "We are in it up to our necks," he said, "but we can't stay here." He paused as several bullets imbedded themselves in the wall. "We have to get out of here sooner or later, no matter what the risk."

"How about giving us the directions to headquarters now?" asked Mikhail. "We might get separated, or some of us might not make it."

Slonimov shook his head. "Sorry. Security requires that we take no chances. You get there with one of us or not at all."

After a while the firing in the area abated and an uneasy quiet set in, broken only by the whistling and bursting of far-off shells. On the wall of the house hung a picture of a pretty, smiling girl which shook and swung precariously with every blast, but did not fall. Kalugin smiled.

"Do you have a wife?" he asked Mikhail.

"What's it to you?" Mikhail replied coldly.

"It's none of my business, but I just feel like talking. I don't like the sudden quiet out there. It gives me the shivers."

"Coming from you, Kalugin, this is an admission. But I'm glad. You can't put your trust in a man who claims to have a monopoly on courage."

"Your talk is brilliant. No wonder they made you a political commissar."

"And you are a real tough soldier, Kalugin. Tell me, how did you get that way? You couldn't have been born that tough."

"I don't know much about my birth. My parents died when I was a child. I was raised in an orphanage—and you had to be tough to survive there." Suddenly he paused and struck his brow. "That's it! Now I know why the name Kruger sounded familiar. There was a girl in the orphanage—I had quite a crush on her. Her name was also Kruger, Manya Kruger."

Manya! That was the name of his little sister. Could it be?

He had often tried to find where his brothers and sister had been sent after he had visited them years ago, but he had given up, fearing that if he probed too deeply he might be forced to reopen the Odessa incident. Where had Kalugin said he was from—Tashkent? Bukhara? Children were often sent to orphanages on the border. It was one way of saturating the area with Russians. "Where is she now?" he asked as casually as he could.

"Too bad," said Kalugin. "I lost track of her when I left for military school. You know me, Tovarisch Major. I'm not the kind who pines long over a woman. Out of sight, out of mind, is my motto. Still—"

"Did she have any brothers?"

"Yes—two. One was a tall, skinny reed who never stopped coughing. He died. The other could never get enough to eat and was always fighting. They had to transfer him to another home equipped with isolation cells. I don't know what happened to him."

"Is that all? Can you remember anything else?"

"Look here, Tovarisch Major. I know you are political commissar of Marshal Ivanov's army, but you are pumping me like a G.P.U. agent."

Mikhail did not probe any further. It was an ironical moment in which to receive the last word about his sister and his two brothers: lying half buried in the ruins of a tottering house which he might never leave alive. What difference did it make now?

Later, under cover of darkness, Slonimov told them to get ready to crawl out of the ruined house.

"It is risky, even at night," Slonimov cautioned Mikhail. "If we stop firing, the Germans might decide to rake the street around the house. So I will stay and keep up a covering fire."

"But what about yourself? Who will cover for you?"

"Don't worry about me, Tovarisch Major. I do not die easily. Besides, we are almost at the marshal's headquarters. Once we are out of this rattrap, the going is easy. All right—here we go."

The men crawled out, one by one, under the cover of Slonimov's sporadic firing. Mikhail and Kalugin helped with their rifles until it was their turn to go. Kalugin went first and Mikhail followed him. As he crawled across the rubble-strewn street to the appointed rendezvous, he heard the occasional report of rifle fire. By the time he joined the rest of the patrol, the firing had stopped. Then there was an eerie silence. Mikhail held his breath. He figured Slonimov to be a little more than halfway to their haven by now. Suddenly the deadly staccato of a machine gun broke the silence. Rat-tat-tat, the bullets spattered close to the spot where Mikhail was crouched and he could hear them thud on the ground he had just crawled over. There were a few more bursts and then silence again. A soldier grabbed Mikhail's arm.

"Come, Tovarisch Major," he whispered. "We must move out before the Germans decide to move in."

"But the lieutenant—"

"His orders were to move on with or without him, Tovarisch." He insisted. "Come. We are very close now and we cannot risk capture."

Mikhail followed the soldier into the darkness.

What was left of the patrol—Mikhail, Kalugin and two of the soldiers—found Ivanov without further trouble. The marshal's headquarters were in the cellar of what had been a bakery in the very center of Stalingrad. Petya and a few key aides were with him.

Ivanov had miraculously penetrated into the heart of the besieged city and, despite constant enemy pressure, had managed to maintain an open supply line. It was a notable achievement, but the marshal was depressed by the appalling—and in his opinion unnecessary—losses he had been forced to incur to hold Stalingrad. And he was disturbed by the prospect that sooner or later he would have to unleash a mass assault against the Germans. *Stalingrad is worth all human lives*! So Stalin had said. And everyone around him seemed to agree, including the "Hero of the Soviet Union," his son.

Mikhail's return cheered up the marshal. He was glad to be able to talk to someone who he knew shared his own doubts and anxieties. More and more he had come to think of Mikhail as the son which he always looked for but could never find in Petya. The pride he should have felt in his son's meteoric career long ago had been blotted out by the pain of Petya's slavish devotion to Stalinism. The marshal's ache went deep. Loyalty was one thing, and this he had taught his son well; but bondage was another matter, and that he had never taught him. He wondered where he might have gone wrong and he thought that one of these days, perhaps after the war, he would discuss it with Mikhail.

Kalugin was assigned not to reconnaissance, as he had expected, but to an aide's post at a division headquarters. He was very much put out and when he came to say good-bye to Mikhail, his embarrassment was written all over him.

"That's how things go, Tovarisch Major," he complained. "They yell emergency and pack me off to this hell without even a briefing. Now I'm to be an aide. If it was a division vacancy, why didn't they say so? I don't think one-half of the army knows what the other half is doing."

Mikhail felt a sudden sympathy for the boisterous lieutenant. He had come to like him during the few days they had been together. Kalugin was a roustabout and would always remain one, but he had shown true courage and even a grain of sensitivity. The thought struck him that his own brother probably would have been like this. Perhaps Kalugin was his brother. He bore a resemblance to him as he recalled him. The names were not too far apart—Kruger, Kalugin—and orphanage officials were often semi-literate. Who could tell? And that story about the boy who fought with everyone and had to be kept in an isolation cell—perhaps Kalugin was that boy and had changed the story. No, it was too fantastic. His imagination was playing tricks again. Kalugin was Kalugin. And even if he wasn't he obviously *wanted* to be Kalugin. He said finally, "Don't take it so hard. Neither rank nor assignment means anything. You are a top soldier."

There was gratitude in Kalugin's eyes. "You really mean that, don't you, Tovarisch Major? I am complimented, and I will never forget it." He saluted and turned to go, then hesitated.

"Yes, Lieutenant?"

"Tovarisch Major, allow me to say that I am very sorry I didn't know you earlier."

He did an about face and left.

A few days later, Ivanov sent for Mikhail and his son and told them,

"I have been ordered to Moscow by Stalin for a military conference. As per my instructions, this is top secret. Colonel Ivanov, you are to take command during my absence."

Petya's eyes glistened. "I will do my best, Tovarisch Marshal."

The marshal smiled. "I want you to maintain my tactics wherever possible. Proceed with caution. I advise against heavy engagements unless the enemy attacks in force. You may get your wish for a mass assault when I return—if I return," the marshal added pointedly, "but until then you are to follow my strategy."

"*If* you return?" Mikhail asked. "There is nothing wrong, I hope, Marshal."

"I expect the Generalissimo will wish to start a mass assault to break out of here. I shall oppose it, of course."

"But Father—Marshal—" began Petya.

"No more. I have thought this out. It is my considered military opinion. Tovarisch Major," he added, turning to Mikhail, "you are to keep your eyes open here and assist the colonel in any way you can."

"Yes, Tovarisch Marshal."

"Good. That is understood. Now let us breakfast."

An orderly brought in a heated samovar, bread, and honey. As they ate and drank, the marshal seemed to have recovered his spirits and talked about lighter things, scrupulously avoiding the subject of war.

That evening Ivanov left with one of the patrols.

The marshal left just in time. The next week the Germans renewed their assault on the center of the city. They were repulsed, but fresh reserves moved up and continued to press the Russian positions. Slowly, street by street, the Red Army fell back. Petya and Mikhail and the staff officers prepared to burn what official documents they could not carry to the nearest divisional headquarters.

On the third day, Petya gave the order to move out. They abandoned the basement and climbed up to the ruins of what had once been the bakery. Shells were whining overhead and exploding dangerously nearby. The din was ear-shattering.

"It's worse than it was when I got here," Mikhail shouted to Petya. "I can hardly hear myself think enough to be afraid."

"The time to worry about a shell," Petya remarked as they scurried for cover, "is when you don't hear it whine."

The next moment a shell exploded to their left with a great roar and they were blown, with a cloud of dirt and rubble, against the frame of the building. Mikhail had not heard a thing. One instant he was running for shelter; the next he felt himself hurtling through the air. Even that sensation was only momentary, for just as the realization of what had happened set in, blackness closed around him.

PART SIX

The Cry of Mother Russia

CHAPTER ONE

Ten days later Mikhail awoke to the sight of a long line of hospital cots. He was lying on his right side. His left side felt extremely sensitive and his head was swathed in bandages.

I must be alive, he thought. *Thank God.* He started to turn over but the pain in his left side was too great. A nurse came quickly to his bedside.

"Ah, Major, you mustn't try to move. Doctor's orders. How do you feel? Can you talk now?"

"Yes," Mikhail said weakly. His voice sounded strange to him, but it was a welcome sound. He moved his arms and legs. "I seem to have everything," he said to the nurse with a wan smile, "even if not in very good shape."

The nurse smiled. "Yes, Major, you are all there. Here comes the doctor now."

A short, stout man in uniform with a captain's epaulets came up to him. "Tovarisch Major," he said jovially, "I am glad to see you awake. You had us worried for a while. We must have taken a pound of shrapnel out of your side and skull. You are a lucky man."

"How long have I been here?" Mikhail asked.

"Here? Let me see—It will be a week tomorrow. You were in pretty bad shape when you got here. But we are fortunate. We have here one of the best neurosurgeons in all Soviet Russia."

"Colonel Ivanov—how is he?" Mikhail asked. "Is he all right?"

"Colonel Ivanov? The son of the late marshal? He is a national hero! He rallied our glorious forces in Stalingrad and held off the whole German army until reinforcements could be brought up. Like father, like son."

"The *late* marshal?" Mikhail repeated. "The *late* marshal, did you say? What do you mean?"

"Oh, I am sorry, Tovarisch Major. I forgot you have been out of things for a while. Marshal Ivanov died almost two weeks ago."

"He was killed at the front?"

"No, he died in Moscow while in conference with Generalissimo Stalin."

Mikhail didn't want to believe it. He asked, "How did he die?"

"A heart attack, I believe *Pravda* said. He was a great man, a great soldier. I understand his funeral was the greatest state occasion since Lenin's burial."

"And Petya—Colonel Ivanov—he is still at the front?"

"Yes, Tovarisch, and the front is slowly moving west. I hear rumors that Hitler's failure to take Stalingrad in the big putsch broke his back. The Germans are retreating. But that is enough conversation for one morning," he added. "Come, let me take a look at your side."

The doctor examined Mikhail's wounds and redressed them. Then he pronounced him in satisfactory condition and left, promising to look in on him every few days.

In the next few weeks the wounds began to heal. Some of the bandages were removed and Mikhail was able to sit up. He spoke little to anybody, except to answer the questions of the doctors and nurses; he read nothing and listened only vaguely to the radio news broadcasts. The siege of Stalingrad had been lifted and the Germans were retreating in many sectors. The broadcaster predicted that soon the war would move to German soil.

In the convalescent ward they put him next to a captain with long chin-whiskers, thin, tight lips, and gray cat's eyes. The moment he saw Mikhail he began to complain.

"This, brother, is suffering. It is the Russian who has to suffer. Everybody suffers except the Jew. The Jew is somewhere in Tashkent, far from the noise of war, doing business, speculating and having the time of his life."

Mikhail, remembering Kalugin, ignored him and the captain who thought that Mikhail was still too weak to carry on a conversation, left him alone for that day. The next day he asked Mikhail how he felt. Beyond feeling sore all over, he seemed all right, Mikhail told him. That was the signal for the captain to grumble.

"We Russians were born to suffer," he said, "but the Jews have it easy. There isn't a single Jew along the whole front from the Arctic to the Caspian. Where are they? Back home, living in the lap of luxury."

Mikhail controlled his indignation and listened. He was tired, his body ached and it was easy to pretend to be asleep for hours at a time. But on the third day when the captain persisted, Mikhail could stand it no longer. He wanted to turn around, but he was under doctor's orders to lie on his right side.

"Tovarisch Captain," he said, "I can't turn around and I would like to see your face."

The captain got off his cot, took his crutches and swung himself around the room until he faced Mikhail, who saw a fine, intelligent face—obviously a man of culture and education. Mikhail compared him with the coarse and vulgar Kalugin. He found it in his heart to forgive the other's accusations because of his ignorance, but this person he could not forgive.

"What you say sounds interesting, Tovarisch Captain, but I didn't catch it all. Would you mind repeating it?"

"I say," the captain said with vicious emphasis, "that we Russians are suffering and that there are no Jews at the front. Jews are living in clover while our blood is being drained."

"Where did you learn all this?"

"I happen to know."

"Are you a Communist?"

"Certainly. What a question to ask!"

"Do you hate all the minorities?"

"I don't hate any minorities. I just hate the Jews because they are cowards and parasites."

"Then let me tell you. I am a Jew and I have just come from the front. Where do you think I picked up all this shrapnel?"

"You are lying. You are no Jew. Your wounds prove it. The Jew is too yellow to fight."

"I didn't hear you," Mikhail almost shouted, feigning deafness. "My head is bandaged down to my ears. Say it again."

As thc captain leaned over and opened his mouth to speak, Mikhail suddenly lifted himself on his elbow and spat in the man's face. The captain recoiled from the shock, his crutches flew from under him and he landed on his back with a thud. He raised a blood-curdling cry. The nurses and attendants rushed in, raised him and carried him back to his cot. He was shaking.

"Take me out of here," he begged.

A doctor came in, heard about the fall and looked him over. "You aren't hurt," he decided, "just reacting a little to the shock of your fall. Why do you want to be moved?"

"I'll tell you why," yelled Mikhail. "If you don't, I'll kill him with my own hands, that's why."

The doctor looked at Mikhail. "Ah, yes, I know your case. Head shrapnel wounds, rather serious, but healing nicely. Still, they can cause a lot of stress. Let's not take any chances."

They took the captain out.

CHAPTER TWO

One morning Mikhail asked the doctor, "When are you signing me out?"

"Tovarisch Major, you are an intelligent man. When your wounds are healed, you will be discharged."

"I feel in excellent shape right now."

"Of course you do. You *are* in fine shape except for some unhealed wounds. I know how impatient you must feel. Besides, it isn't entirely up to me. I can only recommend. The discharge itself must be approved by the medical committee. You have a family, relatives, friends outside?"

"I have nobody."

"Nobody?" The doctor nodded sadly. "Well, Tovarisch Major, in my opinion you will be here for another month. It is doubtful if the medical committee will release you for active duty. The war will be over soon anyway and you will probably not be needed. You have earned a rest and you need people. Since you have nobody, as you say, I can recommend a sanitorium for a few months so that you can fully recuperate. There will be others like you there and you will find it interesting—and therapeutic. In the meantime, be patient."

Mikhail nodded to the doctor, who smiled and left. A month, he thought, is a long time.

When the doctor came a few days later, Mikhail told him, "There is somebody—sort of a relative. Would you please write to her for me and ask her to come?"

The doctor smiled. So this woman was "sort of a relative." "Tovarisch Major," he said, "I think I understand. But why ask me to write when you are quite capable of writing yourself? There is nothing wrong with your hands."

"It's a long story, doctor. It takes more than hands. It takes courage."

The doctor looked at him for a moment. "Very well. I'll write," he said.

"Thank you," Mikhail said. "Here is her address." He gave him Katya's Moscow address.

Mikhail now began to live in anticipation of Katya's visit. The hospital was not too far from Moscow. She would come. She had to. She had believed in him once, had given him courage. Once again, with his world in ruins, he needed her. She was the only one he could turn to now.

He was now well enough to be on his feet and he began to walk the corridors, visit the wards and spend time with other officers and men. The doctor watched his progress with satisfaction. One day he remarked,

"Tovarisch Major, it won't be long now before we discharge you. Be patient."

"I am patient, doctor, and I'm no longer in a hurry. What will be, will be."

"Fine," said the doctor.

A few days later Mikhail lay on his cot, gazing up at the ceiling.

"Why don't you go out and get some sun?" asked the doctor as he breezed through.

"Too lazy."

The doctor stopped at the door. "Too lazy to receive a visitor?"

Mikhail leaped from the cot. "Yekaterina Petrovna!"

"Right! Take it easy, Tovarisch."

"Give me a minute by myself before you show her in, please."

He was calmer when she walked in. She stopped before him and smiled. She had all of her proud, stately grace. To see her sorrow, he had to look into her eyes. She kissed him and took both his hands in hers. "Mikhail," she said tenderly. "If you only knew how we have worried about you—Polya and Boris and I. But you look well again, thank God, and that is all that matters—You are well, are you not?"

For a moment he didn't answer. He looked at her. The gray in her hair, now more gray than reddish, did not make her look any older. In Mikhail's eyes she was as lovely as ever.

"Yes, Katya, I am almost mended, the doctor tells me." He offered her a chair and she sat down.

"Why didn't you write to us, Mikhail? For months we knew nothing, only that you had been badly wounded."

"How did you find that out?" he asked.

"Petya wrote to me about your accident. He says you probably saved his life by shielding him from the explosion."

"It happened so quickly, I still don't remember anything. It was pure luck, I'm sure."

"Well, whatever it was, I am grateful—Russia is grateful—Russia is grateful, for you have saved a national hero."

"If saving your son, no matter what the circumstances, earns your gratitude, I am happy."

"He is my son, Mikhail, but in name mostly. Oh, he loves me, I am sure, and he loved his father. But we—do not see things much alike. He is one of the new, fanatical Communists and I—I am not even sure I'm an old one—"

"Have you seen him lately?"

"No, not since—not since Stalingrad. He is very busy these days. I understand he is slated for a high post in the military."

"And how are Boris and Polya?"

"They are well and they send their love. They would have come with me if Boris were more mobile. Boris insists that you visit him as soon as you come to Moscow. 'Tell him that is an order,' he said to me." She laughed. "Isn't that just like Boris? But tell me," she added, "how do you feel? Shall I tell you what I see? I see a worried, tired young man trying desperately to appear bitter and old. But it is no use, Mikhail. You cannot play the part."

"I am not so sure it is a part, Katya."

"Nonsense. When you are discharged," she said, trying to sound austere, "you are to come directly to me. I will not have it otherwise. You can stay at my home until you get your bearings. You will need time to plan, to think. You are a writer and it would be tragic if you let go now. I expect a great deal from you. It is the privilege of one who loves you deeply."

"I will come to you," he said simply.

She was standing looking down at him, and he saw that her hands were tightly clasped. Her eyes were now like dark wells.

"Mikhail, I have one question to ask you before I go. You were at the front, at headquarters, when my husband left for the Kremlin. What last impression do you have of Ivan?" As Mikhail tried to avert his eyes, she continued, "No, don't lower your head. This is why you didn't write, isn't it? Look at me. I must know. I want you to be perfectly frank."

"I will be frank. Marshal Ivanov left me with the impression that he did not expect to return."

She put her hand softly on his shoulder.

"But he didn't die in the Kremlin, Mikhail. He died at home."

"I see. Then he died a natural death?"

"Let us think of it that way."

They said nothing further on the subject. After a while, Katya kissed him on both cheeks and left.

A few weeks later, the medical committee discharged Mikhail and recommended that he be released from military duty in view of his original reserve status and the absence of a national emergency. He was offered a period of convalescence at a sanitorium, but he declined and instead took the first train to Moscow.

CHAPTER THREE

Mikhail arrived in Moscow tired out by his trip and went straight to Katya's, where he slept all afternoon. The next day they set out to visit Boris and Polya. At the railroad station they saw scrawled on the station house wall in huge, white ungainly letters:

KILL THE JEWS AND SAVE RUSSIA!

Mikhail went looking for a police officer and brought him back. The officer read the scrawl, smiled and went off shrugging his shoulders. Mikhail was about to follow him and protest, but Katya pulled his sleeve.

"Don't, Mikhail. You will get no action on this. It's been going on for some time now. It's the aftermath of German propaganda. It is only temporary. It will blow over."

"I can't accept that. To me, it's a blatant injustice. Tell me that injustice is built into the fabric of life here and I will understand."

"Stop, you foolish boy! You are only hurting yourself. Leave justice alone for a few minutes or we will miss the train."

Mikhail followed her reluctantly. They found Boris at home. Boris shouted for joy when he saw them, startling the elderly maid who was busy polishing the furniture. His face beaming, Boris propelled himself expertly in his wheelchair and proudly showed them the improvements he had recently made in the house. Then he waved them into chairs, banged his fists down on the wheels and roared,

"You are alive and well. That's all that counts." Boris added, "And now that you are no longer a soldier, you look quite dashing again in your civilian clothes. The military uniform never suited you."

"How are things?" Mikhail asked, repressing a smile.

Boris' face darkened a bit. "Not too bad, but there is still a food shortage. Polya is out there right now, on some long queue. They used to send my supplies over, but not any more."

"Why don't you send the maid?"

"She can't read the ration cards. Too often she gives away a high value for a cheap item. We can't depend on her. Polya has to do it. I don't like to send her, but I have to."

"The golden era —new Russia!"

"I'm not complaining. The war will soon be over and we'll go back to the old days."

"And how were the old days, Boris?"

"The old days were the old days. Things will be even better some day," Boris answered, ignoring the sarcasm.

Still the same Boris, thought Mikhail, still invincible, regardless of what he knows or may sometimes feel.

Polya came in, her arms full of packages. She was perspiring and her face was flushed with exertion. Mikhail quickly saw that she was on the verge of crying. When she saw Mikhail and Katya she burst into tears, but refused to offer any explanation.

At the table Boris was quiet, almost as quiet as he had been in the days of his service, when he shrouded himself in silence. But unlike the old days, he dipped freely into the brandy. Mikhail watched the unhappy Polya as she served them. He was almost certain he knew what had caused her tears. He had to be sure.

"Boris, what do you think of this new situation?" he asked, hoping to bring it out in the open.

"What are you referring to?"

"I'm talking about the anti-Semitic outbreaks."

"It's temporary," answered Boris. "A by-product of war."

"Overlooked, I suppose, by the Party and government?"

"Nonsense. My wife thinks as you do but it is still nonsense. Every time some drunken sot yells 'Sarah' at her, she comes home crying and convinced that there is open and official anti-Semitism in Russia."

Polya burst out, "It is I who have to face it every day, not you. 'Dirty Jew,' they yell, and some of them even recognize that I am the wife of Boris Garber, a man honored by Stalin himself, and still they have no respect."

"You see, Boris. I was right," Mikhail insisted.

"That's enough!" Boris commanded.

"Can you say honestly that you are not troubled by this situation?"

"It is a topic I would rather not discuss," Boris shouted, losing his temper.

Katya intervened. "Enough of this," she reprimanded them. "You seem to forget that we are alive through a miracle. You are old friends. Enjoy the present."

Mikhail shrugged his shoulders and laughed. "Boris and I have always fought. But he knows what he has done for me and what I would do for him."

Boris now filled a glass with brandy. It was unusually large and they all looked at one another. He drank it with slow relish, wiped his lips and turned to Mikhail. He was by now quite drunk.

"You, Mikhail, don't know when you are well off. Let me tell you something. You are a writer. Now who are writers? Mostly, they are people who treat their art as a trade, the only one they know. Take it away from them and they starve. The trade of writing in this country is built on the Party line. It follows that writers who abandon the Party line must starve, to say the least. A writer is also a man in love with his culture. Take away his trade, throw him in jail, and he still walks to the gallows quoting Pushkin. For me, Mikhail, you are a Russian, not a Jew, and you have to live and die as a Russian. Now take your case as a Russian writer—a Soviet Russian writer. You write Party line but your conversation is always anti-Party. I am not an educated man, but to me this means only one thing: you don't believe a word you write! What is your problem? You are a crusader! Fortunately, you have been very lucky so far. Eventually you will be found out and you will be shot." He paused and slowly refilled his glass with brandy.

"So you promise me death," Mikhail said. "This, then, is your solution for me."

Boris, with agonizing deliberation, drank down the brandy. When he had finished, he inverted the glass and shoved it away from him. His eyes were red-rimmed. He looked at them all in turn and then fixed his eyes on Mikhail.

"Stop living two lives! You have been speaking treason for twenty years but you are still alive, I notice. My opinion is that you don't belong in this country."

He was very drunk and Polya helped him as he wheeled himself away to his bedroom.

Katya was sitting opposite Mikhail.

"What do you think he means?" Mikhail asked her, his voice touched with fear and his eyes full of pain.

A slight tremor went through Katya. "I was thinking how cruel he can be and how much he loves you."

"Yes, and I love him too. But perhaps he is right—"

"Mikhail, I think we should go now. Boris will sleep it off. He will most likely apologize tomorrow."

On the train back to Moscow they talked very little, their thoughts filled with the unpredictable and grim note on which the visit had ended. Mikhail kept seeing before him the drunken face of Boris and hearing his ominous warning. He heard again the words of his lifelong friend: "Stop living two lives! You have been speaking treason for twenty years . . ."

When Katya looked up at him her heart contracted with pain. He looked so forlorn as he stared into space like a man who had lost everything.

"Talk to me, Mikhail," she said, reaching over and taking both his hands in hers. They were cold and lifeless. "I can't bear to see you suffer."

Gently he withdrew his hands from hers. "Give me a little time, Katya. I'll get over it."

She wanted to say something, to console him, but suddenly he stood up and walked out to the open platform at the rear of the car. Katya followed discreetly behind him.

The train crawled across a bridge spanning two hills. Far below, a long freight train chugged along, the locomotive sending up little white puffs of smoke. It passed and left a vacuum. In the distance lay Moscow suffused in the ruby glow of a late afternoon sun. Mikhail watched the city sink into a sea of gloom.

Without turning around, he felt Katya standing beside him. When he spoke, his voice seemed to come from an abysmal pit below. "Please Katya, go back inside. I'd like to be alone." He saw no way out. He had lost all belief in the ideal, in people, and in himself.

Reluctantly she started to walk away while Mikhail remained staring fixedly into the valley. Then she stopped and looked back. Mikhail was bending over the railing. All at once the blood rushed to her head. She could see his body hurtling over the edge to the tracks below. She leaped to his side, grasped his shoulders and spun him around.

"No, Mikhail! No!" she cried out in terror. She took him in her arms, moaning and sobbing. "You can't do it, Mikhail. I need you."

Like a man who had returned from the dead, Mikhail shuddered as Katya's warm embrace brought him back to reality. He was no longer alone. There was someone who cared.

"Dear Katya," he repeated over and over again. He put his arm around her and slowly they walked back to their seats. When they arrived in Moscow it was already quite dark.

The spacious apartment that Katya occupied was lonely and dreary until Mikhail's arrival. She had prepared her late husband's room, trying to make it as comfortable for Mikhail as possible. Although he knew that Katya cared for him he had neither the audacity nor the conceit to think he could ever replace the marshal or fill his shoes, yet the hours and days they spent together reading or taking long walks brought contentment and serenity into their lives. There was a tacit understanding that they would observe every propriety and each one stayed within the boundary.

It was the nights that plagued them. They lay in their beds, restlessly tossing and turning until spent with exhaustion, sleep overtook them. And mornings over breakfast and nights before retiring they would avert their eyes as if to hide what could be seen there.

Only once, on the occasion of Katya's birthday, when they had returned from a performance of *Eugene Onegin* given at the Bolshoi Theater, Mikhail kissed Katya before saying goodnight. It had started innocently enough, but the fire in Katya's lips—he could still feel it burning on his mouth as he lay in bed. He had never dreamed it could be possible, but now all his pure and chaste feelings, all his resolve never in any way to offend Katya either in thought or deed, was drowned in an unquenchable desire to possess her. He must go to her, talk to her, touch her.

Katya stood in front of the mirror in her robe, loosening her thick hair. She lifted her hands above her head and let her fingers run through her hair like a comb. She remained standing that way, staring at herself in the mirror, and did not hear the door open. Suddenly Mikhail appeared before her, his eyes clouded with desire, his mouth twisted as if in pain. Without saying a word, he lowered himself on the floor near her and embracing her legs, nestled his feverish face between her knees. Katya stood motionless. Through the robe she could feel the heat of his breath on her legs. She reached down and softly caressed his head.

"Dear, sweet Mikhail. Don't!"

It was more of a plea than a protest. Mikhail threw open the folds of Katya's robe and pressed his head between her thighs.

"Please, Mikhail. I beg you. Don't!" she gasped, shuddering and drew her robe around her.

Slowly Mikhail stood up, looked at her like a sinner begging forgiveness. "It's all my fault, Katya. I had no right . . ."

She pushed him gently toward the door.

"But Katya, I love you. I have always loved you, believe me."

"And you know my feelings for you." She sighed. "But Ivan's grave is still fresh."

"I'm sorry, Katya." He bent down and tenderly kissed her hand. "Please forgive me."

CHAPTER FOUR

On Sunday Katya bought a bouquet of flowers. "I am going to visit Ivan's grave," she told Mikhail. "Would you like to come with me?"

Mikhail was deeply moved. "Of course I would."

They went together to the military cemetery just outside of Moscow. The marshal's grave was bedecked with flowers. A white marble plaque bore the simple words:

MARSHAL IVAN IVANOV
HERO OF THE SOVIET UNION
Sept. 16, 1885–Dec. 27, 1942

Mikhail and Katya sat together in silence on a white marble bench at the graveside. Above them stretched a reddish sky. The small trees planted about the marshal's grave bowed and swayed gently in the breeze.

Mikhail felt Katya's hand in his. Her eyes were dry as she stared at the grave, but her lips were set in a hard, thin line.

"The truth can be told here, Mikhail, at his graveside. He was destroyed. To you, I can tell it. Ah, he was not poisoned or shot. No. He was spiritually and morally destroyed. Ivan could not bear it any longer. His sensitive heart gave way."

Mikhail looked quickly around him. "I beg you, Katya, don't say it. For your sake. Even here, the time has not come for us to tell the truth."

"But it's true, Mikhail. I know it."

Mikhail put his arm around her shoulder, pressed her close to him and said hopelessly,

"I believe you, Katya. But what can we do? Can we protest? Can we fight? There is only one thing we can do—weep here at his grave and drown the truth in our tears."

She looked into his face and suddenly forgot her own unhappiness.

"I'm worried about you, Mikhail. I'm worried about your future. Especially after what Boris said. Even if he said it in a drunken stupor, still he was right. You don't belong in this country."

"Why? What terrible crime have I committed? I was a loyal Communist, a good citizen, a fearless soldier, and even as a writer I was my own censor before I sat down at my desk."

"My poor Ivan, rest his soul, he was so devoted, so patriotic, and see how he was repaid—"

"In death at least he is beyond the reach of the Kremlin," Mikhail said bitterly. "Perhaps that is the best way out. I often thought about it in the hospital and later on. I believe I would have killed myself if it had not been for you, Katya." He took her hand in his. "You are all I have left. I need you, Katya."

"I will do anything I possibly can."

"Come away with me. Our life here is finished. Somewhere, together, perhaps we will find a reason for living."

"All the gates of this country are closed, Mikhail."

"We must find a way out."

She shook her head, her eyes glistening with tears. "Yes, Mikhail, for you, but not for me." She began to cry. It seemed to him it was the cry of Mother Russia—

"Why not?" he asked her although he guessed the reason.

"I have too much here." She turned toward the marshal's grave.

"I understand," he said.

"But you," she said fervently, "you can go. You must go. You have nothing to keep you here. Anyhow, you need a change even if it's temporary."

"And leave you? Don't ask me to do that."

"You must! And I will help you. I'm sure you heard that Petya was recalled from the front and is now on a military mission abroad."

"Yes, I heard. He follows in his father's footsteps."

She shivered. "Let's go now. It's getting chilly here. I'll tell you my plan on the way home."

When Mikhail came in to breakfast several days later, Katya greeted him excitedly. "Here they are," she said, holding up two permits. "One—a permit for me to fly to England to visit my son who is attached to the Russian Embassy there. And two—a permit for the writer Mikhail Kruger to escort me on this trip and do an article on the second front! You see!" she added breathlessly, "I still have some influence in the Foreign Ministry!" She sighed. "Later you will have to make your own decision—either to come back with me or to disappear from sight."

Mikhail was speechless. He didn't want to go, but he knew that he had to.

"Hurry," Katya added before he could say anything. "We have only two hours before the plane leaves, and the permit expires in three days."

When Mikhail came down to the living room with his valise, he found Katya at the window, staring into space. He came up behind her and whirled her around. Her eyes were moist. He kissed her hand.

"Any more tears and I will change my mind," he threatened.

She smiled bravely as he helped her into her coat. At the door, he turned.

"There's one more thing I must do, Katya."

"What is it?" she asked, startled.

"I want to call Boris."

"In heaven's name, don't!"

"I won't say anything. I just want to hear his voice."

He went to the telephone, asked for Boris' number and waited. When the answering voice came, he listened a moment, hung up and pressed his forehead against the wall.

"Was that Boris?" Katya asked from the doorway.

"Yes, it was Boris."

They said nothing in the limousine that drove them to the airport. They boarded the plane only a few minutes before takeoff. It was a gray morning.

The two engines roared into action and the plane glided down the runway and into flight. The city of Moscow seemed to rotate slowly, then it settled at a sharp angle as the plane banked and executed a great arc over the city and began its long journey westward. Beneath them, the familiar villages quickly diminished in size until they looked like clusters of pins stuck into a huge map. The plane knifed through a layer of clouds and leveled off.

Above the clouds the sun was shining brightly.

THE END